PUBLISHER'S NOTE

Ancient Chinese classic poems are exquisite works of art. As far as 2,000 years ago, Chinese poets composed the beautiful work *Book of Poetry* and *Elegies of the South*. Later, they created more splendid Tang poetry and Song lyrics. Such classic works as *Thus Spoke the Master* and *Laws Divine and Human* were extremely significant in building and shaping the culture of the Chinese nation. These works are both a cultural bond linking the thoughts and affections of Chinese people and an important bridge for Chinese culture and the world.

Mr. Xu Yuanchong has been engaged in translation for 70 years. He won the Lifetime Achievement Award in Translation conferred by the Translators Association of China (TAC) in 2010, and won the "Aurora Borealis" Prize for Outstanding Translation of Fiction Literature, conferred by the Federation of International Translators (FIT) in 2014. He is honored as the only expert who translates Chinese poems into both English and French. After his excellent interpretation, many Chinese classic poems have been further refined into perfect English and French rhymes. This collection of Classical Chinese Poetry and Prose gathers his most representative English translations. It includes the classic works *Thus Spoke the Master*, *Laws Divine and Human* and dramas such as *Romance of the Western Bower*, *Dream in Peony Pavilion*, *Love in Long-life Hall* and *Peach Blooms Painted with Blood*. The largest part of the collection includes the translation of selected poems from different dynasties. The selection includes various types of poetry. The selected works start from the pre-Qin era to the Qing Dynasty, covering almost the entire history of classic poems in China. Reading these works is like tasting "living water from the source" of Chinese culture.

We hope this collection will help English readers "understand, enjoy and delight in" Chinese classic poems, share the intelligence of Confucius and Lao Tzu (the Older Master), share the gracefulness of Tang poems, Song lyrics and classic operas and songs and promote exchanges between Eastern and Western culture. We also sincerely invite precious suggestions from our readers.

出版前言

中国古代经典诗文是中国传统文化的奇葩。早在两千多年以前，中国诗人就写出了美丽的《诗经》和《楚辞》；以后，他们又创造了更加灿烂的唐诗和宋词。《论语》《老子》这样的经典著作，则在塑造、构成中华民族文化精神方面具有极其重要的意义。这些作品既是联接所有中国人思想、情感的文化纽带，也是中国文化走向世界的重要桥梁。

许渊冲先生从事翻译工作70年，2010年荣获"中国翻译文化终身成就奖"，2014年荣获国际译联颁发的"北极光"杰出文学翻译奖。他被称为将中国诗词译成英法韵文的唯一专家，经他的妙手，许多中国经典诗文被译成出色的英文和法文韵语。这套"许译中国经典诗文集"荟萃许先生最具代表性的英文译作，既包括《论语》《老子》这样的经典著作，又包括《西厢记》《牡丹亭》《长生殿》《桃花扇》等戏曲剧本，数量最多的则是历代诗歌选集。这些诗歌选集包括诗、词、散曲等多种体裁，所选作品上起先秦，下至清代，几乎涵盖了中国古典诗歌的整个历史。阅读和了解这些作品，即可尽览中国文化的"源头活水"。

我们希望这套许氏译本能使英语读者对中国经典诗文也"知之，好之，乐之"，能够分享孔子、老子的智慧，分享唐诗、宋词、中国古典戏曲的优美，并以此促进东西文化的交流。也敬请读者朋友提出宝贵意见。

PROJECT FOR TRANSLATION AND PUBLICATION
OF CHINESE CULTURAL WORKS
中国文化著作翻译出版工程项目

CLASSICAL CHINESE POETRY AND PROSE

ELEGIES OF THE SOUTH

TRANSLATED BY XU YUANCHONG

许译中国经典诗文集

楚辞 | 许渊冲 译

五洲传播出版社　　中华书局
China Intercontinental Press　　Zhonghua Book Company

Contents

目　　录

Preface　1	序　147
Qu Yuan	屈原
Sorrow after Departure 19	离骚................162
The Nine Songs 35	九歌................196
The Almighty Lord of the East ... 35	东皇太一................199
To The God of Cloud........ 35	云中君................203
To the Lord of River Xiang... 36	湘君................207
To the Lady of River Xiang... 38	湘夫人................213
The Great Lord of Fate 39	大司命................219
The Young Goddess of Fate .. 41	少司命................224
The God of the Sun........... 42	东君................228
The God of the River......... 43	河伯................232
The Goddess of the Mountain 44	山鬼 236
For Those Fallen for the Country 45	国殇 241

The Last Sacrifice 46	礼魂 244
Asking Heaven 47	天问 246
The Nine Elegies 68	九章 273
I Make my Plaint 68	惜诵 276
Crossing the River 72	涉江 284
Lament for the Chu Capital ... 75	哀郢 290
Sad Thoughts Outpoured .. 78	抽思 297
Longing for Changsha 81	怀沙 305
Thinking of the Fair One ... 85	思美人 312
The Bygone Days Regretted ... 88	惜往日 317
Hymn to the Orange Tree ... 91	橘颂 325
Grieving at the Whirlwind ... 93	悲回风 329
The Far-off Journey 99	远游 339
Divination 107	卜居 354
The Fisherman 109	渔父 358
Song Yu	**宋玉**
Nine Apologies 111	九辩 363
Qu Yuan	**屈原**
Requiem 122	招魂 383
Great Requiem 134	大招 401

CLASSICAL CHINESE POETRY AND PROSE

Elegies of the South

TRANSLATED BY XU YUANCHONG

China Intercontinental Press   Zhonghua Book Company

Preface

> There lies a glassy oblong pool,
> Where light and shade pursue their course.
> How can it be so clear and cool?
> For water fresh comes from its source.
>   Zhu Xi (1130–1200)

Chinese poetry is a vast ocean where light and shade pursue their course. Its source is *the Book of Poetry* compiled in the 6th century B. C. and *Elegies of the South* composed in the 3rd. *The Book of Poetry* is the earliest anthology of realistic poems written by common people along the Yellow River in North China, including the richest State of Qi in the east, the most thickly populated States of Zheng and Wei in the Central Plain, and the most powerful State of Qin in the west. In the Valley of the Yellow River Confucius and his disciples had rationalized ancient tradition, myth and shamanism, humanized divinities and transformed extraordinary chaos into ordinary world order. On the other hand, *Elegies of the South* may be said to be the earliest collection of romantic poems written by poets of the largest State of Chu along the Blue River or the Yangzi Valley, permeated with time-hallowed tradition, fantastic imagination and violent emotions of a mythical world.

Qu Yuan (340–278 B. C.) was the most important Chu poet who lived at a time when romanticism or shamanism in the South came into contact with realism in the North. He became the greatest lyrical poet in ancient China as a result of the contact. At first, he had won the confidence of the king of Chu, and held the high post of "left minister". In view of the danger threatening Chu from the powerful State of Qin, Qu Yuan proposed reform in the government and alliance with the rich State of Qi to ensure the safety of Chu. But the king of Chu was surrounded by self-seekers who, having accepted bribes from Qin's envoy, not only dissuaded the king from taking Qu Yuan's advice, but brought about the poet's estrangement from the king. Therefore, Qu Yuan wrote his autobiographic long poem *Sorrow after Departure*.

This long poem is not only one of the most remarkable works of Chinese poetry, but it ranks as one of the greatest poems in world literature. It describes the poet's patriotism, his disillusionment with a society fallen into evil ways and his imaginary journeys in a chariot drawn by dragon and phoenix to a supernatural world.

> The Moon's Charioteer goes before, oh!
> The curtain-rolling Wind runs after.
> To clear the way the phoenixes soar, oh!
> The Lord of Thunder bursts in laughter.

By means of rich imagery and skilled similes, the poet expresses his loyalty to the king of Chu referred to as "Fair One" or "Sacred One."

> The Sacred One neglects his duty, oh!
> He will not look into my heart.
> The Slanderers envy my beauty, oh!
> They say I play a licentious part.

Preface

Thus he builds up the tradition of using the beauty to symbolize the sovereign, and fragrant plants to represent loyal ministers. He also depicts, directly or indirectly, the social condition of that time and the destinies of the States of ancient China, for example:

> The last king of Xia's stormy age, oh!
> Abused all laws and he lost his crown.
> That of Shang burned alive his sage, oh!
> His dynasty was overthrown.

The conflicts between the ruling groups are repeatedly described while the poet affirms his determination to seek his ideal or beauty.

> All men delight in what they please, oh!
> Alone I always love the beauty.
> My body rent, my heart at ease, oh!
> Can I change and neglect my duty?

> I bid the Driver of the Sun, oh!
> To Holy Mountains slowly go.
> My way ahead is a long, long one, oh!
> I'll seek my beauty high and low.

His love for the ideal or beauty was so passionate that he could not bear the stern reality and finally he drowned himself in the River Milo on the fifth day of the fifth lunar month, which has become a holiday for Chinese people to commemorate his death, when a race of dragon boats is held, it is said, to the rescue of the drowned poet.

    In a certain sense, *Sorrow after Departure* may be compared with Homer's *Odyssey* composed 500 years earlier and with Dante's *Divine Comedy* composed 1,500 years later. Homer describes in *Odyssey* Ulysses' voyage on sea, his wisdom and his physical sufferings on his way back to his native State; Qu Yuan describes in his *Sorrow* his imaginary journey to Heaven, his qualities and his mental sufferings on leaving his native State in quest of an ideal prince or beauty as personified in the Nymphean Queen, the Swallow's Bride or the young prince's fair lady, or embodied in jasper tree, fragrant flower or sweet grass. Dante records in the *Divine Comedy* his moral and spiritual experience of illumination, regeneration and beatitude by describing his imaginary journeys down to the Hell and up to the Purgatory and then up to the Paradise. As Qu Yuan follows the ancient sages and consults the witch and wizard, Dante is guided by Reason in the person of Virgil and then by Beatrice, an incarnation of beauty and virtue, an image of goodness and divine wisdom. In *Sorrow after Departure*, Qu Yuan glorifies the three ancient kings and the founders of the Xia and Shang dynasties, and condemns their last monarchs; in the *Divine Comedy*, Dante glorifies only Christian saints and condemns pagans, including the wise Ulysses and the brave Caesar. But modern attitude toward pagan heroes has changed in the West, while the glorification of ancient sages and the condemnation against evil and vice in China remain unchanged throughout the ages. This shows Qu Yuan's sorrow represents that of Chinese intellectuals down to the present century. Thus we may say *Sorrow after Departure* is no less important in the East than *Odyssey* and *Divine Comedy* in the West.

Other poems attributed to Qu Yuan include *the Nine Songs and the Nine Elegies*. The former are songs dedicated to gods or goddesses. Their form is suggestive of drama, in which a male or a female shaman donned elaborate costume and make-up, and singing and dancing, invited the god or goddess to an amorous encounter. As sacrifices to the gods were occasions for courtship, the mention of love in these poems is natural. Since the Han Dynasty the *Nine Songs* had always been attributed to Qu Yuan, until in recent years some scholars advanced the theory that they were ancient folk songs and not the work of any individual poet.

The Nine Songs can be divided into different types. The first type describes the sacrifice itself, as in *The Almighty Lord of the East and The Last Sacrifice*. The second type describes the god's delight in the sacrifice, as in *The God of the Sun*. The third type describes the love professed by the witch or sacrificial priestess for the god, as in *The God of Cloud* and *The Great Lord of Fate*. It would be interesting to compare Qu Yuan's cloud with Shelley's. The fourth type is a dialogue between two gods, for instance, between the Lord and the Lady of River Xiang paying court to each other. The third and fourth verses to the Lady are beautiful lines:

> The autumn breeze, oh! ceaselessly grieves
> The Dongting waves, oh! with fallen leaves.

The poet describes the lake rippled by the breeze with fallen leaves and reveals the grief of the Lady waiting for the Lord, in other words, at the sight of the rippled lake, we see not only the face, but also the heart of the grieved lady, that is to say, a discription of the outer world reveals the inner world of the heroine. Another example of the fourth type is *The God of the River*, dialogue between the God of the Yellow River and the Goddess of River Luo. The fifth type portrays lovesick goddesses, as in the *Young Goddess of Fate*, who says:

> None is so sad, oh! as those who part;
> Nor so happy, oh! as new sweet heart.

The Goddess of the Mountain portrays the lovesick fairyqueen of Mount Wu waiting for King Xiang of Chu. The first stanza describes the Goddess as follows:

> In mountain deep, oh! looms a fair lass,
> In ivy leaves, oh! girt with sweet grass.
> Amorous looks, oh! and smiling eyes,
> For such a beauty, oh! there's none but sighs.

This beautiful lass in ivy leaves can be found in a picture drawn by Xu Beihong (1895–1953), a famous Chinese painter. The last type is the poem praising the fallen warriors:

> Their spirit is deathless, oh! although their blood was shed;
> Captains among the ghosts, oh! heroes among the dead.

This is the only poem in the *Nine Songs* to make no mention of love.

The Nine Elegies are *Sorrow after Departure* enlarged, said Liang Qichao (1873–1929), a famous Chinese scholar. Of the nine poems *the Hymn to the*

PREFACE

Orange differs in style and mood from the rest and was probably written by Qu Yuan in his earlier days. This ode praises the orange, which is symbolic of the poet's virtue.

> Within you're pure; without you're bright,
> Like a man virtuous and right, oh!...
> You stand alone in this world wide,
> Unyielding to the vulgar tide, oh!

The other eight elegies were written during the poet's banishment. Most of them voice the author's extreme anguish. Probably *I Make My Plaint* was the first written just after banishment, followed by *Grieving at the Whirlwind*, *Thinking of the Fair One* and the *Bygone days Regretted*, which is the simplest and clearest of all the elegies.

> Though, loyal, I have done no wrong, oh!
> I suffer from slanders in throng…
> I'd drown myself and leave my name behind, oh!
> But to the light my lord's still blind.

Lament for the Chu Capital was probably written in 298 B. C. when the capital fell to General Bai Qi of Qin. Liang Qichao was moved to tears on reading the following epilogue:

> Gazing with longing eyes, I stand, oh!
> When may I come back to my homeland?
> A bird flies nowhere but home-bound, oh!

> A dying fox turns its head to its mound.
> Guiltless but banished, I take flight, oh!
> Can I forget my home day and night?

Of *Crossing the River* the first part is a portrait of the poet himself, the second a realistic description of his journey and the third tells us why he cannot but roam about.

> Darkness replaces light;
> The time is far from right, oh!
> Faithfulness becomes doubt.
> How can I not set out? oh!

Sad Thoughts Outpoured tells us his ideal:

> He (the king) might imitate the three and five kings, oh!
> And I might learn from Peng to do good things.
> Is there an end that cannot be attained? oh!
> Could a world-wide renown be stained?

Longing for Changsha is believed to be the poet's last work for it ends by the following verse:

> I know that none can avoid death.
> Why should I grudge my breath? oh!
> I declare to those I revere,
> I will take you as my compeer, oh!

Preface

Asking Heaven is the most extraordinary of Qu Yuan's poems. Reflecting the poet's rational approach to nature and history, this work provides us with rich material on ancient Chinese myths and legends. In this poem Qu Yuan asks questions regarding what existed before the universe, the creation of the heavenly bodies and the structure of the earth. Over one hundred and seventy questions are raised, and none of them answered. From them we can see the poet's concern with nature, and the richness of his imagination and the heights reached by Chinese science in his time. This long poem may be compared with the *Book of Job* in the *Holy Bible*.

The *Far-off Journey* could be described as a Taoist's answer to *Sorrow after Departure*. Without any of the allegory and symbolism of the *Sorrow*, it describes a celestial journey which ends not in despairing gloom but in triumphant fulfilment. Therefore, its authenticity is in doubt. The first part of this poem describes the poet's thoughts before the journey:

> Between the boundless earth and sky, oh!
> Forever man must toil, I sigh.
> Beyond my reach are bygone days, oh!
> Can I hear what the future says?

The Taoist thought is revealed in the following stanza:

> Empty-minded you may await, oh!
> Do not strive to be first or great!
> Let all things be formed as they may, oh!
> Then you'll find the door to the Way.

The last stanza describes how Unity is attained:

> Below it's bottomlessly deep, oh!
> Above it's heavenlessly steep.
> I look but see not what changes fast, oh!
> I listen but hear nothing in space vast.
> I transcend Inaction to Purity, oh!
> Then I come near the Realm of Unity.

Divination and *the Fisherman* are two narrative poems in which Qu Yuan is described as a rationist who believes neither in gods nor in divination. This is consistent with *Sorrow after Departure* and *Asking Heaven*. In *Divination* the poet asks:

> Which way will lead to weal and which to woe?
> Which way should I dodge and which should I go?

In *the Fisherman* the poet says:

> When all the world in mud has sunk,
> Alone I am clean;
> When all the people are drunk,
> Sober I'm seen.

But the old fisherman advises him to "adapt himself to the time" and sings the following song.

Preface

> When the river is clear, oh!
> I'll wash my headdress here.
> When water is not neat, oh!
> I may wash here my feet.

Nine Apologies is a cycle of nine or ten poems attributed to Song Yu (298–265 B. C.), a literary follower of Qu Yuan. These poems are uneven in quality. Parts of them possess a rare beauty which represents the highest peak of perfection ever attained in *Elegies of the South*. The atmosphere of melancholy grandeur, the heavy richness of the language, the masterly use of assonances, double words and parallelism combine to produce an indescribable effect. We may read for example stanzas from the first and the last part.

> Ah! sad as death
> Is autumn's breath.
> What a bleak day, oh!
> Leaves shiver, fade, fall and decay.
> Forlorn and dreary, oh!
> As on a journey weary,
> Climbing the hill, oh!
> To see a friend off across the rill.

> I'd ride the ether round on round, oh!
> And race with gods sky-bound, sky-bound.
> I'd drive the rainbow white, so white, oh!
> And pass through the stars bright, so bright.
> At left the Red Bird beats its wing on wing; oh!

> At right the Dragons Green swing and swing.
> The Lord of Thunder rumbles past, past, oh!
> The master of Wind flies ahead, fast, fast.
> In front, light coaches ring bell on bell, oh!
> Behind, the heavy waggons utter yell on yell.

In ancient China, when a man fell ill, his relatives and friends would, at midnight, in mournful and loving tones, call upon his spirit to return. *Requiem* and *Great Requiem* are magnificent poems developed from simple folk tunes of this type, showing the poetic imagination of which these ancient people were capable. The main content of these two poems is a detailed description of the charms of the native land of the spirit, compared with which all other places appear uninhabitable. Through his patriotism, rich imagery and colorful language, the poet makes clear what he hated and loved. *Requiem*, said Liang Qichao, may be compared with Goethe's Faust.

There have been different theories regarding the subject and authorship of these two poems. However, according to Sima Qian, the great Chinese historian of the second century, they are the works of Qu Yuan. According to some, it was the king of Chu whose soul Qu Yuan was recalling. Others believe they were composed by Song Yu to call back Qu Yuan's spirit, so they are the best poems written in memory of Qu Yuan. For instance, the charm of the beautiful dancers is described in the following stanzas:

> The beauties are drunk with wine;
> Their rosy faces shine, eh!
> Their flirting glances look
> Like amorous waves in a brook, eh!

PREFACE

> The belts and strings untied
> Run riot far and wide, eh!
> Fair dancers come from east or west
> Sit together with the guest, eh!
> Without cease they make merry and drink
> Till days into night sink, eh!

The charm of the beauties of the Chu State and the horrors of the four corners of the world are described in detail in order to arouse the soul's love for his country. The eagerness of the people to call back the soul also shows their deep love for the poet.

"Few poets indeed in the world," concludes Guo Moruo, an authority on Qu Yuan studies and a poet himself, "can rival Qu Yuan in his sincerity, imaginative power and brilliance, nor in the wealth of imagery, lyrical qualities and diversity of forms of his poems. A poet who had such deep love for his country and his people, for freedom and justice, will for ever be remembered."

* * * *

Important as *Elegies of the South* is, it was not translated into European languages until the 19th century. In 1852, Dr. A. Pfizmaier published a German translation at Vienna. In 1870, the Marquis d'Hervey de Saint Denys published a French translation at Paris. Neither of these attracted much attention. In 1879, E. H. Parker published *The Sadness of Separation*, or *Li Sao* in the *China Review*, VII, pp. 309–314. The lilt of his first verse impressed very favorably professor H. A. Giles of Cambridge:

Born of the stock of our ancient princes,
(My father, Peh Yung by name,)
The Spring-star twinkled with cheery omen
On the lucky day I came.

But the lilt did not last. And Professor David Hawkes of Oxford said, "It is really more a paraphrase than a translation, and its bouncing Victorian verse could have been written by a clever schoolboy."

In 1884, Professor Giles published in Shanghai his *Gems of Chinese Literature*, which contains translations of *Divination*, the *Fisherman* and the *Goddess of the Mountain*. "Like most of Giles's translations from the Chinese," said Hawkes, "these are elegant and extremely readable, but free in a rather arbitrary way and sometimes tiresomely Europeanized, e. g.

Should I yoke myself a fellow in the shafts with Bucephalus, or shamble along by the side of Rozinante? Should I vie with the wild goose in soaring to heaven, or scramble on a dunghill with hens?
(Divination)

In 1895, James Legge published *The Li Sao Poem and its Author* in *Journal of the Royal Asiatic Society*, XXVII, pp. 847−864. "J. Legge's translation of Li Sao," Said Hawkes, "… faithfully reproduces the interpretation of Wang Yi's commentary and probably owes a good deal to the French translation of the Marquis d'Hervey de Saint-Denys. It is certainly more accurate than Parker's translation,…Legge had no feeling for poetry of any kind, and would appear to have undertaken this translation because *Li Sao* was deemed an important literary work by Chinese scholars."

An excellent Japanese translation with notes and commentaries by Shaku Seitan appeared in the early part of the 20th century. A German scholar, E. Erkes, translated *Requiem* into German in 1914; his word-for-word English translation of *Great Requiem* appeared in *Asia Major*, Hirth Anniversary Volume, pp. 67–86, in 1923. This was followed by translations of *The Great Lord of Fate* and *The Young Goddess of Fate* contained in his *God of Death in Ancient China* published in 1939. "Erkes's translations," said Hawkes, "make painful reading, but they would be useful to a student beginning to study Chinese literature in the original." The following is a brief example:

> Cold and damp (look) the monkeys and bears.
> If you think, (how much) you resemble them,
> then you will become sad.

In 1918, Arthur Waley published *A Hundred and Seventy Chinese Poems* which contains a translation of *For Those Fallen for the Country*. In 1919, he published *More Translations from the Chinese* which contains "a brilliant translation" — in the words of Hawkes — of *Great Requiem*. Both these translations reappeared in 1946 in *Chinese Poems* published by Allen and Unwin, the first of them considerably revised.

In 1928, F. X. Biallas published his *Ku Yuan, His Life and Poems* in *journal of the North China Branch of the Royal Asiatic Society*, LIX, pp. 231–253, which includes English translations of *the Almighty Lord of the*

East, the Goddess of the Mountain, the first twelve lines of *Asking Heaven, I Make My Plaint, Divination and the Fisherman*. "These are workmanlike literal translations," said Hawkes, "with no pretensions to literary merit." Most of Biallas's translations of *Elegies of the South* are in German.

In 1929, Dr. Lim Boon Keng, president of the University of Amoy, published in Shanghai *The Li Sao, an Elegy on Encountering Sorrows*. This was the most important version published in the 1920s, for which the famous Indian poet Tagore and Professor Giles had written prefaces. "The *Li Sao*" said Giles, "is a wonderful poem; a pindaric ode. It was written more than three hundred years before Christ. When I first tried to read it, in 1872, the verses seemed to me like flashes of lightning, blinding me so that I could only catch the sense here and there… this elaborate study of an ancient and difficult poem seems to me to go far to leave the British Empire precisely where it was." "The verses of this poem," said Dr. R. Tagore in his preface, "carry in them a lament, political in character, which makes vivid to us the background of a great people's mind, whose best aspiration was for building a stable basis of society founded upon the spirit of moral obligation…" We feel through the whole poem the pervasive sadness of a day's end that has discovered the promise of its morning betrayed. The following verse has in it the sigh of a dying breeze in the twilight sending its farewell whisper across all the leaves of this book:

> Time flows, meseems, I cannot keep pace with it;
> I fear it gives me not the years I need;
> At morn, I pluck magnolias on the hill;
> At eve, I pick the islet's evergreen."

But Hawkes said on the contrary, "Lim Boon-Keng's translation of *Li Sao*... is a good student's crib. It has very copious and on the whole useful notes. But the translation is less accurate than Legge's and about equally void of literary merit."

In 1947, Robert Payne published in New York *The White Pony, an Anthology of Chinese Poetry from the Earliest Times to the Present Day*, which contains translations by Payne, professors and students of National Southwest Associated University of the *Nine Songs*, *Crossing the River* and *Sorrow after Departure*. Hawkes said, "the translations are fresh and readable, — the only extensive English translations of *Chu Tzu (Elegies of the South)* apart from Waley's which do not positively deter the reader."

In 1953, the Foreign Languages Press at Beijing published *The Li Sao and Other Poems of Qu Yuan* translated by Yang Xianyi and Gladys Yang in English rhymes. "The result," said Hawkes, "is a monument of ingenuity, but to my mind bears about as much relation to the original as a chocolate Easter egg to an omelette. The first and last lines of the translation will serve as an example:

> A Prince am I of Ancestry renowned,
> Illustrious Name my royal Sire hath found. *(Li Sao)*
> A thousand Miles away my Heart doth yearn,
> Beyond the Wailing Stream, O Soul return! *(Requiem)*"

In 1955, Arthur Waley published his translation of the *Nine Songs*, which is "invaluable" in Hawkes's word.

In 1959, Oxford University Press published *Chu Tzu, the Song of the South* translated by Hawkes, which includes all the works compiled by

Wang Yi of the Han Dynasty. The first and last lines mentioned above of his translation will serve as an example:

> Scion of the High Lord Kao Yang,
> Po Yung was my father's name. *(Li Sao)*
> The eye travels on a thousand Li, and the heart breaks for sorrow.
> O soul, come back! Alas for the Southern Land! *(Chao Hun)*

Hawkes considers his own translation "to be somewhere midway between a literal and a 'free' one." From a microscopic point of view, his version is perhaps more accurate than others, but from a macroscopic point of view, it is as void of literary merit as other prosaic translations, including those of 1975 and 1984. Therefore, I offer this rhymed version, which I hope will bring out the original beauty in sense, in sound and in form.

Xu Yuanchong
April 18, 1994
Peking University

Qu Yuan

Sorrow after Departure

Descendant of High Sunny King, oh!
My father's name shed sunny ray.
The Wooden Star appeared in spring, oh!
When I was born on Tiger's Day.

My father saw my birthday bright, oh!
He gave me an auspicious name.
My formal name was Divine Right, oh!
I was also called Divine Flame.

I have so much beauty inside, oh!
And add to it a style ornate.
I weave sweet grass by riverside, oh!
Into a belt with orchids late.

Like running water years will pass, oh!
I fear time and tide wait for none.
At dawn I gather mountain grass, oh!
At dusk I pick secluded one.

The sun and the moon will not stay, oh!
Spring will give place to autumn cold.
Grass will wither and trees decay, oh!
I fear that beauty will grow old.

Give up the foul while young and strong, oh!

Elegies of the South

Why won't you my lord, change your style and way?
Ride your fine steed, gallop along, oh!
I'll go before you lest you stray.

Three ancient kings were pure and true, oh!
Around them flocked all fragrant things.
Pepper and cassia also grew, oh!
Sweet orchids were formed into rings.

The first two monarchs were so bright, oh!
That they followed and gained the way.
The two last kings were in sad plight, oh!
They sought by paths and came to bay.

Your partisans love stolen pleasure, oh!
Their way is dark, with perils sown.
Do I dread my personal woe? oh!
I fear the royal cab o'erthrown.

I run before it and behind, oh!
I wish you would follow your sire.
To my loyalty you're unkind, oh!
You heed slander and burst in fire.

With frank advice you won't comply, oh!
I endure and cannot have done.
Be my witness, Ninth Heaven high, oh!
I've done all for you Sacred One.

SORROW AFTER DEPARTURE

The word you've given still remains, oh!
But you go back on it and stray.
Departure causes me no pains, oh!
Of your fickleness what to say?

I grow spring orchids in fields nine, oh!
And a hundred acres of clover.
I plant peonies line by line, oh!
Mixed with fragrant grass all over.

I'd see their leaves green and blooms red, oh!
And reap the fruit in season due.
I am not grieved they're withered, oh!
But they decay 'mid weeds in view.

All vie in avarice and greed, oh!
Their lust is never gratified.
Judging others by their own deed, oh!
They're jealous-minded and green-eyed.

I am not so eager as they, oh!
To run after wealth here and there.
Old age draws near from day to day, oh!
Have I a name lasting and fair?

From magnolia I drink the dew, oh!
And feed on aster petals frail.
My spirit being pure and true, oh!
Do I care to grow lank and pale?

ELEGIES OF THE SOUTH

I string clover with gathered vine, oh!
And fallen stamens thereamong.
I plait cassia tendrils and twine, oh!
Some strands of ivy green and long.

I'll imitate the ancient sage, oh!
Not the vulgar world of today.
Though I displease the modern age, oh!
I will follow the ancient way.

I sigh and wipe away my tears, oh!
I'm grieved at a life full of woes.
Good and just, I hear only jeers, oh!
Morning and night I suffer blows.

I make a belt of grasses sweet, oh!
And add to it clovers and thymes.
My heart tells me it's good and meet, oh!
I won't regret to die nine times.

The Sacred One neglects his duty, oh!
He will not look into my heart.
The slanderers envy my beauty, oh!
They say I play licentious part.

The vulgar praise what is unfair, oh!
They reject common rules with pleasure
They like the crooked and not the square, oh!
Accommodation is their measure.

Sorrow after Departure

Downcast, depressed and sad am I, oh!
Alone I bear sufferings long.
I would rather in exile die, oh!
Than mingle with the vulgar throng.

The eagle cleaves alone the air, oh!
Since olden days it has been fleet.
The round cannot fit with the square, oh!
Who go different ways ne'er meet.

I curb my will and check my heart, oh!
Endure reproach as well as blame.
I'd die to play a righteous part, oh!
The ancient sages would bear no shame.

Regretting I've gone a wrong way, oh!
I hesitate and will go back.
Before I go too far astray, oh!
I wheel my cab to former track.

I loose my horse by waterside, oh!
At Pepper Hill I take a rest.
I won't advance to turn the tide, oh!
I will retire to mend my vest.

I'll make a coat with lotus leaves, oh!
And patch my skirt with lilies white.
Unknown, I care not if it grieves, oh!
My heart will shed fragrance and light.

Elegies of the South

I raise my headdress towering high, oh!
And lengthen pendants sparkling long.
My fragrance 'mid the dirt won't die, oh!
My brilliancy ne'er wanes thereamong.

I look around and feast my sight, oh!
On scenes north and south, east and west.
My pendants seem all the more bright, oh!
My fragrance outshines all the rest.

All men delight in what they please, oh!
Alone I always love the beauty.
My body rent, my heart at ease, oh!
Can I change and neglect my duty?

My sister gently comes downcast, oh!
She warns me again and again:
"The flood-fighter selfless, steadfast, oh!
By mountainside at last was slain.

"Fond of beauty, why are you straight? oh!
Why hold alone your virtue high?
When thorns and weeds o'errun the State, oh!
Could you despise them and stand by?

"You can't dissuade them one by one, oh!
Who would then understand your heart?
There're many cliques under the sun, oh!
Why hear me not and stand apart?"

Sorrow after Departure

I follow sages of ancient day, oh!
I judge by heart from fall to spring.
I cross the streams and go south way, oh!
I state my case to ancient king:

"The second king of Xia loved songs, oh!
He was indulged in his desire.
He heeded nor dangers nor wrongs, oh!
His five sons threw the land in fire.

"The hunter loved each shot to tell, oh!
Shooting fox, he led a wild life.
Such wantonness could not end well, oh!
His friend slew him and stole his wife.

"The traitor's son with might and main, oh!
Did what he would without restraint.
All day long he sought pleasures vain, oh!
At last he lost his head blood-stained.

"The last king of Xia's stormy age, oh!
Abused all laws and he lost his crown.
That of Shang burned alive his sage, oh!
His dynasty was overthrown.

"Kings Tang and Yu full of respect, oh!
And that of Zhou went the right way.
The good and wise they did select, oh!
They followed the rule as kings may.

"Heaven august was fair and square, oh!
It gave to ministers their due.
Only the sages were employed there, oh!
They might rule o'er the land in view.

"Looking before and after then, oh!
I find the rules for livelihood.
None would employ those unjust men, oh!
Nor obey those who are not good.

"I've risked my life and braved death, oh!
I don't regret I've held my ground.
The sage would lose his life and breath, oh!
Like square pegs unfit for holes round."

Melancholy and sad I stay, oh!
Why live I at a time that grieves?
With soft grass I wipe tears away, oh!
Which have streamed down and wetted my sleeves.

I kneel aground and plead my ease, oh!
My heart is glad to find the true.
Dragon and phoenix start my race, oh!
I rise on wind into the blue.

At dawn I leave the E'ergreen State, oh!
At dusk I reach the mountain's crest.
I halt before Celestial Gate, oh!
To see the sun sink in the west.

SORROW AFTER DEPARTURE

I bid the Driver of the Sun, oh!
To Holy Mountains slowly go.
My way ahead's a long, long one, oh!
I'll seek my Beauty high and low.

I drink my steeds in the Sun's Bath, oh!
I tie their reins to giant tree.
I break a branch to brush Sun's path, oh!
I wander for a while carefree.

The Moon's Charioteer goes before, oh!
The curtain-rolling Wind runs after.
To clear the way the phoenixes soar, oh!
The Lord of Thunder bursts in laughter.

I order giant birds to fly, oh!
All day long, by night as by day.
The whirlwinds gather up on high, oh!
The rainbow greets me all the way.

They part and join in proper order, oh!
In various hues and up and down.
To open I bid Heaven's Porter, oh!
He looks at me with a deep frown.

The day grows dark, its end is nigh, oh!
Twining orchids, I linger there.
The beauty's oft viewed with green eye, oh!
The foul can't be told from the fair.

ELEGIES OF THE SOUTH

I tether steeds on Endless Peaks, oh!
After I crossed the Deathless Stream.
Gazing back, tears run down my cheeks, oh!
On high I find no beauty of my own.

I visit Verhal Temple hall, oh!
Adorn my belt with jasper bough.
Before the jasper blossoms fall, oh!
I'll send them to my Beauty below.

I bid the Lord of Cloud above, oh!
To find astream the Nymphean Queen.
I give my belt as pledge of love, oh!
To Lord of Dream as go-between.

She comes and goes, we meet and part, oh!
Irreconcilably, I deem.
She passes the night with her sweetheart, oh!
And washes her hair in the stream.

She's arrogant, though fair and bright, oh!
She is wanton beyond compare.
She's beautiful but impolite, oh!
I will seek a beauty elsewhere.

I look around from side to side, oh!
Go down after circling the sky,
And find the Swallow's beauteous bride, oh!
Alone in Jasper Tower high.

Sorrow after Departure

The falcon wooes for me her love, oh!
He tells me that she is not good.
I bid the singing turtledove, oh!
He flies away with false birdhood.

I hesitate like fox in doubt, oh!
I'd go myself but that won't do.
With gifts the phoenix has set out, oh!
Lest before me my rival woo.

I take no rest and go misled, oh!
I rove and wander here and there.
If the young prince were not yet wed, oh!
I'd stay with his two ladies fair.

My clumsy match-maker, I fear, oh!
Cannot give convincing advice.
The foul, dark world will not revere, oh!
The fair and bright but praise the vice.

From inner hall kept far apart, oh!
The prince won't wake, though wise and fair.
To whom can I lay bare my heart? oh!
Can I go on like this fore'er?

With magic herbs and slips of bamboo, oh!
I bid the witch for me to divine.
He says, "Two beauties will meet, true, oh!
Who won't admire the fair and fine?

"The Nine States are vast in and out, oh!
Can you find beauties only here?
Go far away and put off doubt, oh!
Beauty-lover will call you dear."

"Where can you not find fragrant grass, oh!
Why linger in old neighborhood?"
The world is dark, a dizzy mass, oh!
Who can tell evil from the good?
"Likes and dislikes depend on taste, oh!
This gang appears strange and unfair.
They gird foul mugwort on their waist, oh!
And say orchids unfit to wear."

"They cannot tell good plants from bad, oh!
How can they know the precious gem?
In filthy clothes they are clad, oh!
But pepper's fragrance they condemn."

I'd follow the witch's advice, oh!
But still I doubt and hesitate.
At dusk I prepare peppered rice, oh!
For the wizard to tell my fate.

All angels shade with wings the sky, oh!
Nine fairies come from Shady Peaks.
The wizard comes in splendor high, oh!
All lend their ear to what he speaks.

Sorrow after Departure

"Go up and down, look high and low, oh!
For one who'd share your common fate!
As ancient kings share weal and woe, oh!
With ministers and magistrate.
If you love beauty above all, oh!
Why do you need a go-between?
A convict pounding earthen wall, oh!
Was employed by his sovereign.

"A butcher brandished his knife, oh!
King Wen raised him to Master Great.
A cowherd sang and played his fife, oh!
Duke Huan made him Lord of the State.

"You're still in the prime of your years, oh!
Time has not yet run out, though fleet.
But autumn birds may cry in tears, oh!
And fragrant grass no longer sweet."

"Your jasper branch gleams low and high, oh!
All try to darken it with shade.
On partisans you can't rely, oh!
Through envy they will make it fade."

The age disordered changes pell-mell, oh!
How can I linger here so long?
Sweet orchids have lost fragrant smell, oh!
Sweet grass turn to weeds stinking strong.

ELEGIES OF THE SOUTH

How can sweet plants of days gone by, oh!
Turn to weeds and wormwood unfair?
Is there another reason why? oh!
For beauty no one seems to care.

On orchids I thought to rely, oh!
They're not so good as they appear.
Beauty is spurned in vulgar eye, oh!
Weeds grow and rise in fragrant sphere.

The pepper flatters and looks proud, oh!
It wants to fill a noble place.
It tries to climb upon the cloud, oh!
But it has nor fragrance nor grace.

All men do so on such a day, oh!
Who can remain unchanged at heart?
Orchid and pepper act this way, oh!
Let alone stream-sage and halt-cart.

I prize my jasper pendant rare, oh!
Despite what other people say.
It's flower-like, fragrant and fair, oh!
Its sweetness lingers still today.

To wear my pendant I take pleasure, oh!
In search of Beauty I will rove.
In an adorned dress which I treasure, oh!
I'll seek her below and above.

The witch foretold good luck for me, oh!
I choose to start on a day nice.
I eat the fruit on jasper tree, oh!
I grind fine jasper into rice.

The flying dragons draw my cart, oh!
Bright with ivory on display.
The gang differs from me at heart, oh!
I'll leave them and go far away.

I turn to Kunlun Mountains high, oh!
The winding way is wide and long,
The rainbow banners veil the sky, oh!
The phoenix bells ring merry song.

At dawn I start from Heaven's Ford, oh!
At dusk I reach the Western End.
The phoenixes sing in accord, oh!
Their wings with rainbow banners blend.

I go across the Sandy Ridge, oh!
I rove along the River Red.
I bid a dragon serve as bridge, oh!
For me to cross and go ahead.

The way is perilous and long, oh!
I bid cars go another way,
I turn left round Mount Pillar Strong, oh
"Let's meet at Western Sea," I say.

A thousand chariots in my train, oh!
On wheels of jade run side by side.
I drive eight dragon-steeds amain, oh!
Cloud banners spread like rising tide.

I slow down speed and curb my will, oh!
My spirit soars far, far away.
I sing nine songs and dance my fill, oh!
I steal the pleasure of a day.

I rise to see the splendid sky, oh!
I bow to find my home below.
My horses neigh and my glooms sigh, oh!
Looking back, they won't forward go.

Epilogue:

Alas! none understands me in the State, oh!
Why regret me native village?
Since I can't rule my kingdom's fate, oh!
I'd drown myself like ancient sage.

The Nine Songs

The Almighty Lord of the East

Auspicious hour, oh! of lucky day!
With deep respect, oh! we worship our lord.
His jade pendants, oh! chime on display;
He holds the hilt, oh! of his long sword.

Jade weights fasten, oh! his mat divine
Adorned with gems, oh! and flowers sweet.
We pour pepper sauce, oh! and laurel wine
And serve in orchids, oh! the spiced meat.

We raise the rod, oh! to beat the drum;
The drumbeats rise, oh! into the cloud.[①]
In slow rhythm, oh! we sing and hum;
To pipes and flutes, oh! we chant aloud.

In fair array, oh! our lord appears;
His fragrance fills, oh! the ritual hall.
Five sounds mingle, oh! and charm our ears;
Our lord is glad, oh! and gladdens all.

To The God of Cloud

Bathed in orchid's, oh! sweet-scented dews

---

① This line, missing in the original, is supplied hy the translator.

And dressed in robes, oh! of varied hues,
With fleecy hair, oh! you slowly rise
To beautify, oh! the morning skies.

In deathless hall, oh! you stay at noon;
Your whiteness rivals, oh! sun and moon.
The dragon is, oh! your charioteer;
You waft and wander, oh! far and near.

In silver drops, oh! you come with rain;
On wings of wind, oh! you rise again.
Upon the land, oh! you come with ease;
You float over, oh! and beyond four seas.
Longing for you, oh! I can't but sigh;
My yearning heart, oh! to you would fly.

To the Lord of River Xiang

Why don't you come, oh! still hesitating?
For whom on midway isle, oh! are you waiting?
Duly adorned, Oh! and fair, I float
On rapid stream, oh! my cassia boat.
I bid the waves, oh! more. slowly go
And the river, oh! tranquilly flow.
I wait for you, oh! who have not come;
Playing my flute, oh! with grief I'm numb.

In dragon boat, oh! for north I make
And zigzag up, oh! to Dongting Lake,

The Nine Songs

Ivy behind, oh! lotus before,
Orchid for flag, oh! cedar for oar.
I gaze on the lake, oh! and its farthest side;
My soul can't cross, oh! the river wide.
Across the river, oh! I cannot fly;
For my distress, oh! my handmaids sigh.
My tears stream down, oh! and slowly flow;
Longing for you, oh! I hide my woe.

With orchid rudder, oh! and cassia oar,
I break the ice, oh! and snow before,
As plucking ivy, oh! from the stream
Or lotus from trees, oh! in a dream.
The go-between, oh! cannot unite
Two divided hearts, oh! whose love is light,
As on a shallow stream, oh! a dragon boat,
Though its wings beat fast, oh! can't keep afloat.
Faithless as you're, oh! you deceive me;
Breaking our tryst, oh! you say you're not free.

At dawn I drive my cab, oh! by riverside;
At dusk on northern isle, oh! I stop my ride.
Under the eaves, oh! the birds repose;
Around the house, oh! the river flows.
I throw in water, oh! my jasper rings
And cast away, oh! my offerings.
I pluck sweet flowers, oh! on the island

And give them to maids, oh! inferior hand.
For time once lost, oh! can't be found again;
From thinking of you, oh! I would refrain.

To the Lady of River Xiang

Descend on northern isle, oh! my lady dear,
But I am grieved, oh! to see not clear.
The autumn breeze, oh! ceaselessly grieves
The Dongting waves, oh! with fallen leaves.
I gaze afar, oh! 'mid clovers white
And wait for our tryst, oh! in the twilight.
Among the reeds, oh! can birds be free?
What can a net do, oh! atop a tree?

White clover grows, oh! beside the creek;
I long for you, oh! but dare not speak.
I gaze afar, oh! my beloved one,
I only see, oh! rippling water run.
Could deer find food, oh! within the door?
What would a dragon do, oh! upon the shore?
At dawn by riverside, oh! I urge my steed;
Across the western stream, oh! at dusk I speed.

For you bid me, oh! to come today;
Together we are, oh! to ride away.
A midstream palace, oh! shall soon be made;
Over its roof, oh! lotus weave a shade.

In purple court, oh! thyme decks the wall;
With fragrant pepper, oh! is spread the hall.
Pillars of cassia, oh! stand upright,
And rooms smell sweet, oh! with clover white.
We weave the ivy, oh! into a screen
And spread the ground, oh! with its leaves green.
The corner stones, oh! shall be white jade,
And fragrance of orchids, oh! shall never fade.
On lotus roof, oh! let vetch be found
And azaleas, oh! are fresh around.
The courtyard is filled, oh! with herbs so fair;
The corridor, oh! with perfume rare.
All gods will come, oh! from mountains high
Like rainbow clouds, oh! o'erspreading the sky.
I throw when I wake, oh! from my sweet dream,
My shirt with sleeves, oh! into the stream.

I pluck sweet flowers, oh! upon the bay;
I'd give to strangers, oh! far, far away.
For time once lost, oh! can't be found again;
From thinking of you, oh! I would refrain.

The Great Lord of Fate

Open wide, wide, oh! the Heaven's door!
I will descend, oh! on cloud blue-black.
I bid whirlwind, oh! to go before
And icy rain, oh! to wash the track.

The lord in flight, oh! comes into view.
I'll cross mountains, oh! to follow you.
The young and old, oh! of the nine Lands,
Your life or death, oh! is in my hands.

I soar up high, oh! serene in flight;
I ride on air, oh! on shade and light.
I will speed up, oh! with our lord divine;
I will lead him, oh! to holy peaks nine.

My cloudlike dress, oh! floats in the breeze;
My pendants hang, oh! in rainbow hue.
I control light, oh! and shade with ease.
The people know not, oh! what I will do.

Of Holy Hemp, oh! I pluck the flower
To give to our lord, oh! going away.
Old age draws nearer, oh! with each passing hour.
The farther he's, oh! the sadder I stay.

My dragon chariot, oh! rumbles loud.
I drive my steeds, oh! into the cloud.
Laurel in hand, oh! I wait and sigh;
The longer I wait, oh! the sadder am I

With a broken heart, oh! what can I do?
Better keep fit, oh! in mind and heart!
Each man is fated, oh! to have his due;
It's not up to us, oh! to meet or part.

The Young Goddess of Fate

Autumn orchids, oh! and flowers sweet
Like silver stars, oh! grow at our feet.
Their leaves are green, oh! and blossoms white;
Fragrance assails us, oh! left and right.
All women have, oh! fair ones they love.
Why are you sad, oh! lonely above?

Autumn orchids, oh! are lush with shoots;
Their leaves so green, oh! with purple roots.
The fair ones fill, oh! the hall with glee.
Why is amorous look, oh! but cast on me?

Wordless you come, oh! wordless you go
As cloud-flags spread, oh! and whirlwinds blow.
None is so sad, oh! as those who part;
Nor so happy, oh! as new sweetheart.

In lotus dress, oh! a belt at the waist,
Suddenly you come, oh! and you go in haste.
At dusk you lodge, oh! on Heaven's plain.
Why on the clouds, oh! should you remain?

I'd bathe with you, oh! in pools divine
And dry your hair, oh! in the sunshine.
But you won't come, oh! and I wait long;
Lost in the wind, oh! I sing a song.
With plumed banners, oh! and peacock canopy,

You grasp Broom Star, oh! to sweep the sky.
You wield long sword, oh! to grasp the young;
You are the one, oh! to right the wrong.

The God of the Sun

Before my light, oh! dawns in the east,
I take a bath, oh! by Sacred Tree.
I stroke my steed, oh! with reins released;
The night brightens, oh! the day set free.

My dragon car, oh! is drawn by thunder;
My cloud-flags wave, oh! and undulate.
I sigh, go up, oh! and then look under,
My heart lingers, oh! I hesitate.

For ears and eyes, oh! what great delight!
Those who behold, oh! forget their land.
"Smite zither strings, oh! which are made tight,
And strike the bells, oh! till rocks their stand."

They play the flutes, oh! and the pipes blow.
The witch dances, oh! so bright and fair
As a green bird, oh! flies high and low.
All sing in glee, oh! and dance in pair.

All in accord, oh! to drums keep time;
The fairies come, oh! and shade the sun
In rainbow white, oh! and cloud sublime.

I shoot the Wolf, oh! it is undone.

I downward sink, oh! and grasp the Bow;
The Dipper's used, oh! to ladle wine.
I hold my reins, oh! by night I go,
For in the east, oh! at dawn I'll shine.

The God of the River

On rivers nine, oh! with you I roam
The whirlwinds rise, oh! and billows foam.
My water chariot, oh! lotus-canopied,
Two dragon-steeds, oh! run side by side.

On Mount Kunlun, oh! I look around;
My heart surges up, oh! beyond the bounds.
Homesick at dusk, oh! why not go back?
I gaze afar, oh! to find lost track.

You've fish-scaled house, oh! and dragon's hall,
Purple towers, oh! and pearly wall.
What would you do, oh! lord, after all?

I'd chase spotted fish, oh! on turtle white,
And roam with you, oh! on sands in delight,
While melted ice, oh! drifts left and right.

Let us go eastward, oh! hand in hand!
I'll see you off, oh! for southern land.
Waves on waves rise, oh! to welcome you;

Fish on fish leap, oh! to bid adieu.

The Goddess of the Mountain

In mountains deep, oh! looms a fair lass,
In ivy leaves, oh! girt with sweet grass.
Amorous looks, oh! and smiling eyes,
For such a beauty, oh! there's none but sighs.

Laurel flags spread, oh! over fragrant cars
Drawn by leopards, oh! dotted with stars.
Orchids as belt, oh! and crown above,
She plucks sweet blooms, oh! for her dear love.

"The bamboo grove, oh! obscures the day;
I come too late, oh! hard is the way.
Standing alone, oh! on mountain proud,
I see below, oh! a sea of cloud.

"The day is dark, oh! as dark as night;
The east wind blows, oh! rain blurs the sight.
Waiting for you, oh! I forget hours.
Late in the year, oh! who'd give me flowers?

"Amid the mountains, oh! I seek herbs divine,
Here rock on rock, oh! there vine on vine.
Longing for you, oh! I forget to return.
Are you too busy, oh! for me to yearn?

"Amid the mountains, oh! I feel not at ease;

I drink from springs, oh! beneath pine trees.
From missing you, oh! I am not free;[1]
I doubt if you, oh! are missing me.

"Thunder rumbles, oh! rain blurs the eye;
At night apes wail, oh! and monkeys cry.
Winds sigh and sough, oh! leaves fall in showers.
Longing for you, oh! how to pass lonely hours!"

For Those Fallen for the Country

We take our southern spears, oh! and don our coats of mail;
When chariot axes clash, oh! with daggers we assail.
Banners obscure the sun, oh! the foe roll up like cloud;
Arrows shower crisscross, oh! forward press our men proud.
Our line is broken through, oh! our position overrun;
My left-hand horse is killed, oh! and wounded my right-hand one.
The corpses block my wheels, oh! my chariot is stayed;
I beat the sounding drum, oh! in vain with rods of jade.
By angry Power's order, oh! our warriors are slain;
Their corpses and horses strew, oh! here and there on the plain.

They came out not to return, oh! to where they belong;
The battlefield's so vast, oh! their homeward way so long.
With their long sword in hand, oh! and bows captured from the west,

---

[1] This line, missing in the original, is supplied by the translator.

Though head and body sever, oh! their heart's not repressed,
They were indeed courageous, oh! and ready to fight,
And steadfast to the end, oh! undaunted by armed might.
Their spirit is deathless, oh! although their blood was shed;
Captains among the ghosts, oh! heroes among the dead!

The Last Sacrifice

The rites performed, oh! all beat the drum;
Flowers passed round, oh! fair dancers come,
With drums keep pace, oh! and sing with grace.
From spring to fall, oh! flowers will blow;
From age to age, oh! the rites will go.

Asking Heaven

Who could tell us at last
When did begin the past?
How could anyone know
The formless high and low?

Who knows where darkness did end
When light and shade did blend?
How to imagine things
In air but not on wings?

How could darkness turn bright
When was day divided from night?
How did light and shade strange
Originate and change?

Who did take measure of
The Ninth Heaven above?
Who built the firmament
Of such boundless extent?

What string could bind the sky?
How was the Pole raised high?
Where did Eight Pillars[①] stand?

[①] The Eight Pillars were the eight mountains which held up the sky. The Fury (See Stanza 18) butted against the north-west Pillar, causing the earth to tilt. Up and the sky to fall in that region, with the result that in the south-east the Pillar no longer touched the sky.

Elegies of the South

Why lowered southeast land?

How did Nine Spheres divide
And join up side by side?
How many ins and outs
Of Heaven's whereabouts?

On what rests Heaven wide?
How did twelve hours divide?
And sun and moon shed rays
And stars in fine arrays?

Rising from Vale of Beam
And setting by Dark Stream,
How many leagues had run
From dawn till dusk the sun?

How could the moon be bright
And wax and wane by night?
What advantage was there
To keep in it a hare[①]?

Unwed was Star Divine.
How could she have sons nine?
Where is Wind Star who frees
The freshening warm breeze?

What door, when closed, made night

[①] According to some traditions the moon had inside it a toad, a laurel tree and a hare who pounded the drug of immortality.

And, when opened, gave light?
Where behind the closed gate
Did the sun hide and wait?

To stem the flood Kun was unfit.
Why was he ordered to do it?
"No one cares for the worst.
Why not let Kun try first?"

Bird-turtles[①] made a sign.
How could Kun think it divine?
He would not sink but swim.
Why should the Lord punish him?

For three years cast away,
Why did his corpse[②] not decay?
How was his son Yu born
Out of his belly torn?

How did his son succeed
In accomplishing his deed?
How did the plan begun
Become a different one?

---

① The bird-turtles, were turtles with bird's heads and snake's tails. The story would seem to be that Kun saw a procession of them walking beak to tail and built his dike on the ground they had covered. turtles, like dragons, had power over the waters.

② Three years after his death on Feather Mountain Kun's body was cut open and his son Yu came out. His body then turned into a yellow dragon and dived into a lake.

ELEGIES OF THE SOUTH

How did Yu try to fill
Up the deep flood at will?
To build riverbanks and
To protect land on land?
How did the Dragon's tail[①]
Braze on the earth a trail?
How did the rivers flow
And towards oceans go[②]?
How could Yu well succeed
In Kun's miscarried deed?
And the Fury[③] o'ergrown
Knock the southeast Peak down?

Why are the nine lands dry
And wet the valleys lie?
Who knows why streams east go
And seas never overflow?

How far is east to west
Or north to southern crest?
Is it longer than wide
From north to southern side?

[①] Yu was assisted by a Dragon who traced lines on the ground to show where he should dig water-courses.

[②] Here two lines are missing in the original, and this stanza is expanded by the translator.

[③] See Note on Stanza 5.

ASKING HEAVEN

The Hanging Garden's high[①].
But where did its base lie?
Kunlun walls were ninefold.
How high were they, all told?

Who went with rapid strides
Through the gates in four sides[②]?
And what wind passed before
The open northwest door?

Could Torch Dragon[③] shed light
When the sun was not bright?
How could flowers divine
Before the sun's chariot shine?

Where's winter warm and old?
Where's summer young and cold?
Where could be found stone trees?
Where could beasts talk with ease?

Where's Dragon without horn
Swimming with bears airborne?
Where's the nine-headed Snake

---

① The Hanging Garden was in the Magic Mountain of Kunlun, which was the seat of the Lord on earth and the doorway into Heaven.
② The Archer went through the gates of Kunlun. See Stanza 29.
③ The legend said that it was day when the Torch Dragon opened his eyes and it was night when his eyes were closed.

ELEGIES OF THE SOUTH

Moving without a break?
Where would man never die?
Where lived giants on high?
Where's the nine-branched weed
And the hemp's blooming seed?
What serpent could devour
An elephant beyond its power?

Where's Mount Perils and goes
Black Stream dyeing one's toes?
How could a deathless man
Live as long as he can?

Where lived man-fish unheard
Of and white-headed giant bird?
How did the Archer[①] shoot down
Nine suns with golden crown
And the Raven in the sun
With its feathers undone?

Yu made flood-water flow
Through nine channels below.
How with a Southern lass could
He make love in the wood?

[①] At one time there were ten suns in the sky which dried up the earth, and the great Archer was ordered to shoot down nine of them. It was believed that there was a golden raven in the sun just as there was a hare of jade in the moon, that is the reason why the sun was called Golden Raven and the moon, the Hare of Jade.

Asking Heaven

If he loved the fair one,
He should have loved their son.
Why did he make up his mind
To leave their son behind?

How did Qi[①] take Yi's place
After he met disgrace?
Put in prison by Yi,
How could Qi be set free?

All shot at Qi with bows;
He was not hurt by blows.
How was Yi overthrown?
How did Qi win the crown[②]?

Qi sought favor divine
And got melodies nine.
How could his stony breath
Entail his mother's death[③]?

The Lord sent Archer down

[①] Qi was the son of Yu who chose Yi to be his successor. Qi fell in disgrace and was put in prison by Yi.

[②] The people of Xia preferred Qi as Yu's successor.

[③] According to the legend, Yu's consort, the Southern lass (See Stanza 30), ran away in disgust when he changed himself into a hear. When Yu pursued her she turned into a stone. She was pregnant at the time, and Yu called to her to give him his child, whereupon the stone burst open, revealing Qt. In a sense Qi killed his stone mother.

Elegies of the South

That Xia's evils be mown.
Why did he shoot the Lord of Stream
And wive his Lady Dream[1]?

He bent to the full his bow
And killed the big swine below.
Why was his sacrifice
Not accepted as nice?

The traitor wed his wife
And plotted against his life.
How was he boiled and slain,
Piercing seven shields in vain?

Barred from returning west,
Could Kun[2] cross Mount Crest?
Turned into a yellow fish,
Could he revive at wish?

Kun had black millet sown
And weeds and grasses mown.

---

[1] The Archer usurped the position of Yu's descendants. His wife and a traitor plotted against him, had him killed when he was returning from the hunt, and served up his flesh to his son.

[2] Kun was father of Yu, the Flood Hero and founder of the Xia dynasty (2205—1766 B. C.). Kun tried unsuccessfully to alley the flood by building dykes, and was punished by Yao for his failure (See Stanzas 12—14). His body turned into a water-monster. The poet showed an unusual tenderness for this unpopular figure.

Asking Heaven

Why should he bear the blame
And have ever a bad name?

Adorned with rainbow white,
Why should the Belle① take flight
With herbs divine to hide
Herself at the moon's side?

Heaven rules left and right;
Death comes when there's no light.
Should not the Golden Raven cry
When shot down from the sky?

How did the Lord of Rain shout
And showers fall all about?
How did the wings of Deer②
Raise the wind far and near?

How could the Turtles great③
Bear the five islands' weight?
Without the giant boat,
How could the island float?

---

① The Belle was wife of the Archer (see Stanzas 29, 35—37), stole his drug of immortality, fled to the moon and became the Moon Goddess (See Stanza 9).
② The Lord of Wind had a horned bird's head and a snake's tail on the body of a deer.
③ According to the legend, the five islands in the Eastern Sea were supported on the backs of giant turtles.

ELEGIES OF THE SOUTH

What did Strong Ao[①] ask for
At his brother's widow's door?
Was Strong Ao's head cut down
By the Hunter wearing crown?

The sewing widow kept
Ao at home and they slept.
How did she lose her head
By mistake while in bed?

How was Ao's armor planned
The stoutest of the land?
Boats overturned, by what way
Was the foe brought to bay?

King Jie[②] attacked Meng State.
How did this change his fate?
His queen with charm was filled.
How by Tang was she killed?

How did Shun's father blind
Leave unwed his son kind?

---

① The Strong Man Ao was the son of the Archer's wife and the Traitor (see Stanza 37). He had incestuous relations with his sister-in-law. The Hunter whose father was killed by Ao went to kill Ao by night and brought away his sister-in-law's head by mistake.

② Jie was the last king of the Xia Dynasty. His infatuation with his charming queen got from the Meng State precipitated his conquest by Tang and the founding of the Shang Dynasty in 1766 B. C.

ASKING HEAVEN

And Yao give him princess[①],
Telling not the sightless?

Who did at the first sign
Foretell the Shang's decline[②]?
By whom was built and made
The ten-floored tower of jade?

When Snake-queen[③] mounted the throne,
Who said it was well done?
Who made her body change
Into seventy shapes strange?

Shun yielded to his brother[④],
Still he was harmed by the other.
How could the dog prevail
And his tricks never fail?
Old Wu State extended far
Southward up to Mount Bar.
How did two princes great[⑤]
Come to rule over the State?

---

① Yao chose Shun as his successor and gave him his two daughters.
② Prince Ji Zi foretold the decline of the Shang Dynasty when the last Shang king built the tower of jade.
③ The Snake-queen bad a snake's tail instead of legs.
④ Shun's jealous brother did him harm by playing tricks like a dog.
⑤ The two princes were uncles of King Wen of the Zhou Dynasty.

In cauldron decked with swan of jade
The sacrifice was made.
King Jie of Xia received the crown.
Why was he overthrown?

How did Lord Tang advise
Yi his minister wise
To have King Jie destroyed
And people overjoyed?

How did King Ku's favor shower
On fair Janedy[①] in the tower?
How did the Swallow's egg
Make her conceived, I beg?

Hai[②] was Qi's worthy son;
He did as Qi had done.
Why did he go and keep
In Youyi ox and sheep?

How was the Youyi queen entranced
When shield in hand Hai danced?
How could the oxherd win

[①] Janedy was ancestress of the House of Shang. She was shut up in a tower. King Ku, first ancestor of the Shang people, sent her a swallow, and she became pregnant by swallowing its egg.

[②] Hai was son of Qi, an early ancestor of the Shang kings. He was the first Herdsman. He committed adultery with the queen of Youyi, where he was pasturing his flocks and herds, and he was killed by the lord of Youyin revenge.

Asking Heaven

The queen with lovely skin?

How did a herdsman find
Them making love and from behind
Strike and miss them in bed
And they lost not their head?

How could Heng① tend his flocks
And get back his fat ox?
Why did he, gifts in hand,
Not come back to his land?

Wei② followed up Hai's trace
And put Youyi out of place.
Why should he risk his life
To make love with his son's wife?

His brother full of lust
Did him harm, so unjust.
How could one doing wrong
Have descendants in throng?

Lord Tang the victor great③

---

① Heng, the younger brother of Hai, went to Youyi, gifts in hand, to get back his fat ox but did not come back to his State.
② Wei, the son of Hai, conquered Youyi and killed its lord.
③ Lord Tang was the first king of the Shang Dynasty. He needed a wise minister, discovered Yi Yin who was then the cook of the lord of Youshen, and arranged for him to be sent in the train of Youshen's fair daughter when he married her.

Elegies of the South

Went east to Youshen State.
How could he need a cook
And win a princess of good look?

In a riverside tree
Was found a baby free①.
How did the minister mean
Come with Youshen's fair queen?

Jailed in the Double Spring,
What wrong did Tang do the king?
Who provoked him to overthrow
The Xia by blow on blow?

How did lords in array
Arrive on battle day?
Who made grey eagles fly
And flock up in the sky?

Fa beat the corpse of Yin's king bad,
Why was Fa's② brother sad?
When Fa ruled the Zhou State,
Why did his brother sigh over Yin's fate?

When Yin had divine grace,

---

① The baby was Yi Yin, who became minister of Tang, the first king of the Shang Dynasty(1766—1122 B. C.).
② Fa, the first king of the Zhou Dynasty (1122—255 B. C.), led the lords to overthrow the Shang or Yin in 1122 B. C.

Asking Heaven

What had they done in place?
Thriving and then overthrown,
What crimes committed the crown?

Who made Zhou's ranks proceed
With weapons at full speed,
Keep pace and forward go
And smite the wings of the foe?

How was King Zhao's tour planned[1]
As far as the Southern land?
How was he drowned at sight
Of a great pheasant white?

King Mu[2] was fond of steed.
How did he tour with speed
The western land all o'er?
What was he searching for?

What did a man and his wife base
Cry in the market place?
Did King You[3] kill the pair
To get Bao Si the fair?

---

[1] Zhao, fourth of the Zhou kings, was drowned in the south.

[2] Mu, fifth of the Zhou kings, was famous for his steeds.

[3] A base man and his wife selling in the market place bow and quiver which, according to the rumor, would destroy the kingdom of Zhou, fled to Bao with an abandoned fatherless child, who grew up to be King You's queen, Bao Si, whose follies hastened the downfall of Western Zhou.

Elegies of the South

Capricious is the Fate
To punish and to compensate.
How was Duke Huan[1] denied
To be buried long after he died?

How could King Zhou's crowned head[2]
Into folly be led?
How did he hate advice,
And not flattery and vice?

What wrong did Pi Gan do[3]
That his heart was pierced through?
What good did Yesman Kai
To be raised to rank high?

Why did men excellent
Have a fate different?
Mei Bo was minced, so sad;
Ji Zi pretended mad!

Ji was King Gu's first-born[4].
How was he made Lord Corn?

---

[1] Duke Huan of Qi was the first Great Hegemon(died 643 B. C.).
[2] King Zhou was the last king of the Shang Dynasty, led astray by his vicious wife Da Ji.
[3] Pi Gan, Mei Bo and Ji Zi were lords under the last Shang king.
[4] Ji was ancestor of the Zhou people. All attempts at killing him by exposure were miraculously frustrated.

Asking Heaven

Why, left out on the ice,
Was he warmed by birds nice?

How did he bend his bow
And special talent show?
His birth surprised the king.
Could he teem with offspring?

Lord Chang at Yin's decline[1]
Became a herdsman fine.
How did he move his altar great
From Qi to replace the Yin State?

How did the people free
Bring their wealth and move to Mount Qi?
How much did the jeered king[2] care
For the bewitching fair?

Given the minced flesh of his son[3],
Lord Chang denounced the deed done.
Should not God punish the Yin State
If its last king cursed its own fate?

How could Lord Chang recognize

---

[1] Lord Chang was King Wen of Zhou, whose home was under Mt. Qi.
[2] The last Shang king was jeered because he was too much infatuated by the bewitching Da Qi to listen to any protest.
[3] Yin's last king killed Chang's son and sent him some of his flesh.

ELEGIES OF THE SOUTH

The butcher as master wise[①]?
Hearing the butcher's knife ring,
How glad was the future king?

When Yin's last king was killed,
Why was Wu[②] with sorrow filled?
Carrying the corpse of the knight,
Why was he so eager to fight?

Why should Yin's last king be
Hanged on a cypress tree?
What on earth did he tread?
Who would tremble in dread?

Heaven ruled royal fate.
How did it warn Yin State?
Yin's kings ruled over the land.
Why were they replaced by the grand?

At first Yi Yin was Tang's slave,
Then he became a lord brave.
How did he share Tang's nice
Ancestral sacrifice?

He Lu[③] was Meng's grandson;

---

① Master Jiang, famous minister of King Wen was once a butcher.
② King Wu carried the corpse of his dead father in his chariot to battle.
③ King He Lu of Wu (reg. 514—496 B. C.)was grandson of Shou Meng.

Asking Heaven

While young, he was a vagrant one.
Grown up, strong he became.
How did he spread his fame?

How did God like to eat
Peng-cooked pheasant's meat?
Peng lived eight hundred years.
Why should he still shed tears?

Lords ruled the Central State.
Why was the king in anger great[①]?
How could the ant-like throng
Be powerful and strong?

The two brothers[②] ate no fern.
How did the doe show its concern?
In northern waterside retreat,
Why were they glad to meet?

Why should the duke's younger brother[③]
About the duke's dog bother?

---

① When the unpopular King Li of Zhou was driven by rebellion from his capital, there was for some years a regency of lords.
② The brothers Bo Yi and Shu Qi disapproved of the conquest by Zhou of their overlord the Shang king and retired to northern waterside mountains, resolved "not to eat the corn of Zhou." They would have starved but for the miraculous appearance of a white doe which suckled them.
③ The younger brother of Duke Jing of Qin would take hold of the duke's dog but lost hold of his rank.

He would for it give gold,
But of his rank lost hold.

At dusk a tempest roared.
Why, on backward way feel bored
And without dignity
Appeal to His Majesty?

When hidden in a cave[1],
For what could one still crave?
Repent and mend your way!
What more have I to say[2]?

Why raise an army vast
And how could it long last?
How beaten ever since
He fought against Wu prince[3]?

Why go by winding way
To the hill far away,
Where to make love in mirth
And to Zi Wen give birth[4]?

---

[1] King Zhao of Chu, defeated by Wu in 506 B. C, was hidden in a cave for several months.

[2] Stanzas 91-95 are rearranged by the translator.

[3] Chu raised a vast army and lea a successful campaign against Wu in 538 B. C. but Wu prince He Lu put an end to Chu's run of victories.

[4] Zi Wen, famous minister of King Cheng of Chu, was born as a result of a "union in the fields".

Asking Heaven

Why say the king did wrong
And his State would not last long?
Why kill him and replace
Him and win divine grace[①]?

[①] King Cheng of Chu killed his elder brother and replaced him in 676 B. C.

ELEGIES OF THE SOUTH

The Nine Elegies

I Make my Plaint

I make my plaint and tell my grief, oh!
I vent my wrath to seek relief.
If what I say is not in honesty, oh!
I ask Heaven my witness be.

I bid the Five[①] and Six Lords[②] to, oh!
Judge if I am guilty or true.
I call on streams and mountains here and there, oh!
To be magistrates fair and square.

I serve my prince with soul and heart, oh!
Unwanted, I am set apart.
I nor flatter nor please the mass, oh!
My prince should know me from an ass.

My word can find in deeds its trace, oh!
I've changed nor feeling nor face.
No judge is better than my king, oh!
Proofs are not far to seek or bring.

It's right to put before myself my prince, oh!
But I have earned the crowd's enmity since.

[①] Lords of the North, South, East, West and Centre.
[②] Lords of the wind, rain, stars, etc.

The Nine Elegies

I care for none but my prince dear, oh!
But this has caused hatred and fear.

Whole hearted, I don't hesitate, oh!
But I cannot secure my state.
My devotion will only to him go, oh!
But it's the way to bring me woe.

None's truer to the prince than me, oh!
But I forget my poverty.
I serve him and ask for nothing more, oh!
But to win his favor I ignore.

I ask myself from time to time, oh!
Why I am punished without crime.
Peerless. I am turned upside down, oh!
The crowd jeers at the overthrown.

Slanders and blames are laid on me, oh!
So many that from them I can't be free.
My feelings stifled, I'm set apart, oh!
Screened from my lord, I can't open my heart.

Heavy with sorrow and despair, oh!
To whom can I lay my feelings bare?
My disordered words find no vent, oh!
My thought has no way to present.

If I'm retired and silent, who will know, oh!

Who will bear if I cry and onward go?
My mind feels troubled and suppressed, oh!
How can my sorrow be expressed?

Once I dreamed to ascend the sky, oh!
Halfway I could not go more high.
I bade the Dream Lord to divine;
He said, "None'd help your aspiration fine.

"At last a stranger should face peril alone, oh!
The prince might be thought of, not relied on.
Many tongues could even melt gold, oh!
Good men risk failure as of old.

"Burnt by broth, you blow on cold food, oh!
Why don't you change your attitude?
Ladders cast down, skyward you'd go, oh!
Such were your ways long, long ago.

"Frightened, all turn their hearts against you, oh!
How can you find companions new?
Different ways lead to the same end, oh!
Who would help you as your old friend?

"Prince Shen Sheng was a filial son, oh!
Slandered, not loved, he was undone.
Kun would not change, so stiff and straight, oh!
He failed in work at any rate."

They said that loyalty might lead to hate, oh!
I thought they did exaggerate.
Wounds would make a physician good, oh!
At last I know it's not falsehood.

The cross-bow is set overhead, oh!
And the bird-nets below are spread.
Traps are laid to mislead His Grace, oh!
Where by his side can I find a place?

If I tarry in such a state, oh!
I fear there would fall a heavier fate.
If I fly and perch far away, oh!
Won't my prince ask, "Where will you stay?"

If I a winding path pursue, oh!
Would my strong will allow me to?
My back and breast are split with pain, oh!
My heart is torn and aches again.

Magnolia and orchid I pound, oh!
And pepper flowers for food are ground.
I sow and plant asters to bring, oh!
Savors for provender in spring.

I fear none would believe my heart, oh!
So I say again and again my part.
I will retire to think and stay, oh!
With these sweet flowers far away.

ELEGIES OF THE SOUTH

Crossing the River

While young, I loved rare brilliant dress; oh!
When old, my love grows none the less.
My long sword dazzles far and nigh; oh!
My cloud-cleaving crown towers high.

My robe adorned with pearls moon-bright, oh!
My belt with gems shedding rare light①.
The world is foul and knows not me; oh!
I won't look down when up I flee.
I'd ride on dragons blue, oh! and white snakes as I please,
I would tour with King Shun, oh! the Garden of Jade Trees.

I would ascend, oh! the Kunlun Mountains,
Eat jade flowers, oh! and drink from fountains.
I'd live as long, oh! as earth and sky,
I would outshine, oh! sun and moon on high.
Misunderstood, oh! my heart will ache.
I'll cross the river, oh! at daybreak.

I look back, coming to the Beach, oh!
Where autumn or winter winds screech.
By mountainside I pace my steeds good, oh!
I stop my chariot near the wood.

---

① One line is missing here in the original and this line is expanded into two by the translator.

The Nine Elegies

I take a boat and upstream go, oh!
We beat the waves with oars and row.
Slowly it makes little headway, oh!
The whirling waves cause its delay.

At dawn I leave for farther west; oh!
At night in Southern Star I rest.
But since my heart is true and straight, oh!
What if I'm in a distant state?

By poolside I pace to and fro, oh!
Perplexed, I know not where to go.
Amid deep woods in twilight gloom, oh!
There are the haunts where monkeys loom.

The sun is screened by mountains steep; oh!
It's clark with rain in valleys deep.
Sleet and snow fall without an end; oh!
The heavy clouds with roof-tops blend.

About my joyless life I groan, oh!
Living in the mountains alone.
To please the crowd I cannot change my heart; oh!
I'd live a poor, sad life apart.

…oh!
   …①

---

① Two lines are missing here in the original.

His head shaved, Jie Yu was called mad; oh!
The recluse ran about, unclad.
A loyal man may not be used; oh!
A wise man is often refused.
General Wu suffered his last defeat; 'oh!
Lord Bi Gan was cut into minced meat.

Of former times this was the way, oh!
Why should I complain of today?
I will go straight and do no wrong; oh!
I'll live in the dark all my life long.

Epilogue:

The phoenixes from day to day
Fly farther and farther away, oh!
Swallows and sparrows, crows and pies all
Build their nests o'er the temple hall, oh!

Daphnes and lily-magnolias die
On the verge of the woods nearby, oh!
Stinking weeds overrun the place;
Fragrant flowers, cannot gain grace, oh!

Darkness replaces light;
The time is far from right, oh!
Faithfulness becomes doubt;
How can I not set out? oh!

The Nine Elegies

Lament for the Chu Capital

Inconstant is Heaven on high. oh!
How people tremble far and nigh!
Scattered, all men are lost in woe; oh!
Just in mid-spring eastward I go.

I leave my home for far-off place; oh!
Exiled, along the stream I pace.
I pass through city gate with heavy heart, oh!
On the first day[①] at dawn I part.

Leaving the capital of Chu, oh!
I am at a loss what to do.
In time we dip slowly the oar; oh!
My prince is not seen, I deplore.

Gazing on high trees, I heave sighs; oh!
Like sleet sad tears fall from my eyes.
Passing Summer Head, westward[②] we float, oh!
The Dragon Gate can't be seen from my boat.

Hurt by an invisible wound, oh!
I know not where to stand aground.
I follow the waves and the breeze, oh!
As if I traveled at my ease.

---

① The first day of a ten-day week.
② The poet sailed eastward, passed the Head of the Summer River and turned westward to gaze on the Dragon Gate in the capitall of Chu.

ELEGIES OF THE SOUTH

I ride on waves which overflow, oh!
Like birds in flight knowing not where to go,
My heart is in unresolved doubt, oh!
My thought in a maze can find no way out.

I let my boat float downstream through, oh!
The Dongting Lake and River Blue.
I've left the home where I lived since old days, oh!
At random I go eastward way.

Not for a moment does my soul not yearn, oh!
To the old capital to return.
Gazing westward on Summer Bay, oh!
I'm grieved each day to be farther away.

I climb the bank to look afar, oh!
To ease the sorrow of my heart.
I'm sad to see the land so wide, oh!
And the old ways of the riverside.

Where will the waves in the south flow? oh!
Crossing the river, where shall I go?
Who could foresee the ruined palace great, oh!
With its two ruined eastern gates?

My heart feels unhappy for long, oh!
And grief and sorrow come in throng.
The capital in mist is lost, oh!
The Summer River can't be crossed.

Unbelievably olden time disappears; oh!
I have not been back for nine years.
My sadness cannot be expressed; oh!
In despair my grief is compressed.

By outward flattery you're charmed, oh!
How could the weak not be disarmed?
Loyal, I tried to come near you; oh!
Jealousy cut me off from your view.

Kings Yao and Shun's deeds spread far and nigh; oh!
Their glory reaches to the sky.
The backbitters envious of their fame, oh!
Give them a false and unkind name.

You dislike the straightforward beauty, oh!
And say the braggarts doing their duty.
They press forward and win each day more grace; oh!
True beauty's forced to far-off place.

Epilogue:

Gazing with longing eyes, I stand; oh!
When may I come back to my homeland?
A bird flies nowhere but home-bound; oh!
A dying fox turns its head to its mound.
Guiltless but banished, I take flight; oh!
How can I forget you day and night?

Sad Thoughts Outpoured
Part I

Of gloomy thoughts my heart not eased, oh!
Alone I sigh, my grief increased.
My mental knot can't be untied; oh!
The night is long; the world is wide.

I'm grieved the autumn wind's changed the world's face; oh!
There're whirls and ebbs from place to place.
My gracious lord is moved to ire; oh!
My heart is drowned in sorrow dire.

I would rise up and elsewhere go; oh!
I refrain when I see people in woe.
I put my feelings into word, oh!
In homage to my gracious lord.

My lord made once a tryst with me, oh!
Saying the dusk our time should be.
Half-way he went back on what he said, oh!
And turned his mind upon another head.

Proud of his beauty on display, oh!
He showed me all his fine array.
From keeping his words he was free; oh!
Why should he vent his ire on me?

I'd take my chance to tell my part; oh!

The Nine Elegies

I did not dare with trembling heart.
Hesitating, I'd still go near, oh!
But my heart was wounded with fear.

Put in words my feelings true; oh!
Feigning deafness, he'd not listen to.
An honest man pleased not his master; oh!
The crowd said I would bring disaster.

What I said first in a plain way, oh!
Can it be forgotten today?
How could my advice give me delight? oh!
But I wish my lord's beauty shine bright.

He might imitate the three and five kings, oh!
And I might learn from Peng to do good things.
Is there an end that cannot be attained? oh!
Could a world-wide renown be stained?

Good virtue comes not from outside, oh!
Nor can good name be falsified.
If you don't give, what reward can you keep? oh!
If you don't sow, what can you reap?

Intermezzo:

I pour out thoughts to my prince fair and bright; oh!
There is no witness day and night.
He showed his beauty in high glee; oh!
He's too proud to listen to me.

Part II

A bird comes with the southern breeze, oh!
And perches on northern riverside trees.
How fair and bright alone he stands, oh!
Forsaken in these foreign lands.

Alone and cast off from the mass am I, oh!
None would recommend me near by.
My home's forgotten day by day, oh!
I would explain but find no way.
I gaze on hills with tearful eyes, oh!
By riverside I heave long sighs.

Though summer nights so short appear, oh!
They seem to me as long as a year.
The capital's so far away, oh!
My soul haunts it nine times a day.

Know not the road's twists and turns, oh!
For southern moon and stars my soul yearns.
In vain I dream to go there straight, oh!
My soul is busy early and late.

Why should my soul be true and fine? oh!
Other hearts are not the same as mine.
My recommender is so weak; oh!
None knows I am so hard to seek.

Epilogue:

Water runs fast in shallow long;
I go against the current strong, oh!
With wild glances southwards I go
To ease my heart of grief and woe, oh!

Before me stands a craggy hill,
Barring me from doing what I will, oh!
Shall I go back or forward through?
I am at a loss what to do.

I bend my head and hesitate;
I pass the night at Northern Gate, oh!
With troubled looks I'm tired and weary;
On my long journey I feel dreary, oh!

With knitted brows I heave long sighs;
High up and far away my soul flies, oh!
The way is long, the place obscure,
I have no recommender sure, oh!

I pour my thoughts out in this verse
To save myself from getting worse, oh!
My sorrow can find no way out.
To whom can I complain about? Oh!

Longing for Changsha

Early summer runs like a stream, oh!

Elegies of the South

The blooming trees and grasses teem.
Laden with endless grief, my heart, oh!
For far-off southern land should part.

Into the hazy gloom my eyes strain,
Where silence and quietude reign.
Tormented and tortured, I go, oh!
I've suffered long in grief and woe.

Over my feelings and thoughts I brood, oh!
I restrain myself though misunderstood.
You may fit the square into the round, oh!
I will stand on my proper ground.

To change my course and first intent, oh!
Is what good men disdain and resent.
Making with ink a picture clear, oh!
From former path I do not veer.

Outwardly straight and inwardly sound, oh!
Great men extol you all around.
If the carpenter cuts no line, oh!
Who could tell if it's curved or fine?

The sightless old man could not mark, oh!
Out colored brocade in the dark.
The keen-eyed peered in broad daylight; oh!
The dim-eyed thought him dim in sight.

The Nine Elegies

The black is changed into the white, oh!
The low is put onto the height.
The phoenix shut up in a cage, oh!
The hens and ducks gambol with rage.

Jewels are mixed up with stone, oh!
Into the same measure they're thrown.
The partisans whom I despise, oh!
Do not know what in me I prize.

When laden with a heavy load, oh!
I sink in the mire on the road.
I hide within me jade and gem, oh!
But do not know how to show them.

The dogs of the village bark, oh!
At what they see not in the dark.
It is the vulgar attitude, oh!
To condemn the wise and the good.

Within and without fair and square, oh!
The crowd know not my talent rare.
I store material to excess, oh!
But no one knows what I possess.

I multiply what's good and right, oh!
Generous, careful, fair and bright.
I have not met Shun, the sage king, oh!
Who knows my ease when I take wing?

Few kings and lords meet as of old, oh!
The reason why cannot be told.
Kings Yu and Tang lived long before, oh!
Too remote for me to adore.

I'll curt my pride and check my ire, oh!
Restrain my heart and my desire.
I will not change my mind in woe, oh!
To give an example I'll go.

I will halt on my northward way, oh!
At sunset dusky turns the day.
I'll give out a sorrowful breath, oh!
Lest it should blow after my death.

Epilogue:

The mighty rivers roll along,
Singing a gurgling song, oh!
The long, long road looks dim and grey,
Stretching far, far away, oh!

I cherish feelings pure
Have no witness sure, oh!
The connoisseur is dead,
Who knows the steed well-bred? oh!

All mortals live and die,
Ordained by Heaven high, oh!

My heart is calm and broad my mind.
Of what am I afraid behind? oh!

Long grieved, I vent my discontent;
Sighing, I oft lament, oh!
To me the world is foul and cold;
The heart of man cannot be told, oh!

I know that none can avoid death.
Why should I grudge my breath? oh!
I declare to those I revere,
I will take you as my compeer, oh!

Thinking of the Fair One [1]

Thinking of the Beauty[2] on high, oh!
I wipe my tears and gaze with longing eye.
The way is blocked, there's no go-between, oh!
How to send word to the unseen?

Laden with wrong on wrong, my cart, oh!
Sunken and stayed, I cannot start.
Pouring forth my feelings all day, oh!
Could a sinking heart express what I'll say?
I'd trust my word to floating cloud, oh!
But Feng Long[3] says I'm not allowed.

---

[1][2] The Fair One or the Beauty refers to the king of Chu.
[3] Feng Long was the Lord of Cloud.

I'd confide it to homing birds, oh!
But they're too high and fast to hear my words.

When King Ku sought for a fair queen, oh!
The swallow served as go-between.
If I should follow vulgar ways, oh!
How could I change my mind of former days?

I passed through woes from year to year, oh!
I would nor shift my ground nor veer.
I'd rather endure to end my life, oh!
Than alter my course in the strife.

I know the road is rugged before, oh!
But I won't change my way of yore.
Though my chariot's turned upside-down, oh!
Alone, I'll pursue the way of my own.

I harness my steed for a trip, oh!
The best charioteer flips my whip.
My steed falters and won't run fast, oh!
I take time and let it go past.
I point to western mountainside, oh!
Let dusk be the end of my ride!

When spring ushers in the new year, oh!
The bright sun shines long far and near.
I'll go along the stream carefree, oh!
And feast my eyes on scenes with glee.

The Nine Elegies

I cull in woodland clovers white, oh!
And on the isle herbs of the night.
I have not seen the sages of yore, oh!
Who will enjoy beauties before?

I gather herbs of various hue, oh!
To twine a garland girdle new.
The girdle's wreathed with flowers around, oh!
Withered, they're rejected on the ground.

I roam to pass sorrowful days, oh!
And see southerners' varied ways,
I find joy hidden in my heart, oh!
And I put my sorrow apart.

With the foul is mingled the fair, oh!
But fragrance will emerge from there.
The fragrance reaches far and wide, oh!
Full within, it will waft outside.
Its form and matter safe and sound, oh!
Unseen, it will spread all around.

I'd ask the fig to plead for me, oh!
I fear to climb into the tree.
I'd bid lotus as go-between, oh!
I fear my skirts wet with water unclean.

I do not like to climb up high, oh!
And I cannot go down and lie.

My body will not yield, I wait, oh!
Undecided, I hesitate.

I will pursue my former plan, oh!
And will not change the course I ran.
In the gloaming I find no outlet, oh!
Still I will go before sunset.
Alone, I go my lonely southward way, oh!
Can I not think of the ancient sage's day?

The Bygone Days Regretted

In the past the king trusted me, oh!
I published the royal decree.
The ancestors' deeds shone about, oh!
Made laws plain to those in doubt.

The law on rich, strong land held sway, oh!
The king confided in me each day.
The secret locked in my heart, oh!
Casual misdeeds were put apart.

My heart was pure and free from wrong, oh!
But slanders' jealousy was strong.
Angry with me the king became, oh!
And cared not if I'm free from blame,

The king's eyes and ears were deceived, oh!
What was wrong and false was believed.

The Nine Elegies

Unjustified, I met disgrace, oh!
And was removed to tar-off place.
To trust traducers he was free, oh!
Angry, he would find fault in me.

Though, loyal, I have done no wrong, oh!
I suffer from slanders in throng.
Ashamed before the sunny scene, oh!
I hide myself behind the screen.

Of the dark river on the brink, oh!
Could I bear to plunge in and sink?
I'd drown myself and leave my name behind, oh!
But to the light my lord's still blind.

Without measure to judge man's deeds, oh!
He let sweet herb hidden in weeds.
Could I express my feelings fine? oh!
I would rather die than repine.
Screened from my lord and hidden in the shade, oh!
How could loyal request be made?

Bai Li[①] was once a prisoner, oh!
A cook became Shang minister[②].
Master Jiang[③] was a butcher strong, oh!

[①] Bai Li became minister of Duke Mu of Qin in 660 B. C.
[②] Yi Yin was a cook and became minister of the first Shang king.
[③] Master Jiang became minister of the first Zhou king.

Ning Qi[1] fed ox while singing a song.
If they had not met connoisseurs, oh!
Could they have become counselors?

Wu[2] trusted in slanderers' words, oh!
Killed his general and rued afterwards.
Loyal Jie[3] would rather be burned, oh!
When his forgetful Duke Wen for him yearned.
The Duke made Mount Jie a holy place, oh!
To requite his service with grace.
The Duke thought of his old compeer, oh!
Clad in white, he shed tear on tear.

As martyrs loyal friends may die, oh!
Those are not doubted, who cheat and lie.
Acting nor with care nor on truth, oh!
One would believe slanders, forsooth.
The foul is mixed up with the fair, oh!
Who could discern between them anywhere?
Why are sweet herbs withered and lost, oh!
Before descends the hoary frost?
The unwise are more deaf each day, oh!
When flattery and slander hold sway.

---

[1] Ning Qi became minister of Duke Huan of Qi.

[2] King Fu Chai(?—473 B. C.)of Wu killed his general Wu Zixu.

[3] Jie was a loyal follower of Duke Wen of Jin and once fed him on a piece of his own flesh. Forgotten, he fled to Mount Jie.

As of old, jealous of the fair, oh!
They say orchids unfit to wear.
Jealous of fragrant beauty sweet, oh!
The ugly queen thought herself neat.
The Western Lady had a lovely face, oh!
Jealous women would take her place.

I would explain what I have done, oh!
They say I am a guilty one.
The wrong done me becomes each day more clear, oh!
Like stars in the celestial sphere.

I'd ride my steed and gallop to and fro, oh!
Without bit and rein, how could I go?
I'd mount a raft and downstream float, oh!
Where could I find oars for my boat?
A lawless heart can never rule, oh!
Nor can a boat go without tool.

I would rather unburied die, oh!
Lest disasters come by and by.
Should I plunge in the stream with much unsaid, oh!
Could I clear my lord's muddled head?

Hymn to the Orange Tree

Fair tree on earth without a peer,
Laden with oranges, you grow here, oh!
You are destined not to be moved

Elegies of the South

In the southern land you are loved, oh!

Your root's too deep from us to part;
What's more, you have a single heart, oh!
You have green leaves and flowers white.
What an exuberant delight! oh!

Your branches thick armed with sharp pine
Are laden with fruit round and fine, oh!
A riot of yellow and green,
What a dazzling splendid scene! oh!

Within you're pure; without you're bright,
Like a man virtuous and right, oh!
Luxuriant and trimmed, you thrive;
No blemish but charm's kept alive, oh!

While young, you aspire as you please,
Quite different from other trees, oh!
Grown up, independent you stand.
How you're admired in southern land! oh!

You're too deep-rooted to transplant;
Seeking nothing, you're so exuberant, oh!
You stand alone in this world wide,
Unyielding to the vulgar tide, oh!

You seal your heart and act with care;
You've done nothing wrong anywhere, oh!

So selfless, you have virtues high,
And become one with earth and sky, oh!

All the trees fade by the year's end;
I will forever be your friend, oh!
You're free from sin, so pure and bright,
And your trunk is ever upright, oh!

Although you appear young in view,
Even the old may learn from you, oh!
You're an example and inspirer,
And I am your humble admirer, oh!

Grieving at the Whirlwind

The whirlwind shakes the orchids down, oh!
My heart is drowned in grief overgrown.
A little thing is easy to fall, oh!
The faintest sound may arouse all.

Why ancient sages do I admire? oh!
I can't forget to what they aspire.
Who can conceal his change of heart, oh!
And play for long a deceitful part?

Birds and beasts seek their kind and meet, oh!
Herbs amid weeds are no longer sweet.
Fish show their scale's flickering light, oh!
The dragon hides its patterns bright.
Sweet herbs don't share the same field with the dead, oh!

ELEGIES OF THE SOUTH

When alone, orchids' fragrance will spread.

A beauty will always be fair, oh!
For the changing world I don't care.
Far away aspire my thoughts proud, oh!
Like the pitiable floating cloud.
Lest my thoughts should aspire in vain, oh!
I write songs to make myself plain.

Over beauties alone I brood, oh!
I pluck flowers from fragrant wood.
I heave deep sigh upon deep sigh, oh!
Alone and pondering, I lie.

Dreary tears stream from nose and eyes, oh!
Sleepless, I ponder till sunrise.
The pace of long, long night is slow, oh!
The grief I would suppress won't go.

I rise and slowly rove with ease, oh!
I try my sorrow to appease.
I utter a pitiable sigh, oh!
My stifling sorrow will not die.

I twist my longing round my breast, oh!
And weave my grief into a vest.
I break a branch to shade from light, oh!
And follow the wind left and right.

The world seems something vague which sleeps, oh!

The Nine Elegies

My heart like boiling water leaps.
I clutch my belt to calm my heart, oh!
Lost in sorrow, slowly I start.

Quickly, quickly elapsed a year, oh!
Slowly, slowly my time draws near.
Withered grasses break one and all, oh!
Unrivaled fragrant flowers fall.

My longing heart cannot be cured, oh!
My stinging words must be endured.
Exiled, I'd die to find relief, oh!
Rather than bear this endless grief.

The orphan sobs and rubs his tears, oh!
The exile goes and disappears.
Who could think of this without pain? oh!
Did ancient sages hear this in vain?

I climb a rock and look afar, oh!
How silent the far-flung roads are!
No echo of shivering shade, oh!
I strain my eyes and ears, but all fade.
Sad and dreary I cannot stay, oh!
My sorrow can't be put away.
My heart is tied with unloosed care, oh!
My breath is twisted into despair.

Immensity mute has no border, oh!

ELEGIES OF THE SOUTH

Vast wilderness can have no order.
Sound unseen can be felt and heard, oh!
Things uncreated can't be put in word.

The farthest can't be measured out, oh!
The endless can't be turned about.
Grief in silence is sadder plight, oh!
Flight in darkness affords no delight[①].
On wind and waves I'd find the road, oh!
Toward the ancient sage's abode.

I mount the steepest mountain height, oh!
And ride the upper rainbow bright.
I dance the lower one near by, oh!
And stroke with hand the azure sky.

I sip from floating source the dew, oh!
And rinse my mouth with frost in view.
I rest in the Cave of the Breeze, oh!
Awake, I rove again with ease.
Into the mist on Mount Kunlun I peer, oh!
From Mount Min flows the River clear,
Angry torrents dash on boulders before, oh!
I hear violent billows roar.

The River overwhelms its border, oh!

---

① The two Lines following this verse in the original ave transposed to Stanza 25.

The Nine Elegies

Its water runs and rolls in disorder.
It churns, I know not whence it flows, oh!
It winds its way, I know not where it goes.

Waves fall and rise and reach their height, oh!
They swirl and sway from left to right.
The waves before are pressed by those behind, oh!
As if flood and ebb were combined.

I watch the heated vapor rise, oh!
Condensed into dew in the skies.
I'm grieved it falls in frost and snow, oh!
And shocks with tidal bore below.

I'd borrow daylight to make a trip, oh!
And use a crooked yellow thorn for whip.
I seek the hermit's dwelling place, oh!
I see the royal brothers' trace[①].
My mind once made up won't depart, oh!
I'll be true to the measure of my heart.

Epilogue:

I grieve for hopes of days gone by, oh!
And mourn for those that will come nigh.
I would float down the River Blue, oh!
To the sea ruled by General Wu.

---

① These two lines are transposed from Stanza 17.

ELEGIES OF THE SOUTH

On Yellow River's isles I gaze, oh!
And mourn over Shen Tu of olden days[1],
Who rebuked his lord in vain, oh!
What good to be drowned in the main?

---

[1] Shen Tu Di was a contemporary of the last king of Shang, When his remonstrances against the king's folly were ignored he drowned himself clasping a great stone.

The Far-off Journey

Hard pressed by the world's ways and woe, oh!
I'd become light and upwards go.
Weak within and helpless without, oh!
On what can I ride and float about?

Fallen in the mire far and wide, oh!
To whom can I my grief confide?
Sleepless throughout the endless night, oh!
My lonely soul roves till daylight.

Between the boundless earth and sky, oh!
Forever man must toil, I sigh.
Beyond my reach are bygone days, oh!
Can I hear what the future says?

I pace and ponder here and there, oh!
Frustrated, I'm lost in despair.
My mind is bewildered in cloud, oh!
My heart with grief is overflowed.

My spirit goes and won't return, oh!
My body withered must sojourn.
I look in to learn to do right, oh!
And seek to know from where comes light.

I'm glad my mind is abstinent, oh!
With inaction I feel content.

Elegies of the South

I've heard how Red Pine[1] was carefree, oh!
I'd learn from what he had left me.

I know the Real Beings'[2] ways, oh!
And Immortals of bygone days.
They're deified and disappear, oh!
Their names will last from year to year.

I marvel how Fu[3] to a star could run, oh!
And how Han[4] with the Way could become one.
Their bodies tranquil go afar, oh!
Their spirit leaves the world for the star.

Transformed in air, I upward rise, oh!
As swift as gods and spirits in surprise,
The world is hazy, viewed from far, oh!
Spirits come to and fro, bright as star.

Leaving the dust, carefree I stand, oh!
I won't go back to my native land.
I'm not troubled by the world's woe, oh!
Nobody knows where I will go.

The seasons will change without rest, oh!
I fear the sun will ever go west.

---

[1] A Fairy Man much spoken of in Taoist mythology.

[2] Real Beings have won perpetual youth.

[3] Fu was translated into a star after death.

[4] Han sought for the drug of immortality and became immortal.

The Far-off Journey

Hoar frost will fall, I am afraid, oh!
And fragrant grass and flowers will fade.

I try to wander far and near, oh!
Nothing's achieved from year to year.
Who would enjoy with me fragrance at ease? oh!
At dawn I bare my heart to the breeze.
The wise king long ago was gone, oh!
Who can I model myself on?

Again I say:
Spring and autumn will pass away, oh!
How in old home can I long stay?
The Yellow Emperor lived long ago, oh!
I'd play with Prince Qiao[①] high and low.

I'd eat six essences and drink dew, oh!
I'd rinse my mouth with cloud and sunbeams new.
I'd keep my spirit pure and divine, oh!
Exhale the foul and inhale the fine.

I'd ride south wind to southern nest, oh!
Enjoy my fill and take a rest.
I'd greet the prince in serenity, oh!
And ask him how to attain unity.

---

① Prince Qiao was the son of King Ling of Zhou (reg. 571—545 B.C.) who flew away on a great white bird and became an Immortal.

He says, "We may learn the Way, oh!
Which we can't to others convey.
Small, nothing within it is found; oh!
Great, there is no boundary around.
If to disorder not inclined, oh!
Naturally will work your mind.
If your spirit is unified, oh!
At midnight it's kept pure inside.

"Empty-minded you may await, oh!
Do not strive to be first or great!
Let all things be formed as they may, oh!
Then you'll find the door to the Way."

Having learned this secret, I part, oh!
In a twinkling I start.
I see at Red Hill the Spirits with wings, oh!
They stay in the land of eternal springs.

At dawn I wash my hair in Val Divine, oh!
At dusk I dry myself beneath suns nine.
I sip the foam of Flying Spring, oh!
My breast adorned with gems in ring.

My jade-like face looks fair and bright, oh!
My spirit pure grows strong and light.
My body languishes by and by, oh!
My carefree soul flies upward high.

THE FAR-OFF JOURNEY

I like the warmth of Southern State, oh!
And laurel blooms in winter late.
The mountains without beast look dreary, oh!
The wilds seem lonely with no man weary.

My soul on rainbow cloud looks bright, oh!
Veiled in floating cloud, I reach the height.
I bid the porter open the door, oh!
He does and looks me o'er.

I bid the Lord of Cloud to lead the way, oh!
And ask where does Divinity stay.
I reach the ninth sphere's palace hall, oh!
From Morning Star I view the capital.

At dawn I leave Heaven's Arcade, oh!
At dusk I reach Mountain of Jade.
Ten thousand chariots smoothly ride, oh!
The steeds go forward side by side.
We drive eight dragons serpentine, oh!
Cloud banners undulate in a line.

I make a flag of rainbow bright, oh!
Five colors form a dazzling sight.
The york-steeds run with their heads bowed, oh!
The trace-steeds arch, curve and look proud.

We hear the din and bustle rise, oh!
Our colorful train dazzles the eyes,

I hold my reins and flip my whip, oh!
We'll pass by the wood in our trip.

We cross the eastern sky and turn right, oh!
The Wind Lord leads the way in flight.
Before sunrise the Heaven's cool, oh!
We fly across the Heaven's Pool.

The Lord of Wind leads the way on high, oh!
Dust cleared away, clean and cold is the sky.
Phoenixes spread their wings like flags unrolled, oh!
And in the west we meet the Lord of Gold.

For banner I seize the Broom Star, oh!
For baton the Dipper's Handle stretching far.
Up and down all look strange, oh!
Into fleeting mist the drifting waves change.

Obscured and dimmed the stars appear, oh!
I bid the Black Star to bring up the rear.
The Star of Letters leads my trains, oh!
All gods go abreast holding reins.

The endless road stretches afar, oh!
We slow down to the highest star.
Left and right the Master of Rain Hard, oh!
And of Thunder serve as my guard.

I'll leave the world and forget home, oh!
Carefree, I'll enjoy my fill and roam.

The Far-off Journey

My heart content will find delight, oh!
I'll make merry in my wild flight.

I cross the clouds and freely go, oh!
When suddenly I see my home below.
My groom homesick, my heart downcast,
My steeds look back and won't go past.

I picture in fancy my dears, oh!
With heavy sighs I brush away my tears.
I float with ease and go farther still, oh!
Must restrain my heart and my will.

To Fiery God I gallop straight, oh!
Then to Mount Mysteries of Southern State.
I see the wilds beyond the main, oh!
I float over the watery plain.

The Fiery God warns me not to go, oh!
I send for the Goddess of River Luo.
She plays music to Cloud and Lake, oh!
Two princesses sing the nine songs they make.

The Fairies of the Xiang on zither play, oh!
The Sea God and River God dance in spray.
The water monsters come in and out, oh!
Their bodies coil and whirl about.
The lower rainbow circles over, oh!
The phoenixes soar up and hover.

The music swells without end, oh!
Leave them and continue to ascend.

I give free rein to my steeds running forth, oh!
Till the Cold Gate of Extreme North.
I overtake the swift wind at Clear Spring, oh!
Over piled ice I follow the Northern King.

I meet the Water God on rugged way, oh!
I look back as night yearns for day.
I bid the Creator to appear, oh!
And pave the way as pioneer.

I tour north and south, east and west, oh!
Down to the depth and up to the crest,
Up to the heaven's crack, oh!
And then down to the abyss black.

Below it's bottomlessly deep, oh!
Above it's heavenlessly steep.
I look but see not what changes fast, oh!
Listen but hear nothing in space vast.
I transcend Inaction to Purity, oh!
Then I come near the Realm of Unity.

Divination

Qu Yuan exiled from the capital
For three years obtains no recall.
He served his prince loyally as he may,
But slanderers have barred his way.
His troubled mind is full of woe;
He does not know which way to go.
He calls on the diviner great
And asks about his fate.
"In my mind," he says, "I have doubt.
Will you please help me to work it out?"
The diviner sets out magic herb and tortoise shell
And says, "What would you have me tell?"

"Should I spare no effort to plough and hoe up weeds
Or make a name by singing the great men's deeds?

"Should I risk my life to say frankly what is right
Or save my skin by pleasing the rich and the might?
Should I preserve my purity and lofty stand
Or flatter and curry favor with a woman grand?

"Should I be honest, blameless, pure and hold my ground
Or be slippery as leather, lard or pillar round?

"Should I hold high my head like a steed running free
Or drift in water up and down like ducks in glee?

"Should I with the swiftest stallion keep pace
Or follow a broken hackney's trace?

"Should I fly with the skylark wing to wing
Or dispute with barnyard fowls for trifling thing?
Which way will lead to weal and which to woe?
Which way should I dodge and which should I go?
The world is dire
In mud and mire.
They call heavy cicada's wings
And think metal weights are light things.
Bronze bells are destroyed without cause;
Earthen vessels win thunderous applause.
Slanderers have renown
While wise men are unknown.
Alas! silent, what can I do?
Who knows I am loyal and true?"

The diviner then puts away
His magic herb and tortoise shell to say:
"A foot may be too short for something long;
For something weak an inch is strong.
Everything has its weak points;
Sometimes a wise man disappoints.
There's something which to fate we must resign,
And other things beyond the power divine.
So you may act according to your mind and heart;
My magic herb and tortoise shell can play no part."

The Fisherman[1]

Banished, Qu Yuan wanders by riverside,
Singing alone.
At the sight of his haggard face,
All skin and bone,
A fisherman asks,
"Are you not Lord of the Three Clans? Alas!
What has brought you to such a pass?"
Qu Yuan says,
"When all the world in mud has sunk,
Alone I'm clean;
When all the people are drunk,
Sober I'm seen.
How can I not get banished?"
The fisherman says,
"A wise man will not stick to any climes
But should adapt himself to the times.
If all others are dire,
Why not wallow with them in mud and mire?
If all the men are drunk,
Why should you from liquor have shrunk?
If you should above others rise,
Can you not get exiled? Can you think yourself wise?"

---

[1] The original is a poem in prose with rhymed lines.

Qu Yuan replies,
"I've heard it said:
After you wash your hair,
You should keep your hat fair.
After a bath, none the less
You should keep clean your dress.
How could I darken my mind bright
And blacken my skin white?
In River Xiang I would rather wish
To bury myself in the belly of the fish
Than spoil my spotless purity
With dirt and dust of vulgarity."
The fisherman has nothing more to say;
He faintly smiles and sings while paddling away:
"When the river is clear, oh!
I'll wash my headdress here.
When water is not neat, oh!
I may wash here my feet."

Song Yu

Nine Apologies

Ah! sad as death
Is Autumn's breath.
What a bleak day, oh!
Leaves shiver, fade, fall and decay!
Forlorn and dreary, oh!
As on a journey weary,
Climbing the hill, oh!
To see a friend off across the rill.
Empty and bare, oh!
The sky is high with chilly air.
Silent and drear, oh!
The river sinks with water clear.
Grieved, I heave sigh on sigh, oh!
Penetrated with the cold drawing nigh.
Heart-broken at the view, oh!
I leave the old for the new,
Rugged the way, oh!
The jobless poor is discontent with the day.
Lost in space endless. oh!
I stay on my journey friendless.
So desolate, oh!
I secretly pity my fate.
Swallows fly wing to wing home-bound, oh!
Forlorn cicadas make no sound.

Elegies of the South

The honking wild geese southward fly, oh!
Clattering partridges mournfully cry.
Waiting for dawn alone I cannot sleep, oh!
The crickets fighting at night makes one weep.
Fast, fast, half my days have passed, oh!
I have done nothing that could last.

Hard-pressed and grieved, oh! alone I dwell apart
Like a fair one, oh! so sad at heart.
I've left my homeland, oh! and go far away;
I rove here and there, oh! where to go today?
I love my lord, oh! all my life through;
My lord knows not, oh! what can I do?
I complain, oh! and repeat;
My mind troubled, oh! I forget to eat.
I'd see him once, oh! and tell for what I pine,
But his heart is, oh! different from mine.
My chariot ready, oh! I come back again;
I can't see him, oh! my heart feels grief and pain.
I sigh and lean, oh! on the board of my car;
A stream of tears, oh! wet the chariot-bar.
I can't cut off, oh! and leave him behind;
I'm at a loss, oh! with a disordered mind.
I grieve without end, oh! for what I can't do;
My heart still beats, oh! honest and true.
High Heaven divides the four seasons, oh!
I grieve at autumn for no reasons.

Dew drops on grasses in the breeze, oh!
Withered leaves fall from the plane trees.
Gone are the sunny days so bright, oh!
Invaded by the long, long night.
I've left behind my years in bloom, oh!
And sink into deepening gloom.

Autumn warns us first by white dew, oh!
Winter's severe frost falls anew.
No more splendor of summer high, oh!
All are sickly and buried lie.
Discolored, leaves turn pale and fade, oh!
Branches criss-cross in disorderly shade.
Trees look languid and no longer fair, oh!
They yellow when their trunks turn bare.
I grieve at sparse trees in this land, oh!
Like wounded skeletons they stand,
Their leaves and grasses wilt and wither, oh!
My time is also gone, but whither?
I seize the reins and use no whip, oh!
I rove as if on a pleasure trip.
But the end of the year draws near, oh!
I can't live to old age, I fear.
I mourn I was born in a wrong age, oh!
When the world is red-hot with rage.
I lean on rails in Western Hall for long, oh!
To hear alone the crickets' mournful song.

Elegies of the South

My heart trembles without relief, oh!
I have so much sorrow and grief.
Looking up, I sigh at the moon so bright, oh!
And pace beneath the stars till comes daylight.

I grieve for orchids once in bloom, oh!
Which beautify the capital room.
But no fruit is borne by the flower, oh!
Which flies away in wind and shower.
My lord prefers not orchid fair, oh!
To any other flower there.
My matchless thought I can't to him convey, oh!
So I leave him and fly away.
I pity myself sad and drear, oh!
I'd see him once to make all clear.
I cannot, but I won't complain, oh!
Although my heart is gnawed by pain.
Could I not long for my lord great? oh!
I can't go through his ninefold gate.
His fierce, snarling dogs bark and roar, oh!
None can pass the bridge and closed door.
High Heaven overflows with autumn rain, oh!
When will the Earth get dry again?
Alone by waterside I heave long sighs, oh!
And gaze at floating cloud with longing eyes.

The vulgar world's crafty and fine, oh!

NINE APOLOGIES

They turn away from the ink-line.
They won't ride a swift horse, oh!
But take the road on a nag of weak force.
Is there in this age no fine steed? oh!
There is no man who can drive at full speed.
If a wrong rider takes the rein, oh!
The steed will bolt and run amain.
Wild ducks and geese eat water-weed, oh!
On which high-soaring phoenix will not feed.

If you put a square peg in a round hole, oh!
Can the peg fit and play its role?
The common birds all have a nest, oh!
Only the phoenix has nowhere to rest,
I'd gag my mouth and nothing say, oh!
Having received favor in former day.
Master Jiang[①] throve at ninety years, oh!
Before then he'd not met his peers.
Where goes the fine steed in flight, oh!
Where will the phoenix alight?
The ways of the world become flat, oh!
The fancier of today like the fat.
The hidden steed will disappear, oh!
The flying phoenix won't come near.

---

① Master Jiang assisted the Martial King of Zhou to overthrow the Shang dynasty in 1122 B. C.

Even birds and beats know their way, oh!
Why not good men choose where to stay?
Without good driver won't run a fine steed, oh!
Nor will phoenix take food for greed.
My lord neglected and rejected me, oh!
I wish to be loyal, how can I be?
I'd be estranged from him without a word, oh!
But I can't forget the favor he conferred.
I suffer more without a friend, oh!
How can my sorrow have an end?

Bitter frost and dew fall along, oh!
My heart is glad they've done no wrong.
But when snow and sleet aggravate, oh!
I know my inevitable fate.
I'd wait for better chance from high, oh!
With vast expanse of grass I'd die,
Straight to my lord I wish to go, oh!
But the road is blocked high and low.
I wish to follow an easy way, oh!
But I can't find it night and day.
I stop midway in perplexity, oh!
What can I do but recite poetry?
But dull, I know not how to please, oh!
How can I recite verse with ease?

NINE APOLOGIES

I love Shen's[①] loyal sentiment, oh!
But fear the time is different.
The vulgar world is crafty and unfair, oh!
They destroy the compass and square.
Staunch, I won't follow the age, oh!
But the teachings left by former sage.
In a foul world to appear bright, oh!
Won't give my heart the least delight.
I won't by foul means win a fame, oh!
But live poor and free from blame.
I may eat any food not bad, oh!
I need to be but warmly-clad.
I admire the old poet's style, oh!
I would be only worth my while.
Much grieved for no reason I stand, oh!
On this immense expanse of land.
I have no furs against winter's cold, oh!
I fear I'd die before spring I behold.

In lonely late autumn's long night, oh!
Tormented, my heart is in sad plight.
As spring and autumn alternate, oh!
I sadly grieve for my hard fate.

---

① Shen Baoxu, nobleman of the State of Chu, fled to the State of Qin when the Chu capital was overrun by Wu armies, wept in the Qin court continuously for seven days, sang "Comradeship" (in *The Book of Poetry*) and induced the ruler of Qin to take the field against Wu on Chu's behalf.

Four seasons come and go, a year will end, oh!
And light and dark will never blend.
The sun will rise and set again, oh!
The moon, however bright, will wane.
The year will quickly pass away, oh!
Old age will come, all will decay.
Distraught, my heart still hopes for the best, oh
Disappointed, I cannot rest.
Anguish and grief rise and rerise, oh!
What can I do but heave long sighs!
The years roll by from day to day, oh!
Where, old and lonely, can I stay?
Affairs press me to forward go, oh!
How can I hesitate in woe?

How does the cloud overspread so soon, oh!
As to cover up the bright moon?
I wish my loyalty shine bright, oh!
But veiled in mist, it's out of royal sight.
I wish the bright sun to come out, oh!
But it is overcast all about.
I'll be loyal without thinking of fame, oh!
But others try to stain my name.
Kings Yao and Shun had virtues high, oh!
Their glory reaches to the sky.
But jealous persons backbite from behind, oh!
Defaming them as kings unkind.

NINE APOLOGIES

Bright as the sun and the moon are, oh!
Still neither is a flawless star,
Not to speak of the state affair, oh!
More complicated beyond compare.

A lotus coat is soft to wear, oh!
But too flimsy a girdle to bear.
If you are proud and boast of your might, oh!
None will be loyal to you left and right.
You dislike the straightforward beauty, oh!
And say the braggarts doing their duty.
They press forward and win each day more grace, oh!
True beauty's forced to far-off place.[①]
If farmers idly put their plough down, oh!
The fields with weeds will be overgrown.
Preoccupied with private affair, oh!
Who of the State would take good care?
If blind, you just repeat what people says, oh!
Can you know whom to blame and whom to praise?
If you, adorned, look in the glass, oh!
You may hide your defects and pass.
I'd send my message by a shooting star, oh!
But soon it's away, I know not how far.
At last the sky is veiled by floating cloud, oh!
The earth below is wrapped in a dark shroud.

[①] See Qu Yuan's "Lament for the Chu Capital," Stanza 16.

ELEGIES OF THE SOUTH

Kings Yao and Shun used able men, oh!
They could sleep sound and carefree then.
None was against them here or there, oh!
Their hearts were free from fear and care.
If you ride your steed for a trip, oh!
Why should you force it with a whip?
You can't be safeguarded by town wall, oh!
What avails heavy armor at all?

Why am I worried endlessly, oh!
And gnawed by grave anxiety?
Passenger between earth and sky, oh!
I have accomplished nothing, why?
I will disappear and subside, oh!
Still I long for fame far and wide.
Look for connoisseur about, oh!

I wear myself foolishly out.
There's water everywhere below, oh!
Where can a wandering bird go?
None in the State can ride a fine steed, oh!
Yet they search for one fast in speed.
When Duke Huan of Qi heard Ning's[1] song, oh!
He knew Ning could make his State strong.
Without a connoisseur of horse, oh!

---

[1] Ning was a merchant who became a leading minister of Duke Huan of Qi (reg. 658—643 B. C.), the first of the Five Great Hegemons.

Who could discern one of great force?
I weep and brood over the day, oh!
I know where there's a will, there's a way.
I'll be loyal with a pure heart, oh!
But the jealous courtiers keep me apart.

If my worthless body allowed, oh!
My spirit to soar amid the cloud,
I'd ride the ether round on round, oh!
And race with gods sky-bound, sky-bound.
I'd drive the rainbow white, so white, oh!
And pass through the stars bright, so bright.
At left the Red Bird beats its wing on wing, oh!
At right the dragons green swing and swing.
The Lord of Thunder rumbles past, past, oh!
The Master of Wind flies ahead, fast, fast.
In front, light coaches ring bell on bell, oh!
Behind, the heavy waggons utter yell on yell.
Clouds undulate like banners serpentine, oh!
A train follows of horsemen fine.
I'll never change my loyal, loyal mind, oh!
My wish fulfilled, I will not be unkind.
If Heaven's favor should last long, oh!
I'd come back to see my lord free from wrong.

ELEGIES OF THE SOUTH

QU YUAN

Requiem

While young, I was spotless and pure, oh!
To do what is right I was sure.
I served my lord with virtuous deeds, oh!
Entangled then amid vulgar weeds.
My lord of my deeds was not clear, oh!
I suffered and felt sad and drear.[①]

The Lord God to the wizard said,
"To someone I'd give aid,
Whose soul's dispersed below.
To help him you should go."

The wizard said, "It seems
Hard to fulfil your dreams.
If you insist I should divine,
I'm afraid I could not decline."

The wizard came down to play his role:
Come back, O soul!
Why should you leave your breast
And roam north, south, east, west? oh!
Why desert your place of delight
And fall in a sad plight? oh!

---

① The first six lines appear to be said by the soul whom the wizard tries to call back in the following stanzas.

Requiem

O soul, come home!
Don't eastward roam, oh!
The eastern giants are nine fathoms tall;
They seek and catch souls they enthral, oh!
Ten suns together shine,
Melting stone and metal fine, oh!
The giants are accustomed to the day,
But you souls would melt away, oh!
Come home, come home!
Don't eastward roam, oh!

O soul, come back!
Don't stay with southerners whose teeth are black!
They have tattooed forehead;
They sacrifice the flesh of the dead,
Whose bones are pounded to shred, eh!
There huge serpents defile,

And foxes run from mile to mile, eh!
The nine-headed snakes go
Swiftly to and fro
And swallow men high and low, eh!
Come back, come back!
Do not stay with those with teeth black, eh!

O soul, come back from the west vile
Where quicksands quake from mile to mile, eh!
If you fall in the thunderous whirlpool,

You would be swallowed by water cool, eh!
If you're by luck not drowned,
You'll find vast wilderness around, eh!
Where wasps are big as gourds; red ants
As huge as elephants, eh!
No grain grows there; man feeds
On dry and thorny reeds, eh!
The barren earth would make men rot;
No water could be got, eh!

You'll find no shelter near at hand
In such a boundless land, eh!
Come back! Don't westward go,
Or you would fall in woe, eh!

O soul, come back, do not go forth!
You can't stay in the north, eh!
Where ice rises pile on pile
And snowflakes fly from mile to mile, eh!
Come back! Do not go forth!
You cannot stay long in the north, eh!

O soul, come back! Don't hie
Up to the sky, eh!
Where the man-eating tiger guards
The nine gates with leopards, eh!
The nine-headed monsters without cease
Pull up nine thousand trees, eh!

REQUIEM

The wolves and jackals go
With hostile eyes to and fro, eh!
They hang out man for sport and throw
Him into the abyss below, eh!
They wait for orders from on high,
Then man may shut his eyes and die, eh!
Come back, come back at my call,
Or in danger you'll fall, eh!

O soul, come back! Don't go
To the Hell down below, eh!
Its guardian has nine tails;
The horn on his head ails, eh!
With shoulders huge and bloody thumb,
He pursues men, fearsome, eh!
His three-eyed tiger's head.
And bull-like body would cause dread, eh!
On human flesh he'd feed,
…eh!
Come back! Don't go below
Or you'll be lost in woe, eh!

O soul, come back! Do not be late
To enter the capital's gate, eh!
The wizard calling you will retreat
Backward to lead your feet, eh!
Basket and strings from east and west,

And central banners and the rest, eh!
Magic instruments ready one and all,
You hear the wizard's wailing call, eh!
O soul, come on your backward road
To your former abode, eh!

No quarters of the world are paradise
But full of harm and vice, eh!
Think of the house of your own,
Quiet and reposeful up and down, eh!
Great halls and deep rooms on high ground
With railings on railings around, eh!
Pavilions and terraces far and nigh
Look on the mountains high, eh!
The lattice doors and crimson stairs
Are richly carved with squares on squares, eh!
Draughtless is the winter room;
The summer gallery is full of gloom, eh!
Streams murmur in and out
Of the gully and thereabout, eh!
The mililotus sway at ease
With lofty orchids steeped in breeze, eh!
The inner hall and rooms o'erspread
With floors and ceilings red, eh!

How bright the wall of polished stone looks
With hangings green on jasper hooks, eh!

The pearly kingfisher bedspread
Dazzles by the light those pearls shed, eh!
Walls are adorned with soft tapestries
And silken canopies, eh!
Ribbons of varied hues displayed
With precious stone and jade, eh!

The sight in inner room is fair
With decorations rare, eh!
The orchid-perfumed candles shine
On flower-like faces fine, eh!
Young ladies of sixteen are bright;
In turn they share your bed at night, eh!
Noble maidens come from many a land;
Above other beauties they stand, eh!
With rich and varied headdress tall,
They throng the palace hall, eh!
Each has an unsurpassed fair face
And an unrivaled grace, eh!
Each slender body stands straight,
Silent but intimate, eh!
Their lovable, amorous looks
Illumine nuptial chamber nooks, eh!
Their moth-like brows and eyes bright
Glisten with gleams of light, eh!
Their delicate flesh and soft skin
And seductive glances will ever win, eh!

ELEGIES OF THE SOUTH

In the tent or garden of pleasure,
They're waiting for your leisure, eh!

In lofty hall there hang curtain and screen
Adorned with kingfisher feathers green, eh!
Red walls with panels are inlaid
As the roof-beams with jet and jade, eh!
O'erhead the carved rafters wake
With painted dragon and snake, eh!
Seated in the hall, leaning on railings, you
May have a winding pool in view, eh!
The lotus begins its blooming hours,
Mingled with caltrop flowers, eh!
The purple-stemmed plants with grace
Ripple green water's face, eh!
Attendants in skins of leopard,
Ranged by the steps, stand guard, eh!
When you arrive in tilbury fine,
Footmen and riders wait in line, eh!
Orchids carpet the ground about the door,
With hibiscus hedge-row before, eh!
O soul, come back! Why stay
So far away? eh!

Your household pays homage at your shrine
With all kinds of food and wine, eh!
With yellow millet, early wheat and rice

REQUIEM

Offered in your sacrifice, eh!
Salt, bitter, sour and pepper hot,
Honey sweet and what not, eh!
The fatted beefsteak is so well
Cooked that it gives a nice smell, eh!
If you like ginger or vinegar,
There's soup of Southern connoisseur, eh!

You'll find stewed turtle and roast kid again
Served up with sauce of cane, eh!
Swans cooked in sour sauce, ducks side by side
With geese and big cranes fried, eh!
Seethed tortoise and chicken braised,
Delicious, not to spoil your taste, eh!
Fried honey-cakes of rice
And malt-sugar sweetmeats nice, eh!
The jade-like wine fills up
The bird-shaped cup, eh!
After wine strained of dregs and ice-cold drink,
Into refreshening coolness you'd sink, eh!
A sumptuous feast is displayed
With wine which looks like jade, eh!
Come home where you may expect
Nothing wrong but respect, eh!

The feast is in full swing;
Fair maidens come and dance and sing, eh!

ELEGIES OF THE SOUTH

Drums are beaten and bells are rung,
And newly composed songs are sung, eh!
"Gathering Caltrops," "Crossing the Stream Wide,"
And "Sunny Riverside," eh!
The beauties are drunk with wine;
Their rosy faces shine, eh!
Their flirting glances look
Like amorous waves in a brook, eh!
They are clad in silks fine,
Splendid without freak design, eh!
From chignon high falls their long hair
Adorned with jewels rare, eh!
The dancers in two rows of eight
Perform a dance of Central State, eh!
Their sleeves cross like bamboo stems
And come down bright with gems, eh!
In sound the pipes and zithers vie;
Thunderous drums run high, eh!
The palace walls tremble with fear
At the uproar they hear, eh!
Then songs are sung from west or east
And music played for the feast, eh!
Men sit by women's side;
In disorder they hide, eh!
The belts and strings untied
Run riot far and wide, eh!

Requiem

Fair dancers come from east or west
Sit together with the guest, eh!
The songstress singing best
Finds favor o'er the rest, eh!

Ivory chess with chips of jade,
The game of six pieces is played, eh!
The two divided sides commence
Their attack and defence, eh!
It's hard to win his fight;
The winner cries, "Five White!" eh!
He Wins a rhino hook;
Bright as day it would look, eh!
Some strike the bell till its frame swings;
Some sweep the wooden zither's strings, eh!
Without cease they make merry and drink
Till days into nights sink, eh!
Candles of orchid-perfumed fat shed light
On their stands of carved bronze so bright, eh!
Guests rack their brain to make songs new,
Sweeter than orchid blooms in view, eh!
Each has his weak points and his strong!
Together they make a better song, eh!
When their pleasure reaches its height,
They drink to the departed with delight, eh!
O soul, come on your backward road
To your former abode, eh!

ELEGIES OF THE SOUTH

Epilogue[①]:

In the new year begins spring day, oh!
I hurry on my southward way.
Green duckweed sprouts in rows, oh!
And white clover grows.
I pass by River Lu[②], oh!
To my left stretches water blue.
I go along the waterside, oh!
And see an expanse far and wide.
The four black horses go along, oh!
Before a thousand chariots strong.
The wood is burned and flames rise high, oh!
A pal! of smoke darkens the sky.
The footmen follow on the way, oh!
And vie to lure the hunted prey..
The steed is reined, the prey in sight, oh!
The chariot is turned to the right.
In Dream Lake with the king I'd race, oh!
To see who would win the first place.
The king himself shoots at the head, oh!
Of a rhino which falls dead.
Dawn follows night on the run, oh!
Time and tide wait for none.

---

① The epilogue seems to be the words of the soul.
② In modern Jiangxi Province.

REQUIEM

Covered by orchids and grass green, oh!
The waterside path can't be seen.
Deep, deep the river flows at ease, oh!
On rivershores stand maple trees.
I gaze for miles and miles with longing eyes, oh
For spring could I not heave deep sighs?
"O soul, come back to southern shore, oh!
Over your homeland can you not deplore?"[1]

---

[1] The last two lines are the words of the wizard.

ELEGIES OF THE SOUTH

Great Requiem[①]

Green spring replaces winter drear;
The sun shines bright far and near, eh!
The breath of spring revives the earth
And quickens every creature's birth, eh!
Ice in the dark will melt by day;
The soul has nowhere to run away, eh!
O soul, come back to your own home!
Do not go far away and roam, eh!

O soul, come back and take a rest,
Don't go north or south, east or west, eh!
In the east there is the sea;
Its angry waves would drown you and me, eh!
The dragons swim side by side,
Up and down with the tide, eh!
The fog is mingled with the rain;
The sky appears one with the main, eh!
O soul, don't go to eastern state,
Where the valley is desolate, eh!

O soul, don't go south for a while,
Where fire is burning from mile to mile
And coiling cobras beguile, eh!

[①] Written to summon the soul of the sick king of Chu, or that of the deceased poet Qu Yuan.

GREAT REQUIEM

In dangerous mountain and wood,
Tigers and leopards eat man as food, eh!
The cow-fish and spit-sand[①]
And roaring serpents overrun the land, eh!
O soul, be not bewitched by southern charm!
The monsters would do you great harm, eh!

O soul, do not go to the western state,
Where the moving sands undulate
Like a boundless ocean great, eh!
The beasts with head like swine stare
With slanting eyes and shaggy hair, eh!

Their wild, mad laughter hides beneath
Their long claws and serrated teeth, eh!
O soul, do not go to the west
Infested with dangerous pest, eh!

O soul, do not go north, behold!
Where tower frozen mountains cold,
And glares the red Torch Dragon old, eh!
The northern river's deep, we're at a loss
How we can go across, eh!
The sky is white with snow;
The earth congealed below, eh!
O soul, do not go forth

---

① The spit-sand was said to be a bogey which lurked in riverbanks and killed the passer-by by spitting sand at him.

ELEGIES OF THE SOUTH

Beyond the extreme north, eh!

O soul, do come back please!
To enjoy leisure and ease, eh!
Do what you will in your southern state,
You'll be untroubled and sedate, eh!
Fulfil your wish, enjoy your best
And set your mind at rest, eh!

You will be happy and gay,
And live as long as you may, eh!
O soul, come back like birds,
You will be happy beyond words, eh!

The five grains are heaped up high,
With corn of zizania near by, eh!
The cauldrons seethe in view,
Sweetened with blended savors new, eh!
Plump waterbirds, geese and pigeons sweet,
Flavored with broth of jackal's meat, eh!
O soul, come back with delight!
Indulge your appetite, eh!

Fresh turtle, chicken succulent,
With southern sauces blent, eh!
Pickled pork, dog's meat dried,
With slices of zingiber beside, eh!
Sour salad of the South
Savory to the mouth, eh!

Great Requiem

O soul, come back and rejoice
And indulge in your own choice, eh!

Roast crane is served up and quails boiled,
Stewed magpies and goose broiled, eh!
Duck is served up in steam,
Together with fried bream, eh!
O soul, come back and go ahead!
Before you choicest things are spread, eh!

Four kinds of matured wine
Won't rasp on your throat fine, eh!
Do not drink to excess with cheer
The fragrant ice-cooled liquor clear, eh!
White yeast is mixed with must of Wu
To make the clearest wine of Chu, eh!
O soul, come back, come here!
You may drink without fear, eh!

The Northern, Southern and Central Plains
Play their pipe music and refrains, eh!
And "Emperor Fu Xi's Defence"
And "Southern Grief" intense, eh!
We chorus "Sunny Rivershore"
To Eastern flute songs of yore, eh!
O soul, come to hear the melody
Made by the lute of mulberry, eh!

Girls of sixteen join in the dance;

Elegies of the South

The songs they sing entrance, eh!
Musicians strike the bells in time,
Sing the refrain and sound the chime, eh!
They vie in piping to satiety
And give a pleasing variety, eh!
O soul, come back and come along
To listen to your choicest song, eh!

With vermeil lips and teeth jade-white,
The girls are fair and bright, eh!
They're elegant with winning grace,
Accustomed to leisurely pace, eh!
With nicely rounded flesh and bones delicate,
They'll please and fascinate, eh!
O soul, do come back please!
You may enjoy comfort and ease, eh!

Over their smiling dreamy eyes,
The long, smooth eyebrows rise, eh!
They look fresh, beautiful and nice,
Their rosy faces would entice, eh!
Richly adorned and slender,
They are lovely and tender, eh! [1]
O soul, come back! It's good
To enjoy quietude, eh!

---

[1] These two lines are misplaced at the beginning of the next stanza in the original.

Great Requiem

Their plump cheeks and small tilted ears,
The arched eyebrow like compass appears, eh!
Their bearing shows generous heart,
Their beauty brought out without art, eh!
The long slender neck and small waist
Would satisfy even foreign taste, eh!
O soul, come back! Don't lag behind!
Get rid of sorrow in your mind, eh!

The dancer fair has clever heart;
She's apt to act her part, eh!
Her eyebrow black and powder white
Give off a perfume light, eh!
Her face hidden behind sleeves long
Detains the guest like a song, eh!
O soul, come back! Don't stay away!
Make merry till night turns to day, eh!

Her straight black eyebrows rise
Over her captivating eyes, eh!
Her dimpled cheeks and fine teeth would beguile
The guest with bewitching smile, eh!
With plump flesh and bones delicate,
Her body would intoxicate, eh!
O soul, do come back please!
You may enjoy your ease, eh!

The northern hall is large with beams overspread

Elegies of the South

With woodwork painted red, eh!
Between pavilions and southern hall
There is a courtyard small, eh!
Beside the loggia long
Beasts are exercised in throng, eh!
O soul, come back!...
...eh!①

The horses gallop and hounds bark;
The hunters go to vernal park, eh!
The chariot has golden flowers inlaid
In wood and hubs of jade, eh!
Wild parsnip, orchid, cassia swing and sway,
So thick along the way, eh!
O soul, come back if you will!
You may enjoy your fill, eh!

Peacocks fill the garden wide;
Phoenixes are kept by their side, eh!
At dawn storks chorus with cranes,
And fowls sing the refrains, eh!
Large swans fly to and fro with ease;
All around wander green geese, eh!
O soul, why not come over?
See the phoenixes for you hover, eh!

---

① Here two lines are missing in the original.

Great Requiem

Your face is beaming with delight
Of sanguine health at the height, eh!
To preserve life your body's fit,
Its lamp of life ever lit, eh!
Your family and household fill the court
In high rank of every sort, eh!
O soul, come back! Don't go away!
It's better in your house to stay, eh!

For miles and miles the crowd
Comes back and forth like cloud, eh!
Lords of three sceptres in a line
Listen to orders divine, eh!
They watch over and uphold
Orphans and widows, young and old, eh!
O soul, come and defend
The weak from beginning to end, eh!

You have thousands of fields by the stream,
Where people prosper and teem, eh!
You'll reign all over the state
By virtue and favor great, eh!
You'll rule first by might and then by right,
With goodness at its height, eh!
O soul, come back anew!
Here punishment and reward are due, eh!

Your fame as bright as the sun

ELEGIES OF THE SOUTH

Shines over everyone, eh!
Your virtue rises heaven-high,
Well-known to people far and nigh, eh!
It spreads from northern frontier
To southern countries far and near, eh!
From the narrow western Gorge free
To the farthest eastern sea, eh!
O soul, come back if you would
Revere the wise and the good, eh!

Proclaim your rule and act!
Restrain oppressors with tact, eh!
Raise to power the brave and keen,
And get rid of the mean, eh!
The good and just reign in the land
Most like King Yu in his command, eh!
The brave and wise hold sway in capital;
From them flows favor over all, eh!
O soul, come back! Don't hesitate!
Come back for the good of the State, eh!

Majestic you appear
With Heaven's virtue clear, eh!
The stately dukes one and all
Ascend and descend in the hall, eh!
The princes come all with their maces,
The nine ministers in their places, eh!

Great Requiem

White targets are set up there
Where is stretched the leather of bear, eh!
Bow under arm, arrow in hand,
On ceremony they stand, eh!
O soul, come back to your own door!
Revive the ways of the Three Kings of yore, eh!

许译中国经典诗文集

楚 辞

许渊冲　英译
林家骊　中文译注

五洲传播出版社　中华书局

序

> 半亩方塘一鉴开，天光云影共徘徊。
> 问渠哪得清如许？为有源头活水来。
> 　　　　　　　　朱熹《观书有感》

中国文化是"天光云影共徘徊"的一片汪洋大海，而它的"源头活水"就是《诗经》和《楚辞》。《诗经》是中国最早的现实主义诗集，编于公元前六世纪，地区包括华北的黄河流域，东起富庶的齐国，西至强盛的秦国，中原地带有人口稠密的郑、卫等国。在华北，儒家把远古传统、神话、巫术逐一理性化，把神人化，把奇异传说化为君臣父子的世间秩序。《楚辞》却是中国最早的浪漫主义诗集，作于公元前三世纪，地区是华南的长江流域，当时主要是版图广大的楚国。楚国保持和发展着绚烂鲜丽的远古传统，弥漫在一片奇异想象和炽烈情感的神话世界中；而楚文化的代表，是把个体的人格情操和想象的神话世界融合为一、开创了中国抒情诗光辉典范的屈原（约公元前340—前278）。

从屈原起，开始了中国诗人个体创作的时代。屈原的作品，最初是单篇流传的。现在所能看到的《楚辞》版本，最早是东汉王逸的《楚辞章句》，前十篇的次序如下：一、《离骚》，二、《九歌》，三、《天问》，四、《九章》，五、《远游》，六、《卜居》，七、《渔父》，八、《九辩》，九、《招魂》，十、《大招》。后面还有几篇汉时人作品。一般说来,《楚辞》只收战国时期的楚国作品,所以本书只译了《楚辞章句》的前十篇。

《诗经楚辞鉴赏辞典》序言中说:"今传屈原二十余篇作品,可以分成三类,构成一个序列。首先应说《九歌》十一篇,它本是楚地的祀神乐曲,经屈原加工润色,刮垢磨光,成为精美的诗篇。这组诗的抒情主人公或为神祇,或为主祭者。诗是代言体,尚非诗人的咏怀。它们更多地展现了诗人从继承到创新的创作轨迹。其次是《天问》,它是屈原根据神话、传说材料创作的古今无两的煌煌大篇,着重表现了诗人的历史观与自然观,显示了哲理与抒情的两重性。第三是《离骚》、《九章》等作品,是屈原的政治抒情之作,它们有事可据,有义可陈,情感充沛,形象鲜明,气象磅礴,达到了思想与艺术的完美结合。《天问》《九歌》和《离骚》……各自代表了楚辞的最高成就。"

《离骚》是中国古代最早、最辉煌的长篇抒情诗,其气魄之宏伟、抒情之深刻、构思之奇幻、辞采之绚烂,在古典诗歌的宝库里首屈一指。屈原在楚怀王时曾担任过"左徒"的要职,一度得到怀王的信任。他主张改革内政,联合东方富庶的齐国,抵抗西方强盛的秦国;但秦国的使臣贿赂了楚国的大臣,大臣向楚王进谗言,楚王不但不接受屈原的意见,反而把他放逐。所以他在《离骚》中写道:

怨灵修之浩荡兮,终不察夫民心;
众女嫉余之蛾眉兮,谣诼谓余以善淫。

序

关于"离骚"二字的意义,司马迁说是"离忧",班固说是"罹忧",王逸说是"别愁",本书的译名采用司马迁和王逸的说法。《离骚》既是政治抒情诗,又是伟大心灵的悲剧,全诗可以看作是由"述怀"、"追求"、"幻灭"三部分组成的三部曲。他"述怀"的名句如:

> 民生各有所乐兮,余独好修以为常。
> 虽体解吾犹未变兮,岂余心之可惩?

他"追求"的名句如:

> 吾令羲和弭节兮,望崦嵫而勿迫。
> 路曼曼其修远兮,吾将上下而求索。
> ……
> 前望舒使先驱兮,后飞廉使奔属。
> 鸾皇为余先戒兮,雷师告余以未具。

诗人的理想冲不破现实环境的束缚,所以感到"幻灭";但是远游自疏的念头又终于被眷恋故国之情所压倒。例如:

> 陟升皇之赫戏兮,忽临睨夫旧乡。
> 仆夫悲余马怀兮,蜷局顾而不行。

这四句诗,显然受了《诗经·周南·卷耳》的影响:"陟彼砠矣,我马瘏矣,我仆痡矣,云何吁矣!"后来甚至影响到元代马致远的《秋思》"古道西风瘦马",使马和思乡之情紧密地联系起来,甚至成为与乡思有关的意象了。

《离骚》在艺术表现上的最大特色,就是"比兴"、象征手法的运用。"比兴"在《诗经》里已开其端,但是大多作为特定的修辞手段。《离骚》却将这种手法扩展到诗篇的整个艺术构思上,借以塑造出一组组富于象征色彩的意象群来。朱自清说过,"比体诗"有四大类——咏史(以古比今),游仙(以仙比俗),艳情(以男女比君臣),咏物(以物比人)。《离骚》中借男女恋情来比喻君臣离合的很多,如上面引用的"众女嫉余之蛾眉兮";借仙比俗的也不少,如上面引用的神话意象群:羲和、望舒、飞廉、雷师;以物比人,主要是用香花芳草比喻忠臣,用野花杂草比喻奸臣;以古比今如:

> 夏桀之常违兮,乃遂焉而逢殃。
> 后辛之菹醢兮,殷宗用而不长。

就是用夏商灭亡的前车之鉴,来警告楚王。但是楚王不听忠言,国事日益混乱,楚国危亡在即,屈原悲愤交加,最后在夏历五月五日投汨罗江而死。后人缅怀他进步的理想、卓绝的人格、不幸的遭遇,在他离世的每个周年纪念日举行龙舟竞渡,象征性地要挽救诗人的遗体,这种风俗长达两千多年之久,甚至传到日本、朝鲜、东南亚去了,由此可见他的事迹感人之深。

《离骚》可以和西方荷马的史诗《奥德赛》及但丁的《神曲》先后媲美。荷马比屈原约早五百年,《奥德赛》描写特洛伊战争的英雄奥德修斯,在回国途中经历的海上风险,他过人的智力和身受的痛苦。《离骚》写的却是诗人追求理想的天路历程,他高尚的品德和离乡背井的内心悲哀。奥德修斯追求的是现实生活,是回到故国和妻子家人团聚;屈原寻求的却是理想的君主或美人,如洛水的宓妃,有娀之佚女、有虞之二姚等。

但丁比屈原约晚一千五百年。茅盾在《世界文学名著杂谈》中把《神曲》和《楚辞》作比较说:"但丁的《神曲》的基本思想是基督教的禁欲主义……也有异教的传说和神话。同样地,屈原所'上下而求索'者,虽然是尧舜的'纯粹',可是他也喜言'巫俗'。《神曲》是'梦的故事',而《离骚》和《九章》也是'神游'的故事。《神曲》开头的文豹、狮子和牝狼是象征或隐喻的,《离骚》等篇的椒兰凤鸠也是隐喻。《神曲》托毗亚德里采为天堂之向导,但丁是把这个纯洁的女子作为信仰之象征的;同样地,《离骚》也托言求'有娀之佚女'。《神曲》包罗了中世纪的社会的、政治的现象,交织着中世纪之哲学和科学的思想;屈原在他的一气发了一百八九十个疑问的《天问》内,也颇有包举一切……古代文化的气概。不过有一个大不同在,即但丁是站在自己的立场肯定地批判了一切,而屈原则是皇皇然求索。"

有趣的是,钱稻孙把《神曲》译成中文,用的就是"骚"体,如《地狱》曲一的前六行:

  方吾生之半路
   恍余处乎幽林,

> 失正轨而迷误。
> 　　道其况兮不可禁
> 林荒蛮以惨烈
> 　　言念及之复怖心!

这真是中西文化交流的一段佳话了。

《九歌》是祭祀神灵的乐歌,相传是夏朝的音乐,流传于楚国民间。屈原流放时,看到民间祭祀的歌舞之乐,感到乐曲很美但歌词鄙陋,于是就在原来的基础上加以润色,创作了一套新的歌词。这就是流传至今的《九歌》,共十一篇,前九篇祀神,第十篇《国殇》祭鬼,第十一篇是尾声。有人认为第一篇《东皇太一》是总的迎神曲,最后一篇《礼魂》是总的送神曲,所以只写祭祀,没有颂神。第二篇本是《云中君》,据闻一多考订,认为是错简,《东君》应当在《云中君》之前,因为在《史记》《汉书》中,"皆东君、云中君连称",二者本是"依农业社会观念,象征着两个对立的重要自然现象——晴与雨的"。《东君》是男巫扮太阳神的唱词,而十一、十二句是女巫唱的。太阳神的形象,从红日东升到丽日当空,到夕阳西下,都是雄伟而壮美的,祭祀场面也写得热闹。《云中君》是写云神的,第一、二句有人说指女巫,有人说指朝霞;第三句可和雪莱的《云》比较,最后两句是女巫的唱词。《湘君》和《湘夫人》两篇合起来是一个整体,由男巫扮湘君,女巫扮湘夫人,男女对舞对唱。《湘君》写湘夫人的心理活动,由希望而失望,而怀疑,而痛伤,而埋怨,入情入理,曲尽其妙。《湘夫人》则写湘君赴约、失望,怀想,盼望,望之不见,遇之无因等情节,开头四句借景写情,情景交融,是历代诗家所推崇的佳句;《大司命》是扮寿命之神的男巫和人间凡女的对唱,是神凡恋爱的悲剧。《少司命》一说是写送子娘娘;郭沫若说是写爱情女神失恋,所以说:"悲莫悲兮生别离。"《河伯》写黄河水神对洛水女神的相思。《山鬼》写巫山神女的相思之苦,徐悲鸿还画了《山鬼图》。《国殇》则是追悼秦楚交战阵亡将士的哀歌。

《九歌》虽是祭祀用的乐章,但主要内容却是恋歌。古代的祀神祭节,也正是青年男女欢会游乐的大好时光,用恋歌作祭词是自然的事;因为祭神的目的是为了得到神的保佑,所以用恋歌来娱神、悦神;而《九歌》中的恋歌如《湘君》《湘夫人》《少司命》《山鬼》等,艺术形式完美,对后来两千多年的文学有深刻的影响。

《九章》就是"九篇",包括九篇内容与《离骚》近似、篇幅较小的作品。第八篇《橘颂》的风格与其他各篇不同,说到"嗟尔幼志","年岁虽小",有人认为是屈原早期的作品。这是一首咏物诗,赞美橘树,同时借咏橘来自喻,比喻自己的品德,像橘树一样,是"独立不迁"、"苏世独立"、"闭心自慎"的。这首诗写得不即不离,不离开橘,又不局限于橘,而是把橘和自己结合起来写,写出了诗人自己的品格。其他八篇梁启超说是"《离骚》的放大",不过主要是用写实的方法,反映诗人一些具体的生活片断,及当时的思想情绪。如《史记》没有记载屈原流放的地点,《抽思》写他初放汉北,《哀郢》写他流放郢都以东,《涉江》写他从今天的武汉一带,流落到荒凉的湘西,《怀沙》写他从湘西奔赴长沙，最后死节，这四篇填补了流放地点的空白。

《九章》之中，《惜诵》可能是屈原流放后写的第一篇，接着可能是《悲回风》《思美人》《惜往日》。《哀郢》可能作于公元前289年，那时秦将白起攻陷了郢都。"乱曰：曼余目以流观兮，冀壹反之何时？鸟飞反故乡兮，狐死必首丘。信非吾罪而弃逐兮，何日夜而忘之？"梁启超认为是"最沉痛的"文字。"这等作品，真所谓'一声河满子，双泪落君前'。任凭是铁石人，读了怕都不能不感动哩！"《涉江》是屈原流放江南时所作，抒情才悲戚深沉，叙事则历历如见，议论则引古证今，随文变幻，各达极致。《抽思》一篇写得情意缠绵，如怨如慕，充摄诗篇灵魂的，是屈原高尚的理想："望三五以为像兮，指彭咸以为仪。夫何极而不至兮，故远闻而难亏。"《怀沙》是屈原临终的作品，通篇以赋为主，比兴兼施，灵感因岁序景物而生发，事理借形象比喻以辨明；融思想美、艺术美、自然美于一炉。梁启超说：

> 他最后觉悟到他可以死而且不能不死，他便从容死去。临死时的绝作说道：
> 知死不可让，愿勿爱兮。
> 明告君子，吾将以为类兮。

《天问》是哲理诗，思想、历史价值很高。诗人提出了一百七十多个问题，问到宇宙起源，天地形成，天象变化，洪水灾难，四方异物，神话传说，历史变迁等。鲁迅在《摩罗诗力说》中赞叹道："怀疑自遂古之初，直至百物之琐末,放言无惮,为前人所不敢言。"《天问》素以难懂著称,闻一多《天问疏证》中精义较多。《天问》的形式在两千多年的古典诗史上是独一无二的;在国外,则有《旧约·约伯记》可以比较。

《远游》是中国第一篇游仙诗。梁启超说:"《远游》一篇,是屈原宇宙观、人生观的全部表现,是当时南方哲学思想之现于文学者。"《远游》写凡人修炼得道而神游太空,不同于《离骚》写的神话人物游天。因为《远游》表现的主要是道家思想,和屈原的思想不同,有人认为不是屈原所作;也有人说屈原思想不限一家,某一时期具有道家思想是可能的。《远游》之前,诗人的思想表现在下列句中:

> 惟天地之无穷兮,哀人生之长勤。
> 往者余弗及兮,来者吾不闻。

《远游》中的道家思想,主要表现在仙人王子乔的下列句中:

> 道可受兮,不可传;
> 其小无内兮,其大无垠;
> ……
> 虚以待之兮,无为之先;
> 庶类以成兮,此德之门。

得道之后,诗中最后一段也有描写:

> 下峥嵘而无地兮，上寥廓而无天。
> 视儵忽而无见兮，听惝恍而无闻。
> 超无为以至清兮，与泰初而为邻。

《卜居》和《渔父》是两首叙事诗，采用对话的形式表达作者的思想。梁启超说："《卜居》是说两种矛盾的人生观（此孰吉孰凶？何去何从？），《渔父》是表自己意志的抉择。"如屈原说"举世皆浊我独清，众人皆醉我独醒"，而渔父则劝他"与世推移"，并且唱道："沧浪之水清兮，可以濯吾缨；沧浪之水浊兮，可以濯吾足。"王逸说这两篇都是"屈原之所作"；又说《渔父》是"楚人思念屈原，因叙其辞，以相传焉"。无论作者是谁，作品思想都与《离骚》是一致的。

《九辩》的作者是宋玉（约公元前298—前265）。王夫之在《楚辞通释》中说："辩，犹遍也；一阕谓之一遍。"所以"九辩"就是"九遍"，就是分成九个乐章的组诗。宋玉在诗中把自然的季节、楚国的政治气候、个人的身世，有机地融合在一起，而以秋天的萧瑟之气贯穿全诗，达到了情景交融的境界，使"宋玉悲秋"成了文学史上的习语。诗中多是低沉幽怨的哀音，也有高亢激昂的调子，那多是从屈原的作品改装过来的。屈原为自己的政治理想不能实现而愤慨，宋玉却是为个人的失意而痛苦。《九辩》洋溢着忧郁美，第一乐章被古人誉为描写悲秋的绝唱："悲哉，秋之为气也！萧瑟兮，草木摇落而变衰。"宋玉在诗中表现了对事物的怜悯感，自己才华出众的优越感，发泄苦闷后的痛快感。他创造了情景交融的美感，包括天上地下多层次的空间美，季节转换的时间美，社会生活的动态美，内心矛盾的传神美，双声叠字的音乐美。尤其是最后一个乐章，用了"拊拊""湛湛""习习""丰丰""芰芰""跃跃""阗阗""裔裔""锵锵""从从""容容"等叠字，取得了难以形容的效果，前无古人的成就。后来汉武帝、魏文帝、李白、杜甫、李贺等写悲秋诗，没有一个人不受宋玉启发的。

《招魂》和《大招》，有人说是屈原所作，招的是楚怀王的魂；有人说是宋玉所作，招的是屈原的生魂。楚国巫风盛行，有病垂死的人，可以请巫招魂；所以宋玉托上帝的意旨，借巫语招屈原的魂，寄托楚人对他的厚望，盼他还朝的深意。《招魂》开始一段写屈原自诉洁身服义，君主却不察知他的盛德。于是上帝告诉巫阳，把灵魂招还给屈原。以下便是巫阳招魂之辞，可以分为两大层次。前一层次把天地四方的害人事物，写得神怪无以复加：长人、十日、雕题、黑齿、蝮蛇、封狐、雄虺、木夫、土伯等，都不同于儒家后来加工修饰过的神话，而是险恶壮美的形象。后一层次列述宫室、起居、饮食、燕乐、声色之美，王夫之说："盖人君待贤之礼，自当极致其丰。"所以极尽夸张、想象之能事，写得淋漓尽致。如"美人既醉，朱颜酡些。娭光眇视，目曾波些。""士女杂坐，乱而不分些。放陈组缨，班其相纷些。"王逸说"外陈四方之恶，内崇楚国之美"，是希望楚王觉悟，召屈原来挽救危亡的。后一层次的欢乐气氛，是和前一层次诡怪可怕的景象形成对比，在艺术上达到平衡的。《招魂》最后一段和开始一段对应，用第一人称代屈原写魂归来后，将和楚王射猎于云梦，真是怀念屈原的最好诗篇。《文心雕龙》说："《招魂》《大招》，耀艳而深华。"可见这两篇的词采之艳、意蕴之美，"衣被词人，非一代也！"梁启超说：《招魂》可和歌德的《浮士德》先后争辉。

《楚辞》在中国流传了两千多年，直到十九世纪才有西方译本。1852年，在维也纳出版了普费兹梅尔博士的德文译本。1870年，在巴黎出版了德尔韦侯爵的法文译本。最早的英译文，是1879年《中国评论杂志》第七期309—314页上发表的派克英译的《离骚》，译文韵，得到剑桥大学翟理斯教授赞赏，但他认为开始很好，后面就难以为继了。牛津大学霍克思教授认为：派克释义多于翻译。现将他的译文摘抄在英文序中，以见一斑。

1884年，翟理斯教授在上海出版了英文本的《中国文学精华》，其中选译了《卜居》《渔父》和《山鬼》三篇。他的译文优雅可读，但是过分欧化，现将他译的《卜居》也摘抄在英文序中。1895年，英国皇家亚洲学会的《亚洲学刊》第二十七期847—864页发表了理雅各英译的《离骚》。他的译文忠实地翻出了王逸的解释，可能还参考了德尔韦侯爵的法译本，显然比派克的英译本更加准确，但和他英译的《诗经》一样，一点不能引人入胜，读来毫无诗意，仿佛他译《离骚》只是责无旁贷，自己完全没有兴趣。理雅各之后，日本还出版了质量很高的《离骚》日译本。

有个德国学者艾尔克，在1914年曾把《招魂》译成德文，到1923年又把《大招》译成英文。到1939年，他发表的《古代中国的死神》中，包括了他英译的《大司命》和《少司命》。

他的译文基本上是逐字直译，对开始学习中文的外国学生倒还有用。现将《招隐士》中两行摘抄在英文序中，以见一斑。

1918年，韦理出版了他英译的《中国诗选一百七十首》，其中包括《九歌》中的《国殇》；1919年，他又出版了《中国诗选续集》，其中包括《大招》，霍克思认为是光辉灿烂的译文。1946年，韦理再出版了《中国诗选》，这两篇都收在其内，《国殇》修改较多。

1928年，英国皇家亚洲学会《华北分会学刊》第五十九期231—253页，刊登了比亚拉斯的《屈原的生平和诗作》一文，其中包括他英译的《东皇太一》《山鬼》，《天问》前十二行，《惜诵》《卜居》《渔父》几篇，完全是机械式的直译，毫无文学价值可言。此外，他还曾将部分《楚辞》译成德文。

1929年，在新加坡出生的华侨、英国爱丁堡大学博士、厦门大学第一任校长林文庆，在上海出版了英译《离骚》。英国汉学大师翟理斯，印度著名诗人泰戈尔，都为林译本写了序。翟理斯说："《离骚》是一篇奇妙的抒情诗，可以和古代希腊诗人品达比美争辉。诗篇是公元前三百多年写的。我在1872年第一次读到的时候，诗句有如闪耀的电光，使我眼花缭乱，觉得美不胜收。"他还说林译使英国显得瞠乎其后，停滞不前了。泰戈尔说：

> 这篇政治抒情诗是一首哀歌，使人栩栩如生地看到一个伟大民族的心灵，如何渴望在道德精神的基础上，建立起一个稳定的社会……我们感到整部诗篇弥漫着时

代末日的悲哀，并发现希望的曙光也是如梦如幻。读读下面这四句诗：

汩余若将不及兮，恐年岁之不吾与。
朝搴阰之木兰兮，夕揽洲之宿莽。

我们仿佛听到黄昏的微风发出了临终前的叹息，诗句的字里行间吐露了生离死别的衷情。

但是霍克思的看法不同，他认为林译只适宜学生用来作中英对照本，译文不如理雅各的准确，而且同样缺乏文学价值。现将林译摘抄两段在英文序言中，以见一斑。

1947年，英美出版了白英和西南联大师生合译的《白驹集》（古今中国诗选），闻一多参加了选题，包括《九歌》《涉江》《离骚》几篇。霍克思认为译文清新可读，除了韦理的译本外，《白驹集》要算最好的，它不会使读者望而却步。但白英把有韵的骚体译成散文了。

1953年，北京外文出版社出版了杨宪益夫妇合译的《离骚》等诗，包括《九歌》《九章》《卜居》《渔父》《招魂》《天问》在内，除中间两篇外，全部译文押韵。霍克思说这是匠心独运的一座丰碑，但像蒲伯译的荷马史诗一样，并不忠实于原文。

1955年，韦理又出版了他英译的《九歌》，霍克思认为译文是无价之宝。1959年，牛津大学出版社出版了霍克思自己译的《楚辞》，包括王逸《楚辞章句》中的全部作品，内容最为广泛。他的译法介乎直译与意译之间，从微观的角度来看，比前人更准确；但从宏观的角度看来，却只能使人知之，不能使人好之、乐之。

1975年，纽约出版了柳无忌等编译的《葵晔集》，其中选译了《离骚》《湘君》《大司命》《哀郢》《橘颂》五篇。1984年，美国哥伦比亚大学出版了华逊编译的《中国诗选》，其中选译了《离骚》《云中君》《湘君》《山鬼》《国殇》五篇。柳无忌和华逊都把有韵有调的《楚辞》译成无韵无调的分行散文；也就是说，最多只能传达原诗的意美，但是不能再现原诗的音美和形美。而《楚辞》的英译本如果只有意美而没有音美、形美，那就会使人觉得奇怪：怎么能把《离骚》和《奥德赛》及《神曲》、把《天问》和《约伯记》、把《招魂》和《浮士德》相提并论呢！

《诗经楚辞鉴赏辞典》序言中说："在一个民族文化中，如果只有山峦而没有高峰，只有江河而没有大海，只有大合唱而没有最强音，是断难彪炳于世界文化之林的。"屈原就是中国文化史上的第一座"高峰"，大合唱中的第一个"最强音"。而散体译者却把《楚辞》译成"山峦"，译成"大合唱"了。而我认为，英译《楚辞》一定要再现原诗的意美、音美、形美，才能使这座高峰屹立于世界文化之林。

许渊冲
1994年4月18日
北京大学畅春园舞山楼

楚辞

屈原

离 骚

【题解】

关于"离骚"的解释自古以来就歧义迭出,大致分为以下九种:

一、遭受忧患说。汉刘安《离骚传序》称:"离骚者,犹离忧也。"此说为司马迁采纳,他在《史记·屈原贾生列传》中引用刘安《离骚传序》的内容,并称:"故忧愁幽思而作《离骚》。离骚者,犹离忧也。"又"屈平之作《离骚》,盖自怨生也"。汉班固《离骚赞序》称:"离,犹遭也;骚,忧也;明己遭忧作辞也。"后世如颜师古、朱熹、钱澄之、段玉裁、王念孙、朱骏声等均持此说。

二、离别的忧愁说。汉王逸《离骚经序》称:"离,别也。骚,愁也。经,径也。言己放逐离别,中心愁思,犹依道径,以风谏君也。"明汪瑗《楚辞集解》、姜亮夫《重订屈原赋校注》亦持此说。

三、散去的忧愁说。宋项安世《项世家说》卷八称:"《楚语》伍举曰:'德义不行,则迩者骚离,而远者距违。'韦昭注曰:'骚,愁也;离,畔也。'盖楚人之语,自古如此。屈原《离骚》,必是以离畔为愁而赋之。其后词人仿之,作《畔牢愁》,盖为此矣。畔谓散去,非必叛乱也。"王应麟《困学纪闻·左氏传》卷六亦同此说。

四、离为卦名,代表火与光明。明周圣楷《楚宝》称:"离,明也;骚,扰也。何取乎明而扰也?离为火,火在天则明,风则扰矣。"

五、牢骚。清戴震《屈原赋注初稿》称:"离骚,即牢愁也,盖古语,扬雄有《畔牢愁》。离、牢,一声之转,今人犹言牢骚。"游国恩同此说。

六、楚古曲名,即《劳商》曲。游国恩《楚辞概论》称:"《大招》云:'楚《劳商》只。'王逸曰:'曲名也。'按'劳商'与'离骚'为双声字,古音劳在'宵'部,商在'阳'部,离在'歌'部,骚在'幽'部,宵、歌、阳、幽,并以旁纽通转,故'劳'即'离','商'即'骚',然则《劳商》与《离骚》原来是一物而异其名罢了。"郭沫若《屈原研究》、何剑熏《楚辞拾沈》赞同此说。

七、远离忧愁说。钱钟书《管锥编·楚辞洪兴祖补注一八则》称:"'离骚'一词,有类人名之'弃疾'、'去病'或诗题之'遣愁'、'送穷';盖'离'者,分阔之谓,欲摆脱忧愁而遁避之,与'愁'告'别',非因'别'生'愁'。"

八、骚为楚地名,即蒲骚说。李嘉言《〈离骚〉丛说》一文称:"'骚'应解作地名。'离骚'就是离开'骚'那个地方。"其引《左传·桓公十一年》、《元和郡县图志》卷二七,认为"骚"即汉水之北应城县境的蒲骚,并由此推断屈原住在汉北时很可能住在蒲骚,本篇则是离开蒲骚时所作。

九、离骚即离疏说。徐仁甫《楚辞别解》称:"疏骚双声,有方言读此二字同音者可证。知骚离即疏离,则离骚即离疏,而此作品之时期可考。《离骚》作于屈原初被疏远之时,《史记》本传说甚明确。"

楚辞

  虽然"离骚"释义异说纷呈，但为学界广泛认同的并不多。因此，在新材料发现之前，本书认为汉司马迁的离骚犹离忧说、班固的明己遭忧作辞说、王逸的离别忧愁说等比较符合实际。

  《离骚》可分十二章。依次追述家世、姓名的由来，历数上古圣王、尧、舜、桀、纣等人的为政得失，申述作者远大的政治理想和在政治斗争中遭受的迫害，对社会政治的黑暗进行了揭露和批判，对幻想中的美政理想境界进行了热情的讴歌。此篇集中反映了屈原追求自身价值及社会理想的坎坷过程和最终美政理想破灭却忠于故国、独立不迁的人格，以及志洁行廉、上下求索的傲岸情怀。

  据《史记·屈原贾生列传》，本篇的写作时间应在被楚怀王疏远之后；而司马迁《报任安书》又说"屈原放逐，乃赋《离骚》"，则当在楚顷襄王当朝，诗人再放江南时。至今尚无定论。

  《离骚》以其无与伦比的思想艺术价值得到千百年来文人学者的推崇，并在创作中进行模拟，例如扬雄《反离骚》《广骚》《畔牢愁》，班彪《悼离骚》，梁竦《悼骚赋》，应奉《感骚》三十篇，挚虞《愍骚》，黄祯《拟骚》，黄道周《謇骚》《续离骚》《丛骚》，张灿《拟离骚》二十篇等，清人嵇永仁甚至还作有杂剧《续离骚》。明人胡应麟《诗薮·内篇》评价《离骚》对后世的影响说："屈原式兴，以瑰奇浩瀚之才，属纵横艰大之远，因牢骚愁怨之感，发沉雄伟博之辞。上陈王道，下悉人情，中稽物理，旁引广譬，具网兼罗，文词钜丽，佳制闳深，兴寄超远，百代而下，才人学士，追之莫逮，取之不穷。"作为与《诗经》并称的文坛双璧，《离骚》及其他优秀楚辞作品必当在世界文学殿堂中绽放出永恒的艺术魅力！

离骚

　　帝高阳之苗裔兮①,朕皇考曰伯庸②。摄提贞于孟陬兮③,惟庚寅吾以降④。皇览揆余初度兮⑤,肇锡余以嘉名⑥。名余曰正则兮⑦,字余曰灵均⑧。纷吾既有此内美兮⑨,又重之以修能⑩。扈江离与辟芷兮⑪,纫秋兰以为佩⑫。汨余若将不及兮⑬,恐年岁之不吾与⑭。朝搴阰之木兰兮⑮,夕揽洲之宿莽⑯。日月忽其不淹兮⑰,春与秋其代序⑱。惟草木之零落兮⑲,恐美人之迟暮⑳。不抚壮而弃秽兮㉑,何不改此度㉒?乘骐骥以驰骋兮㉓,来吾道夫先路㉔。

【注释】

①帝：帝之本义为花蒂（吴大澂说）或胚胎（姜亮夫说），引申为始生之祖。在夏、商、周三代，称已死的君主为帝。屈原与楚王同宗，故也以帝高阳颛顼为始生之祖。高阳：集《史记》《山海经》《左传》《吕氏春秋》等书及长沙出土帛书考之，颛顼有天下，号高阳。高阳是南楚神话中的地方神，始由天神所派，后逐步由地方神演变为楚人之祖先。苗裔(yì)：子孙后代。兮(xī)：语气词，楚地方言。一说可读若"啊"。

②朕(zhèn)：上古时代第一人称，至秦始皇二十六年（前221），诏定为皇帝自称。这里是屈原自称。皇考：对亡父的尊称。皇，大，美，光明。考，指亡父。但也有学者提出皇考是指先祖或祖父。伯庸：屈原父亲的名或字。一说是屈原先祖或祖父的名或字。

③摄提：此处为"摄提格"的省称。岁星名。古代岁星记年法中的子、丑、寅、卯、辰、巳、午、未、申、酉、戌、亥十二辰之一，相当于干支纪年法中的寅年。《尔雅·释

天》："太岁在寅曰摄提格。"也有学者认为"摄提"不是"摄提格"的省称，而是星名。贞：古与"鼎"字同。鼎，当也。孟陬(zōu)：孟春正月。正月为陬，又为孟春日，故称。

④庚寅：屈原出生的日子，庚寅日为楚民间习俗上的吉宜日，古有男命起寅的传说。降(古音hōng)：诞生，降生。本义为自天而降，这里屈原自言天生。

⑤揆(kuí)：度量，揣度。初度：有四解：一释为刚出生时的器度。度，态度，器度，气象。二释为年时。三释为吉度。四释为天体运行纪数之开端。

⑥肇(zhào)：开始。一说认为"肇"通"兆"，占卜的意思。锡：同"赐"，送给。

⑦正则：公正而有法则。《史记·屈原贾生列传》："屈原者，名平。"正则是对"平"字进行的解释。

⑧字：取表字。灵均：灵善而均调。王夫之《楚辞通释》："原者，地之善而均平者也。"

⑨纷：美盛。内美：先天具有的内在的美好德性。

⑩重(chóng)：加上。一说是轻重之重。修能：即"修态"，即"美好的外表仪形"。能，通"态"。一释为"长才"，即"很强的才干和能力。"能，通"耐"。

⑪扈(hù)：披，楚地方言。江离：亦作"江蓠"，又名"蘼芜"，香草名。一说江离是生于江中的香草。辟芷(zhǐ)：幽香的芷草。一说为生长在幽僻处的芷草。

⑫纫：搓，捻。一释为续，接。又可释为结、贯。

⑬汩(yù)：疾行；快速。

⑭不吾与：即"不与吾"之倒言。

⑮搴(qiān)：拔取。陛(pí)：有六解：一为山名。二为陛同陴，即崖岸。三为南楚语，小阜曰毗，大阜曰陛，即大山。

四为坒之借，依《说文•土部》，"地相次比也"之意。五为水边小山。六为阰与陂同。木兰：香木名，又名杜兰、林兰，皮似桂而香，状如楠树。
⑯揽(lǎn)：采摘。洲：江河中的陆地。宿莽：经冬不死的草。
⑰忽：通"飍"，迅速。淹：通"延"，逗留，停留。
⑱序：通"谢"，过去，逝去。
⑲惟：思。
⑳美人：此处指楚怀王。迟暮：比喻晚年。
㉑不抚壮而弃秽兮：诸本此句无"不"字，非是。抚，凭，持。壮，指盛壮之年。一说指国势强盛。秽，指污秽的行为。一说指杂乱的政事。又一说指小人。
㉒此度：指上文"不抚壮而弃秽"的态度。
㉓骐骥(qí jì)：骏马。驰骋：纵马疾驰，奔驰。
㉔来：相招之辞。道：通"导"，引导。夫(fú)：语气词。先路：先王的道路。

【译文】

我是远祖高阳氏的后裔啊，我父亲的名字叫伯庸。岁星正好运行到寅年正月啊，我呱呱降生。父亲端详我初生时的气度啊，从那时起他赐予我这贞祥的名字：他给我起名叫正则啊，起字作灵均。我欢喜自己刚出生已有如此众多的惠质啊，又加上具有出众的才能。披戴着江离和幽香的白芷啊，缀结秋兰作为腰间配饰。我快速前行看似追寻不上目标啊，担心岁月不再留给我更多的时间！早上拔取坡地上的木兰啊，傍晚采摘水洲中的宿莽。日月倏忽不返从不停下脚步啊，春天与秋天季节在更替。想到草木都要凋零啊，就怕楚王步入衰残的暮年。为什么不趁着壮年抛弃污秽啊，就此改变你的态度？骑上骏马奔驰吧！来吧，我在前面为你开路！

楚辞

　　昔三后之纯粹兮①，固众芳之所在②。杂申椒与菌桂兮③，岂维纫夫蕙茞④？彼尧舜之耿介兮⑤，既遵道而得路⑥。何桀纣之猖披兮⑦，夫唯捷径以窘步⑧。惟夫党人之偷乐兮⑨，路幽昧以险隘⑩。岂余身之惮殃兮⑪，恐皇舆之败绩⑫。忽奔走以先后兮，及前王之踵武⑬。荃不察余之中情兮⑭，反信谗而齌怒⑮。余固知謇謇之为患兮⑯，忍而不能舍也。指九天以为正兮⑰，夫唯灵修之故也⑱。曰黄昏以为期兮，羌中道而改路⑲。初既与余成言兮⑳，后悔遁而有他。余既不难夫离别兮㉑，伤灵修之数化㉒。

【注释】

①三后：有五解：一说指夏禹、商汤、周文王（王逸）；二说指三皇，即少昊、颛顼、高辛（朱熹）；三说指楚之先君（汪瑗）；四说指伯夷、禹、稷（蒋骥）；五说指黄帝、颛顼、帝喾（王树枬）。当以汪瑗"楚之先君"说为是。纯粹：纯正不杂，引申指德行完美无缺。

②众芳：喻众多有才能的人。

③杂：会集，兼有。申椒：生得重累而丛簇的花椒。菌桂：像竹子一样圆的桂树。

④维：仅，只。蕙茞(zhǐ)：均香草名。

⑤尧舜：唐尧和虞舜的并称，远古部落联盟的首领，古史传说中的圣明君主。耿介：光大圣明。

⑥遵道而得路：遵，循。道，正途。路，大道。

⑦桀纣(jié zhòu)：夏桀和商纣的并称。猖披：衣不系带，散乱不整貌。引申为狂妄偏邪之意。

⑧捷径：原意指近便的小路，此处喻不循正轨、贪便图快的做法。窘(jiǒng)：困窘，窘迫。

⑨夫：彼。党人：朋党。偷乐：贪图享乐。一作"苟且偷安"解。
⑩幽昧(mèi)：昏暗不明。险隘(ài)：危险狭隘。
⑪惮(dàn)：畏惧，害怕。
⑫皇舆：君王乘的车子，比喻国家政权。败绩：原意指车之覆败，引申指事业的败坏、失利。
⑬前王：姜亮夫《屈原赋校注》认为即上文之"三后"与"尧舜"。踵(zhǒng)武：足迹。踵，足跟。
⑭荃(quán)：香草名，多喻君主。中情：谓内心真诚。
⑮齌(jì)怒：疾怒，暴怒。齌，炊火猛烈，引申为暴烈。
⑯謇謇(jiǎn)：直言的样子。患：害。
⑰九天：谓天之中央与八方。正：通"证"，验证。
⑱灵修：能神明远见者，此处当指楚怀王而言。
⑲"曰黄昏"以下二句：此为衍文。
⑳成言：定言。
㉑难：畏惮，畏惧。
㉒化：变化。一作"讹"解。

【译文】

　　从前楚国三位贤王德行完美、纯正无私啊，因而成为群贤毕集的所在。花椒与菌桂聚集一处啊，缀结的何止蕙和茞？尧舜光大圣明啊，他们遵行正道使国家走上正途。桀纣一样荒乱偏邪啊，贪图近便小径以致走投无路。结党营私之徒享乐啊，国家的前途晦暗不明危险难行。难道我是害怕自身遭受灾殃吗？我是怕君王的车子遭到颠覆。我匆促奔走于君王鞍前马后啊，希望他能追踪先王的足迹。君王却不明察我内心的真情啊，反而轻信了逸言而勃然大怒。我本来就知道正道直行会引起祸患啊，宁可忍受痛苦却无法改变初衷。手指天地作为我起誓的明证啊，这都是因为君王的缘故。说好在黄昏时分相约会面的啊,走到半路又中途改道。当初已经跟我订下誓约啊,随后又反悔另有他求。我已不再为君臣分隔而难过啊,只是哀惋君王朝令夕改。

余既滋兰之九畹兮①,又树蕙之百亩②。畦留夷与揭车兮③,杂杜衡与芳芷④。冀枝叶之峻茂兮,愿竢时乎吾将刈⑤。虽萎绝其亦何伤兮,哀众芳之芜秽⑥。众皆竞进以贪婪兮,凭不厌乎求索⑦。羌内恕己以量人兮⑧,各兴心而嫉妒⑨。忽驰骛以追逐兮⑩,非余心之所急⑪。老冉冉其将至兮⑫,恐修名之不立。朝饮木兰之坠露兮⑬,夕餐秋菊之落英⑭。苟余情其信姱以练要兮⑮,长顑颔亦何伤⑯?擥木根以结茝兮⑰,贯薜荔之落蕊⑱。矫菌桂以纫蕙兮⑲,索胡绳之纚纚⑳。謇吾法夫前修兮㉑,非世俗之所服。虽不周于今之人兮㉒,愿依彭咸之遗则㉓。

【注释】

① 滋:栽,栽种。九畹(wǎn):极言其多。畹,古代面积单位,十二亩田曰畹,一说三十亩田曰畹。
② 树:种植。蕙:香草名,所指有二:一指薰草,俗称佩兰。古人佩之或做香焚以避疫。二指蕙兰。
③ 畦(qí):分畦种植。留夷:香草名。一说即芍药。揭车:香草名。
④ 杜衡:亦作"杜蘅",香草名,俗名马蹄香。芳芷(zhǐ):香草名,即白芷。
⑤ 竢(sì):等待。刈(yì):割取。
⑥ 哀:悯惜。众芳:指上文所言之六物——兰、蕙、留夷、揭车、杜衡、芳芷,喻众贤。芜秽:荒芜,谓田地不整治而杂

草丛生。此处比喻自己所培养的人才变质了,它们竟变成了一片恶草。

⑦凭:满足。楚人名"满"曰"凭"。

⑧羌(qiāng):楚地方言,发语词。恕己以量人:谓以自己之心来忖度他人,犹俗语所云"以小人之心,度君子之腹"。

⑨兴心:生心。

⑩驰骛(wù):疾驰,奔腾。

⑪非余心之所急:此句屈子自表其心不同于众,而众人不必嫉妒他。

⑫老:老景。冉冉(rǎn):形容时光渐渐流逝。

⑬饮:小口吸食。

⑭餐:吞食。落英:坠落的花朵。一释为"初生的花朵"。

⑮信姱(kuā):真正美好。姱,美好。练要:谓精诚专一,操守坚贞。要,约束。

⑯顑颔(kǎn hàn):因饥饿而面黄肌瘦。

⑰擥(lǎn):执持。木根:兰槐之根。

⑱薜(bì)荔:香草名,又称木莲。蕊(ruǐ):花心。

⑲矫:有三解:一释为举;二释为直,即使之直的意思。三释为搓揉使柔软而易于缝纫。菌桂:香木名,姜亮夫《屈原赋校注》以为即今之肉桂、桂属中的一种。

⑳索:绞合使紧。胡绳:香草名。纚纚(xǐ):长而下垂的样子。

㉑謇(jiǎn):为楚地方言,发语词。一说为用心竭力、艰难勤苦之意。前修:犹前贤。

㉒周:调和,适合。

㉓彭咸:王逸《楚辞章句》:"彭咸,殷贤大夫,谏其君不听,自投水而死。"以后各家释彭咸者均承此说。

【译文】

我栽下了九畹的兰花啊,又种上了百亩的蕙草。将芍药和揭车分畦种植啊，其间兼有马蹄香和白芷。希望它们枝繁叶茂啊，我愿等待时机将它们采摘。即使枯黄凋落又有何伤感啊，悲哀的是这许多花草变成遍地荒棘！众人都争名逐利、贪得无厌啊，孜孜以求从不满足。他们以自己的心肠来猜度我啊，各自私念丛生又充满妒忌。急切奔跑追逐名利啊，并不是我的心中所求。人生暮景渐渐就要降临啊，我担心的是人生的美名没有树立！早上啜饮木兰上滴下的露水啊，傍晚含咀坠落的秋菊。只要我的情志美好、精纯如一啊，长久以来的神形消损又怎值得悲戚！持取木根绕结茝花啊，将薜荔刚绽放的花心联结成串。使菌桂变直并缀结上蕙草啊，再把胡绳绞合起来而彰显飘逸身姿。我效法前贤的装束啊，并非流俗之辈所能服习。即使不能迎合当世的人啊，我愿依从彭咸留下的范型！

长太息以掩涕兮，哀民生之多艰。余虽好修姱以靰羁兮①，謇朝谇而夕替②。既替余以蕙纕兮③，又申之以揽茝④。亦余心之所善兮，虽九死其犹未悔。怨灵修之浩荡兮⑤，终不察夫民心⑥。众女嫉余之蛾眉兮⑦，谣诼谓余以善淫⑧。固时俗之工巧兮，偭规矩而改错⑨。背绳墨以追曲兮⑩，竞周容以为度⑪。忳郁邑余侘傺兮⑫，吾独穷困乎此时也。宁溘死以流亡兮⑬，余不忍为此态也⑭。鸷鸟之不群兮⑮，自前世而固然。何方圆之能周兮⑯，夫孰异道而相安？屈心而抑志兮，忍尤而攘诟⑰。伏清白以死直兮⑱，固前圣之所厚。

【注释】

①虽：通"唯"。修姱(kuā)：修洁而姱美，喻美德。靰羁(jī jī)：马缰绳和络头，比喻束缚。

②謇(jiǎn)：发语词。谇(suì)：谏。一释为诟，让，意即指责，责备。替：废，废弃。
③纕(xiāng)：佩带。一说即今香囊之属。
④申：重复。揽茝(zhǐ)：姜亮夫认为此"揽"字当为"兰"字，"兰茝"与上文"蕙纕"为对。
⑤灵修：指楚国国君。浩荡：犹荒唐。
⑥民：人，屈原自谓。
⑦蛾眉：指女子美丽的容貌，又用以比喻屈原自己优秀的品质。
⑧谣诼(zhuó)：造谣毁谤。淫：邪乱，淫乱。
⑨偭(miǎn)：背，违背。规矩：规和矩，校正圆形和方形的两种工具。错：通"措"，措施。
⑩绳墨：木工画直线用的工具，这里比喻正道直行。追曲：随意曲直，没有一定的法则。
⑪周容：迎合讨好。度：常行之法。一说为态度。
⑫忳(tún)：忧郁，烦闷。郁邑：忧愤郁结，忧懑压抑。侘傺(chà chì)：失意而神情恍惚的样子。
⑬溘(kè)死：忽然死去。流亡：谓淹忽而死，随水以去。
⑭此态：指小人工巧、周容之丑态。
⑮鸷(zhì)鸟：指凶猛的鸟。一说鸷鸟当为忠贞刚特之鸟。不群：猛禽不与众凡鸟为群，喻刚正之君子不与阘茸之小人为伍。
⑯方圜：同"方圆"。周：合。
⑰忍尤：容忍罪过。尤，罪过。攘诟(rǎng gòu)：容忍耻辱。以上"屈心"与"抑志"、"忍尤"与"攘诟"均为对文。
⑱伏：通"服"，信服。

【译文】

长长地叹息我掩面拭泪啊，感伤人生的道路是多么的艰难。

我虽爱好美德却遭受羁縻啊,早上向君王进谏傍晚就被废弃。废弃我的原因是因为我身佩蕙草啊,又加上我用兰茝作为佩饰。它们都是我心头之好啊,为此即使万死我也不后悔。埋怨怀王行事荒唐啊,终究不明察我的忠心。女人们都嫉恨我美丽的容貌啊,恶语中伤说我善于淫逸。本来流俗善于取巧啊,背弃原则篡改措施。违反标准并无原则啊,争相迎合讨好且以之为常行之法。忧郁压抑我失意不乐啊,偏偏独有我受困于时。宁肯突然死去形体不存啊,我不忍心作出那副样子!鸷鸟高飞远走、卓特不群啊,先世以来就一向如此。圆凿方枘如何能够互容啊,谁可以道不同却彼此相安?委屈本心压抑情志啊,包容过错含垢忍耻。坚持清白之躯为正义而死啊,那才是先贤们所珍视的事。

悔相道之不察兮^①,延伫乎吾将反^②。回朕车以复路兮,及行迷之未远。步余马于兰皋兮^③,驰椒丘且焉止息^④。进不入以离尤兮,退将复修吾初服^⑤。制芰荷以为衣兮^⑥,集芙蓉以为裳^⑦。不吾知其亦已兮,苟余情其信芳^⑧。高余冠之岌岌兮^⑨,长余佩之陆离^⑩。芳与泽其杂糅兮^⑪,唯昭质其犹未亏^⑫。忽反顾以游目兮,将往观乎四荒^⑬。佩缤纷其繁饰兮^⑭,芳菲菲其弥章^⑮。民生各有所乐兮^⑯,余独好修以为常^⑰。虽体解吾犹未变兮^⑱,岂余心之可惩^⑲?

【注释】

①相(xiàng)道:观察道路。一释为寻找道路。察:详细察看。
②延伫(zhù):长久地站立。一释为长望。
③步余马:骑着我的马慢慢走。一释为训练我的马。兰皋

(gāo)：长着兰草的水边高地。
④椒丘：尖削的高丘。一释为生有椒木的丘陵。焉：于此。
⑤退：有二释：一释为退去，回去；一说作隐退解。初服：未入仕时的服装。
⑥制：裁剪。芰(jì)荷：指菱叶与荷叶。一说芰荷为一物。衣：上衣。
⑦芙蓉：荷花的别名。裳：古代称下身穿的衣裙，男女皆服。
⑧其：句中衬字，无义。
⑨岌岌(jí)：高高的样子。
⑩佩：身上佩带的剑。陆离：长的样子。
⑪芳：草香，亦泛指香，香气。泽：有三解：一释为"玉之润泽"；二释为"垢腻、污垢"；三，姜亮夫《屈原赋校注》认为此为"臭"字之讹变。糅(róu)：混杂，混合。
⑫唯：有三解：一释为独。二释为辞也，即发语词。三说同惟，表明心中冀望之意。三说均可通。昭质：明洁的品质。亏：损。
⑬"忽反顾"以下二句：有一种意见认为屈原是想"求贤君""求知己"等，另一种意见认为屈原欲离朝去野，隐居避祸。后一种意见更有道理。忽，不经意。游目，放眼纵望。四荒，四方荒远之地。
⑭缤纷：繁盛的样子。繁饰：众多的彩饰，盛饰。
⑮菲菲：香气很盛。
⑯民生：即人生。
⑰好修：喜作修饰。常：常规，习惯。
⑱体解：分解人的肢体，古代酷刑之一。
⑲惩(chéng)：克制，制止。

【译文】

悔恨选择道路时未曾看清啊，站在那里久久凝望而后我就要回返。调转我的车头重归正确的路啊,趁误入迷途还不是太远。让我的马漫步在长满兰花的湿地上啊,跑到遍是椒树的土坡上在那里休憩。进谏不被君王接纳却承受过错啊,我将隐退重新穿回当初的衣冕。裁制菱叶作为上衣啊,缀合莲花以作下裙。没有人理解我也就算了吧,只要我的情志真正高洁芳郁。加高我的帽子使之显得危耸啊,加长我的佩剑使之更加奇诡斑斓。芳香和腐臭混杂在一处啊,只有明洁的品质尚未缺损。倏忽间回首远望啊,我将去四方荒远之地游览。戴上众多华美的佩饰啊,浓郁的芳香使它们更加耀眼。人生各有各的乐事啊,我偏好美洁已习惯成自然。即使躯体分解我也不会改变啊,我的心中还有何畏惧?

女嬃之婵媛兮①,申申其詈予②。曰鲧婞直以亡身兮③,终然夭乎羽之野④。汝何博謇而好修兮,纷独有此姱节⑤。薋菉葹以盈室兮⑥,判独离而不服⑦。众不可户说兮⑧,孰云察余之中情?世并举而好朋兮,夫何茕独而不予听⑨。

【注释】

①女嬃(xū):有六解:一释为屈原之姊。二释为屈原之妹。三释为女巫或神巫。四释为女伴、侍女。五释为贱妾,比喻党人。六释为一个假想的女性。婵媛(chán yuán):有四解:一释为牵引,情思牵萦;二释为女嬃之容貌形态;三释为喘息之貌;四释为痛恻婉转陈辞。
②申申:有三解:一释为重(zhòng)重;二释为重复、多次;三释为和舒、婉转的样子。詈(lì):责骂。
③曰:说。以下至"夫何茕独而不予听"是女嬃责备屈原的话。鲧(gǔn):传说中古代部落酋长名,号崇伯,禹之父。

据说奉尧之命治水,未成,而被舜杀于羽山。一说被舜幽囚在羽山,最后死在那里。婞(xìng)直:倔强,刚直。一说为"刚愎自用"之意。亡身:一作"方身"。一说当作"方命",是不听指挥,不服从命令之意。 释为忘身。

④殀(yāo):早死。一释为死。又释为不得善终而死。亦释为拥塞,遏制。羽:羽山,地名。

⑤纷:纷然、美盛。姱(kuā)节:美好的节操。一释为奇异的行为。

⑥薋(cí):积聚。菉(lù):草名。葹(shī):草名。

⑦判独:分别离散,与众不同。服:用,使用。

⑧户说:一家一户地去说,又释为遍说。

⑨茕(qióng)独:孤独。不予听:即不听予。予,我,女媭自谓。

【译文】

女媭满心痛彻啊,重重责骂我。她说鲧因为刚直而遭流放啊,最后幽殁在羽山的郊野。你为什么还博采众芳而爱好美洁啊,美好的节操显得如此与众不同!蒺藜、荩草、地葵充满屋子啊,你却迥异于众人偏偏不肯佩用在身上。不可能向每个人都详尽说明心中的想法啊,谁能明白我们内心的真诚呢?世人相互推举而好朋比为奸啊,你为什么茕然独立却不听我的劝告。

依前圣以节中兮①,喟凭心而历兹②。济沅湘以南征兮③,就重华而陈词④。启《九辩》与《九歌》兮⑤,夏康娱以自纵⑥。不顾难以图后兮⑦,五子用失乎家巷⑧。羿淫游以佚畋兮⑨,又好射夫封狐⑩。固乱流其鲜终兮⑪,浞又贪夫厥家⑫。浇身被服强圉兮⑬,纵欲而不忍。日康娱而自忘兮⑭,厥首用夫颠陨⑮。夏桀之常违兮⑯,乃遂焉而逢殃⑰。后辛之菹醢兮⑱,

177

殷宗用而不长⑲。汤禹俨而祗敬兮⑳,周论道而莫差㉑。举贤而授能兮,循绳墨而不颇㉒。皇天无私阿兮㉓,览民德焉错辅㉔。夫维圣哲以茂行兮㉕,苟得用此下土㉖。瞻前而顾后兮,相观民之计极㉗。夫孰非义而可用兮,孰非善而可服㉘。阽余身而危死兮㉙,览余初其犹未悔。不量凿而正枘兮㉚,固前修以菹醢㉛。曾歔欷余郁邑兮㉜,哀朕时之不当㉝。揽茹蕙以掩涕兮㉞,沾余襟之浪浪㉟。

【注释】

①节中:犹折中,取正。
②喟(kuì):叹息,叹声。凭:满。历兹:至此。
③沅(yuán):沅江,古称沅水,源出贵州省云雾山,东北流经黔阳、常德到汉寿入洞庭湖。湘:即湘江,源出广西,流入湖南省,为湖南省最大的河流。
④重(chóng)华:虞舜的美称。一说舜重瞳,故名。
⑤启:指夏启,大禹之子,夏朝君主。一释为"开启"。《九辩》:夏代乐名。一说天帝乐名。《九歌》:古代乐曲,相传为禹时乐歌。一说《九歌》也是天帝乐名。
⑥夏:有四解:一释为大;二释为太康,即启子太康;三释为下;四释为夏王。一般取第一种解释。康娱:逸乐,安乐。
⑦不顾难:不回顾其最初取得天下之不易。以图后:为后代作谋划。
⑧五子:有四解:一释为启的五个儿子。二释为太康昆弟五人。三释为启之第五子。四释为启的兄弟。用失乎:即"用乎","失"字为衍文,用乎,因之,因而。家巷(hòng):内讧。巷,通"閧"。

⑨羿(yì)：传说中夏代有穷氏之国君，因夏氏以代，善射，不修民事，为家臣寒浞所杀。佚(yì)：放纵。畋(tián)：畋猎，打猎。

⑩好(hào)：喜好。封狐：大狐。一释为大猪。"狐"是"狶"之误。

⑪乱流：乱逆之流。鲜(xiǎn)终：少有善终。

⑫浞(zhuó)：传说中夏时有穷氏后羿之相。羿不理政事，寒浞遂杀羿自立。厥(jué)：其，这里指代羿。家(gū)：通"姑"，古时对妇女的一种称谓，这里指羿的妻室。

⑬浇(ào)：即过浇。传说中夏代寒浞之子。被(pī)服强圉(yǔ)：负恃有力，即依仗自己强大的力量。一释为穿着坚甲。

⑭自忘：忘怀自身安危。

⑮用夫：因而。颠陨(yǔn)：坠落。

⑯夏桀：夏代最后一个君主，名履癸，相传为暴君。常违：经常违背天道和人理。

⑰逢殃：遭到祸殃。夏桀之结果，有二说：王逸《楚辞章句》："终为殷汤所诛灭。"朱熹《楚辞集注》："逢殃，为汤所放也。"

⑱后辛：即殷纣王。后，君主。辛，纣王之名。菹醢(zū hǎi)：亦作"葅醢"，古代把人剁成肉酱的酷刑。后亦用以泛指处死。

⑲殷宗：殷商之国祚。用而：因而，因此。

⑳汤禹：商汤与夏禹。一释为大禹。俨(yǎn)：恭敬，庄重，庄严。祗(zhī)敬：恭敬。

㉑周：周文王或周文王与周武王。一释为周密谨慎地选择有道之士。

㉒循(xún)：顺着，遵从。绳墨：木工画直线用的工具，此处喻规矩、准则和法度。

㉓皇天：对天及天神的尊称。私阿(ē)：偏爱，曲意庇护。

㉔民德：在皇天看来，人君也是臣民，故此"民德"是指那些得了天下的君王而言。错辅：安排辅助。错，通"措"，安排。

㉕维：同"唯"，独。圣哲：此处指具有超人的道德才智的人。茂行：德行充盛。

㉖苟：于是。用：拥有，治理。下土：天下。

㉗相(xiàng)：看，观察。计极：兴亡的原因。

㉘服：行，行事。

㉙阽(diàn)：临近危险。危死：濒临死亡。

㉚凿(záo)：榫眼。正：审定，确定。枘(ruì)：器物的榫头。

㉛前修：古代的贤人，此处指因忠言直谏而遭到葅醢之刑的贤人，如龙逢、梅伯等。

㉜曾：通"增"，屡屡。歔欷(xū xī)：悲泣，抽噎。郁邑：即"郁悒"，苦闷，忧愁。

㉝哀朕时之不当：哀叹自己生不逢时。当，引申为"值"，逢，遇之义。

㉞茹：柔软。一释为香草名。

㉟沾：浸湿。浪浪：泪流不止的样子。

【译文】

依从先贤的价值标准进行评判啊，满怀感喟为何遭此厄运。渡过沅、湘向南进发啊，到帝舜跟前大声陈说：夏启创制《九歌》、《九辩》啊，恣意寻欢作乐以致放纵堕落。不顾念先王创业艰难并为后代打算啊，五位王公因此内讧相争。后羿过度沉溺于狩猎啊，又喜欢射杀大猪以取乐。本来恣肆妄行就没有好下场啊，寒浞夺权又占有了他的妻子。浇恃强尚武啊，放纵欲念不肯放弃糜烂生活。每天沉浸于燕舞笙歌浑然忘我啊，他的头颅因此而掉落。夏桀所行与常情有违啊，最后终究遭受了灾祸。纣王辛发明将人剁成肉酱的酷刑啊，殷商因而不能国祚绵长。大禹庄穆而敬畏神灵啊，周详地施行仁政而没有差错。推举贤德、任用能臣啊，遵守法则而不偏颇。上苍不会偏袒谁啊，视民心向背加以辅佐。只有贤达睿智、德行充盛啊，才能拥有这整个天下。回顾历史展望将来啊，考察人世治变的道理。谁不是因为忠义而被任用啊，谁不是因为纯良美好而成为奉行的楷模！我身陷危难几蹈死地啊，静观初心从未后悔。不度量凿孔而选用合适的榫头啊，这本是前贤被剁成肉末的原因。我频频悲叹抑郁忧伤啊，哀惋自己生不逢时。拿起柔软蕙草掩面痛哭啊，泪珠滚滚滑落打湿我的前襟。

跪敷衽以陈辞兮①，耿吾既得此中正②。驷玉虬以桀鹥兮③，溘埃风余上征④。朝发轫于苍梧兮⑤，夕余至乎县圃⑥。欲少留此灵琐兮⑦，日忽忽其将暮。吾令羲和弭节兮⑧，望崦嵫而勿迫⑨。路曼曼其修远兮⑩，吾将上下而求索⑪。饮余马于咸池兮⑫，总余辔乎扶桑⑬。折若木以拂日兮⑭，聊逍遥以相羊⑮。前望舒使先驱兮⑯，后飞廉使奔属⑰。鸾皇为余先戒兮⑱，雷师告余以未具⑲。吾令凤鸟飞腾兮⑳，继之以日夜。飘风屯其相离兮㉑，帅云霓而来御㉒。纷总总其离合兮㉓，斑陆离其上下㉔。吾令帝阍开关兮㉕，倚阊阖而望予㉖。时暧暧其将罢兮㉗，结幽兰而延伫。世溷浊而不分兮㉘，好蔽美而嫉妒㉙。

【注释】

①敷：铺开。衽（rèn）：衣之前襟。
②耿：耿介，光明正大。此中正：此中正之道，即上文所说明

主贤臣相得、昏君乱臣相残的道理。
③驷(sì)：古代一车套四马，因以称驾一车之四马，或四马所驾之车。这里意思是以四虬龙驾车。虬(qiú)：传说中的一种无角龙。椉(chéng)：同"乘"。鹥(yì)：传说中的鸟名，凤凰之属，身有五彩花纹。
④溘(kè)：忽然。埃：微小的尘土。征：行，此处指乘坐四龙所拉的凤车飞上天空。
⑤发轫(rèn)：拿掉支住车轮的木头，使车前进。借指起程，出发。苍梧：一名九疑，在湖南省宁远县东南。
⑥县圃：又作玄圃、悬圃，传说中神仙居处，在昆仑山顶。
⑦灵琐：君门。姜亮夫《屈原赋校注》以为即玄圃之门。
⑧羲(xī)和：古代神话传说中驾御日车的神。弭(mǐ)节：缓慢行驶。节，车子行驶的步调。
⑨崦嵫(yān zī)：山名，在甘肃天水西境，传说以为日落的地方。迫：迫近。
⑩曼曼：形容距离远或时间长。修远：长远。
⑪上下而求索：求索的对象，各家说法不一，主要有三说：一谓求与己同志的贤人；二谓求贤君；三谓求天帝之所在。联系上下文，当以第三说近是。
⑫咸池：神话中谓日浴之处。
⑬总：系，结，束结。辔(pèi)：驾驭马的缰绳。扶桑：神话中的树名。传说日出于扶桑之下，拂其树杪(miǎo)而升，因谓为日出处。
⑭若木：古代神话中的树名。一说即扶桑。
⑮聊逍遥以相羊：聊逍遥、相羊，是联绵词的不同变体，意思相同，都有徘徊之义。
⑯望舒：神话中为月驾车的神。先驱：原指军队中的前锋，此处引申指向导。

⑰飞廉：即风神。一说能致风的神禽名。奔属(zhǔ)：奔跑着紧跟在后面。
⑱鸾(luán)皇：亦作"鸾凰"。鸾与凰，皆瑞鸟名，常用以比喻贤士淑女。
⑲雷师：神话中的雷神。或说就是丰隆。未具：驾御未备。
⑳凤鸟：凤凰，传说中的瑞鸟。
㉑飘风：旋风，暴风。屯：聚集。离：附丽。
㉒帅：通"率"，率领。霓(ní)：虹的一种，又称副虹(相对于主虹而言)。
㉓总总：聚集一处的样子。罢：有三解：一释为"极"，疲惫；二释为罢散；三释为月魂初生的时光。
㉔斑：荣盛。陆离：光辉灿烂的样子。
㉕帝阍(hūn)：天帝的看门人。阍，看门人。
㉖阊阖(chāng hé)：神话中的天门。
㉗暧暧(ài)：昏暗的样子。罢：有三解：一释为极，即疲惫；二释为罢散；三释为月魂初生的时光。
㉘溷(hùn)浊：混乱污浊。
㉙美：品德、才能皆优秀的人。

【译文】

衣襟铺开跪着慷慨陈辞啊，我得到无私正道心中豁然通明。驾驭四条无角玉龙所拉的凤车啊，倏忽间我依托风云直上天空。早上从苍梧出发啊，傍晚到县圃停歇。我打算在神门前稍歇片刻啊，日头渐渐偏移入暮。我让羲和徐徐前行啊，看到崦嵫山暂且止步。前途漫长遥远无边啊，我将上天入地寻求出路。在咸池饮我的马啊，将马缰系在扶桑神木。攀折若木遮蔽日光啊，姑且逍遥徜徉自由自在。使月神望舒在前面开路啊，让风伯奔跑于后。早有鸾凤为我戒严道路啊，雷神却告诉我严装未备。我命凤鸟们腾翔于九天啊，日以继夜不得疏忽。暴风骤集欲使队伍离散啊，统率着前来迎接的云雾。来势盛大忽散忽聚啊，上下翻转光彩夺目。我命天帝的看门人打开天门啊，他却倚靠在天门外视而不见。此刻光线暗淡日将西落啊，只得编结幽兰长久停驻。世道混乱良莠不分啊，喜欢掩蔽贤才妄加嫉妒。

朝吾将济于白水兮①，登阆风而绁马②。忽反顾以流涕兮，哀高丘之无女③。溘吾游此春宫兮④，折琼枝以继佩⑤。及荣华之未落兮⑥，相下女之可诒⑦。吾令丰隆乘云兮⑧，求宓妃之所在⑨。解佩纕以结言兮⑩，吾令蹇修以为理⑪。纷总总其离合兮⑫，忽纬繣其难迁⑬。夕归次于穷石兮⑭，朝濯发乎洧盘⑮。保厥美以骄傲兮⑯，日康娱以淫游。虽信美而无礼兮，来违弃而改求⑰。览相观于四极兮⑱，周流乎天余乃下。望瑶台之偃蹇兮⑲，见有娀之佚女⑳。吾令鸩为媒兮㉑，鸩告余以不好。雄鸠之鸣逝兮，余犹恶其佻巧㉒。心犹豫而狐疑兮㉓，欲自适而不可。凤皇既受诒兮㉔，恐高辛之先我㉕。

【注释】

①白水：神话传说中源出昆仑山的一条河流，相传饮之可以不死。

②阆(làng)风：山名。神话传说中神仙居住的地方，在昆仑之巅。绁(xiè)马：系马。

③高丘：楚国山名。一释为传说中的神山。

④春宫：神话传说中东方青帝居住的地方。

⑤琼枝：神话传说中的玉树。

⑥荣华：原意指草木茂盛、开花，此处喻美好的容颜或年华。

⑦相(xiàng)：视。下女：有多种解释，洪兴祖《楚辞补注》认为"喻贤人之在下者"。朱熹《楚辞集注》认为"谓神女之侍女也"。蒋骥《山带阁注楚辞》认为"指下处宓妃诸人；对高丘言，故曰下"。诸说较之，蒋骥之说可取。诒(yí)：通"贻"，赠送。

⑧丰隆：神话传说中的雷神，后多用作雷的代称。一说是云神。

⑨宓(fú)妃：神话传说中的洛水女神。

⑩纕(xiāng)：佩带。结言：用言辞订约。

⑪蹇修：人名，传说中伏羲氏之臣，古贤者。一释为以钟磬声乐为媒使。理：使者，媒人。

⑫纷总总：此处形容使者纷纷攘攘，络绎于道。

⑬纬繣(huà)：乖戾，不合。

⑭次：留宿。穷石：神话中传说的地名。

⑮濯(zhuó)：洗涤。洧(wěi)盘：神话传说中的水名。据说发源于崦嵫山。

⑯保：依靠，仗恃。厥(jué)：其，指宓妃。

⑰来：回来吧！这是招回丰隆的话。违弃：抛开，丢开。

⑱览相观：三字同义，看。四极：泛言四方之边极。

⑲瑶台：美玉砌的楼台。偃(yǎn)蹇：高耸。

⑳有娀(sōng)：传说中的古国名。殷始祖契之妃简狄，即有娀氏女。有，词头。佚女：美女。指有娀氏美女简狄。

㉑鸩(zhèn)：传说中的一种毒鸟，以羽浸酒，饮之立死。

㉒恶(wù)：讨厌，憎恨。佻(tiāo)巧：轻佻巧佞。

㉓犹豫：迟疑不决。狐疑：猜疑，怀疑。

㉔凤皇：即凤凰。受诒：指凤凰已接受了送给简狄的聘礼，准备前去说媒。诒，通"贻"，指聘礼。

㉕高辛：帝喾初受封于辛，后即帝位，号高辛氏。事迹详见《史记·五帝本纪》。

【译文】

早上我将渡过白水啊,登上阆风山系马驻足。忽然回首眺望潸然泪下啊,哀伤楚地高丘没有美女。我迅疾游历青帝所居之春宫啊,攀折那琼枝来补充我的佩饰。趁着缤纷的花草还未零落啊,我寻访美女赠送给她。我让雷神驾云而去啊,探寻宓妃所在的居处。解下佩戴的香囊来订下誓约啊,我命蹇修来当媒人。纷繁盛多来去不定啊,善变乖戾难以迁就。晚上回穷石过宿啊,早上在洧盘濯洗秀发。倚仗她的美貌心骄气傲啊,每天安然享乐游玩无度。虽然她确实美丽却缺乏礼教啊,回来吧蹇修,让我们丢开她再去别处寻求。察考天下四方啊,绕天巡行后我降临下土。望见玉台高拔耸立啊,我看到有娀氏的美丽公主。我命鸩去为我做媒啊,鸩告诉我她的种种不好。雄鸠高叫着远去啊,它轻佻讨巧实在令我厌恶。犹豫不定狐疑满腹啊,我打算亲自造访又不合礼数。凤凰虽已接受信物啊,又怕帝喾比我提前一步。

欲远集而无所止兮,聊浮游以逍遥①。及少康之未家兮②,留有虞之二姚③。理弱而媒拙兮,恐导言之不固④。世溷浊而嫉贤兮⑤,好蔽美而称恶。闺中既以邃远兮⑥,哲王又不寤⑦。怀朕情而不发兮,余焉能忍与此终古。

【注释】

①浮游:不知所求,无目的地漫游。逍遥:徘徊不进,与"浮游"义近。
②少康:夏代中兴之主,帝相之子。
③有虞:相传是虞舜后裔的部落国家,故址在今河南虞城。二姚:有虞国君的两个女儿。

④导言:传达疏导之言。
⑤世溷(hùn)浊:时世混乱污浊。
⑥闺中:宫室之中。邃(suì)远:深远。
⑦哲王:明智的君王。寤(wù):醒悟,觉醒。

【译文】

想在远方栖身却无处落脚啊,姑且漫游天地飘荡不前。趁少康还未成家啊,有虞氏的二姚尚待字闺中。使者无能媒人拙劣啊,恐怕无法传达心曲不能让人信服。时世混乱嫉恨贤良啊,喜欢遮蔽美善称扬邪恶。宫闱如此深远啊,明君却偏不觉悟!怀有我这样的衷情却不能舒泄啊,我怎能强忍郁闷抱恨过此一生?

索藑茅以筳篿兮①,命灵氛为余占之②。曰两美其必合兮③,孰信修而慕之?思九州之博大兮④,岂唯是其有女⑤?曰勉远逝而无狐疑兮⑥,孰求美而释女⑦?何所独无芳草兮⑧,尔何怀乎故宇⑨?世幽昧以眩曜兮⑩,孰云察余之善恶。民好恶其不同兮,惟此党人其独异⑪。户服艾以盈要兮⑫,谓幽兰其不可佩。览察草木其犹未得兮,岂珵美之能当⑬?苏粪壤以充帏兮⑭,谓申椒其不芳。欲从灵氛之吉占兮,心犹豫而狐疑。巫咸将夕降兮⑮,怀椒糈而要之⑯。百神翳其备降兮⑰,九疑缤其并迎⑱。皇剡剡其扬灵兮⑲,告余以吉故。曰勉升降以上下兮⑳,求矩矱之所同㉑。汤禹严而求合兮㉒,挚咎繇而能调㉓。苟中情其好修兮,又何必用夫行媒㉔。说操筑于傅岩兮㉕,武丁用而不疑㉖。吕望之鼓刀兮㉗,遭周文而得举㉘。宁戚之讴歌兮㉙,齐桓闻以该辅㉚。及年岁之未晏兮㉛,时亦犹其未央。恐鹈鴂之先鸣兮㉜,使夫百草为之不芳。何琼佩之偃蹇㉝,众薆然而蔽之㉞。惟此党人之不谅兮,恐

187

嫉妒而折之。时缤纷其变易兮㉟,又何可以淹留。兰芷变而不芳兮,荃蕙化而为茅㊱。何昔日之草兮,今直为此萧艾也㊲。岂其有他故兮,莫好修之害也。余以兰为可恃兮㊳,羌无实而容长㊴。委厥美以从俗兮㊵,苟得列乎众芳。椒专佞以慢慆兮㊶,樧又欲充夫佩帏㊷。既干进而务入兮㊸,又何芳之能祗㊹。固时俗之流从兮㊺,又孰能无变化。览椒兰其若兹兮,又况揭车与江离㊻。惟兹佩之可贵兮,委厥美而历兹㊼。芳菲菲而难亏兮㊽,芬至今犹未沫㊾。和调度以自娱兮㊿,聊浮游而求女。及余饰之方壮兮㉛,周流观乎上下。

【注释】

①夐(qióng)茅:即旋花,一种多年生的茅草,可用于占卜,又称灵草。筳篿(tíng zhuān):筳,木棍,一说为竹片。篿,楚人用茅草加木棍或竹片的占卜方法的统称。隋唐以前折竹为卜,为筳篿本义。

②灵氛:有多种说法,一说"灵"即神巫,"灵氛"即神巫名。一说为神名。又说指天地间灵气。今以第一种说法为善,可从。占(zhān):占卜吉凶。

③曰:以下四句是灵氛的答语。一说"曰"字以下四句是屈原问卜之词。两美其必合:这里"两美"有象喻义,承上文"求女"而来,指男女匹合。其深层象喻意义则是指圣君贤臣的遇合,屈原作品经常以男女关系比喻君臣关系。

④九州:《书·禹贡》中称当时中国有冀、徐、梁、雍、兖、荆、扬、青、豫九州,而此处似为更加宽泛,与邹衍所言"赤县神州"之大九州说近。

⑤是:此处,这里,指楚国。一说指上文所云天地四方,即宓

妃、简狄、二姚之所在。女：美女。承上文"求女"而来。
⑥曰：以下四句也是灵氛劝告作者的话。
⑦女：通"汝"，你。
⑧芳草：与上文"女"一样，都有象喻意义，喻指贤人。
⑨故宇：指家园，旧居。宇，屋檐。
⑩眩曜(xuàn yào)：迷惑混乱。眩，一作"炫"。曜，通"耀"。
⑪党人：特指楚国谄上欺下的结党营私之徒。关于"党"存在两说：一说为地方区划单位，此指楚国；二说为朋党。兹从第二种说法。
⑫服：佩带。艾：白蒿，一种恶草。盈要：满腰。
⑬珵(chéng)：美玉。当：得当，得宜。
⑭苏：即"索"一音之转，有拾取义。帏(wéi)：香囊。
⑮巫咸：古神巫名，史有其人，而后人加以神化。
⑯椒糈(xǔ)：以椒香拌和的精米，类似粽子。椒为香料。糈，精米。要(yāo)：同"邀"，迎候。
⑰翳(yì)：华盖。此处用作动词，遮蔽。备降：一同降临。
⑱九疑：即九嶷，山名，在湖南宁远县南。此指九嶷诸神。
⑲皇剡剡(yǎn)：皇，大。剡剡，光华四溢的样子。扬灵：显扬神灵。
⑳曰：以下至"使夫百草为之不芳"都是巫咸劝告诗人的话。升降以上下：上天入地，周游四方，有寻找贤君知己之意。
㉑矩矱(yuē)：即规矩、规约。矩，本指画直角或方形的工具，后引申为法度。矱亦指尺度。
㉒严：通"俨"，庄重，恭敬。合：匹合，这里指与自己志同道合的贤臣。
㉓挚(zhì)咎繇(gāo yáo)：挚，商汤名臣伊尹。咎繇，舜臣，又作"皋陶"。调：有三种说法：一说意为调和，协调；二

说作"适"解，合适；三说作"选拔、进用"解。
㉔媒：本指出使以通聘问之人。此指通达己意于君王左右的媒介、使臣。
㉕说(yuè)：即傅说，殷时贤臣。操筑：版筑。操，持。筑，捣土。傅岩：地名，傅说服贱役的地方，在今山西平陆东。
㉖武丁：殷高宗，一代中兴之君。
㉗吕望：即姜子牙，晚年出仕，助武王破商，受封齐地。鼓刀：指运刀镞时虎虎有声。鼓，舞动。
㉘周文：周文王姬昌，韬光养晦，广求贤才，到儿子武王时一举实现灭殷大业。
㉙宁戚：卫人。《史记·鲁仲连邹阳列传》："宁戚饭牛车下，而桓公任之以国。"
㉚齐桓：春秋五霸之一，曾九次召令诸侯拱卫周室，并为盟主。该辅：征用以备辅佐之选。该，备。
㉛晏：晚。
㉜鹈鴂(tí jué)：鸟名，即子规、杜鹃，或作鹭鸪。
㉝琼佩：玉佩，这里象征美好的德行。琼，美玉。偃蹇：形容美盛的样子。
㉞薆(ài)然：遮蔽的样子。
㉟缤纷：这里形容时世纷乱混浊。
㊱茅：茅草，这里比喻谗佞小人。
㊲直：竟然。萧艾：贱草，这里比喻谗佞小人。萧即白蒿。艾，艾草，生于山原，茎直，色白，高四五尺，霜后始枯。
㊳兰：指子兰，乃怀王少子，襄王弟。一说此处"兰"并非实有所指，只是喻指变节之人。
㊴无实：徒有其表，缺乏内在实质。容长：外貌美好。容，外貌。长，华硕，美好。本句历来多认为有影射时事之意。
㊵从俗：追随世俗，与小人同流合污。

㊶椒：一种说法认为是影射当时楚国大夫子椒。另一种说法认为只是对于一班变节之人的比喻说法。慢慆(tāo)：怠惰佚乐。

㊷樧(shā)：似茱萸而小，赤色。夫：于，乎。

㊸干进：即汲汲于进退之间。干，求。进，进身。务入：即务必求进，与"干进"同义。

㊹祗(zhī)：尊敬，爱护。

㊺流从：如水流顺势而下，滔滔不返，比喻时俗盲目从众，不辨是非。

㊻揭车与江离：借喻贤才之变节者。

㊼委：丢弃，这里是遭人抛弃的意思。历兹：到这步田地的意思，意即遭遇祸殃，以至于此。又说是到现在，到如今的意思。

㊽亏：亏损，消歇。

㊾沫(mèi)：这里是香气消散的意思。

㊿调度：格调和法度。调，格调。度，法度。

�饰：佩饰，服饰，这里比喻年岁。壮：壮大，壮健，这里比喻年富力强。

【译文】

取竹片、茅叶来卜筮啊，命灵氛为我占知。他说两种美好事物一定能会合啊，哪个真正美好的人不会招人思慕？想一想九州之地的广大啊，难道只有这里才有美女存在？他说勉力远走不要迟疑啊，哪个真心追求美好的人会把你放弃？哪里没有芬芳的花草啊，你为何必单恋旧居？世道昏暗使人迷乱啊，谁说能明察我心的善恶！人的好恶尺度有别啊，只有这些党徒们格外令人不可思议。家家户户将艾草挂满腰间啊，说幽谷香兰不能作佩饰。察考选用的草木都不得当啊，难道能公正地衡量玉石的美质？拾取粪土装满香囊啊,他们说大椒毫不芳馨。我打算听从灵氛吉祥的卜辞啊,心里却还怀疑彷徨。巫咸傍晚就要降临啊,我怀揣香粽前往迎候。众神遮天蔽日纷纷降临啊,九嶷山灵纷纷也来迎接。煌煌威灵神光特显啊,他们告诉我灵氛吉卜的缘故。我上天入地周游四方啊,只为寻求君臣间同心戮力。汤禹虔敬求索与己合德的贤臣啊,伊尹、皋陶得以与之调和共济。只要内心崇尚修洁啊,又何必用那使臣来进行沟通。傅说在傅岩操杵筑土啊,武丁任用他毫无猜疑。吕尚挥刀屠肉啊,遇到文王而得到重用。宁戚击牛角高歌啊,齐桓公听到后让其入朝辅弼。趁年龄还不算老大啊,时机还未尽失。唯恐鹈鸠早早啼叫啊,使花卉凋零黯淡了芳香。为何玉佩那么卓然高贵啊,人们却群起把它光芒遮蔽?只有这些党徒不诚信啊,恐怕会出于嫉妒将它摧折伤害。时代纷乱变幻莫测啊,又有什么理由长期逗留?兰草、白芷被同化而不香醇啊,荃、蕙变得与茅草无异。为什么曾经的香草,如今竟与白蒿、艾草同处一地!难道还有别的缘由吗?这是不喜好修洁带来的危害!我以为兰草可以依靠啊,却不知它华而不实只是外貌修顽。委弃它的美好而随波逐流啊,苟且偷生得以列入芳香花草的行列!椒专断谄佞飞扬跋扈啊,樧又想混进人们佩带的香囊里。既然一心只想钻营汲汲于名位啊,又怎能对芳华本有的品格抱有敬意?本来时俗就随大流啊,谁又能固持原则坚定不移。看到椒和兰也是这样啊,又何况揭车和江离?想到这佩饰如此可贵啊,它的美质遭人唾弃竟到如此田地。我的香囊芬芳浓郁难以消损啊,馨香至今还未散去。调节自我以求欢娱啊,姑且飘浮观览寻找知己。趁我恰当年富力强啊,巡行天地上下游历。

灵氛既告余以吉占兮,历吉日乎吾将行。折琼枝以为羞兮^①,精琼靡以为粻^②。为余驾飞龙兮,杂瑶象以为车^③。何离心之可同兮,吾将远逝以自疏^④。邅吾道夫昆仑兮^⑤,路修远以周流。扬云霓之晻蔼兮^⑥,鸣玉鸾之啾啾^⑦。朝发轫于天津兮^⑧,夕余至乎西极^⑨。凤皇翼其承旂兮^⑩,高翱翔之翼翼。忽吾行此流沙兮,遵赤水而容与^⑪。麾蛟龙使梁津兮^⑫,诏西皇使涉予^⑬。路修远以多艰兮,腾众车使径待^⑭。路不周以左转兮^⑮,指西海以为期^⑯。屯余车其千乘兮^⑰,齐玉轪而并驰^⑱。驾八龙之婉婉兮^⑲,载云旗之委蛇^⑳。抑志而弭节兮^㉑,神高驰之邈邈^㉒。奏《九歌》而舞《韶》兮^㉓,聊假日以媮乐^㉔。陟升皇之赫戏兮^㉕,忽临睨夫旧乡^㉖。仆夫悲余马怀兮^㉗,蜷局顾而不行^㉘。

乱曰^㉙:已矣哉,国无人莫我知兮,又何怀乎故都?既莫足与为美政兮^㉚,吾将从彭咸之所居。

【注释】

①羞:同"馐",美味。
②精:精细制作,去杂取纯。琼靡(mí):玉屑,玉粒。粻(zhāng):干粮。
③瑶象:珠玉象牙。瑶,美玉,一说似玉的美石。象,象牙。
④自疏:自我疏离,即离开楚国远行。
⑤邅(zhān):调转,转向。昆仑:古代神话传说中山名。
⑥晻蔼(yǎn ǎi):遮天蔽日。
⑦鸾:通"銮",马铃。啾啾(jiū):形容铃声如鸟鸣。
⑧天津:天河渡口。
⑨西极:最为辽远的西疆,传说为日落之处。
⑩翼:这里形容凤旗庄重严整的样子。承旂(qí):指凤旗与龙

旗随风飘展,交互掩映。承,相接,相连。旍,竿头系铃,绘有双龙缠斗图样的旗。

⑪遵:沿着。赤水:神话传说中水名。容与:徘徊。

⑫麾(huī):举手号令。蛟龙:传说中龙的两种。梁津:即在渡口间架起浮桥。梁,浮桥。

⑬诏:告诉,这里有命令的意思。西皇:西方之神,传说为少皞。一指蓐收。少皞为西天之皇,蓐收则为西天之神使。

⑭腾:传言,告诉。径侍:径直侍候。径,径直,直接。侍,侍卫。

⑮不周:古代神话传说中山名。

⑯西海:古代神话传说中西部大湖名。

⑰乘(shèng):四马驾一车称乘。

⑱軑(dài):车辖,即车轮与车轴固定在一起的插栓。

⑲婉婉:曲折蜿蜒。

⑳委蛇(wēi yí):形容车旗迎风飘舞的样子。

㉑抑志:按压或安定心志。弭(mǐ)节:停车。弭,止。节,车行的节度。

㉒邈邈(miǎo):高远貌。

㉓《九歌》:上古乐曲名。《韶》:相传为夏启之乐舞。

㉔假日:假借时日。媮(yú):一作"喻"解,愉悦。一作"偷"解,苟且。

㉕陟(zhì):上升,从低处往高处走,与"降"相对。皇:天。赫戏:辉煌隆盛貌。

㉖睨(nì):斜视。旧乡:即楚国。

㉗仆夫:为诗人驾车的人。怀:眷恋,思念。

㉘蜷(quán)局:拘挛回环,徘徊不前。

㉙乱:楚辞篇末结束全篇的标志称为乱,与结束曲、尾声相似。

㉚美政:指作者心目中的理想政治。

离骚

【译文】

　　灵氛已告诉我吉祥的卦辞啊，选好良辰我即将出行。攀折琼枝当作美味啊，精制玉屑作为点心。为我驾起奔腾的龙车啊，珠玉象牙缀饰车身。离心离德如何能同归一途啊，我将远走离开故国。调转车头我取道昆仑啊，路途遥远绕四方巡行。张扬云霓旌旗遮天蔽日啊，玉铃啾啾作响发出清鸣。早上由天河渡口出发啊，晚上我要到达日落的西方。凤旗庄严肃穆连绵不断啊，高高飞翔凌空舒展。我快行走到流沙地带啊，沿赤水岸边徘徊不前。指挥蛟龙在渡口间架起浮桥啊，命少皞帮我涉险过关。路途遥远艰险重重啊，传令众车径直侍候身边。路经不周山转而向左啊，遥指西海作相会地点。聚集我的车队足有千驾啊，使玉轮一起并驾齐驱。驾乘八匹龙马蜿蜒飞驰啊，载着迎风飞舞的绘有云霓的旗帜。气定神闲徐缓前进啊，神思飞扬超越无边。弹奏《九歌》应和《韶》乐而舞啊，姑且借这辰光娱乐身心。登临光明浩大的苍天啊，忽然向下一瞥看到楚地故园。车夫悲伤我马哀恋啊，徘徊不前无限顾念。

　　尾声：算了吧，国中没有贤士，无人理解我啊，又何必苦苦眷恋我的故国？既然没有谁能与我一起致力于政治革新啊，我将追随彭咸到他栖息的居所。

楚辞

九 歌

【题解】

《九歌》是一组祭祀神祇的乐歌,原本在楚国民间流传,后经屈原加工改写而具有了新的体制特点与精神面貌。《九歌》共有十一篇,"九"字为虚指还是实指?如果是实指,如何使总题与篇目相符?这是古今学者们争论的焦点。《文选五臣注》中张铣主张虚指,他认为:"九者,阳数之极,自谓否极,取为歌名矣。"朱熹《楚辞集注》则采取存疑的做法,认为:"篇名《九歌》而实十有一章,盖不可晓。旧以九为阳数者,尤为衍说。或疑犹有虞、夏《九歌》之遗声,亦不可考。今姑阙之,以俟知者,然非义之所急也。"他批评了张铣的看法,但并未自出新解。自明朝以来,主张实指的学者增多,汪瑗、林云铭、胡文英等人都有论及。其中,汪瑗率先提出较为合理的解释,其《楚辞蒙引》认为:"(《九歌》)末一篇固前十篇之乱辞也。《大司命》、《少司命》固可谓之一篇,如禹、汤、文武谓之三王,而文武固可为一人也。《东皇太一》也,《云中君》也,《湘君》也,《湘夫人》也,二《司命》也,《东君》也,《河伯》也,《山鬼》也,《国殇》也,非九而何?"总之,如何将十一篇中某些篇目进行合理归并,成为论说的重心所在。近代以来,上述"循名责实"的意识渐趋淡化,如陆侃如认为:"《九歌》是楚

九歌

国民间祭歌,共十一篇,前十篇每一篇祭一个神,最后一篇《礼魂》是送神曲。"这既是对汪瑗等人观点的继承,又不再主使《九歌》篇目与总题相符强作解人。现在一般认为,《九歌》前五篇《东皇太一》《云中君》《大司命》《少司命》《东君》为祭祀天神之歌,其演唱形式由饰为天神的主巫与代表世人的群巫共同参与、轮流演唱。但《东皇太一》中,主巫只出现于祭坛,并不演唱;后四篇《湘君》《湘夫人》《河伯》《山鬼》为祭祀地祇之歌,以饰为地祇的主巫独唱独舞,没有群巫歌舞穿插其中;《国殇》为祭祀楚国阵亡将士的哀歌,因对祭祀对象的敬重,与祭神相似,也由主巫与群巫轮流对唱;最后一篇《礼魂》为送魂曲,表明祭礼结束。"天神""地祇""人鬼"的体制安排,体现了《九歌》的完整性及系统性特点。姜亮夫认为东君与云中君、大司命与少司命、湘君与湘夫人、河伯与山鬼是四对配偶神。

王逸《楚辞章句》云:"《九歌》者,屈原之所作也。昔楚国南郢之邑,沅、湘之间,其俗信鬼而好祠,其祠必作歌乐鼓舞以乐诸神。屈原放逐,窜伏其域,怀忧苦毒,愁思沸郁。出见俗人祭祀之礼,歌舞之乐,其词鄙陋。因为作《九歌》之曲,上陈事神之敬,下见己之冤结,托之以风谏。故其文意不同,章句杂错,而广异义焉。"肯定了《九歌》为屈原吸纳楚风遗俗而作。朱熹《楚辞集注》进一步提出,《九歌》是屈原在既有的民间祭歌的基础上加工润饰而成的,似乎更加符合屈子创作的原貌。品味歌中情感,多委婉多情,基于悲欢离合的爱恋之情,而辞句甚为典雅清丽,正是文学家与民间大胆抒情歌曲的优秀结合。不管《九歌》是否为屈原被流放之后的作品,将其拿来与屈原的政治遭际相比附固然有相通之处,但处处皆求于此,就脱离了《九歌》作为乐神祀曲的实际，而后者才是我们今天进行欣赏评价的出发点。

以往的《九歌》研究多从政治、神话等角度进行阐释，包括上面提及的几个研究流派多不能出此范围。姜亮夫从《九歌》的宗教色彩出发，认为它与《离骚》有一共同的情怀，即"宗教情感"；至于在这种情感的处理方面则略有不同，《离骚》侧重理想化之描写，而《九歌》则侧重写实化之描写："离骚等十三篇，与九歌十一篇，有一相同之情怀，曰'宗教情感'。离骚十三篇所最景仰之情，为远游帝宫，西涉昆仑，寄意圣贤，匹偶圣姬，就重华而陈辞，依彭咸以为仪，求宓妃之所在，望瑶台之偃蹇，胥是也。而九歌之咏十神，天地、日月、山川、人先、鬼伯、国殇，无一非宗教之所崇祀。其所仰之神异，而其情则类也。虽然，其处理方法，则两者实大异：十三篇之所神祀者，以思想、情愫之景仰之主，从理智分析，得其美蔽善恶之辨。而自理想中结构一别然之宇宙，与个人修姱自洁之理想相结合，而欲归依与影从；或个人情思无法处理之时，欲依神圣为自解之计。自神化中有个人理性存在，为高度之自觉感。至九歌十一篇，则全部为神鬼事迹之描写，其写情处，亦纯从神鬼自身事象上立意，或借其神威灵感，以赞叹欣赏之，或借神鬼夫妇燕昵之情，以歌咏之；即有所寓寄，亦仅能于同底窥测一二，非十三篇之直述冀望感念者之可比。故九歌宗教感情之处理，乃写实化之描写也；十三篇宗教情感之处理，乃理想化之描写也。"(详见《重订屈原赋校注》页167、168)。另外，需要指出的是，《九歌》中所体现出的宗教情绪既不是迷狂畏惧的，也不是轻佻玩亵的——无论是《云中君》"思夫君兮太息，极劳心兮忡忡"的告白，还是《湘君》《湘夫人》《河伯》《山鬼》等篇什中的质朴真挚的情感，均表明了楚民与众神之间亲和、挚密的依恋关系，通过向赋予了平等人格的神的自由对话来实现祈愿、祝福等仪式过程。总之，孕育产生《九歌》的楚地民间具有的质朴、热情、重祀等特点，亦赋予了《九歌》欢腾的场面、华美的器饰、缠绵的情怀、虔敬的祷祝等等艺术美感和人文特质，读者可从中找到诗意的憩园。

关于《九歌》的创作时间，王逸认为是屈原放逐江南时所作，当时屈原"怀忧若苦，愁思沸郁"，故通过制作祭神乐歌，以寄托自己的思想感情。但现代研究者多认为作于放逐之前，仅供祭祀之用。

东皇太一

【题解】

《东皇太一》是祭祀最高天神的乐歌，因居《九歌》之首，被称为迎神曲。"太一"之名在先秦的一些典籍中不是天神的名称，而是一个抽象的哲学概念，或指形成天地万物的元气，或指老庄思想中所谓"道"的概念。《吕氏春秋·仲夏纪·侈乐》有"太乙"一词，本指神名，疑"太乙"与"太一"相通。姜亮夫《楚辞通故·天部》引本篇"穆将愉兮上皇"、宋玉《高唐赋》"醮诸神礼太一"，并下按语称"上皇即上帝之称变，言上皇者，以协韵之故，以此知战国时已以太一为上帝矣"。既而又进一步引申说："细考先秦故籍，以一字表事物最高概念浸假而为造化之原，自《易》至《老》《庄》莫不有此思想。……道立于一，则一之又一曰太一，太者更加神圣之谓，故以太一为造物主，亦即为以太一为帝。惟此说北土渐衰(重人事故)，故惟屈子、道家尚存其说。"汉景帝至汉武帝之时，太一渐成为天神、上帝的专名。另一方面，汉代以来天文家及道家又以天极最明亮之星为太一。《史记·封禅书》"宜立太一而上亲郊之"，《天官书》："中宫，天极星，皇其一明者，太一常居也。"张守节《史记正义》："泰一天帝之别名也。"可知，汉代星名与神名联为一体，祭太一亦成为郊祀的内容之一。直到宋代，祭祀太一的风俗犹存，据《楚辞通故·书篇部》称，当时祭于东方则称东太一，于西方则称西太一，于中央则曰中太一。本篇"东皇太一"之"皇"字亦指天帝，有复指强调之义。将"太一"视为天神并加以祭祀最早见于《九歌》，因此，祭祀"太一"可能是楚国特有的风俗。

因东皇太一高踞众神之上，从篇中表述的祭祀形式看，主巫所饰东皇太一在受祭过程中略有动作而不歌唱，以示威严、高贵。群巫则载歌载舞，通篇充满馨香祷祝之音，使人油然而生庄穆敬畏之情，以此表现对东皇太一的虔敬与祝颂。

吉日兮辰良①，穆将愉兮上皇②。抚长剑兮玉珥③，璆锵鸣兮琳琅④。

【注释】

①辰良："良辰"的倒文，为押韵之故。好时光。
②穆：恭敬。愉：娱乐。上皇：天帝，指东皇太一。
③珥(ěr)：即剑珥，剑鞘出口旁像两耳的突出部分，又叫剑鼻。
④璆(qiú)：美玉。锵(qiāng)：金属发出的音响。琳琅：美玉名。

【译文】

吉祥的日子啊美好时刻,恭敬地取悦啊天上的帝王。手抚长剑啊玉石为珥,身上玉佩啊锵锵相鸣。

瑶席兮玉瑱①,盍将把兮琼芳②。蕙肴蒸兮兰藉③,奠桂酒兮椒浆④。

【注释】

①瑶席:装饰华美的供案。瑶,美玉。席,此为呈献美玉的供案。玉瑱(zhèn):玉器。瑱,通"镇"。
②盍(hé):通"合",会集。琼芳:美好的芳香植物。琼,本义美玉,引申为美好。
③蕙肴:与"桂酒"相对。即用蕙草包裹的佳肴。蕙为香草名,又名薰草。蒸:姜亮夫《屈原赋校注》认为当作"荐",即进献;而且放置于"蕙肴"之前,即此句应为"荐(蒸)蕙肴兮兰藉。"这样与下句"奠桂酒兮椒浆"结构完全相称。兰藉:垫在祭食下的兰草。兰,香草名。藉,古时祭礼朝聘时陈列礼品用的草垫。
④桂酒:用桂花泡制的酒。椒浆:用椒泡制的酒浆。桂、椒都是香料。

【译文】

献祭供案上啊放着宝瑱,还摆上成把啊芳香的植物。蕙草包裹着祭品啊下面垫有兰叶,桂椒泡制酒浆啊敬献上神。

扬枹兮拊鼓①。疏缓节兮安歌,陈竽瑟兮浩倡②。

【注释】

①扬枹(fú)兮拊(fǔ)鼓：疑此句下脱去一句。闻一多《楚辞校补》以为"本篇通例，无间两句叶韵者，此不当独为例外，疑此句下脱去一句"。枹，击鼓槌。拊，轻轻敲打。

②竽(yú)瑟：都是古代乐器。竽，古吹奏乐器，笙类中较大者，管乐，有三十六簧。瑟，古弹拨乐器，琴类，弦乐，其形制颇多异说。浩倡：声势浩大。倡，一作"唱"。

【译文】

祭巫举起鼓槌啊轻轻敲击鼓面。鼓节舒缓啊歌声安闲，竽瑟齐鸣啊声势震天。

灵偃蹇兮姣服①，芳菲菲兮满堂。五音纷兮繁会②，君欣欣兮乐康③。

【注释】

①灵：代表神的巫者。偃蹇(yǎn jiǎn)：形容巫师优美的舞蹈姿态。一称美盛貌，即美好众多的样子。

②五音：宫、商、角、徵、羽合称五音。繁会：音调繁杂，交会在一起。

③君：指东皇太一。

【译文】

巫师翩翩起舞啊衣服亮丽，祭殿芳香馥郁啊让人心旷神怡。乐声纷繁啊众音交会，天帝喜悦啊安乐无边。

云中君

【题解】

云中君，当指常出现在云中的一位神。历来多解为云神丰隆。如洪兴祖《楚辞补注》："云神丰隆也。一曰屏翳。"朱熹、汪瑗、戴震等人均主此说。清代以来对此渐有异议，如徐文靖《管城硕记》卷十四认为"云中君"当为云梦泽中之神，其称："《左传·定公四年》：'楚子涉睢济江，入于云中。'杜注：入'云梦泽中'。是'云中'，一楚之巨薮也。云中君犹湘君耳。《尚书》：'云土梦作。'《尔雅》：'楚有云梦。'相如《子虚赋》：'云梦者，方九百里。'湘君有祠，巨薮如云中，可无祠乎？"此种说法曾得到王闿运、陈培寿等人的支持，但因与本诗文义不合，遭到后来学者批评，如游国恩《〈云中君〉非祀水神说》一文。今人何剑熏《楚辞拾沈》认为云中君当为电神，其称："余意云中君者，电神也。"姜亮夫认为云中君为月神，其在《屈原赋校注》中提出："《云中》在《东君》之后，与东君配，亦如大司命配少司命，湘君配湘夫人，则云中君月神也。又以本篇文义证之，曰'烂昭昭'，曰'齐光'，曰'皇皇'，皆与光义相连。云师宜与电雨相属，不得言光。且既降又突然举，此亦与月出没之情态相类。而'横四海'即《尚书》所谓'光被四表'之义，故曰'无穷'，与云神意象亦不合。且春秋以来，无祀云神者，楚云即特殊，其大齐必不能出入太甚，则与其谓为云神之无据，不如指为月神之有根矣。"此解甚新，有学者指出既为月神，则文中不应称"蹇将憺兮寿宫，与日月兮齐光"。按"寿宫"，王逸《楚辞章句》解为"供神之处也，祠祀皆欲得寿，故名为寿宫也。"洪兴祖《楚辞补注》称："汉武帝置寿宫神君。臣瓒曰：寿宫，奉神之宫。""蹇将憺兮寿宫"殆指云中君受祀之处灯火通明、光华夺目之状，"与日月兮齐光"一句实为喻指，未见有不当之处。倒是称云神行动倏忽，光齐日月，威及四海，颇令人费解。因此本书取云中君为月神一说。

关于本篇题旨，朱熹《楚辞集注》认为："此篇言神既降而久留，与人亲接，故既去而思之，不能忘也，足以见臣子慕君之深意矣。"这其实是对王逸、洪兴祖"忠君"说的进一步申述；但同时，它也启发了后来"人神相恋"说的产生，影响较为深远。从《九歌》整体来看，云中君应为东皇太一的属神，篇中称"灵连蜷兮既留，烂昭昭兮未央。蹇将憺兮寿宫，与日月兮齐光"，说明其祭处火烛通明，其祭礼似在晚上举行，这亦突出其月神的身份。至于篇末"思夫君兮太息，极劳心兮忡忡"，疑与楚地自由恋慕的民风有关。云中君除在观测天象、制定历法、安排农事等方面有重要作用外，也有着催化男女婚恋的浪漫意义。楚人祭祀云中君的用心，大概即在此。

《云中君》按韵可分为两章，每章都采用主祭的巫与扮云中君的巫对唱的形式来颂扬月神。除了描述祭祀"云中君"的全过程之外，无论人的唱词、神的唱词，都从不同角度叙说了月神的特征，表现出人对云中君的热切期盼和思念，以及对云、雨的渴望和云中君对人们祭礼的报答。

浴兰汤兮沐芳[1]，华采衣兮若英。灵连蜷兮既留[2]，烂昭昭兮未央[3]。

【注释】

①浴：洗身体。兰汤：煮兰为汤。汤即洗浴用的热水。沐：洗头发。芳：白芷。
②灵：即云中君，这里指扮月神的巫。连蜷(quán)：形容身姿矫健美好的样子。
③烂昭昭：指天色微明。昭昭，光明，明亮。未央：未尽，未已。央，极，尽。

【译文】

主祭者用芳香兰汤浴身啊以白芷水洗发，穿上华美的五彩衣裳啊芬香宜人绚丽如花。神灵附身啊巫师身姿美好而让人流连，天色微明啊夜犹未尽。

蹇将憺兮寿宫①，与日月兮齐光。龙驾兮虎服②，聊翱游兮周章。

【注释】

①蹇(jiǎn)：发语词。憺(dàn)：安居。寿宫：供神之宫。
②龙驾：用龙拉的车。驾，把车套在马等牲口身上。虎服：驾着虎。服，车右边所驾之物。

【译文】

月神将要安居啊在那寿宫，那里灯火通明啊与日月同辉。月神乘着龙车啊鞭策着虎，在空中回旋飞翔啊周游盘桓。

灵皇皇兮既降①，猋远举兮云中②。览冀州兮有余③，横四海兮焉穷④。

【注释】

①灵：指云中君。皇皇：同"煌煌"，指云中君下降时神光灿烂盛明的样子。
②猋(biāo)：迅速前行。云中：云霄之中，高空，常指传说中的仙境。这里指云中君原来居住的地方。
③冀州：古九州之一。有余：还有其他地方。这里指所望之远，不止此一州。
④横：遍及。四海：指中国以外的地方。焉穷：哪有穷尽。焉，安，何。穷，尽，完。

【译文】

月神光明灿烂啊已经降临，既而疾入云霄啊远远高翔。俯瞰冀州啊还有其他所在，光芒照耀九州啊直到宇外八荒。

思夫君兮太息①，极劳心兮忡忡②。

【注释】

①夫(fú)：与"此"相对，即"彼"。君：指云中君。
②忡忡(chōng)：形容忧愁的样子。

【译文】

月神啊！我如此思念你啊不由悠声长叹，每日忧心百转啊神思不安。

湘　君

【题解】

"湘君"和"湘夫人"是湘水的配偶神。将神话传说融入自然景观，赋予自然物以特别含义，是初民自然崇拜的一种表现。在《九歌》产生的时代，神话传说中帝舜及其妃子娥皇、女英分化而成湘神中男神和女神，使湘神有了具体的化身。

关于舜与二妃的传说由来已久。舜葬苍梧之说见于《山海经》中多处，如《山海经·海内南经》："苍梧之山，帝舜葬于阳，帝丹朱葬于阴。"二妃死于湘江之说，见于多书之记载，《山海经·中山经》："洞庭之山……，帝之二女居之，是常游于江渊。"《礼记·檀弓上》："舜葬于苍梧之野，盖二妃未之从也。"郑玄注："《离骚》所歌'湘夫人'，舜妃也。"张华《博物志·史补篇》卷八："尧之二女，舜之二妃，曰湘夫人。舜崩，二妃啼，以涕挥竹，竹尽斑。"可知舜初南行，二妃未同往。二妃后来赶到洞庭湖滨，听到舜崩于苍梧的消息，南望痛哭，自投湘水而死，成为湘水之神。这一传说长期流传，渐渐演变成舜为湘水之男神(湘君)，二妃为湘水之女神(湘夫人)。后人又加以演化，衍生了许多关于他们的凄美的爱情故事。从《湘君》、《湘夫人》两篇的内容来看，他们之间的热烈思恋，一方面反映了人们对超自然力量的崇拜，另一方面反映了人们对纯真爱情的向往和对幸福生活的追求。

围绕着湘君和湘夫人与舜的关系，历史上曾经产生过很多纷争。近人陆侃如、冯沅君在《中国诗史》中曾归纳为以下几种：

一、湘君为舜之二妃，与湘夫人无关，见《史记·始皇本纪》、刘向《列女传》卷一；

二、湘君为水神，湘夫人为舜之二妃，见王逸《楚辞章句》；

三、湘夫人为舜之二妃，与湘君无关，见《礼记·檀弓》郑玄注、张华《博物志》卷八《史补篇》；

四、湘夫人为舜之二女，与湘君无涉，见《博物志》卷六《地理考》；

五、湘君为娥皇，湘夫人为女英，见《昌黎先生集》卷三十一《黄陵庙碑》；

六、湘君为湘水神，湘夫人为其配偶，见王夫之《楚辞通释》，高秋月、曹同春《楚辞约注》，陈本礼《屈辞精义》；

七、湘君、湘夫人为湘水神的两位夫人，见顾炎武《日知录》卷二十五；

八、湘君、湘夫人为楚俗所祀湘山神夫妇二人，见赵翼《陔余丛考》卷十九；

九、湘君、湘夫人为天帝之二女，见刘梦鹏《屈子章句》。

相比较而言，王夫之以湘君为湘水神、湘夫人为其配偶之说较合理。王逸以湘夫人为二妃，自然易使人将湘君与舜相比附，因大致不妨碍对两篇内容的理解，也可作为参照。至于其他，则多有敷衍不通之处，故不取。从两篇内容来看，似是两人相约会见，却不知何故失之不遇。《湘君》写湘君对湘夫人的思念以及主动追寻爱人的过程，《湘夫人》则体现湘夫人对湘君同样的企盼和忠贞。一对神仙眷侣竟无缘一见，不禁令人扼腕。

全诗共分五章，依次叙述湘君对即将赴约的湘夫人的苦恋和约会前的精心准备，久候湘夫人不至而前去迎接，备尝艰辛却未能相遇，遍寻湘夫人不得又重返约会地点，最终相会成泡影后黯然离去等。情感变化曲折、缠绵悱恻。

君不行兮夷犹①，蹇谁留兮中洲②？美要眇兮宜修③，沛吾乘兮桂舟④。令沅湘兮无波⑤，使江水兮安流⑥！望夫君兮未来⑦，吹参差兮谁思⑧！

【注释】

①君：指湘夫人。行：动身走来，即赴湘君之约。夷犹：犹豫，迟疑不前。

②蹇(jiǎn)：楚国方言，发语词。

③要眇(yāo miǎo)：形容姿态美好。宜修：修饰合宜。

④沛：形容迅疾的样子。吾：我，湘君自谓。桂舟：用桂木造的船。后亦用作对舟船的美称。

⑤沅湘：水名。沅水源出贵州，穿过湖南西部，流入洞庭湖。湘水源出广西，穿过湖南东部，流入洞庭湖。

⑥江水：指长江。一说即指沅、湘之流水。

⑦夫(fú)君：犹彼君，这里指湘夫人。

⑧参差(cēn cī)：一作"篸㢀"，洞箫的别名。谁思：谁会知道。

【译文】

你犹犹豫豫啊终未赴约，究竟为谁驻留在啊你居住的水洲？我已修饰停当啊容仪美好，乘上轻快桂舟啊赶到这里守候。我叫沅湘之水啊不要掀起波浪，让那水流啊能够舒缓向前。我望了又望啊还是不见你的丽影，只有吹起排箫啊谁能听懂我的哀伤？

驾飞龙兮北征①，邅吾道兮洞庭②。薜荔柏兮蕙绸③，荪桡兮兰旌④。望涔阳兮极浦⑤，横大江兮扬灵⑥。

【注释】

①飞龙：即上文之"桂舟"，以龙引舟（或舟形似龙，舟行如龙飞），故曰"飞龙"。

②邅(zhān)：回转，绕道。洞庭：即今洞庭湖。

③薜荔柏：用薜荔编织的帘子。薜荔，植物名，又称木莲。柏，通"箔"，帘子，船屋的门窗上所挂。蕙绸：以蕙草织为帷帐。蕙，香草名。绸，通"帱"，或作"裯"，即床帐。

④荪桡(sūn ráo)：缠绕以荪草的船桨。兰旌(jīng)：以兰草为旌旗。兰，兰草。旌，古代用牦牛尾或兼五彩羽毛饰竿头的旗子。

⑤涔(cén)阳：地名，即涔阳浦，在今湖南省涔水北岸，澧县附近，地处洞庭湖西北岸与长江之间。一说在郢都附近。极浦：遥远的水滨。

⑥扬灵：划船前进。灵，通"舲"，一种有舱有窗的船。

【译文】

驾着龙舟啊直向北行，折转路线啊取道洞庭。薜荔为帘啊蕙草当帐，荪草绕桨啊兰草为旗。远远望见涔阳啊在那遥远水滨，继续横渡大江啊划船找寻。

扬灵兮未极，女婵媛兮为余太息①。横流涕兮潺湲②，隐思君兮陫侧③。桂櫂兮兰枻④，斲冰兮积雪⑤。采薜荔兮水中，搴芙蓉兮木末⑥。心不同兮媒劳，恩不甚兮轻绝！石濑兮浅浅⑦，飞龙兮翩翩。交不忠兮怨长，期不信兮告余以不闲。

【注释】

①女：湘夫人的侍女。婵媛(chán yuán)：忧愁悲怨。
②潺湲(chán yuán)：形容流淌的样子。这里是就流泪而言。
③隐：忧痛。悱(fěi)侧：即"悱恻"，悲痛的意思。
④桂棹(zhào)：桂木做的船桨。棹，船桨。兰枻(yì)：兰木做的船舷。兰，这里指木兰，香木名。
⑤斲(zhuó)冰：在激流中行船，波浪翻滚，水花四溅的景象。这里"冰"、"雪"是对流水的比喻说法。积雪：比喻浪花翻腾，清澈洁白。
⑥"采薜荔"以下两句：这两句比喻采择非其地，枉劳无益。薜荔，缘树而生的香草。搴(qiān)，拔取，采取。芙蓉，荷花。木末，树梢。
⑦石濑(lài)：沙石间的浅水滩。浅浅(jiān)：水流迅疾的样子。

【译文】

我驱舟前进啊未能与你相遇，你身边的侍女也忧愁悲怨啊不禁为我长长叹息。眼泪奔泻而出啊犹如泉涌，痛苦地思念你啊心情多么悲伤。桂木为桨啊木兰为舷，劈波斩浪啊水花飞溅。就像到水中啊采摘薜荔，爬到树梢啊采摘荷花。两人心意不同啊媒人说合也无意义，恩情不深啊就会轻易弃绝。沙石间江水啊在快速流淌，我的龙船啊在水上飞快前行。两人交往不能推心相爱啊难免怨恨绵长，约期相会不守信用啊却告诉我没有闲暇。

鼂骋骛兮江皋①，夕弭节兮北渚②。鸟次兮屋上③，水周兮堂下④。

【注释】

① 鼌(zhāo)：通"朝"，早晨。骋骛(chěng wù)：疾驰，奔腾。这里指行船而言。江皋：江岸，江边高地。
② 弭(mǐ)节：停船。北渚(zhǔ)：洞庭湖北岸的小洲。
③ 次：止宿，留宿超过两天。屋上：迎神用的屋子。
④ 堂：坛，一种方形土台，这里指祭坛。

【译文】

早晨行船到江岸高地上啊把你寻找，傍晚一无所获啊重回北岸。但见鸟儿栖宿啊在屋顶之上，水流环绕啊在祭坛下边。

捐余玦兮江中①，遗余佩兮醴浦②。采芳洲兮杜若③，将以遗兮下女④。时不可兮再得，聊逍遥兮容与⑤。

【注释】

① 捐：舍弃。玦(jué)：古时佩带的玉器，环形，有缺口，常用作表示决断、决绝的象征物。
② 佩：古代系于衣带的装饰品，常指珠玉之类。醴(lǐ)浦：澧水之滨。澧水经澧县入湖一段，正在长江与洞庭之间。醴，通"澧"，水名，是今湖南省境内流入洞庭湖的大河。
③ 杜若：香草名，又名山姜，古人谓服之"令人不忘"。
④ 遗(wèi)：赠送。下女：即前文所说湘夫人的侍女。
⑤ 逍遥：徜徉，缓步行走的样子。容与：义与"逍遥"接近。

【译文】

我把玉玦啊投到江水之中，把玉佩啊丢在醴水之滨。我在芳草丛生的水洲啊采摘杜若，准备送给啊她的侍女。时间一去啊再不复返，暂且漫步啊排遣忧愁。

湘夫人

【题解】

　　本篇承《湘君》文意，写湘夫人同样思念湘君，而终不能相见的惆怅伤怀的心情，可参《湘君》题解。本书认为，就屈原创作的时代而言，湘君、湘夫人与舜及二妃尚未形成固定的互指关系，在一定程度上，湘君、湘夫人的传说与舜、二妃的传说是并行不悖的。《湘君》与《湘夫人》中所反映出的情感纠葛，按常理推，不似一对经年夫妇所应有的表现，因此本书认为湘君与湘夫人为配偶神，两篇内容可看作是其罗曼史的开始部分或者一个不愉快的插曲。至于将湘君比附为舜，湘夫人比附为二妃，则是秦以来的说法，它已较远地背离了舜的传说的本来面目。总之，作为姊妹篇，本篇依《湘君》体制作了平行对称的表述，哀感顽艳，情氛动人。

　　全诗共分四节，依次铺叙湘夫人因不得与湘君相见的忧愁，思念湘君又不敢吐露的矛盾，想象与湘君会面的美景，最终未能与湘君相见的满腹惆怅等。后世以"二湘"为题材的诗文很多，唐人杜甫、贾至、李贺等均有所作，如杜甫《祠南夕望》云："百丈牵江色，孤舟泛日斜。兴来犹杖屦，目断更云沙。山鬼迷春竹，湘娥倚暮花。湖南清绝地，万古一长嗟。"他将"山鬼"与"湘娥"对举，显然已将湘夫人（或湘君）作为"湘娥"的替身，这是文学形象与民间传说发生叠合的表现。诗人们一方面颂扬娥皇、女英的贞烈事迹，另一方面其营造的悲情意象、缠绵意境又多是对《湘君》《湘夫人》的直接借鉴，两方面结合起来构成了影响后世的"二湘"骚怨传统。唐人李贺《帝子歌》曾一改悲情式的构思,使二湘故事焕发出喜乐的亮彩。其称:"洞庭明月一千里,凉风雁啼天在水。九节菖蒲石上死,湘神弹琴迎帝子。山头老桂吹古香,雌龙怨吟寒水光。沙浦走鱼白石郎,闲取真珠掷龙堂。"诗中重新安排了湘神迎见"帝子"亦即湘夫人的场面,前者弹奏琴弦发出美妙的乐声,空气中则弥漫着山头桂树所散发的幽香清韵;他们静听龙吟,闲掷真珠,享受着"逍遥容与"的幸福生活!在千年之后,在"诗鬼"笔下,湘君与湘夫人实现了和解共处!

帝子降兮北渚①,目眇眇兮愁予②。嫋嫋兮秋风③,洞庭波兮木叶下。

【注释】

①帝子:湘夫人。上古"子"既可称儿子,又可称女儿。北渚:指靠近洞庭湖北岸的小洲。
②眇眇(miǎo):瞻望弗及,望眼欲穿之貌。愁予:忧愁。予,通"忬",《说文·心部》:"忬,忧也。"
③嫋嫋(niǎo):又作"袅袅",本义柔弱曼长貌,这里指微风徐徐吹拂的样子。

【译文】

湘夫人以帝子之尊啊降临洞庭湖北岸的小洲,远寻湘君身影啊望眼欲穿悲痛忧伤。萧瑟的秋风啊徐徐吹拂,洞庭湖波涛涌起啊,树叶纷纷飘落。

白薠兮骋望①,与佳期兮夕张②。鸟萃兮蘋中③,罾何为兮木上④。

【注释】

①白蘋(fán)：水草名。骋(chěng)望：放眼远望。
②与(yù)：古多训"为"。佳期：男女约会的日期。佳，美，美好。期，会，会合。夕：傍晚，日暮。张：陈设，布置。
③萃(cuì)：聚集，汇集。蘋(pín)：植物名，多年生草本，生浅水中。
④罾(zēng)：用木棍或竹竿做支架的方形渔网，形似伞。鸟当止于木上，而集于水中；罾当施于水中而置于木上，二物所施不得其所，喻心意难达，与《湘君》之"采薜荔兮水中，搴芙蓉兮木末"用意相同。

【译文】

在白蘋丛中啊放眼远望，为约会的美好时刻啊早已准备停当。但鸟儿怎会聚集在啊水蘋之中，渔网怎会挂在啊树梢之上？

沅有茝兮醴有兰①，思公子兮未敢言②。荒忽兮远望，观流水兮潺湲③。

【注释】

①茝(zhǐ)：香草名，即白芷。
②公子：指湘君。未敢言：不敢说出来，指蕴藏在内心而无法倾吐的深情。
③潺湲(chán yuán)：水缓缓流淌的样子。

【译文】

沅水生有白芷啊澧水长着兰草，我思念您啊却不敢说出来。我神思迷惘啊向远处眺望，却只见那流水啊缓缓流淌。

楚辞

麋何食兮庭中①？蛟何为兮水裔②？朝驰余马兮江皋，夕济兮西澨③。闻佳人兮召予④，将腾驾兮偕逝⑤。

【注释】
①麋(mí)：哺乳动物，毛淡褐色，雄的有角，角像鹿，尾像驴，蹄像牛，颈像骆驼，但从整体上来看哪一种动物都不像，故又俗称"四不像"。
②蛟：古代传说中的一种龙。水裔(yì)：水边。
③澨(shì)：水滨。
④佳人：爱人，即湘君。
⑤腾驾：传车马急驰飞奔。腾，传。偕(xié)逝：一同前往。

【译文】
麋鹿为什么啊在庭堂上吃草，蛟龙为什么啊被困水边？早晨我纵马啊奔驰在江岸，傍晚我渡过啊西边水滨。一旦听到爱人啊召唤我的声音，我就急驰飞奔啊和他一同高飞远去。

筑室兮水中①，葺之兮荷盖②。荪壁兮紫坛③，匴芳椒兮成堂④。桂栋兮兰橑⑤，辛夷楣兮药房⑥。罔薜荔兮为帷⑦，擗蕙櫋兮既张⑧。白玉兮为镇⑨，疏石兰兮为芳⑩。芷葺兮荷屋⑪，缭之兮杜衡⑫。合百草兮实庭，建芳馨兮庑门⑬。九嶷缤兮并迎⑭，灵之来兮如云⑮。

【注释】
①室：古代称堂后为室。
②葺(qì)：用茅草覆盖房屋，亦泛指覆盖。
③荪(sūn)壁：以荪草装饰墙壁。紫坛：用紫贝砌成的中庭的

地面，取其坚滑而有光彩。紫，"紫贝"的简称，水产的宝物。

④㪔芳椒兮成堂：谓两手掬椒泥以涂堂室。㪔，"播"的古字，当为"匊"字形误，即后世"掬"字。芳椒，植物名。椒，实多而香，故名"芳椒"。堂：坛，一种方形土台，这里指祀神之殿堂中的祭坛。

⑤桂栋：桂木作的梁栋。栋，房屋正中最高的大梁。兰橑(lǎo)：用木兰做的椽子，亦作为椽子的美称。橑，搭在栋旁的木条，以承载瓦的重量，又叫椽或榱(cuī)。

⑥辛夷楣(méi)：用辛夷做的房屋的次梁。辛夷，植物名，此指辛夷树或其花。辛夷树属木兰科，落叶乔木，高数丈，木有香气。今多以"辛夷"为木兰的别称。楣，房屋的次梁。药房：以白芷饰房。药，即白芷。房，古人称堂后曰室，室之两旁曰房。

⑦罔：同"网"，绳索交叉编结而成的渔猎用具。这里释为"编结"。薜(bì)荔：植物名，又称木莲。帷：以丝帛制作的环绕四周的遮蔽物。泛指起间隔、遮蔽作用的悬垂的丝帛制品。

⑧擗(pì)：分开，裂开。蕙：蕙草做的隔扇。櫋(mián)：隔扇。

⑨镇：用重物压在上面，向下加重量。亦指压东西的用具。

⑩疏：放置。石兰：香草名，蔓延于山石上，叶如苇而柔韧，亦名石苇。芳：闻一多《楚辞校补》疑为"防"之误。《本草》："防风，一曰屏风。""防"与"屏"音近。上句言"白玉"压席，此句言以石兰为床头的屏风。

⑪芷葺(qì)：以白芷覆盖的屋顶。芷，香草名，即白芷。葺，指加盖。

⑫杜衡：香草名，即杜若，叶似葵，形似马蹄，俗名"马蹄香"。

⑬芳馨(xīn)：犹芳香，也借指香草。庑(wǔ)：堂下周围的走廊、廊屋。
⑭九嶷(yí)：山名，在湖南宁远南。此借指九嶷山诸神。并：共同，一起。
⑮灵：指扮神的女巫。如云：形容盛多。

【译文】

我们将在水中啊筑起房屋，用荷叶啊来做房顶。以荪草装饰墙壁啊用紫贝来铺地面，用芳椒和泥啊涂抹祭坛。以桂木为栋啊用兰木做椽，用玉兰为次梁啊用白芷装饰侧房。编结薜荔啊做成帷帐，蕙草成隔扇啊放置停当。使用白玉啊压住睡席，放下石兰啊为床前屏风。白芷加盖啊荷叶为屋，周围环绕啊还有杜衡。汇集香草啊装满庭院，门旁廊下啊充满芳香。九嶷山神啊纷纷前来恭贺新宅，众神降临啊齐集如云。

捐余袂兮江中①，遗余褋兮醴浦②。搴汀洲兮杜若③，将以遗兮远者④。时不可兮骤得，聊逍遥兮容与！

【注释】

①袂(mèi)：衣袖。
②褋(dié)：禅衣，即无里之衣，指贴身穿的汗衫之类。醴(lǐ)浦：澧水之滨。此处与《湘君》"捐玦"、"遗佩"之意同。
③搴(qiān)：采摘，折取。汀(tīng)：水之平，引申为水边平地，小洲。杜若：香草名。
④遗(wèi)：赠予。远者：指湘君。

【译文】

我把衣袖啊丢在江水之中,将禅衣啊扔向澧水之滨。我到水边小洲上啊采摘杜若,准备真的再见时送给啊远方爱人。美好时光啊不易碰到,只有暂且漫步啊独自排遣忧伤!

大司命

【题解】

大司命,旧说多指星宿。《周礼·春官·大宗伯》载:"以燎祀司中、司命。"孔颖达疏:"《星传》云:三台一名天柱,上台司命,为大尉;中台司中,为司徒;下台司禄,为司空云。司命,文昌宫星者。亦据《星传》云,文昌宫第四曰司命,第五曰司中,天文俱载有司中、司命,故两载之。"又《晋书·天文志》载:"三台六星,两两而居,西近文昌二星,曰上台,为司命,主寿。"其对《周礼》又加以申说,赋予其掌握人的寿运的职责。这种引申是可取的,它与本篇中大司命自言"纷总总兮九州,何寿夭兮在予"亦相一致。

值得注意的是,司命之祭并非楚国的专祀。《史记·封禅书》载:"长安置祠祝官、女巫。其梁巫,祠天、地、天社、天水、房中、堂上之属;晋巫,祠五帝、东君、云中(君)、司命、巫社、巫(祠)、族人、先炊之属……荆巫,祠堂下、巫先、司命、施糜之属。"可知其他国家亦有司命之祭。这与洪兴祖《楚辞补注》引《礼记·祭法》所称"王立七祀,诸侯立五祀,皆有司命"的说法相合。楚早期虽与周朝分庭抗礼,但到战国中后期,它与中原各国的交往日趋频繁,有可能楚祭司命是受了中原礼俗的影响。

关于大司命与少司命职责的划分,王夫之《楚辞通释》认为:"大司命统司人之生死,而少司命则司人子嗣之有无,……大司命、少司命,皆楚俗为之名而祀之。"从《大司命》"高飞兮安翔,乘清气兮御阴阳"、"一阴兮一阳,众莫知兮余所为"、"固人命兮有当,孰离合兮可为"等句,均可看出大司命是掌管人的命数的;而从《少司命》"夫人自有兮美子,荪何以兮愁苦"、"竦长剑兮拥幼艾,荪独宜兮为民正"等句,亦可见出少司命为世人子嗣传承忧虑的情况。因此,王夫之的说法是可信的。

《大司命》《少司命》的体制安排似与《湘君》《湘夫人》不同。二司命因其职责不同而得到楚人的分别祭祀,但并不如"二湘"一样同尊共祀;两篇中的互指称谓均限于主巫与二司命之间,而二司命相互间的交流则未见。今人汤炳正等《楚辞今注》认为"大司命"为男性神,"少司命"为女性神,本篇为女巫迎祭男神之辞,下篇乃男巫迎祭女神之辞,有表现男女相慕之意,可参。

广开兮天门,纷吾乘兮玄云①。令飘风兮先驱②,使冻雨兮洒尘③。

【注释】

①吾:我,大司命自称,其应出于扮演大司命的主巫之口。玄云:黑云,浓云。一说青云。
②飘风:旋风,暴风。

③冻(dōng)雨：暴雨。洒尘：洒水洗尘，用来清洗道路。

【译文】

完全敞开啊天宫大门，我从天门出发啊足下踩踏青云。我让旋风啊在前开路，又令暴雨啊清洗道路灰尘。

君迴翔兮以下①，踰空桑兮从女②。

【注释】

①君：指大司命。迴翔：盘旋飞翔。
②空桑：传说中的山名，产琴瑟之材。女（rǔ）：通"汝"，你，此处当指众巫。

【译文】

您在天上盘旋飞翔啊降临下界，越过空桑山啊来到众巫中间。

纷总总兮九州①，何寿夭兮在予！

【注释】

①九州：古代分中国为九州，此泛指天下，全中国。

【译文】

人数众多啊九州的众民，为什么生老病死啊全掌握在我手中！

高飞兮安翔，乘清气兮御阴阳①。吾与君兮斋速②，导帝之兮九坑③。

【注释】

①阴阳：阴、阳是我国古代哲学思想中两个相对的基本概念，用它们可以表示一切对立的事物。"御阴阳"和"寿夭在予"为同义语，都是控制人类生死之意。
②吾：主祭者自称。君：指大司命。斋：郭在贻《楚辞解诂》认为是"齐"字之讹，即谨畏虔敬之貌。
③帝：天帝。之：往，至。九坑：九州之山。坑，山脊。

【译文】

大司命高高飞起啊从容翱翔，驾乘清明之气啊主宰死生阴阳。我主巫恭敬虔诚啊为您大司命做向导，迎接您来到啊这天帝创造的九州之地。

灵衣兮被被①，玉佩兮陆离②。壹阴兮壹阳③，众莫知兮余所为④。

【注释】

①灵衣：神灵的衣裳。被被(pī)：长大貌。
②玉佩：古人佩挂的玉制装饰品。陆离：有三种说法：一说参差错综的样子；二说光彩绚烂的样子；三说参差绚丽的样子。
③壹阴兮壹阳：犹言或阴或阳，阴代表死亡，阳代表生存。意谓大司命能执掌生死。
④众：指一般世俗的人。余：我，大司命自称。

【译文】

云霞之衣啊长长委落，佩带的玉饰啊绚烂错综。生存啊与死亡，世间人哪知道啊都由我掌握。

折疏麻兮瑶华①，将以遗兮离居②。老冉冉兮既极，不寝近兮愈疏③。

【注释】

①疏麻：传说中的神麻，常折以赠别。瑶华：神麻的花朵。
②离居：巫称即将离去的大司命。
③寝(jìn)：逐渐。

【译文】

我折取神麻啊那白玉般的花朵，准备送给啊那即将离去的神灵。我人已渐渐啊走入暮年，如果再不亲近神灵啊就会日益疏远。

乘龙兮辚辚①，高驼兮冲天②。结桂枝兮延伫③，羌愈思兮愁人④。愁人兮奈何，愿若今兮无亏。固人命兮有当⑤，孰离合兮可为？

【注释】

①乘龙：乘坐用龙驾驶的车。辚辚(lín)：车行声。
②驼：同"驰"，飞驰。
③延伫(zhù)：长久站立。延，长久。
④羌：句首发语词。
⑤"固人命"以下两句：指人的生命和悲欢离合都操纵在神的手中，只有安于现状，以求神的眷顾。这是神巫祭祀大司命后的感叹之词。固，乃。人命，人的生命、命运。有当，有定数。离合，分离与团圆。这里指人与神的离合。为，做。

【译文】

大司命驾乘龙车啊车声辚辚,它飞腾而起啊直入云天。我手执编织好的桂枝啊在原地久久伫立,越来越思念他啊愁心百结。愁心百结啊又能怎样?宁可保持现状啊没有缺损。人的生死啊本来就有定数,面对人神的离合啊谁又能做什么?

少司命

【题解】

早在先秦时,司命即已入祀,汉唐以来称之为星名,在职责划分上一般称大司命为主宰命运之神,但少司命的界定却较含糊。朱熹《楚辞集注》囿于前说,在《少司命》题解下称:"按前篇(指《大司命》)注说有两司命,则彼固为上台,而此则文昌第四星欤?"对章旨的理解并无助益。南宋罗愿《尔雅翼》较早指出少司命的权界,其称:"少司命,主人子孙者也。"(见《释草》卷二"靡芜"条下)就本篇而言,非常恰当。近代以来对少司命的认识日渐清晰。高亨等《楚辞选》认为:"少司命神主宰少年儿童们的命运。楚人祭祀时,可能是由男巫扮少司命,而由女巫迎神,相互酬答着歌唱并舞蹈。所以歌辞是一对男女的对话,有人神恋爱的意味。"不管在《少司命》的体制安排上理解有何异同,人们对于她掌管人类子嗣传承的神职方面的认识还是较为一致的。

本篇为少司命的祭歌。《少司命》遵循对唱形式,共分五部分:女巫登场告慰少司命接受歆飨,少司命离去时群巫合唱追念,祭终祈愿和述说对少司命的爱戴。从篇章安排上明显可见降神、娱神、颂神、送神的祭祀全过程，其中女巫与少司命浓厚缱绻的情谊贯穿始终，给人淡淡的忧思而不失庄重肃穆。从本篇的形象描写来看，少司命亲切随和，为人类子嗣仗剑辟邪，完全没有大司命不可一世的情态和玄秘。篇中多有对"秋兰""绿叶""满堂美人""临风浩歌"等鲜活景物和美好情事的描写，充满生机和欢悦，与《大司命》篇末的忧虑无助也形成了较大反差。

秋兰兮麋芜①，罗生兮堂下②。绿叶兮素枝③，芳菲菲兮袭予④。夫人自有兮美子⑤，荪何以兮愁苦⑥！

【注释】

①麋芜(mí wú)：香草名。麋，通"蘼"，芎䓖(xiōng qióng)幼苗的别称。
②堂下：厅堂阶下，此处指祭堂之下。
③素枝："枝"应作"华"。素华，白色的花。
④予：我，一说"我"为女巫；一说指少司命；又一说认为是饰大司命之巫自称。兹从传统看法，是为群巫自称，与两司命无关。
⑤夫(fú)：那。美子：对他人子女的美称。子，子女。
⑥荪：香草名，这里是对少司命的美称。

【译文】

秋兰啊蘼芜，分散生长在啊厅堂台阶下。碧绿的叶子啊白色的花朵，浓郁的芳香啊沁染着我。世间人都会有啊美好的子女，您又为什么啊忧虑担心！

秋兰兮青青①,绿叶兮紫茎。满堂兮美人②,忽独与余兮目成③。入不言兮出不辞,乘回风兮载云旗。悲莫悲兮生别离,乐莫乐兮新相知。

【注释】

①青青:通"菁菁(jīng)",草木茂盛的样子。
②美人:与"美子"相应,指出众美好的人。这里应是以参与祭祀的众巫来代指人间的女性。
③余:我,据上下文意,应即少司命。目成:通过眉目传情来结成亲好。此处指少司命与群巫情谊融洽,堂上虽然有众多美好的人,但众巫还是把眼光投向少司命。

【译文】

秋兰啊如此繁茂,它有绿叶啊和紫色花茎。厅堂之中啊有众多美好之人,但她们突然看到我啊就以目光传达友好。悄悄降临啊她又总是不辞而行,凭依疾风啊张扬云旗。世上最伤心的事啊莫过于活着的时候分离,最开心的事啊莫过于结交新的知己。

荷衣兮蕙带,儵而来兮忽而逝①。夕宿兮帝郊,君谁须兮云之际②?

【注释】

①儵(shū):迅疾。
②君:少司命。须:等待。

【译文】

以荷为衣啊腰围蕙带,来去迅速啊转瞬即逝。傍晚在天国郊野啊停歇止宿,您在等待谁啊在那遥远天际?

与女游兮九河①,冲风至兮水扬波。与女沐兮咸池②,晞女发兮阳之阿③。望美人兮未来④,临风怳兮浩歌⑤。

【注释】

①"与女游"以下两句:疑是《河伯》中语,应删去。
②女(rǔ):通"汝",你。沐:洗头发。咸池:神话中的天池,日浴之处。
③晞(xī):干,晒干。阳之阿(ē):阳谷,乃日出之处。阿,曲隅,指屈曲偏僻之处。
④美人:指少司命。
⑤怳(huǎng):心神不定,失意的样子。浩歌:大声歌唱。

【译文】

我多想与您啊在天河中畅游,但暴风来临啊水中掀起巨浪。多想陪您啊在天池中清洗秀发,到那日出的地方啊把它晒干。不停张望啊您始终未回,失意的我伫立风中啊忍不住以歌解忧。

孔盖兮翠旍①,登九天兮抚彗星②。竦长剑兮拥幼艾③,荪独宜兮为民正④。

【注释】

①翠旍(jīng):亦作"翠旌",用翡翠鸟羽毛制成的旌旗。
②九天:天极高处。古代传说天有九重,故称"九天"。彗星:绕太阳运行的一种星体,后曳长尾,呈云雾状,俗称"扫帚星"。
③竦(sǒng):执,持。幼艾:泛指少年男女。
④荪(sūn)独宜:即"独荪宜",只有您才适合。荪,对神的敬称。宜,合适,适宜。民正:人民的命运主宰。

【译文】

您以孔雀羽为车盖啊以翡翠羽为旌旗,登上高天啊安抚彗星。您手拿长剑啊保护幼童,只有您才有资格啊成为我们命运的主宰。

东 君

【题解】

东君是古代神话传说中的日神。因日出东方,故称东君。古书记载多称日神为羲和,称之为"东君"应当是楚国地方风俗。姜亮夫《楚辞通故》"东君"条下称:"《周礼》云'大宗伯以实柴祀日月星辰',则古载日月祀典甚明。《仪礼·觐礼》云'天子乘龙,载大旆,象日月,升龙降龙,出拜日于东门之外,反祀方明,礼日于南门外'。《礼记·玉藻》云'天子玉藻十有二旒,前后邃延,龙卷以祭,玄端朝日于东门之外'。则祭日必于东方行之,盖日出于东,故迎日于东,而其神亦曰东君矣。东君,犹后世东王之意云耳。按《觐礼》拜日东门云云,郑注引《朝事仪》曰'天子冕而执镇圭,帅诸侯而朝日于东郊,所以敬尊之也。'盖皆楚之习也。"

《东君》是中国文学史上第一支太阳礼赞曲,赞颂了太阳神普照万物、惩除邪恶、保佑众生的美好品质,体现了人们对太阳神的无限感激和赞颂之情。作为祭祀太阳神的乐歌,《东君》通篇以祭者和神灵两种口吻交替歌唱,既表现了日神战胜邪恶、为民除害的英雄气概和留恋故居的温柔情怀,又描绘了初民对太阳神的崇敬和对光明的无限渴望。尽管《东君》的祭祀规格不及《东皇太一》，但万众聚集的参祭场面犹有过之。特别是篇末"撰余辔兮高驼翔，杳冥冥兮以东行"的点睛之笔，将前进不止、循行不息的日神形象刻画得极为饱满，令人油然而生崇敬之情。

暾将出兮东方①，照吾槛兮扶桑②。抚余马兮安驱③，夜皎皎兮既明④。

【注释】

①暾(tūn)：形容旭日初升的样子，又可指代太阳。
②吾：主祭者自称。槛(jiàn)：栏杆。扶桑：神话中树名。传说日出于扶桑之下，拂其树杪而升，因谓为日出处，此亦可代指太阳。
③余：主祭者自称，这里是其代神立言。
④皎皎(jiǎo)：同"皎皎"，形容明亮的样子。

【译文】

温暖明亮的太阳啊即将从东方升起，照耀着我门前的栏杆啊光芒出自扶桑。轻拍胯下的马儿啊缓步徐行，夜色渐渐散去啊即将天亮。

驾龙辀兮乘雷①，载云旗兮委蛇②。长太息兮将上③，心低徊兮顾怀。

【注释】

①龙辀(zhōu)：即龙驾的车。辀，车辕，这里代指车。乘雷：指车声隆隆似雷。

②委蛇(wēi yí)：指周围用作旗子的云彩飘动舒卷的样子。
③太息：长声叹息。此为将日神拟人化的描写。

【译文】

驾着我的龙车啊车声隆隆如雷，云彩为旗高高举起啊飘动舒卷。我长长地叹息啊即将升起，却又犹豫迟疑啊心中眷念故居。

羌声色兮娱人①，观者憺兮忘归②。

【注释】

①羌：楚国方言，发语词。声色：指日出时的奇景。
②憺(dàn)：安乐。

【译文】

日出景象光辉灿烂啊令人欣喜，观看的人群怡然自得啊留连忘返。

緪瑟兮交鼓①，箫钟兮瑶簴②。鸣篪兮吹竽③，思灵保兮贤姱④。翾飞兮翠曾⑤，展诗兮会舞⑥。应律兮合节，灵之来兮蔽日⑦。

【注释】

①緪(gēng)瑟：张紧瑟上的弦。緪，原指粗绳索，此处引申为绷紧、急促的意思。交鼓：古人悬鼓于架，多二人对击，故曰交鼓。
②箫：本指一种竹制管乐器，此处意为敲击。钟：古代乐器，青铜制，悬挂于架上，以槌叩击发音，祭祀或宴飨时用，战斗中亦用以指挥进退。瑶：应为"摇"，使动摇。簴(jù)：

通"虡",悬挂钟磬的木架两侧的立柱。
③箎:通"篪(chí)",一本即作"篪",古代管乐器的一种。竽:古代竹制簧管乐器,与笙相似而略大。
④灵保:神巫。贤姱(kuā):既贤且美。
⑤翾(xuān)飞:飞翔。翠:鸟名。一说"翠曾"应作"卒翾",迅速高飞的意思。曾(zēng):通"翻"。举起翅膀,飞举。
⑥展诗:赋呈或吟唱诗歌。会舞:指合舞,群舞。一说指歌声舞节相配合。
⑦灵:指其他神灵。蔽日:遮蔽日光,极言侍从众多。

【译文】

绷紧瑟弦啊对敲乐鼓,敲击铜钟啊震动钟架。吹响横篪啊吹奏竽笙,思念神灵啊他既贤又美。飞翔而下啊如翠鸟展翅高举,神人同唱歌诗啊一齐跳舞。应着音乐旋律啊和着节拍,神灵纷纷前来啊遮天蔽日。

青云衣兮白霓裳①,举长矢兮射天狼②。操余弧兮反沦降③,援北斗兮酌桂浆④。撰余辔兮高驼翔⑤,杳冥冥兮以东行⑥。

【注释】

①白霓(ní)裳:以白霓为裳(下装)。
②矢:箭,以木或竹制成。天狼:星名,天空中非常明亮的一颗恒星,属于大犬座,古以为主侵略。一说以天狼比喻秦国。
③余:东君自谓。弧(hú):木弓,亦为弓的通称。沦降:坠落,这里指日渐西下。

④北斗：北斗七星，其形似舀酒酒勺，故有此比喻。酌(zhuó)：斟酒。桂浆：以桂制成的酒浆，意即美酒。

⑤撰(zhuàn)：持，握。余：东君自谓。辔(pèi)：缰绳。高驼翔：高驰飞翔。驼，同"驰"。

⑥杳(yǎo)：幽深。冥冥(míng)：昏暗。

【译文】

我以青云作衣啊以白虹为下裳，举起手中长箭啊射杀凶残天狼。手持我的木弓啊准备返回西方，端起北斗七星啊让它斟满醇香酒浆。握紧手中马缰啊向上高高飞翔，穿越幽黑长夜啊我将再次奔向东方。

河 伯

【题解】

河伯，即神话传说中的黄河之神，本来称为河神，战国时始称河伯。河为四渎之一，是尊贵的地祇。关于河伯的神话传说非常多，流传也很广。朱熹《楚辞集注》认为河伯是黄河之神。本书同意朱熹的看法。

关于河伯的"伯"的意义，王逸《楚辞章句》认为："河为四渎长，其位视大夫。屈原亦楚大夫，欲以官相友，故言女也。"汪瑗《楚辞集解》不同意这种看法，他认为："曰伯者，称美之词，如称湘君、东君之类，非如侯伯之伯、爵位等级之称也。"同时他还以为黄河不在楚国境内，本着祀不越望的原则，此祭为僭越之举。对此，王夫之《楚辞通释》有所解释："楚昭王有疾，卜曰：河为祟。昭王谓非其境内山川，弗祀焉。昭王能以礼正祀典，故已之，而楚固尝祀之矣。民间亦相蒙僭祭，遥望而祀之，《序》所谓'信鬼而好祠'也。"这种将河伯之祭作为楚地淫祀之一例的说法，得到后世学者的广泛认同，本书亦采取这一观点。

关于河伯神话的流传非常多，最为典型的是"以女童祭河伯"的"河伯娶妇"故事。据此，有人认为《河伯》是屈原咏河伯娶妻之辞。其实《河伯》主要描述祭巫在想象中与河神在九河遨游，继而登昆仑，望极浦，入龙宫，游河渚，最后依依惜别的情景。整个游玩过程体现出的是歌者无拘无束的情怀，语言上也全是君子之交的清淡口气，未见恋爱中人的热情，故而将其理解为众巫于水边祭祀河神，并向其表达亲近友睦的情怀较为合理。篇中部分描写在一定程度上保留了某些古代遗俗，如篇末"子交手兮东行，送美人兮南浦"。朱熹《楚辞集注》云："交手者，古人将别，则相执手，以见不忍相远之意。晋、宋间犹如此也。"可知"南浦"已成为后代送别怀人的惯用之典。《河伯》迷离清婉的意境给后人许多启发，是江淹《恨赋》《别赋》等"感别赋"的先声。

与女游兮九河[①]，冲风起兮横波。乘水车兮荷盖，驾两龙兮骖螭[②]。

【注释】

① 女(rǔ)：通"汝"，你。九河：黄河下游河道的总名。传说禹治河，至兖州，为防止河水流溢，把它分成"徒骇""太史""马颊""覆釜""胡苏""简""洁""钩磐""鬲

"津"九道,徒骇在北,为主河道,其余都在东南,成为并行东注的八条支流,相距各大约二百里。

②驾两龙:指河伯以两条龙为自己拉车。骖(cān):古人用四匹马驾车,辕内两匹为"服",辕外为"骖"。这里用作动词,驾驭,乘。螭(chī):古代传说中无角的龙。

【译文】

和你一起游览啊观赏九河,暴风搅动水流啊生成巨涛。我们以水为车啊荷叶为那车盖,两条神龙驾车啊螭龙在旁。

登昆仑兮四望①,心飞扬兮浩荡②。日将暮兮怅忘归③,惟极浦兮寤怀④。

【注释】

①昆仑:古代神话传说中山名。
②飞扬:心情舒展,思绪飘飞。浩荡:这里形容意绪放达,无拘无束。
③怅:姜亮夫《屈原赋校注》认为"怅"为"憺"字之讹,即安乐。
④惟:思念。极浦:遥远的水滨。寤(wù)怀:睡不着而怀念,犹言日夜想念。

【译文】

登上昆仑神山啊极目四望,我心被这壮阔的水势啊深深激荡。太阳即将落山啊乐不知返,我还思念那遥远水滨啊难以入梦。

鱼鳞屋兮龙堂①,紫贝阙兮朱宫②,灵何为兮水中③?

【注释】

①鱼鳞屋：以鱼鳞造屋，取其光彩闪耀。龙堂：以龙鳞装饰之堂。
②紫贝阙(què)：以紫贝做宫门。紫贝，也称文贝、砑螺，海中软体动物名。壳圆质洁白，有紫色斑纹，大者至尺许。阙，宫门，城门两侧的高台，中间有道路，台上起楼观。朱宫：亦作"珠宫"，意即以珍珠为宫殿，与"贝阙"对应。
③灵：神灵，指河伯。

【译文】

以鱼鳞造房啊龙鳞装饰厅堂，紫贝修饰宫门啊珍珠做成宫殿，神灵您为什么啊停留在水中？

乘白鼋兮逐文鱼①。与女游兮河之渚②，流澌纷兮将来下③。

【注释】

①鼋(yuán)：大鳖，俗称癞头鼋。文鱼：有花纹的鱼，或即鲤鱼。
②渚(zhǔ)：小洲，水中的小块陆地。
③澌(sī)：解冻时流动的冰。纷：这里形容河水解冻时水势盛大。

【译文】

驾乘白色大鼋啊五彩鲤鱼跟随。我和你游玩啊在那河中小洲，冰块纷纷解冻啊顺势奔流向前。

子交手兮东行①，送美人兮南浦②。波滔滔兮来迎，鱼鳞

楚辞

邻兮媵予③。

【注释】

①子：指河伯。交手：拱手，即告别之意。
②美人：指河伯。浦：水边，河岸。
③邻(lín)：通"鳞鳞"，比次相连，形容众多。媵(yìng)：送别。予：我，主人公自称，似指祭祀河伯的巫者。

【译文】

您拱手告别啊要向东而行，我特意送您啊到南方水边。滔滔波浪啊奔涌来迎，鱼儿众多啊向我道别。

山 鬼

【题解】

"山鬼"一词较早见于《史记·秦始皇本纪》，其称："使者从关东夜过华阴平舒道，有人持璧遮使者曰：'为吾遗滈池君。'因言曰：'今年祖龙死。'使者问其故，因忽不见，置其璧去。使者奉璧具以闻。始皇默然良久，曰：'山鬼固不过知一岁事也。'"华阴在今陕西省东部，渭河下游，秦始置宁秦县，汉代改称华阴县。因其与楚地南北疏隔，此"山鬼"必非彼"山鬼"，而且"山鬼"在秦汉人看来当是无足称道的小神。清人顾成天认为《九歌》中的"山鬼"乃巫山神女。《文选·别赋》"君结绶兮千里，惜瑶草之徒芳"句下李善注称："宋玉《高唐赋》曰：我帝之季女，名曰瑶姬，未行而亡，封于巫山之台，精魂为草，寔曰灵芝。《山海经》曰：姑瑶之山，帝女死焉，名曰女尸，化为䔄草，其叶胥成，其花黄，其实如兔丝，服者媚于人。"可见"瑶姬"即巫山神女。《高唐赋》中神女形貌及自然环境的描写，与《山鬼》多有相似之处，可见，即使"瑶姬"不是"山鬼"，亦另有山神当之。

山鬼的形象历来颇多歧义，综合看有三种：一是清人顾成天"山鬼即是巫山神女瑶姬"说，郭沫若、马茂元、陈子展、聂石樵、金开诚、汤炳正等认同此说；二是洪兴祖、王夫之的"山鬼为山魈"之精怪说；三是明人汪瑗"山鬼即山神"说。汪瑗在《楚辞集解》中云："诸侯得祭其境内山川，则山鬼者固楚人之所得祠者也。但屈子作此，亦借此题以写己之意耳，无关于祀事也。……此题曰山鬼，犹言山神、山灵云耳，奚必夔魖魍魉魅之怪异而后谓之鬼哉？"本书认为山神说可信。《山鬼》祭祀的是位温柔多情而又遗恨绵绵的山中女性精灵，全篇叙述了山鬼与思慕的人相约却未见的哀怨之情。因她温柔婉丽，不以神力凌人，故与其他法力无边而威严逼人的神祇有极大区别。

《山鬼》共分三部分，依次叙述她满怀柔情盛装赴约，等待恋人却终未出现的欣喜与忧虑，预知约会成空时不能割舍的怨恨等。整篇始终以山鬼约会过程中的心理为主线来刻画"痴情自古空遗恨"的女子形象，微妙细腻、温柔感人，与恋爱中少女的心理特点甚为合拍。其中景物描写与人物心理的刻画可谓珠联璧合、相得益彰。

《山鬼》对后世诗歌创作影响很大。唐代诗人即多将山鬼与巫山神女相比附，创作了一系列的哀婉诗篇，如皇甫冉《巫山峡》"巫峡见巴东，迢迢出半空。云藏神女馆，雨到楚王宫"。

尤其值得指出的是，李贺作有《神弦曲》三首，其一有祭祀山鬼的场面，诗云："女巫浇酒云满空，玉炉炭火香鼕鼕。海神山鬼来座中，纸钱窸窣鸣旋风。……终南日色低平湾，神兮长在有无间。神嗔神喜师更颜，送神万骑还青山。"对"山鬼"出没接受祭礼的描写非常生动，故方扶南《李长吉诗集批注》称："《神弦》三首皆学《九歌·山鬼》。"

若有人兮山之阿①，被薜荔兮带女萝②。既含睇兮又宜笑③，子慕予兮善窈窕④。乘赤豹兮从文狸⑤，辛夷车兮结桂旗。被石兰兮带杜衡⑥，折芳馨兮遗所思。

【注释】

①阿(ē)：山的弯曲处。

②被：同"披"。带：用以约束衣服的狭长或扁平形状的物品，古代多用皮革、金玉、犀角或丝织物制成。此处用作动词。女萝：植物名，即松萝，多附生在松树上，成丝状下垂。或说即菟丝。

③含睇(dì)：含情而视。睇，微微斜视。宜笑：适宜于笑，指笑时很美。

④子：山鬼对所思之人的称呼。予：我，山鬼自称。窈窕(yǎo tiǎo)：娴静、美好的样子。

⑤赤豹：毛呈赤色，有黑色斑点的豹。文狸：毛色有花纹的狸猫。

⑥石兰：香草名。杜衡：即杜若。

【译文】

隐隐约约有人啊在那山的拐弯处，身披薜荔啊腰间系着松萝。我美目含情啊微笑美好，您爱慕我的姿态啊娴静美好。我驾赤豹出行啊后有花狸跟随，车是辛夷所制啊捆结桂枝为旗。身披石兰为衣啊又再佩带杜若，折取那芳香花草啊送我思慕的人。

余处幽篁兮终不见天①，路险难兮独后来。表独立兮山之上②，云容容兮而在下③。杳冥冥兮羌昼晦④，东风飘兮神灵雨。留灵修兮憺忘归⑤，岁既晏兮孰华予⑥。

【注释】

①余：山鬼自称。幽篁(huáng)：幽深的竹林。
②表：特出，迥异于众。
③容容：云气浮动的样子。
④杳(yǎo)冥冥：阴暗。羌：发语词。昼晦(huì)：白日光线昏暗。
⑤灵修：对爱人的尊称。憺(dàn)：安乐。
⑥晏(yàn)：晚，迟。华予：使我如花开般美丽。华，使开花。

【译文】

我住在幽深竹林中啊终日见不到天，道路艰险难走啊使我姗姗来迟。不见思慕的人啊我独立在那山巅，云雾舒卷自如啊在脚下飘荡。天色幽暗无光啊白日如同黑夜，东风迅疾吹过啊雨神为我落雨。想挽留思慕的人啊使他乐而忘返，年华渐渐老去啊谁来使我重现花容。

采三秀兮于山间①，石磊磊兮葛蔓蔓②。怨公子兮怅忘归③，君思我兮不得闲。山中人兮芳杜若④，饮石泉兮荫松柏⑤。君思我兮然疑作⑥，雷填填兮雨冥冥⑦，猨啾啾兮又夜鸣⑧。风飒飒兮木萧萧⑨,思公子兮徒离忧。

【注释】

①三秀:灵芝草的别名,灵芝一年开花三次,故又称三秀。
②磊磊(lěi):形容石头众多堆积的样子。葛:多年生草本植物,茎蔓生。蔓蔓:形容葛草蔓延的样子。
③公子:山鬼称所思之人。怅:怨望,失意。
④山中人:山鬼自称。芳杜若:芬芳似杜若,比喻香洁。
⑤荫松柏:以青松翠柏荫蔽,言居处的清幽。
⑥君:山鬼称爱人。然疑:将信将疑,半信半疑。然,肯定,相信,与"疑"相对。作:兴起,发生。
⑦填填:形容雷声之大。冥冥:阴雨貌。
⑧猨(yuán):同"猿",似猕猴。啾啾(jiū):鸟兽虫的鸣叫声。又:当作"狖(yòu)",长尾猿。
⑨飒飒(sà):风声。萧萧:草木摇落声。

【译文】

我在山间啊寻采灵芝,山石到处堆积啊藤蔓缠结。怨恨思慕的人儿啊惆怅忘返,或许你也想我啊只是没有空闲。我这山中之人啊如杜若般芬芳,渴饮石间清泉啊居于松柏山林。或许您思念我啊却又半信半疑,雷声隆隆大作啊伴着绵绵阴雨,猿声啾啾而响啊长夜呼唤不停。风声飒飒地吹啊树叶纷纷掉落,思念公子啊徒然叫人忧伤。

九歌

国 殇

【题解】

国殇，指为国事而死的人。从歌词来看，应是指在秦楚战争中牺牲的楚军将士。洪兴祖《楚辞补注》曰："谓死于国事者。《小尔雅》曰：无主之鬼谓之殇。"汪瑗《楚辞集解》对此加以申说："《小尔雅》曰：无主之鬼谓之殇。此曰国殇者，谓死于国事者，固人君之所当祭者也。此篇极叙其忠勇节义之志，读之令人足以壮浩然之气，而坚确然之守也。后世《乐府》有《从军行》，其或昉于此乎？汉魏而下，虽多能言之士，何足以逾之。"从年龄角度对"殇"进行明确定义的，始于戴震《屈原赋注》。其称："殇之义二：男女未冠（二十岁）笄（十五岁）而死者，谓之殇；在外而死者，谓之殇。殇之言伤也。国殇，死国事，则所以别于二者之殇也。歌此以吊之，通篇直赋其事。"由此可知，本篇是楚人对为国牺牲战士的祭歌。

楚国从怀王后期即与秦国频繁交战，但均以失败告终。《国殇》从两军激战的惨烈场面开始描绘，依次刻画了楚国战士的英武传神，同时也以钦佩敬仰之情对壮烈牺牲将士的坚强不屈之战斗精神和战死于沙场的英雄灵魂给予礼赞，以此激励民众，实现退敌保国的愿望。

操吴戈兮被犀甲①，车错毂兮短兵接②。旌蔽日兮敌若云，矢交坠兮士争先。凌余阵兮躐余行③，左骖殪兮右刃伤④。霾两轮兮絷四马⑤，援玉枹兮击鸣鼓⑥。天时坠兮威灵怒，严

楚辞

杀尽兮弃原野⑦。

【注释】

①吴戈：兵器名。吴地所产，故称，亦泛指精良的戈。一说指盾。戈，古代主要兵器，青铜制，其突出部分名援，援上下皆刃，用以横击和钩杀。又有石戈、玉戈，多为礼仪用具或明器。被：同"披"，披挂，佩带。犀(xī)甲：犀牛皮制的铠甲。犀皮不常有，或用牛皮，亦称犀甲。

②错毂(gǔ)：轮毂交错。错，交错。毂，车轮的中心部位，周围与车辐的一端相接，中有圆孔，用以插轴。短兵接：犹言短兵相接。短兵，刀剑等短武器。

③躐(liè)：践踏，踩。行(háng)：军队的行列。

④左骖(cān)：古时用四匹战马牵一辆战车，左右两旁的马叫骖，中间两匹叫服。殪(yì)：死亡。刃伤：为刃所伤。一说伤者是车右之辕马，"刃"当为"服"。又一说"刃伤"重文，指创伤，"刃"当为"仞"，意为"伤"。三说并录以参。

⑤霾(mái)：遮掩，掩埋。絷(zhí)：拴住马足。

⑥援玉枹(fú)：古时以击鼓指挥军队进击。"枹"一作"桴"，鼓槌。

⑦严杀：残酷杀戮。

【译文】

手持吴地利戈啊身披犀皮铠甲，战车轮毂交错啊刀光剑影相接。敌军旌旗遮天啊敌人众多如云，流矢坠落如雨啊战士奋战向前。敌军侵犯我军阵地啊冲乱我军队列，左侧骖马已死啊右服也遭重创。深埋车轮啊拴紧马腿，手持鼓槌啊敲起震天战鼓。天道沦丧啊神灵发怒，勇士惨遭杀戮啊抛尸疆场。

出不入兮往不反①,平原忽兮路超远②。带长剑兮挟秦弓③,首身离兮心不惩④。诚既勇兮又以武,终刚强兮不可凌。身既死兮神以灵⑤,子魂魄兮为鬼雄⑥。

【注释】

①出不入:指壮士出征,决心以死报国,不打算再进国门,与"往不反"互文见义。反:同"返",返回。
②忽:恍惚不明的样子。
③挟(xié):夹持。秦弓:秦地所产良弓。秦地产坚硬的木材,用以为弓,射程较远。
④不惩(chéng):不畏惧。
⑤神以灵:精神成为神灵,指精神不死而永生。
⑥子:对战士亡灵的尊称。魂魄:古人观念中一种能脱离人体而独立存在的神灵,附体则人生,离体则人死。附形之灵为魄,附气之神为魂。鬼雄:鬼中之英雄,用以称誉为国捐躯者。

【译文】

当初出征报国啊就没打算活着归来,平野辽阔苍茫啊路途遥远漫长。身佩长剑啊我臂下夹持着秦弓,即使身首异处啊也将无所畏惧。你们实在勇敢啊并且武艺超群,始终刚强不屈啊敌人不可侵凌。如今为国捐躯啊精神不死永生,你们的魂魄啊也是鬼中英雄。

礼 魂

【题解】

洪兴祖《楚辞补注》称:"礼,一作祀。"汪瑗《楚辞集解》称:"礼,一作祀。或曰:礼魂,谓以礼善终者,俱非是。盖魂犹神也,礼魂者,谓以礼而祭其神也,即章首'成礼'之'礼'字。一作祀者,祀与俗'礼'字相似而讹也。"认为古"礼"字与"祀"形近而致讹误。这是一首送神曲,通用于《九歌》前十篇。古代宗教祭典结束时,都有一个表示欢庆的特定仪式。《礼魂》就是运用于这一仪式的祭祀歌曲。歌中不言所祭者,足证是总结前十篇的终结辞。姜亮夫《楚辞通故》释"礼魂"称:"盖魂者气之神也,即神灵之本名,故以之概九神也。按此《九歌》最后之大合乐,盖总概《东君》《云中君》《湘君》《湘夫人》《大司命》《少司命》《河伯》《山鬼》《国殇》九祀作最后之总结,篇首《东皇太一》为迎神曲,与此相合,有叙有结,蔚成套数,故曰《九歌》也。"另外,有称《礼魂》为《国殇》的乱辞(屈复《楚辞新集注》),有称"礼魂"为掌握祭祀神灵礼仪的神祇(何剑熏《楚辞拾沈》)等观点,均可备一说。

歌中描写的场面非常隆重热闹,有密集交汇的鼓声、声势浩大的人群、种类繁多的香花、欢快跃动的舞姿,以及浩荡庄重的合唱队伍,组成了一次热烈隆重的送神场面结束仪式。其中有许多地方与《九歌》首篇《东皇太一》遥相呼应,如前者"会鼓"与后者"扬兮拊鼓",前者"传芭"与后者"灵偃蹇兮姣服",前者"姱女倡兮容与"与后者"疏缓节兮安歌""陈竽瑟兮浩倡""五音纷兮繁会",等等,都可以看出彼此遥相呼应的关系。

成礼兮会鼓①,传芭兮代舞②,姱女倡兮容与③。春兰兮秋菊④,长无绝兮终古。

【注释】

① 成礼:有三解:一说使礼完备;二说指祭祀礼仪结束;三说"成"作"盛","成礼"意为盛大的仪式。会鼓:众鼓齐鸣。如《东君》之"交鼓"。会,会合,聚集。这里指鼓点密集,节奏急疾明快。
② 传芭:这里指舞者手执香草,相互传递。芭,指香草。一说"芭"同"葩",即花。代舞:更迭起舞。
③ 姱(kuā)女:美丽的女子。倡:发声先唱,领唱。
④ 春兰兮秋菊:春秋二季祭祀用的香花。

【译文】

祭礼全部完成啊鼓乐合奏共鸣,芳香花草相互传递啊众人依次起舞,美女领唱乐歌啊仪态闲舒从容。春祀奉献兰草啊秋祀祭以晚菊,永远无终无止啊千秋万代相继。

楚辞

天 问

【题解】

关于《天问》的创作缘起，说法颇多。较具代表性的有：

第一，"呵壁问天"说。王逸《楚辞章句》曰："《天问》者，屈原之所作也。何不言问天？天尊不可问，故曰天问也。屈原放逐，忧心愁悴，彷徨山泽，经历陵陆。嗟号昊旻，仰天叹息。见楚有先王之庙及公卿祠堂，图画天地山川神灵，琦玮僪佹，及古贤圣怪物行事。周流罢倦，休息其下，仰见图画，因书其壁，何而问之，以渫愤懑，舒泻愁思。楚人哀惜屈原，因共论述，故其文义不次序云尔。"

第二，问天自解说。洪兴祖《楚辞补注》曰："《天问》之作，其旨远矣。盖曰遂古以来，天地事物之忧，不可胜穷。欲付之无言乎？而耳目所接，有感于吾心者，不可以不发也。欲具道其所以然乎？而天地变化，岂思虑智识之所能究哉？天固不可问，聊以寄吾之意耳。楚之兴衰，天邪人邪？吾之用舍，天邪人邪？国无人，莫我知也。知我者其天乎？此《天问》所为作也。"

第三，对远古天文及历史的拷问说。姜亮夫《屈原赋校注》认为"天"可引为一切高远神异不可知之事之总称，"天问"即对自然、人事一切不可知的疑问。林庚《天问论笺》认为《天问》乃古代传说中的一部兴亡史诗。

综上，《天问》集中体现了屈原所生活的时代人们对自然社会运行发展规律的探讨，具有强烈的怀疑与批判精神。因此，笔者认为姜、林二先生观点是有道理的。

《天问》的独特之处在于它以"问"为主，全篇共三百七十四句，提出一百七十二个问题，涉及天地生成、历史兴衰、神仙鬼怪等问题。既表现了屈原渊博的知识涵养，又体现了他大胆疑古的求知精神。《天问》通过对历朝兴衰的考察，把屈原对历史和楚国的情绪蕴含在追问中，在纵观历史兴衰的同时，强烈地表达了追求自我价值、实现理想的愿望和对楚国及民族发展、人生命运的深切忧虑。全诗气势磅礴，雄壮奇特。

《天问》虽然向来以晦涩难懂著称，但仍不乏摹拟的作品，据姜亮夫《楚辞书目五种》及崔富章《楚辞书目五种续编》著录，有晋傅玄《拟天问》、梁江淹《遂古篇》、北齐颜之推《归心篇·释一》、唐杨炯《浑天赋》、柳宗元《天对》、明方孝孺《杂问》、王廷相《答天问》九十五首、陈稚言《天对》六篇、黄道周《续天问》等等。因此，《天问》在文学史上的地位亦极重要。

曰：遂古之初①，谁传道之？上下未形②，何由考之？冥昭瞢暗③，谁能极之？冯翼惟像④，何以识之？明明暗暗⑤，惟时何为？阴阳三合⑥，何本何化？圜则九重⑦，孰营度之⑧？惟兹何功⑨，孰初作之？斡维焉系⑩？天极焉加⑪？八柱何当⑫？东南何亏？九天之际⑬，安放安属⑭？隅隈多有⑮，谁知其数？天何所沓⑯？十二焉分⑰？日月安属？列星安陈？出自汤谷⑱，次于蒙汜⑲。自明及晦，所行几里？夜光何德⑳，死则又育㉑？厥利维何㉒，而顾菟在腹㉓？女岐无合㉔，夫焉取九子？伯强何处㉕？惠气安在㉖？何阖而晦㉗？何开而明？角宿未旦㉘，曜灵安藏㉙？

【注释】

①遂古：远古。遂，通"邃"，遥远。
②上下：代指天地。未形：没有形成固定的样子。
③冥昭瞢(méng)暗：紧承上句，描述当天地未分之时，宇宙空间明暗混沌的状态。冥，昏暗。昭，明亮。瞢，昏暗模糊。
④冯(píng)翼：元气充盈貌。姜亮夫《屈原赋校注》认为"冯冀"声转则为"丰融"，即充盈之意。像：指想象中之无形之像，意近《老子》四十一章之"大音希声，大象无形"，亦近二十一章"惚兮恍兮，其中有象"之意。
⑤明明暗暗：指一天分昼夜而有明有暗。
⑥三合："三"同"参"，意即交融。可参考《老子》四十二章："道生一，一生二，二生三，三生万物。"
⑦圜：同"圆"，指天体。则：法度。九重：古说天有九重，极言其高。重，层。
⑧营度：量度营造。营，经营。度，度量。
⑨兹：此，指天分九层而言。何功：何等的工程。
⑩斡(guǎn)：运转的枢纽。古人认为天体运行是围绕一个轴心进行的。维：指系于轴上的绳索，此处指空间维度。
⑪天极：天之轴心的顶端。加：放置，安放。
⑫八柱：指支持天宇的八根柱子。当：支撑。
⑬九天：天之四面八方。
⑭放：至。属(zhǔ)：连接。
⑮隅(yú)：角落。隈(wēi)：弯曲的地方。
⑯沓(tà)：合。

⑰十二：古人认为太阳与月亮在黄道上每年相遇十二次，故将黄道分为十二，以记日月运行之轨迹。后人引申与地之十二分野相对应。

⑱汤(yáng)谷：或作"旸谷"，日出之处。

⑲次：驻扎，止息。蒙汜(sì)：或称"蒙谷"，日落之处。

⑳夜光：月的别名。

㉑死：指月缺而渐没。育：指月没而复圆。

㉒利：黑影。

㉓而顾：犹"而乃"。姜亮夫《屈原赋校注》："顾字当与'而'连续为一词，'而顾'犹言'而乃'。"菟(tù)：有二说：一说即兔。二说"顾菟"连续，或为月兔之名。闻一多《天问疏证》以为即蟾蜍。

㉔女岐：古代传说中的神名。合：婚配。这里有野合之义。

㉕伯强：有五种说法：一为风神名；二为疠鬼；三为水神；四为伯阳，即老子；五为阳气。

㉖惠气：即惠风，和畅的风。一说指彗星，惠，通"彗"。

㉗阖(hé)：闭。晦：暗，指天黑。

㉘角宿：东方星。旦：指日出。

㉙曜(yào)灵：太阳。

【译文】

问道：远古始初的情况，是由谁流传下来的？天地没有形成之前的事情，要如何才能探究清楚？天地蒙昧一片，昏明不分，谁能够将它考察明白？宇宙混沌一团，元气充盈，只是想象中得到的虚拟之"像"，要通过什么才能把握到它？天地已分，昼明夜黑，为什么会是这个样子？阴阳交融而诞生万物，以什么为基础，又化育成了什么？天体分为九重，是谁度量过？这样浩大的工程，一开始又是谁干的？使天体围绕轴心旋转的绳索，系在天轴的什么地方？天轴的顶部，又安置在哪里？支持天体的八根巨柱，安放在哪里？东南方的地面为什么塌下去一块？四面八方的天际，分别在什么地方？它们又是如何连接的？天际的角落曲折很多，谁又知道它们确切的数量？天上日月在何处会合？黄道天体又是怎样划分为十二区的？日月是怎样附着在天上而不掉下来？群星又是如何排列而井然有序？太阳从汤谷出来，歇息在蒙汜。从早晨到傍晚，它走了多少里路？月亮又有什么高尚的德行，可以缺而复圆？它上面的黑色东西是什么？难道是一只蟾蜍在那里面？女岐没有婚配，她怎么能生出九个儿子？风神伯强居住在什么地方？那和畅之风又从哪里吹来？为什么天门闭上就是夜晚，天门打开就是白天？天门没有打开之前，太阳未出之时，阳光又藏在什么地方？

  不任汩鸿①，师何以尚之②？佥曰何忧③？何不课而行之④？鸱龟曳衔⑤，鲧何听焉⑥？顺欲成功⑦，帝何刑焉？永遏在羽山⑧，夫何三年不施⑨？伯禹愎鲧⑩，夫何以变化？纂就前绪⑪，遂成考功⑫。何续初继业⑬，而厥谋不同⑭？洪泉极深，何以窴之⑮？地方九则⑯，何以坟之⑰？河海应龙⑱，何尽何历⑲？鲧何所营⑳？禹何所成？康回冯怒㉑，墬何故以东南倾㉒？九州安错㉓？川谷何洿㉔？东流不溢，孰知其故？东西南北，其修孰多？南北顺椭㉕，其衍几何㉖？昆仑县圃㉗，其尻安在㉘？增城九重㉙，其高几里？四方之门，其谁从焉？西北辟启，何气通焉？日安不到，烛龙何照㉚？羲和之未扬㉛，若华何光㉜？何所冬暖？何所夏寒？焉有石林㉝？何兽能言？焉有虺龙㉞，负熊以游？雄虺九首㉟，儵忽焉在㊱？何所不死？长人何守㊲?靡㵐九衢㊳,枲华安居㊴?一蛇吞象㊵,厥大何如?黑水玄趾㊶,三危安在㊷?延年不死,寿何所止?鲮鱼何所㊸?魃堆焉处㊹?羿焉彃日㊺?乌焉解羽㊻?

【注释】

①汩(gǔ):治理。鸿:同"洪",洪水。

②师:众人。尚:推举,推荐。

③佥(qiān):众人。

④课:试验。

⑤鸱(chī)龟:一种神龟。曳(yè)衔:拉扯。

⑥听:音近"圣",谓圣德。

⑦顺欲:按照鲧的意图。

⑧遏(è):幽闭。羽山:神话中的地名,在今江苏赣榆。一说在今山东蓬莱。

⑨三年:约数,指多年。施:解脱。

⑩伯禹:即禹。伯为禹之封爵,禹曾受封为夏伯,故称伯禹。愎:通"腹",这里指从腹中出来。

⑪纂(zuǎn):继续,继承。

⑫考:死去的父亲。功:事业。

⑬初:继续鲧的事业。

⑭厥谋:指禹的治水方略。厥,指禹。

⑮窴(tián):同"填",填塞。

⑯方:区分。九则:九品,禹分天下土地为上上、上中、上下、中上、中中、中下、下上、下中、下下九等,故曰九则。

⑰坟:区分。

⑱应龙:古代神话传说中有翼能飞的龙。

⑲尽:疑为"画",划的意思。一本此句作"应龙何画,河海

何历。"游国恩《天问纂义》认为此句当是错简倒乱。
⑳营：惑乱。一说为"营造"。
㉑康回：共工。王逸《楚辞章句》："康回，共工名也。《淮南子》（按见《天文训》）言共工与颛顼争为帝，不得，怒而触不周之山，天维绝，地柱折，故东南倾也。"冯(píng)怒：大怒。
㉒墜(dì)：同"地"。
㉓九州：传说禹分天下为翼、兖、青、徐、扬、荆、豫、梁、雍九州。详《书·禹贡》。错：通"措"，安置。
㉔洿(wū)：水深。
㉕椭(tuǒ)：狭长。
㉖衍：多余。
㉗昆仑：神话中的神山，在西部。县圃：神话中的山峰，在昆仑山上。
㉘尻(kāo)：即"尻"，本指脊椎尾骨，或指臀部。引申为山之尾麓，山脊尽处。
㉙增城：神话中的地名，在昆仑山上。九重(chóng)：极言高。
㉚烛龙：神名。洪兴祖《楚辞补注》："《山海经》云：'钟山之神，名曰烛阴，视为昼，瞑为夜，吹为冬，呼为夏，不饮不食，不喘不息，身长千里，人面蛇身，赤色。'注曰：即烛龙也。"
㉛羲(xī)和：神名。扬：日出。
㉜若华：若木之花。《山海经·大荒北经》："大荒之中，有衡石山、九阴山、洞野之山，上有赤树，青叶赤华，名曰若木。"
㉝石林：石柱之林，为喀斯特地貌中的特有景观，多分布在我国云南、贵州、广西等地。
㉞虬(qiú)龙：龙无角为虬。

㉟虺(huǐ)：毒蛇。
㊱儵(shū)忽：行动迅速。
㊲长人：即长寿之人。一说指身材高大之人。守：一说守卫，一说指操守。姜亮夫《屈原赋校注》："此中长寿之人，更有何操守而能长寿乎？"
㊳靡蓱(píng)：分枝众多的浮萍。九衢(qú)：谓分枝众多。引申为枝叶交叠的样子。
㊴枲(xǐ)华：麻的花。
㊵一蛇吞像：洪兴祖《楚辞补注》："一或作灵"。王逸《楚辞章句》："《山海经》云：南方有灵蛇，吞象，三年然后出其骨。"
㊶黑水：古代神话传说中水名，在昆仑山。一说为怒江。玄趾：疑为"交趾"，古地名，泛指五岭南。
㊷三危：地名，说法有许多，总结起来有四种：一、在甘肃敦煌三危山，此为古三危山（《尚书·禹贡》）。二、在甘肃岷山西南（孙星衍《尚书今古文注疏·尧典》）。三、在西藏。姜亮夫《屈原赋校注》引刘逢禄《尚书古今集解》引《西藏总传》："卫在打箭炉西南，俗称前藏，藏在卫西南，俗称后藏。喀木在卫东南之处，统名三危，即《禹贡》'导黑水至于三危也'。"四、仙山。
㊸鲮(líng)鱼：神话中的一种鱼。
㊹魾(qí)堆：魁堆，大雀。魾，同"魁"。
㊺羿(yì)：此处指尧时善射箭者。弊(bì)：射。
㊻乌：传说日中有乌鸦。解羽：指乌死。王逸《楚辞章句》："淮南言尧时十日并出，草木焦枯，尧命羿仰射十日，中其九日，日中九乌皆死，堕其羽翼。"

【译文】

鲧不能胜任治水的重任，众人为什么要推举他？他们都对尧说：您有什么好担心的呢，为什么不让他试试再说？鲧到底有什么德行，可以让神龟来帮他治水？按照鲧的想法治水会成功，尧为什么要惩罚他？把他长久地流放在羽山，为什么那么多年不把他释放？大禹从鲧的肚子里生出来，怎么会有这种变化？禹继承了父亲鲧的事业，成就了去世的父亲未竟的丰功。禹继承了鲧的事业，为什么他们治水的思路却一点儿不一样？洪水那么深，禹是用什么东西把它填平的？九州之地分为九块，禹又是用什么标准进行的划分？应龙的尾巴划过哪些地方？江河入海又经过哪里注入大海？鲧被什么迷惑而治水不成？禹又为什么能治水成功？共工怒气冲天，为什么会使大地向东南倾斜？九州如何设置？河谷的水为什么这样深？水向东流，为什么东方永不满溢？东西南北四边哪边距离更长？南北狭长，它能比东西长多少？昆仑山和县圃，它们的边际在哪里？增城高峻，到底有多高？昆仑山上四面八方都有门，谁从那里通过？西北面的门大开，什么风从那里吹过？太阳可有照不到的地方？烛龙照亮了哪里？太阳没有升起之前，若木之花为何能照亮大地？什么地方冬天温暖？什么地方夏天寒冷？什么地方有石林？哪一种兽类能说话？哪里有虬龙，驮着黄熊游来游去？九个头的毒蛇来往迅疾，到底在哪里？什么地方的人能长生不死？那些长命之人有何操守可以如此？分枝极多的浮萍与麻花生在哪里？一条蛇吞下一头大象，它有多大？黑水、交趾、三危在什么地方？延长寿命以求不死，寿数到什么时候会结束？传说中的鲮鱼在哪里？大雀又在哪里？羿为什么要射九日，太阳中的乌鸦又为什么会死？

禹之力献功①，降省下土四方②，焉得彼嵞山女③，而通之于台桑④？闵妃匹合⑤，厥身是继⑥，胡维嗜不同味⑦，而快鼂饱⑧？启代益作后⑨，卒然离蠥⑩，何启惟忧⑪，而能拘是达⑫？皆归躲籲⑬，而无害厥躬⑭。何后益作革⑮，而禹播降⑯？启棘宾商⑰，《九辩》《九歌》⑱。何勤子屠母⑲，而死分竟地⑳？帝降夷羿㉑，革孽夏民㉒。胡躲夫河伯㉓，而妻彼雒嫔㉔？冯珧利决㉕，封狶是躲㉖。何献蒸肉之膏㉗，而后帝不若㉘？浞娶纯狐㉙，眩妻爰谋㉚。何羿之躲革㉛，而交吞揆之㉜？阻穷西征㉝，岩何越焉㉞？化为黄熊㉟，巫何活焉？咸播秬黍㊱，莆雚是营㊲。何由并投㊳，而鲧疾修盈？白蜺婴茀㊵，胡为此堂㊶？安得夫良药㊷，不能固臧㊸？天式从横㊹，阳离爰死。大鸟何鸣㊺，夫焉丧厥体？蓱号起雨㊻，何以兴之？撰体协胁㊼，鹿何膺之㊽？鳌戴山抃㊾，何以安之？释舟陵行㊿，何以迁之？惟浇在户㉛，何求于嫂？何少康逐犬㉜，而颠陨厥首㉝？女歧缝裳㉞，而馆同爰止㉟，何颠易厥首㊱，而亲以逢殆㊲？汤谋易旅㊳，何以厚之？覆舟斟寻㊴，何道取之？桀伐蒙山㊵，何所得焉？妹嬉何肆㊶，汤何殛焉㊷？舜闵在家㊸，父何以鳏㊹？尧不姚告㊺，二女何亲㊻？厥萌在初㊼，何所亿焉？璜台十成㊽，谁所极焉？登立为帝，孰道尚之？女娲有体㊾，孰制匠之？舜服厥弟㊿，终然为害。何肆犬体㉛，而厥身不危败㉜？吴获迄古㉝，南岳是止㉞。孰期去斯㉟，得两男子㊱？缘鹄饰玉㊲，后帝是飨㊳。何承谋夏桀㊴，终以灭丧？帝乃降观㊵，下逢伊挚㊶。何条放致罚㊷，而黎服大说㊸？

【注释】

①力：勤勉。功：指治理水灾，平定九州。
②降省：到下面视察。
③盍(tú)山：即"涂山"，其地不可确指。王逸《楚辞章

255

句》:"言禹治水,道娶涂山氏女也,而通夫妇之道于台桑之地。"

④通:相会。台桑:地名,其地不可确考。

⑤闵(mǐn):爱怜。匹合:婚配。

⑥厥身:指禹。继:继承,即指生启之事。

⑦胡维:为何。维,朱熹《楚辞集注》本作"为"。嗜:爱好。姜亮夫《屈原赋校注》认为"嗜不同味"之"不"字,误衍,可从。

⑧快:满足。鼂(zhāo):同"朝",指时间很短。饱:满足。

⑨启:禹之子,夏朝国王,中国历史上由"禅让制"变为"世袭制"的第一人。益:禹贤臣,是禹选定的继承人。后:君王。

⑩卒(cù):同"猝",突然。离:遭受。蠥(niè):忧患,灾难。

⑪惟:遭受。

⑫拘:拘囚,囚禁。达:逃脱。

⑬躬籍(jú):此处指交战。躬,一作"射"。籍,一作"鞠",射箭声。

⑭厥躬:指启。

⑮作:通"祚",国祚,国家运命福祉。革:变革,指启代益为王。

⑯播降:繁荣昌盛。

⑰棘:急切。宾:祭祀。商:"帝"之误字。

⑱《九辩》、《九歌》:均为古乐曲名,传说是启所作。

⑲勤子:贤子,指启。屠母:传说启母涂山氏化为石,石破而生启,故曰屠母。

⑳死:通"尸",尸体。竟地:满地,到处都是。

㉑夷羿:指羿,上古羿有多人,此处指有穷氏羿,夏太康、少

康时人。

㉒革：革除。孽（niè）：祸患。夏民：夏朝之民，或泛指民众。

㉓河伯：即黄河水神。一说河伯为古诸侯。王夫之《楚辞通释》："河伯，古诸侯，同河祀者。羿射杀河伯，而夺其妻有雒氏。"

㉔雒嫔（luò pín）：上古神话中的雒水女神。

㉕冯（píng）：持。珧（yáo）：本指小蚌，其壳可以镶嵌于弓上。这里指良弓。利：精良。决：通"玦"，钩弦工具。

㉖封豨（xī）：大野猪。历史传说中羿有多人，尧时之羿有射封豨事，屈原或混杂之。

㉗蒸肉：祭肉。膏：祭肉的膏脂。

㉘后帝：天帝。若：通"诺"，赞许，保佑。

㉙浞（zhuó）：指寒浞，传说为羿之相，后杀羿。纯狐：羿之妻。或云即嫦娥。

㉚眩（xuàn）妻：善于迷惑人的妻子，纯狐。爰（yuán）：于是。

㉛躬革：羿善射，传说可射透七层兽皮。

㉜吞：消灭。揆（kuí）：消灭。

㉝西征：指鲧被放逐到东方海滨的羽山，曾向神巫众多的西方行求救。

㉞岩：险峰，这里指前往羽山。

㉟黄熊：指鲧。《左传·昭公七年》："昔尧殛鲧于羽山，其神化为黄熊。以入于羽渊，实为夏郊，三代祀之。"

㊱秬（jù）黍：黑米。

㊲莆雚（huán）：皆水草名。营：耕种。

㊳并投：一起流放，指鲧与共工等人一起被流放。一说鲧与妻修己一同被流放。

㊴疾：罪恶。修盈：谓罪恶深重。修，长。盈，满。

㊵白蜺(ní)：白色的虹。婴：本指装饰品，这里释为"环绕"。茀(fú)：云雾。
㊶堂：有四种说法：一指屈原"呵壁问天"时的祠堂；二指崔文子学仙的堂室；三指后羿藏药之室；四将"堂"视为形容词解为"盛"。
㊷良药：指不死之药。
㊸固臧(cáng)：妥善保管。固，稳妥。臧，同"藏"，保存。
㊹天式：自然法则。从(zòng)横：即"纵横"，意即阴阳消长、生生死死。
㊺大鸟：王子侨所化之鸟。王逸《楚辞章句》："言崔文子取王子侨之尸，置之室中，覆之以弊筐，须臾则化为大鸟而鸣，开而视之，翻飞而去。文子焉能亡子侨之身乎？言仙人不可杀也。"
㊻蓱(píng)：雨神。号：号令。
㊼撰：通"巽"，柔顺。协：合顺。
㊽鹿：指风神飞廉。膺(yīng)：响应。
㊾鳌(áo)：传说中的大龟。戴：背负，驮。抃(biàn)：拍浮，游动，此指大龟伸足游动。
㊿释：放置。陵：本义是大土山，这里指陆地。
㊱浇(ào)：古史传说中的大力士，夏少康时人，寒浞之子。
㊲少康：夏朝国王，夏后相之子。
㊳颠陨：坠落，此指浇被杀。厥首：指浇的首级。
㊴女歧：亦即女艾。闻一多《天问疏证》："案，'女歧'当从《左传》作'女艾'。"按见《左传·哀公元年》："(少康)使女艾谍浇，使季杼诱豷，遂灭过戈，复禹之绩。"姜亮夫《屈原赋校注》："艾在泰韵，歧在支韵，古支泰相转而又同声，故歧得为艾也。"缝裳：据《左传·哀公元年》的记载，则女歧(艾)是夏少康为报父(夏后相)为浇所杀之

㊾仇,以及复兴夏王朝而派到浇身边去的间谍一类人物,目的在于以女色使浇惑乱,从而伺机杀之。"缝裳"意即缝衣裳,当是女歧(艾)与浇的亲密行为之一。

�55馆同:即"同馆",同房。爰:与,一起。止:止宿,居住。

�56易:换,此处指砍错了。王逸《楚辞章句》:"言少康夜袭得女歧头,以为浇,因断之,故言易首。"厥首:指女艾的头。

�57亲:指女艾。逢殆(dài):遭祸,指被杀。

�58汤:为"康"之误,当指少康。此处所问当为少康中兴之事。易:治理,整顿。旅:军队,部下。

�59斟(zhēn)寻:古国名,与夏同为姒姓,地在今河南巩县西南。

�60桀(jié):夏代最后一位君王。蒙山:古国名。一说指岷山。

�61妺嬉(mò xǐ):夏桀之妃。何肆:姜亮夫《屈原赋校注》:"'何肆'之'何',当读与'何有与我'之'何',训为不。"不肆,意即不恣纵。

�62殛(jí):惩罚。

�63闵:妻室。

�64父:"夫"之误字。姜亮夫《屈原赋校注》:"'父何以鳏',父字讹,当为夫字。'夫何以',《天问》句例。"鳏(guān):同"鳏",男子年长而无妻。

�65姚告:即告姚。姚,王逸《楚辞章句》:"舜姓也。"此处指舜之父母。

�66二女:指尧的两个女儿娥皇、女英。亲:结亲。

�67萌:通"民"。

�68璜(huáng)台:用玉装饰的高台。汤炳正《楚辞今注》认为即指舜登基之台。十成：十层，极言其高。
⑥⑨女娲(wā)：神女名。
⑦⑩弟：指舜弟象。
⑦①犬体：这里是对舜弟象的贬称，言其行径悖谬不法有类于犬。
⑦②危败：指舜弟象行事悖逆，一再谋害舜，却未被追究。
⑦③获：得到。一说认为"吴获"为人名。迄(qì)古：从远古时开始，意为国运长久。
⑦④南岳：泛指南方地区。止：留下居住。
⑦⑤去：一作"夫"。姜亮夫《屈原赋校注》："应作夫，夫、去形近而误。夫在句中作于字解。"斯：这样，指代"吴获迄古，南岳是止"这一情况。
⑦⑥两男子：王逸《楚辞章句》认为指太伯、仲雍。
⑦⑦缘鹄(hú)饰玉：此句指伊尹借助烹调食物供汤享用之际接近汤，向他陈说治国之道。缘、饰，义近，皆装饰之义。鹄、玉，皆鼎上作装饰用的花纹与器物。
⑦⑧后帝：指汤。飨(xiǎng)：赏识。
⑦⑨承谋：指伊尹接受汤的旨意，假意事奉桀，实则探听夏之虚实，图谋灭之。
⑧⑩帝：指汤。降观：四处巡察。
⑧①伊挚：即伊尹。商初名臣，为商朝理政安民五十余载，治国有方，权倾朝野。
⑧②条放：指夏桀被流放到鸣条之事。致罚：受到上天的惩罚。
⑧③黎服：天下众民。服，古代行政区划单位。说：同"悦"。喜悦。

【译文】

大禹勤劳地治理水患，巡查四方。他怎么遇到那个涂山国的女子，和她相爱并私会在台桑的？大禹和那位姑娘成就婚配，他

天问

因此有了后代。为什么他们相隔很远，族姓相同，本不该通婚却很快能被彼此吸引，以求一时之欢？启想取代益成为君王，突然遭到了麻烦。为什么启虽遭难，却能从拘禁中逃脱？益与启两个部族交战，箭如雨下，而启却没有受到伤害。为什么益的统治权被夺去，而禹的后代却能繁荣昌盛？启急切地向上帝祭祀并得到了《九辩》和《九歌》。为什么这样贤良勤勉的儿子却会害死自己的母亲，让母亲的尸骨散落遍地？天帝降生了羿，让他为夏民除去祸害，他为什么要射瞎河伯，又娶了河伯的妻子雒水女神？他拿着强弓利器，射杀了大野猪。为什么他献给上帝肥美的祭肉，上帝却不保佑他？寒浞娶走了羿的妻子，那个善于迷惑人的妻子与浞合谋。为什么羿力大善射，却被他们设计消灭了？鲧化为黄熊，向西方进发，他怎样越过那高峻的山岩？鲧的身体已经化为黄熊，神巫又怎能把他救活？鲧辛勤地耕作，把田地都种上了黑粟，铲除了杂草。为什么他却与共工等人一起被流放？难道他真的罪无可赦？嫦娥佩戴着精美的服饰，她为何要打扮得如此美丽？她从哪里得到了那不死良药，并把它妥善保管在月宫里面？天地之间阴阳消长、生生死死，阳气离开就会死亡。王子侨死了之后怎么会变成大鸟，还会发出鸣叫？他是怎样失去了原有的身体？萍翳发出号令就能下雨，雨又是怎样兴起的？风神性情温顺，它怎么能响应兴云起雨的事情？海中的大龟顶着大山四脚划动，又怎能让大山安稳下来？将船放在陆地上，怎样才能移动它？大力士浇在家，为什么还要求助于他的嫂子？少康驱驰猎犬打猎，为什么能将浇的首级砍下？女艾为浇缝衣裳，并同他一起住宿，为什么少康却砍下女艾的头，亲信之人反而遭殃？少康谋划大兴军事，他靠什么使自己的力量增强？那浇曾经倾覆了斟寻国的战船，少康用什么手段取胜了他？夏桀讨伐蒙山，他得到了什么？妹嬉本人并不十分放纵，为何汤要将她惩罚？舜在家有妻室，为何却称他为鳏夫？尧不告诉舜的父母，又怎能将两个女儿嫁给他？舜当初为民的时候，他怎能料到会有今日登基之事？玉饰的高台，又有谁可以登上？舜被立为君王，是谁引导他上台？女娲躯体变化无穷，又是谁造就了她？舜恭顺地对待他的弟弟象，却终于酿成祸患。为什么象极端地放肆，却没有败亡？吴国立国于南方，国运长久。谁能料到会这样，难道只因为出了泰伯、仲雍这两个贤良男子？伊尹用精美的器具烹制美味的羹肴进献给汤，因而得到了赏识。为什么他要假装为夏桀谋划，使夏桀败亡？汤巡视四方，遇到了伊尹。他在鸣条战胜了夏桀，并将其放逐，为何百姓却非常喜悦？

简狄在台①，喾何宜②？玄鸟致贻③，女何喜④？该秉季德⑤，厥父是臧。胡终弊于有扈⑥，牧夫牛羊？干协时舞⑦，何以怀之⑧？平胁曼肤⑨，何以肥之？有扈牧竖⑩，云何而逢？击床先出⑪，其命何从？恒秉季德⑫，焉得夫朴牛⑬？何往营班禄⑭，不但还来⑮？昏微遵迹⑯，有狄不宁⑰。何繁鸟萃棘⑱，负子肆情⑲？眩弟并淫⑳，危害厥兄。何变化以作诈㉑，后嗣而逢长？成汤东巡，有莘爰极㉒。何乞彼小臣㉓，而吉妃是得㉔？水滨之木，得彼小子㉕。夫何恶之，媵有莘之妇㉖？汤出重泉㉗，夫何罪尤㉘？不胜心伐帝㉙，夫谁使挑之？

【注释】

①简狄：帝喾的妃子。
②喾(kù)：传说中的古帝王名。宜：祭祀。姜亮夫《屈原赋校注》作"祭祀求福"解，可从。

③玄鸟：黑色的鸟，指燕。致贻(yí)：送礼。王逸《楚辞章句》："贻，遗也。言简狄侍帝喾于台上，有飞燕坠遗其卵，喜而吞之，因生契也。"

④喜：一作"嘉"，意即受孕而生子。

⑤该：即殷侯亥。季：王亥之父，殷侯冥。

⑥弊：困厄。《山海经·大荒东经》："王亥托于有易，河伯仆牛。有易杀王亥，取仆牛。"有扈(hù)：王国维《殷卜辞中所见先公先王考》认为即"有易"，"易"与"扈"金文形近。

⑦干：盾。协：和合。时舞：指万舞，古代一种大型乐舞。

⑧怀：挑逗，引诱。

⑨平胁：指体形俊美。曼肤：皮肤细腻。姜亮夫《屈原赋校注》认为此句形容有易之女形体曼泽之状。

⑩有扈：即有易。姜亮夫《屈原赋校注》："按有扈即上文有易，……此有易指王亥所淫之女。"牧竖：指王亥。

⑪击床：姜亮夫《屈原赋校注》认为指有易氏杀亥事。先出：依《山海经》说，王亥已被杀，则"击床先出"之"先"，当为误字，以意校之，或"不"、"未"之属也。

⑫恒：即殷侯王恒，王亥之弟。

⑬朴牛：即服牛，可驾车的大牛。王国维《殷卜辞中所见先公先王考》："服牛者，即《大荒东经》之仆牛，古服、仆同音也。"

⑭营：经营。班禄：颁布爵禄。

⑮但：空。一说疑为"得"之误。

⑯昏微：指殷侯上甲微。迹：道路。

⑰有狄：即有易。不宁：不安宁。

⑱繁鸟萃棘：喻荒淫事。姜亮夫《校注》认为此句或指上甲微晚年的荒淫之行。

⑲负：姜亮夫推测本为"媜"字，亦即"妇"。"妇子"或即劫夺儿媳为己妻之丑行。
⑳眩(xuàn)：惑乱，荒唐。
㉑变化：指改变帝位继承顺序。作诈：行为奸诈。
㉒有莘(shēn)：古国名。
㉓乞：讨，要。小臣：指伊尹。
㉔吉妃：美好的姑娘。得：娶到。
㉕小子：指伊尹。
㉖媵(yìng)：陪嫁，指汤娶有莘氏女为妻，有莘氏以伊尹为陪嫁。
㉗重泉：地名。《史记·夏本纪》记夏桀召汤并囚之于夏台，后又将其释放。重泉，大约是夏台之所在。
㉘尤：过失。
㉙胜心：压住怒气。帝：指夏桀。

【译文】

简狄住在高台之上，帝喾为什么要祭祀求福？燕子给简狄送来了礼物，她为什么会怀孕有子？亥继承了他父亲季的美德，并得到了嘉奖。为什么会最终被困于有易氏，为人牧牛放羊？亥拿起盾，跳起万舞，他用什么来诱惑有易氏的姑娘？姑娘肌体丰满，皮肤细腻，是什么让她如此丰美？他们一个是有易氏的美女，一个是低贱的牧人，为什么会碰到一起？有易氏要杀亥，他在事发之前尚未走出家门，他的命运会有怎样的结局？恒也继承了父亲季的美德，他怎样得到那驾车的大牛？他为什么要去有易氏颁布爵禄？目的没有达到他为什么就回来了？上甲微遵循父祖的美德，有易氏从此不得安宁。为什么他晚年竟会荒淫无度，放纵情欲？荒唐昏乱的弟弟和哥哥一起淫乱，最后谋害了他的兄长。为什么坏人篡夺王位，行为狡诈，却能子孙昌盛？成汤在东方巡视，到了有莘国。他为什么想要小臣伊尹，却得到了美丽的新娘？在水边的树木中，伊尹降生。有莘氏为什么厌恶他，让他做有莘氏姑娘的陪嫁？汤因何种罪过被囚禁在重泉，后来才被释放？汤压抑不住胸中的怒火，讨伐夏桀。这又是谁唆使的？

会鼌争盟①，何践吾期②？苍鸟群飞③，孰使萃之？到击纣躬④，叔旦不嘉⑤。何亲揆发足⑥，周之命以咨嗟⑦？授殷天下，其位安施？反成乃亡⑧，其罪伊何？争遣伐器⑨，何以行之？并驱击翼，何以将之？昭后成游⑩，南土爰底⑪。厥利惟何，逢彼白雉⑫？穆王巧梅⑬？夫何为周流？环理天下⑭，夫何索求？妖夫曳衒⑮，何号于市？周幽谁诛，焉得夫褒姒⑯？天命反侧，何罚何佑？齐桓九会⑰，卒然身杀⑱。彼王纣之躬⑲，孰使乱惑？何恶辅弼⑳，谗谄是服㉑？比干何逆㉒，而抑沉之？雷开阿顺㉓，而赐封之？何圣人之一德，卒其异方㉔？梅伯受醢㉕，箕子详狂㉖。稷维元子㉗，帝何竺之㉘？投之于冰上，鸟何燠之㉙？何冯弓挟矢㉚，殊能将之？既惊帝切激㉛，何逢长之㉜？伯昌号衰㉝，秉鞭作牧㉞。何令彻彼岐社㉟，命有殷国？迁藏就岐，何能依？殷有惑妇，何所讥？受赐兹醢㊱，西伯上告。何亲就上帝罚㊲，殷之命以不救？师望在肆㊳，昌何识㊴？鼓刀扬声，后何喜？武发杀殷㊵，何所悒㊶？载尸集战㊷，何所急？伯林雉经㊸，维其何故？何感天抑墬㊹，夫谁畏惧？皇天集命㊺，惟何戒之？受礼天下㊻，又使至代之㊼？初汤臣挚㊽，后兹承辅。何卒官汤㊾，尊食宗绪㊿？勋阖梦生㊶，少离散亡。何壮武厉，能流厥严？彭铿斟雉㊽，帝何飨㊾？受寿永多㊽,夫何久长?中央共牧㊿,后何怒?蜂蛾微命㊾,力何固?惊女采薇㊿,鹿何祐㊿?北至回水㊿,萃何喜㊿?兄有噬犬㊿,弟何欲㊿?易之以百两㊿,卒无禄㊿。

【注释】

①会鼌(zhāo):即"朝会"。争盟:一本作"请盟",即宣誓于神。

②践:履行。吾期:武王定下的日期。吾,同"武"。

③苍鸟:比喻跟从武王伐纣的将士。

④到:一作"列",分解。朱熹《楚辞集注》:"《史记》言:武王至纣死所,射之三发,以黄钺斩其头,悬之太白之旗,此所谓列击纣躬也。"躬:身体。

⑤叔旦:即周公旦。不嘉:不赞许。

⑥揆(kuí):谋划。发:指周武王姬发。足:当作"定",这里是"使安定"之意。姜亮夫《屈原赋校注》认为"足"当为"定"之形误,且应在下句。

⑦咨嗟(zī jiē):叹息。

⑧反:一本作"及",指殷有天下而又失去了它。

⑨伐器:作战的器具,指军队。

⑩昭后:指周昭王。成:同"盛",盛大。

⑪南土:荆楚地区。底:止,至。此指周昭王南征楚国不还之事。

⑫白雉(zhì):白色的野鸡。

⑬穆王:昭王之子。巧梅:善于驾车。梅,通"枚",马鞭。一说通"挴",贪。

⑭环理:周游。

⑮妖夫:妖人。曳衒(xuàn):当为"曳衔",犹言"相将"。

天问

一说"衒"为"卖"的意思。为"衒"之形误。
⑯褒姒(bāo sì)：周幽王妃。
⑰九会：指齐桓公九会诸侯，以尊周室。
⑱身杀：身死。王逸《楚辞章句》："言齐桓公任管仲，九合诸侯，一匡天下；任竖刁易牙，子孙相杀，虫流出户。"
⑲躬：身躯。
⑳辅弼：忠诚的大臣。
㉑谗谄：指谄邪小人。服：任用。
㉒比干：纣王之叔，劝告纣为善去恶，纣王剖其心而杀之。逆：触犯。
㉓雷开：纣时奸佞之人。阿(ē)：阿谀奉承。一作"何"。姜亮夫《屈原赋校注》："作阿非是，此与上句何逆为相对而相反之问，若为阿，则为陈述语矣。"
㉔卒：最后，最终。方：方式。
㉕梅伯：纣时诸侯。醢(hǎi)：肉酱，此处意为砍成肉酱。
㉖箕(jī)子：纣王叔父。详(yáng)狂：装疯。详，通"佯"。据《史记·殷本纪》，纣王杀比干后，箕子惧而佯狂，为奴。
㉗稷(jì)：周人始祖，姜嫄之子。元子：嫡长子。
㉘帝：指帝喾。竺(zhú)：厚。或指"竺"为"毒"。
㉙燠(yù)：焐热，温暖。即《史记·周本纪》所载帝喾将稷"弃渠中冰上，飞鸟以其翼覆荐之"一事。
㉚冯(píng)弓：拿着弓。冯，同"凭"，持。
㉛惊帝：惊动上帝。《诗·大雅·生民》记稷生"上帝不宁"。"帝"有三说。一说指上帝。二说指纣。三说为高辛氏，即帝喾。切激：强烈。
㉜逢长：繁荣昌盛。长，一说文王所受封西伯或西长一职。
㉝伯昌：周文王姬昌。衰：衰世。
㉞秉鞭：执政。牧：古代地方长官。牧，"牧师"的简称，见

《周礼·夏官》，是我国古代管理牧区的官吏，后引申为地方长官。

㉟彻：放弃，毁弃。岐社：岐地是周氏族祭祀之所。

㊱受：纣王名。兹：子，指纣杀文王子伯邑考，烹以为羹，赐文王食。

㊲亲：指纣。就：受到，遭受。

㊳师望：即太公吕望。肆：店铺。

㊴昌：文王姬昌。

㊵武发：指周武王姬发。殷：指纣王。

㊶悒(yì)：忿恨。

㊷尸：灵位。集战：会战。

㊸伯林：指纣。林，《尔雅·释诂》："君也。"雉(zhì)经：上吊自杀。

㊹墬(dì)：地。

㊺集命：集天命于一身。

㊻礼：同"理"，治理。

㊼至：后来之人。

㊽臣挚：以挚为臣，挚是伊尹名。

㊾官汤：指伊尹辅佐汤。

㊿尊食：指伊尹死后配祀汤。宗绪：宗庙。

51勋：有功绩。阖(hé)：吴王阖闾。梦生：吴王寿梦之孙。

52彭铿(kēng)：彭祖。斟(zhēn)雉：善于调制雉（野鸡）羹。

53帝：天帝。一说帝尧。飨(xiǎng)：享用。

54受寿永多：寿命很长。据说彭祖寿七百六十七岁。

55中央：指周王朝。共牧：共同管理。《史记·周本纪》记厉王暴虐，周人将其流放，由周公、召公共执国政。

56蜂蛾：指百姓民众。

57惊女采薇：指伯夷、叔齐二人不食周粟，采薇为食，从而惊动女子。
㊽ 鹿何祐:为何得到神鹿的庇祐、帮助。闻一多《楚辞校补》:"《琱玉集感应篇》引《列士传》曰:伯夷兄弟遂绝食(薇),七日,天遣白鹿乳之。此即所谓'鹿何祐'也。"
㊾ 回水:首阳山处河曲之中,故以曲水代之。
㊿ 萃:停止,歇宿。
㉑ 兄:指秦景公伯车。噬(shì)犬:咬人的狗。
㉒ 弟:子鍼,秦景公弟。
㉓ 易:交换。两:同"辆",用于车辆。
㉔ 无禄:丧失爵禄。

【译文】

诸侯聚集在一起结盟宣誓,他们如何履行周武王定下的约期?苍鹰一样勇敢的将士,谁把他们招集在一起?武王砍断纣王的躯体,周公并不赞同。他亲自为武王谋划,安定周室,却为何要叹息?上帝把天下交给殷朝,帝位为什么又会转移?先让殷室成功后又让他们灭亡,他们犯了什么罪过?诸侯派出军队,是通过什么指挥的?将士们并驾齐驱,攻击敌军两翼,是谁带领的?昭王进行盛大的游历,到了南方。他到底要贪图什么?难道仅仅是为了寻找那白色的野鸡?穆王心巧善驾,他为什么要周游四方?在国中四处行走,他又有什么追求?妖人相携沿街兜售,他们为什么要到大街上高声叫卖?周幽王要诛灭谁?他怎么得到那个褒姒的?天命反复,它会惩罚谁?又会保佑谁?齐桓公为安定周室,九次大会诸侯,为什么最终却那样身死。那个纣王,是谁使他变得如此昏乱?他为什么厌恶忠心辅佐他的大臣,而任用那些谗佞小人?比干到底哪里冒犯了纣王而被压制?雷开怎样阿谀依顺纣王,为什么会得到封赏?为什么圣人的美德都差不多,而他们最终的结局却不相同?梅伯被砍成肉酱,箕子装疯卖傻。后稷是帝喾的嫡长子，帝喾为什么那么讨厌他？他把稷丢弃在寒冰之上，大鸟为什么会用羽翼去温暖稷？稷善务农，又是什么特殊本领使他能操弓执箭？既然他强烈地惊动了上帝，为何他的子孙反而繁荣昌盛？西伯姬昌在乱世中发号施令，成为地方的霸主。武王姬发为什么放弃了岐地的宗社，却能承受天命占有殷室的天下？周太王携带宝藏迁到岐地，他如何能让部族跟随他？纣王身边有个惑乱的褒姒，还能进谏什么？纣王把文王的儿子做成肉羹赐给文王，文王向上天告状。为什么纣王得到上天的处罚，而殷王室却难以挽救？太公吕望栖身在市井小店，姬昌为什么会认识他？太公操刀割肉，西伯听了为什么会高兴？武王姬发击杀纣王，他为什么如此怨恨？他用车载着父亲的灵位，聚集将士就出征，又为什么这么急切？纣王自缢而死，这是什么缘故？他为什么要向上天呼告？难道他还有所畏惧？上天把天命赐予殷王室，为什么又会有后人去讨伐？纣王治理天下，又为什么让人取代他？当初汤以伊尹为臣子，伊尹承担辅佐的任务。他为什么能成了汤的宰相并配祀商汤，接受献祭？功绩赫赫的阖闾是吴王寿梦的孙子，从小就遭遇流亡的命运。为什么长大后勇武威猛，他的声威四处流播？彭祖调制好的雉羹，天帝为什么喜欢享用？他的寿命极长，为什么能够拥有如此高寿？为什么召、周二人共理国政，厉王发怒是为了什么？百姓身份微贱，他们的力量为何如此强大？伯夷、叔齐采薇为食物惊动了妇人，受到了讥讽，神鹿为何要庇佑他们？他们北行到了首阳山，为什么会那样高兴？秦景公有条猛犬，他弟弟为什么想要拥有？他想用一百辆车来交换它，却最终丢失了性命。

薄暮雷电，归何忧[①]？厥严不奉[②]，帝何求[③]？伏匿穴处[④]，爰何云？荆勋作师⑤，夫何长？悟过改更，我又何言？吴光争国⑥，久余是胜⑦。何环穿自闾社丘陵⑧，爰出子文？吾告堵敖以不长⑨。何试上自予⑩，忠名弥彰？

【注释】

①归何忧：回去有何担忧。此句有五种理解：一指屈原当时"问天"时之事。二指舜时之事。三指周公时之事。四指孔甲时之事。五指楚灵王时之事。
②厥：其，这里指楚国。不奉：不能保持。楚先败于吴，后败于秦，故云"不奉"。
③帝何求：即何求于帝，求天帝有什么用。帝，天帝。
④伏匿(ni)：潜伏，潜藏。穴处：住在山洞里，亦即身处山林荒野的意思。
⑤荆勋：楚国勋旧贵族。作师：犹"兴师"。毛晋本作"荆勋徇师"。
⑥光：吴王阖闾名。争国：吴楚相争。
⑦久余是胜：即"久胜余"。久，长久。余，我们，亦即楚国。
⑧"何环"以下两句：当从洪兴祖、朱熹校语作"何环闾穿社，以及丘陵？是淫是荡，爰出子文？"环，绕。闾，乡里。穿，穿过。社，古代地方基层行政单位，泛言之，即里社、村落。及，至，到。丘、陵，皆指土山。是，指代前面的"闾社丘陵"，"是淫是荡"，即"淫荡于是"。爰，于是。出，生出。子文：春秋时期楚国令尹，成王时人，有贤明之名。据《左传·宣公四年》记载，其父伯比居䢵(即勋，《左传·桓公十一年》杜预注曰："在江夏云杜县东南。"则当在今湖北京山西北)国时，与䢵国国君之女私通，遂生子文。此处所问当指此事。

⑨堵敖：名熊艰，楚文王子，继位五年为其弟成王熊恽所杀。
⑩试上：弑君。自予：自立为君。

【译文】

　　傍晚时分电闪雷鸣，回去又有什么可担心的呢？国家的尊严不保，祈求上帝又有什么用处？我幽居在洞穴中，面对此景又能说些什么？楚国不断地大举兴兵，这样国运怎能长久？如果君王能改过自新，我又何必再说什么？吴王阖闾与我国相争，多年来一直战胜我们。子文的父母穿过村子到了山丘，做出苟且淫秽的勾当，又怎么会生出贤明的子文？我说堵敖不会长久。为何成王弑兄自立，他的忠诚名声更加显著？

九 章

【题解】

所谓"九章",是屈原创作的九篇作品的合称,这九篇作品是:《惜诵》《涉江》《哀郢》《抽思》《怀沙》《思美人》《惜往日》《橘颂》《悲回风》(依今本王逸《楚辞章句》所排次序)。

这九篇作品在其早期流传过程中大约是以单篇形式出现的。《九章》这个总题是后人编辑、整理屈原作品时加上的。司马迁《史记·屈原贾生列传》是现存文献资料中最早提及《九章》中单篇作品的,其曰:"乃作《怀沙》之赋",又曰:"余读《离骚》《天问》《招魂》《哀郢》,悲其志。"随之,《汉书·扬雄传》亦曰:"(扬雄)又旁《惜诵》以下至《怀沙》一卷,名曰《畔牢愁》。"可见,西汉时这组作品是以单篇形式流传的。这组作品至迟当在西汉后已被编辑到一起,以一个整体的面貌出现,并加上了《九章》这个总题了。从现存文献资料来看,最早提到《九章》这一名称的是刘向。他在《九叹·忧苦》中说:"叹《离骚》以扬意兮,犹未殚于《九章》。"此外,宣帝时人王褒作有《九怀》,由九篇作品构成一组,形成一个整体,颇似模拟《九章》体制,可见,《九章》有可能在宣帝或宣帝之前的某一时期便已被编纂在一起了。姜亮夫《楚辞通故·书篇部》说:"然则辑录而名定之者为谁?虽不可确考,而其必后于屈原而前于王褒、刘向之徒。当景、武之前,诸贵盛在朝,能为楚辞者,有贾谊、刘安、枚乘、邹阳、司马相如、朱买臣、严助;而汉廷乐府亦多楚声(当时贾谊、刘安实为楚辞大家,谊所为《惜誓》,俨同《九章》,《鵩鸟》则方物《卜居》,安为《离骚传》,文辞美备);度当时传屈子之作者必甚多。则辑《惜诵》等篇为一卷者,虽不必即贾、刘、司马、朱、严之徒,而亦必为不甚远之专家为之。淮南王聚天下文学之士,大为专书,又曾受诏为《离骚传》,且朝受诏而食时上,自必早有辑定之本,故能迅捷至此。安后虽不得其死,而其侍从文学之士,亦多在朝者,则《九章》之辑,盖必成于淮南幕府无疑。"这种观点是非常具有启发意义的。

关于《九章》这一标题的含义,一般认为"九"乃实指,即指其所包含的九篇作品而言,与有着古代乐曲背景的《九歌》《九辩》不同;"章"则是篇章的意思,其本义是指乐曲的结束部分。《说文·音部》云:"章,乐竟为一章。从音,从十。十,数之终也。"也可指乐曲结构的一个组成部分,引申则可指诗、文的一篇。因此,所谓"九章"意即九篇文章。不过,王逸《楚辞章句》对"章"字却有着不同理解,其曰:"屈原放于江南之野,思君念国,忧心罔极,故复作《九章》。章者,著也,明也。言己所陈忠信之道,甚著明也。"王逸联系着屈原"思君念国,忧心罔极""陈忠信之道"的创作动机与背景,对"章"字作出了"明也""著也"的解释,应该说,这种观点有刻意求深之嫌。

关于《九章》的创作时地,历代观点大致可以分为两大类。

其一认为《九章》所有作品都创作于顷襄王时,当时屈原被流放于江南之野。就现存史料来看,最早提出这种说法的是班固。他在《离骚赞序》中说："至于襄王,复用谗言,逐屈原。在野又作《九章赋》以风谏,卒不见纳。"王逸《楚辞章句》也说:"屈原放于江南之野,思君念国,忧心罔极,故复作《九章》。"这大约是汉人流行观点。嗣后,洪兴祖(《楚辞补注》)、王夫之(《楚辞通释》)、清人刘梦鹏(《屈子章句》)、今人汤炳正(《屈赋新探·九章时地管见》、《楚辞今注》)等,亦主襄王说。其中,汤炳正根据1957年出土于安徽省寿县城郊邱家花园的先秦楚国文物"鄂君启金节"上所记载的当时楚国水陆交通路线,对屈原行踪作了新的探索,较有新意。

其二认为《九章》各篇非作于一时一地。一般认为此种说法肇始于朱熹。他在《楚辞集注》中说:"屈原既放,思君念国,随事感触,辄形于声。后人辑之,得其九章,合为一卷,非必出于一时之言也。"关于具体篇章的创作时间,前人各有论述。晚明黄文焕《楚辞听直》开始指出,《思美人》《抽思》两篇是屈原在怀王时作于汉北。清初林云铭《楚辞灯》进一步指出,《惜诵》《思美人》《抽思》都是屈原作于怀王时,其中《惜诵》最早,《思美人》《抽思》则稍后作于汉北,其余六篇作于襄王朝放于江南之时,其先后次序为:一《涉江》;二《橘颂》;三《悲回风》;四《惜往日》;五《哀郢》;六绝命词《怀沙》。稍后蒋骥《山带阁注楚辞》在林云铭观点的基础上作了进一步的发展与修正,认为:"《九章》杂作于怀襄之世。其迁逐固不皆在江南,即顷襄迁之江南,而往来行吟,亦非一处。……《思美人》《抽思》,乃怀王斥之汉北所为。《涉江》《哀郢》六篇,方是顷襄时作于江南者,……《惜诵》当作于《离骚》之前,……《思美人》宜在《抽思》之后,……《九章》当首《惜诵》,次《抽思》,次《思美人》,次《哀郢》,次《涉江》,

次《怀沙》，次《悲回风》，终《惜往日》。惟《橘颂》无可附……"林、蒋二人的观点对后人的研究颇有影响。

关于《九章》创作时地与次序问题，由于历代众说纷纭，具体可参看本书各单篇题解。本书认为，目前看来较为稳妥的创作次序应当是：《惜诵》最早，当为与《离骚》同时的作品；其次是《抽思》《思美人》，当时屈原谪居汉北，其中《抽思》相对早于《思美人》；其次是《涉江》《哀郢》，是顷襄王时屈原被放流于江南的作品；其次是《悲回风》《怀沙》《惜往日》，是屈原自沉汨罗前不久的作品，其中《惜往日》是屈原绝命辞。另外，《橘颂》作于何时不易判断，或是屈原早年作品。

惜 诵

【题解】

本篇因篇首"惜诵以致愍兮"而得名。这是沿袭了《诗经》中常用的标题方式，此外如《思美人》《惜往日》《悲回风》也是以篇首若干字而标题。

关于"惜诵"二字，主要有以下三种解释。一、贪忠信之道而论之。王逸《楚辞章句》说："惜，贪也。诵，论也。……言己贪忠信之道，可以安君。论之于心，诵之于口，至于身以疲病，而不能忘。"二、爱怜君主而陈言。洪兴祖《楚辞补注》说："惜诵者，惜其君而诵之也。"三、痛惜过去而进谏。林云铭《楚辞灯》说："惜，痛也。即《惜往日》之惜。不在位而犹进谏，比之朦诵，故曰诵。"此篇与《离骚》意旨相近，当是受谗被疏之后的作品。"惜诵"合起来解释，就是以痛惜的心情来称述自己因直言进谏而遭谗被疏之事。正如姜亮夫《屈原赋校注》所说："《周语》有瞍赋曚诵之制，盖古之谏官也。古巫史实掌谏纳之事，屈子为怀王左徒，左徒乃宗官之长，入则图议国事，出则应对诸侯，其职实与汉之太常宗正相类，故得自比于古之瞍曚也。"

关于本篇的写作时期，历来有两种意见，一种认为作于怀王时期，一种认为作于顷襄王时期。大部分学者同意第一种意见。从作品内容看，本篇不如《离骚》那么沉痛，也看不出已遭放逐的景象。汪瑗《楚辞集解》认为："大抵此篇作于谗人交构，楚王造怒之际，故多危惧之词，然尚未遭放逐也。"这一说法比较符合实际情况。至于具体的作时，蒋骥《山带阁注楚辞》认为作于"初失位"时，亦即怀王十六年（前313）前后，林云铭《楚辞灯》则认为作于怀王十七年，姜亮夫《屈原赋校注》认为是"其三十岁初放时之作"，陆侃如《屈原评传》认为作于怀王二十四年。从当时的时代背景来看，怀王十六年是楚国政治的转折点，这一年以后，楚国国势江河日下，屈原也遭谗被疏。所以，本篇作于怀王十六七年是有可能的。

《惜诵》是《九章》的第一篇，作者叙述了自己在政治上遭受打击的始末和自己对待现实的态度，基本内容与《离骚》前半篇大致相似，故有"小离骚"之称。

惜诵以致愍兮①，发愤以抒情。所作忠而言之兮②，指苍天以为正③。令五帝以析中兮④，戒六神与向服⑤。俾山川以备御兮⑥，命咎繇使听直⑦。

【注释】

①愍(mǐn)：忧伤。
②所作：当作"所非"，"假如不是"的意思。
③正：通"证"，证明。
④五帝：古代神话传说中的五位神祇。东方太皞，南方炎帝，西方少昊，北方颛顼，中央黄帝。桥(xī)中：意即依照法律条文来判断是非。桥，即折、析，分判、明辨。中，刑书、律书、法律条文。
⑤六神：即六宗之神，古代神话传说中的六位神祇，其说不一，主要有以下几种说法：一指四时、寒暑、日、月、星、水旱之神。二指星、辰、风伯、雨师、司中、司命。三指日、月、星辰、太山、河、海。向：对证，对质。服：事理，事实。
⑥俾(bǐ)：使。山川：指山川之神。备御：即准备侍御之人以陪审。御，侍从，侍御。
⑦咎繇(gāo yáo)：即"皋陶"，相传是虞舜时执掌刑狱法律的大臣。听直：听审诉讼，裁判曲直对错。

【译文】

哀惜进谏表达忧伤啊，发泄愤懑抒写衷情。发誓忠心陈说心声啊，手指苍天为我作证。令五方天神为我剖白啊，命六宗之神为我证明。让山川神祇来做陪审啊，命法官皋陶辨明对错。

竭忠诚以事君兮，反离群而赘肬①。忘儇媚以背众兮②，待明君其知之。言与行其可迹兮，情与貌其不变。故相臣莫若君兮③，所以证之不远。吾谊先君而后身兮④，羌众人之所仇⑤。专惟君而无他兮⑥，又众兆之所雠⑦。壹心而不豫兮，羌不可保也。疾亲君而无他兮⑧，有招祸之道也。

【注释】

①离群：指离开群体，为众人所不容。赘肬(zhuì yóu)：多余的肉瘤。
②儇(xuān)：聪慧，狡黠，有机巧。
③相(xiàng)：审察，察看。
④谊：即"宜"、"义"，这里是"应当"的意思。凡品质、行为符合人世间道德标准、社会利益，便是合适、适宜的，就可称为"义"。
⑤羌：句首发语词，楚地方言。
⑥惟：思念，牵挂。
⑦兆：众人。雠(chóu)：仇恨，怨恨。
⑧疾：急切，极力。

【译文】

竭尽忠诚服事君王啊，却为众所不容反成多余。不懂谄媚违背众意啊，等待有明君了解我心。言行一致有据可寻啊，内心与外貌成为不变。所以没有谁比君王更清楚臣子啊，他的取证都亲身得来不须远求。我应先顾君王后及自身啊，却成为众人怨恨的对象。一心忠君不作他想啊，又招来众人怨恨。心思专一从不犹豫啊，竟导致自身难以保全。急切亲近君王并无它念啊，竟成招致祸殃的根源。

　　思君其莫我忠兮，忽忘身之贱贫①。事君而不贰兮，迷不知宠之门②。忠何罪以遇罚兮，亦非余心之所志③。行不群以巅越兮④，又众兆之所咍⑤。纷逢尤以离谤兮⑥，謇不可释⑦。情沉抑而不达兮⑧，又蔽而莫之白。心郁邑余侘傺兮⑨，又莫察余之中情⑩。固烦言不可结诒兮⑪，愿陈志而无路。退静默而莫余知兮,进号呼又莫吾闻。申侘傺之烦惑兮⑫,中闷瞀之忳忳⑬。

【注释】

①忽:忽略,忘记。贱贫:这里大约是指遭怀王疏远而失去尊官厚禄的情况。

②迷:迷惑。宠之门:得到君王宠幸的门户、途径。

③志:通"知",知道,明白。

④不群:与众人不同,不合群。巅越:坠落,跌落。

⑤咍(hāi):嘲笑,嗤笑。

⑥逢尤:即遭到罪责。尤,罪过,罪责。离谤:即遭到毁谤。离,遭。

⑦謇(jiǎn):句首发语词。释:解释,解说。

⑧沉抑:指愁闷的情绪沉积、压抑在心底的样子。

⑨郁邑:形容忧郁愁闷的样子。侘傺(chà chì):形容因失意而惆怅,于是彷徨徘徊的样子。

⑩中情:泛指为内心情感,专指则为内心忠信之情。

⑪烦言:指要说的话众多而烦冗、杂乱。诒(yí):赠送。

⑫申:重累,重复。烦惑:形容心里烦乱、迷惑的样子。

⑬闷瞀(mào):形容内心烦乱的样子。闷,烦闷。瞀,迷乱。忳忳(tún):形容忧愁的样子。

【译文】

思念君王有谁比我更忠贞啊,忘记了自己出身贫贱。服事君王忠心不二啊,迷茫不知邀宠之法。忠诚有何罪以至遭到责罚啊,其中的缘由也不是我能明白的。行为与众不同因而栽了跟头啊,又被众人嘲弄嗤笑。那么多次受罪责遭毁谤啊,却没办法解释表白。情绪压抑无法畅快表达啊,又遭壅蔽无处澄清。忧郁愁闷失意彷徨啊，又无人明了我的衷情。本来心里的话就杂乱冗多无法总结在一起给别人说啊，想要陈述心志却没有途径。如果隐退沉默便无人了解我啊，如果奔进呼喊却又无人肯听。心中失意，烦乱迷惑啊，内里苦闷，忧虑重重。

昔余梦登天兮，魂中道而无杭①。吾使厉神占之兮②，曰有志极而无旁③。终危独以离异兮④，曰君可思而不可恃⑤。故众口其铄金兮⑥，初若是而逢殆⑦。惩于羹者而吹齑兮⑧，何不变此志也？欲释阶而登天兮，犹有曩之态也⑨。众骇遽以离心兮⑩，又何以为此伴也⑪？同极而异路兮，又何以为此援也？晋申生之孝子兮⑫，父信谗而不好⑬。行婞直而不豫兮⑭，鲧功用而不就⑮。

【注释】

①中道：半路。杭：渡过。
②厉神：主杀罚的神灵，或又能执占卜之事。
③曰：这里是厉神占卜后把结果告诉求卜者屈原。志极：心志很高，志存高远。旁：辅佐，帮助。
④危独：指处境危险而孤立无援。离异：与他人不同而分离，各走各的路。
⑤曰君可思而不可恃：从这里到"鲧功用而不就"是厉神占卜后根据兆象显示而劝告屈原的话。
⑥铄(shuò)：销熔，熔化。
⑦初若是：这里指"恃君"而言。初，当初，以前。若是，像这样。殆(dài)：危险，险境。
⑧羹：古代用肉和菜调和五味做成的带汁的食物，这里指热

羹。齑(jī)：一种被切细的酱菜，属凉菜。
⑨曩(nǎng)：以前。
⑩骇遽(jù)：惊惶，畏惧。离心：这里指与己心分离、不合。
⑪伴："伴"与下句之"援"都是攀援、求援的意思。
⑫申生：春秋时晋献公太子。献公宠爱骊姬，骊姬欲立己子奚齐为太子，因而向献公进谗言，说申生有杀父之心，于是献公追捕申生，申生乃被逼自杀。
⑬好(hào)：喜爱，喜欢。
⑭婞(xìng)直：刚愎，刚直。豫：安乐，宽和，从容不迫。
⑮鲧(gǔn)：古代传说是禹的父亲，夏族的首领。

【译文】

以前我梦见自己登上天庭啊，魂魄走到半路却无路向前。我让厉神算上一卦啊，他说："你志存高远，却没有同伴。""最终会陷入险境众叛亲离吗？"他说："君王可以思慕，但不可以依靠。所以众口一词说坏话能熔化金子啊，当初你依靠君王却因此遭遇了祸患。有过被热羹烫过的教训见到凉菜也要吹一吹啊，为何你却不改变忠直的志向？想要把梯子撤在一边去登天啊，你仍然还是以前那副模样。众人惊惶畏惧，跟你离心离德啊，又怎能同他们结队同行？都想获得君王的任用却追求不同啊，又怎能让他们出手相帮？晋国申生那样的孝子啊，父亲也会听信谗言而不喜欢。行为刚直而不和顺啊，鲧的功业因此没有完成。"

吾闻作忠以造怨兮，忽谓之过言①。九折臂而成医兮②，吾至今而知其信然。矰弋机而在上兮③，罻罗张而在下④。设张辟以娱君兮⑤，愿侧身而无所⑥。欲儃佪以干傺兮⑦，恐重患而离尤⑧。欲高飞而远集兮，君罔谓汝何之⑨。欲横奔而失路兮⑩，坚志而不忍。背膺牌以交痛兮⑪，心郁结而纡轸⑫。梼木兰以矫蕙兮⑬，鑿申椒以为粮⑭。播江离与滋菊兮⑮，愿春日以为糗芳⑯。恐情质之不信兮，故重著以自明⑰。矫兹媚以私处兮⑱，愿曾思而远身⑲。

【注释】

① 忽：忽略，忽视。过言：被过分夸大的话，言过其实。
② 九折臂而成医：指多次遭受被折断手臂一类的打击、祸殃，于是不断积累经验，改良药方，从而成为好的医生。九，虚数，多次。
③ 矰弋(zēng yì)：用来射鸟的短箭。机：安装并发射。
④ 尉(wèi)罗：用来捕鸟的网。尉，捕鸟小网。
⑤ 张辟：用来捕猎鸟兽的工具，一说为罗网，一说为弓弩。
⑥ 愿侧身而无所：意即想要蛰伏、躲藏而没有地方。侧，伏着身子，蛰伏。
⑦ 儃(chán)佪：徘徊不前。干傺(gān chì)：求得仕进。
⑧ 重(chóng)：增加。离：遭遇。尤：罪过，罪责。
⑨ 冈(wǎng)：得无，莫非，该不会。之：往，到……去。
⑩ 横奔而失路：肆意狂奔，从而迷失正道。
⑪ 膺(yīng)：胸。牌(pàn)：分开。
⑫ 郁结：形容心中忧郁的情思缠结积聚的样子。纡(yū)：弯曲，萦回。轸(zhěn)：痛。
⑬ 梼(dǎo)：通"捣"，舂。木兰：一种落叶小乔木或灌木，早春先叶开花，花大，外面紫色，内面近白色，微香。矫(jiǎo)：糅合，混合。蕙：香草名。
⑭ 鑿(zuò)：这里是舂，从而使之精细的意思。申椒：香草名。
⑮ 江离：香草名。滋：栽种，种植。

⑯糗(qiǔ)芳：芳香的干粮。糗，干粮。芳，形容其气味的芳香，因为这儿的"糗"是用香草做成的。
⑰重(chóng)：反复，一再。著：表明，申述。
⑱矫(jiǎo)：举。媚：美好的东西。
⑲曾(céng)：重复，再三。远身：远远地离开，以躲避祸害。

【译文】

我听说做忠臣会招来怨恨啊，心里却不以为意，认为是夸大其词。多次折断胳臂自然成为良医啊，我现在才明白确实如此。短箭装好对着天上啊，罗网就在地面张设起来。设置机关取悦君王啊，想要躲藏却没有地方。徘徊不定想要求得仕进啊，又怕增加罪责忧患更深。想要远走高飞另觅他处啊，君王该不会说你要去哪里？想要肆意狂奔不循正道啊，但又意志坚定不忍变心。后背前胸如裂开一般疼痛难忍啊，心里忧思纠结愁苦不堪。捣碎木兰再拌上蕙草啊，磨细申椒来做点心。种上江离栽上菊花啊，希望春天能做成芳香的干粮。担心内心本性无人相信啊，所以要反复陈说表明自身。标举美德我将隐退独处啊，希望深思熟虑后全身远祸。

涉 江

【题解】

《涉江》为顷襄王时期，屈原远放江南时，为记叙征程和抒写怨愤而作。本篇记述了他渡过大江，溯沅水而上达溆浦一带，幽然独处于深山的旅程，也穿插了在行程中及到达目的地后的所思所感。洪兴祖《楚辞补注》说:"此章言已佩服殊异,抗志高远,国无人知之者,徘徊江之上,叹小人在位,而君子遇害也。"汪瑗《楚辞集解》说:"此篇言己行义之高洁,哀浊世而莫我知也。欲将渡湘沅,入林之密,入山之深,宁甘愁苦以终穷,而终不能变心以从俗,故以《涉江》名之。"这是对本篇内容与题旨的较好概括。

关于本篇的创作时地,清人蒋骥在《山带阁注楚辞》中认为:"皆顷襄时放于江南所作。然《哀郢》发郢而至陵阳,皆自西徂东。《涉江》从鄂渚入溆浦,乃自东北往西南,当在既放陵阳之后。"其说较为合理。

本篇的特色是用一大段纪行文字,描写了沅水流域的山川景物,如钱钟书《管锥编·楚辞洪兴祖补注一八则·九章(一)写景》所说,"开后世诗文写景法门"。这段文字抓住带有特征性的景物,寥寥数语勾勒,便高度概括地写出深山密林险峻幽邃的景象,而这一景象又恰到好处地映衬烘托了作者寂寞悲怆的心情。这一段文字成为后世山水景物描写及山水诗的滥觞。此外,本篇纪行兼抒情的写法也对后世颇有影响,清人胡文英《屈骚指掌》说:"《涉江篇》,由今湖北至湖南途中所作,若后人述征纪行之作也。"汉赋中即颇有类似作品,例如刘歆《遂初赋》、班彪《北征赋》、蔡邕《述行赋》等。

余幼好此奇服兮,年既老而不衰①。带长铗之陆离兮②,冠切云之崔嵬③。被明月兮珮宝璐④。世溷浊而莫余知兮⑤,吾方高驰而不顾。驾青虬兮骖白螭⑥,吾与重华游兮瑶之圃⑦。登昆仑兮食玉英⑧,与天地兮同寿,与日月兮同光。哀南夷之莫吾知兮⑨,旦余济乎江湘。

【注释】

①衰：衰退，懈怠。
②长铗(jiá)：长剑。陆离：形容其所佩带宝剑之长。
③冠(guàn)：本指帽子，这里释为"戴"。切云：一种很高的帽子。崔嵬(wéi)：形容高的样子。
④被(pī)：穿在身上或披在身上的意思。明月：一种夜间能发光的宝珠。珮：犹"佩"，佩带。璐(lù)：玉。
⑤溷(hùn)：混乱。
⑥虬(qiú)：一种有角的龙。骖(cān)：本义指一车驾三马。又特指驾车时服马两边的马。这里指驾驭车两旁的白螭。螭(chī)：一种无角的龙。
⑦重(chóng)华：古史传说中的五帝之一舜的名号。瑶：美玉。圃(pǔ)：这里的"瑶之圃"或即《离骚》之"县圃"，是神话传说中天帝及众神居住的地方。
⑧昆仑：古代神话传说中西方神山的名称。英：花。
⑨南夷：当时楚国江南一带的土著民族。

【译文】

我从小便爱好这身奇特装束啊，如今进入暮年却仍兴致不减。我腰间佩带长长宝剑啊，头戴高高发冠。身上饰有明月珠啊，美玉佩带在我的腰间。人世污浊无人了解我啊，我正自高飞驰骋不再留恋人间。驾着那有角青龙啊配上无角白龙，我和重华大神一起游览啊在那天上的玄圃。登上昆仑山啊品尝那美玉一般的花朵，要和天地啊有一样的寿命，要和日月啊同样灿烂光辉。哀痛的是南方夷族无人了解我啊，清早我便要渡过湘水，去到江南。

乘鄂渚而反顾兮①，欸秋冬之绪风②。步余马兮山皋③，邸余车兮方林④。乘舲船余上沅兮⑤,齐吴榜以击汰⑥。船容与而不进兮⑦,淹回水而疑滞⑧。朝发枉陼兮⑨,夕宿辰阳⑩。苟余心其端直兮,虽僻远之何伤。

【注释】

①鄂渚(è zhǔ):地名,在今湖北鄂州。
②欸(āi):感叹,叹息。绪风:大风。
③步:使行走。皋:水泽,引申为水边之地。
④邸(dǐ):停留。方林:面积广大的树林。
⑤舲(líng)船:有窗子的船。上:这里是沿沅水逆流而上的意思。
⑥吴榜:船桨。一作"大棹"。汰(tài):水波。
⑦容与:徘徊不前的样子。
⑧淹:停留,滞留。回水:江中急流回旋而形成的涡流,即漩涡。疑(níng)滞:即"凝滞",停滞不前。
⑨枉陼(zhǔ):地名,沅水中的一个河湾,在辰阳以东,沅水下游,今属湖南常德。
⑩辰阳:地名,汉有辰阳县,见《汉书·地理志》,属武陵郡,在今湖南辰溪。

【译文】

登上鄂渚回头远望啊,慨叹秋冬时节大风凄寒。让我的马儿啊在山边泽畔,将我的车子啊停靠在大片林边。乘坐舲船我沿沅水上溯啊,众人一起举桨划开水波。船儿徘徊不往前走啊,在急流漩涡中停滞不前。早晨从枉陼开始出发啊,晚上就留宿在那辰阳。假如我的心正直无偏啊,流放之地即使偏远又有什么可伤感的?

入溆浦余儃佪兮①，迷不知吾所如。深林杳以冥冥兮②，猿狖之所居③。山峻高以蔽日兮，下幽晦以多雨。霰雪纷其无垠兮④，云霏霏而承宇⑤。哀吾生之无乐兮，幽独处乎山中。吾不能变心而从俗兮，固将愁苦而终穷。

【注释】

①溆(xù)浦：地名，在今湖南溆浦一带，或因溆水而得名，因其在溆水之滨的缘故。儃(chán)佪：徘徊不前。
②杳(yǎo)以冥冥：意即幽深晦暗。"杳"与"冥"意义相近，都是幽暗、昏暗的意思。
③猿(yuán)：一种猕猴。狖(yòu)：猿猴的一种。
④霰(xiàn)：小雪珠。垠(yín)：边际，涯岸。
⑤霏霏(fēi)：这里形容云气很盛的样子。承宇：指山中云气旺盛而与屋檐相承接。宇，屋檐。

【译文】

进入溆浦我却徘徊犹豫啊，心中迷惑不知去往何方。幽深的树林昏暗阴沉啊，这是那猿猴栖居的所在。山势高峻陡峭遮住太阳啊，山下幽深晦暗阴雨绵绵。雪珠雪花纷纷扬扬无边无际啊，云层浓重与屋檐相连。哀痛我这一生缺少欢乐啊，孤苦寂寞独居在山中。我不能改变志节去随波逐流啊，理所当然会忧愁苦闷困穷终生。

接舆髡首兮①，桑扈臝行②。忠不必用兮，贤不必以③。伍子逢殃兮④，比干菹醢⑤。与前世而皆然兮，吾又何怨乎今之人！余将董道而不豫兮⑥，固将重昏而终身！

【注释】

①接舆：春秋时楚国人，佯狂避世。髡(kūn)首：剃去头发。
②桑扈(hù)：古代隐士。嬴(luǒ)行：意即裸体而行。嬴，同"裸"。
③以：用。
④伍子：即伍子胥，春秋末吴国大夫，名员(yún)，字子胥。曾辅佐吴王阖闾攻破楚国。继事吴王夫差，力谏灭越国，夫差不纳。后遭太宰伯嚭诬陷，被逼自杀。
⑤比干：殷末纣王的叔伯父。菹醢(zū hǎi)：肉酱，这里指剁成肉酱。菹、醢，均有肉、肉酱的意思。
⑥董：正。豫：犹豫。

【译文】

接舆剃去头发佯狂避世啊，隐士桑扈裸体而行。忠臣不一定能得到任用啊，贤人未必能发挥才能。伍子胥遭遇祸患啊，比干被剁成肉酱。整个前代都是这样啊，我又何必怨恨如今的君王！我将正道而行不再犹豫啊，本就准备在重重昏暗中度过一生！

乱曰①：鸾鸟凤皇②，日以远兮。燕雀乌鹊③，巢堂坛兮④。露申辛夷⑤，死林薄兮⑥。腥臊并御⑦，芳不得薄兮⑧。阴阳易位⑨，时不当兮。怀信侘傺⑩，忽乎吾将行兮！

【注释】

①乱：乐曲的最后一章叫乱。古时诗乐不分，故诗文中最后总括全篇要旨的一段文字也被称作乱。
②鸾(luán)鸟凤皇：古人心目中神异的鸟类，这里比喻贤能之士。

③燕雀乌鹊：都是普通常见鸟类，这里比喻谗佞小人。
④巢：鸟窝，这里是搭窝的意思。堂：古时天子以及诸侯议政、祭祀的朝堂、庙堂。坛：用土筑起的高台。
⑤露申：一种香草。辛夷：一种香草。
⑥薄(bó)：草木丛生的地方。
⑦腥臊：恶臭秽浊的气味，这里比喻奸邪小人。御：进用。
⑧薄：靠近，接近。
⑨阴阳易位：这里比喻当时社会忠奸不辨，是非不分，从而使君子贤士失位，奸邪小人得志。
⑩怀信：怀抱忠贞诚信之心。侘傺(chà chì)：惆怅失意的样子。

【译文】

乱辞称：鸾鸟凤凰，一天天地远去啊。燕雀乌鹊，却在庙堂上公然筑巢安居啊。露申辛夷，在草木丛中干枯死去啊。腥臊恶臭都能得到君王的取用啊，芳香的花草却无法靠近他的身边。阴阳颠倒，生不逢时啊。怀抱忠信却失意彷徨啊，我怅然迷惘，还是远行吧！

哀 郢

【题解】

郢是楚国都城的名称，地在今湖北江陵纪南城。《说文·邑部》："郢，故楚都，在南郡江陵北十里。"《汉书·地理志》："江陵，故楚郢都，楚文王自丹阳徙此。"《水经注·沔水》："江陵西北有纪南城，楚文王自丹阳徙此，平王城之，班固言楚之郢都也。""哀郢"即对郢都的思念与哀痛。

九章

关于本篇的创作背景，自从汪瑗《楚辞集解》指出与顷襄王二十一年秦将白起攻破郢都，楚乃东北退保陈城这一重大事件有关后，后代颇有学者承袭其说，而林云铭、蒋骥、屈复等认为，本篇是屈原在被放九年（恐非实数，或是多年的意思）后回忆初放时情景而作，篇中"忽若去不信兮，至今九年而不复"的词句可为证。如是，则存在这样一些疑问：屈原是否有可能在秦军破郢后多年，情绪稍见平稳从而进入创作状态呢？连如此沉重打击都能忍受的人如何能作出自沉殉国的激烈而非常人所能为的举动？且屈原对于宗国感情极其深厚，秦军拔郢对其来说不啻国破家亡，对其情绪必是深重刺激，其也势必作出激烈反应，但何以篇中情感仅有凄恻低徊、缠绵惆怅？秦军拔郢时屈原年事已颇高，其是否能够在家破国亡、颠沛流离中再苦熬九年光阴？因此，本书认为清人戴震的观点，对我们理解《哀郢》的创作背景，更具启发性。戴震《屈原赋注·音义下》认为："屈原东迁，疑即当顷襄元年，秦发兵出武关攻楚，大败楚军，取析十五城而去。时怀王辱于秦，兵败地丧，民散相失，故有'皇天不纯命'之语。"据《史记·楚世家》记载："顷襄王横元年，秦要怀王不可得地，楚立王以应秦。秦昭王怒，发兵出武关攻楚，大败楚军，斩首五万，取析十五城而去。"戴说未必即是不刊之论，但实可从。襄王即位初的这场战役规模颇大，且发生在楚国政局动荡之时，自会对楚国上下造成不小的震撼与恐慌，民众因而避祸往东逃难，造成局面混乱，离散相失，也并不奇怪；而襄王即位，子兰为令尹，屈原势必遭打击排挤，或则其即于此国难临头的多事之秋被放流而离开郢都，出居陵阳（依蒋骥《山带阁注楚辞》说），并在居陵阳九年后回忆初放时事而创作本篇，也是极有可能的。在本篇中屈原记叙了其离开郢都后东行至陵阳这一路上的行程，抒发了其对宗国、对郢都的刻骨思念之情。

皇天之不纯命兮^①，何百姓之震愆^②？民离散而相失兮^③，方仲春而东迁^④。去故乡而就远兮，遵江夏以流亡^⑤。出国门而轸怀兮^⑥，甲之鼌吾以行^⑦。

【注释】

①皇天：天在古人思想观念里占有至高无上的主宰神地位，以"皇"修饰之是古人对天的尊称。皇，美大。
②百姓：指楚国的贵族。震愆(qiān)：震恐，惊恐。
③民：普通民众。
④仲春：阴历二月。
⑤遵：沿着。江夏：长江和夏水。江即长江。夏指夏水，夏水是古水名，由长江分流而出，注入汉水，今已堙没。
⑥国：这里是国都、京城的意思。轸(zhěn)：痛，哀痛。
⑦甲：甲日。古以十天干记日。鼌(zhāo)：通"朝"，早晨。

【译文】

天命反覆无常啊，为何让宗亲贵戚们惊恐万端？民众流离，亲人失散啊，在这仲春二月向东逃难。离开故土，去向远方啊，沿着江水夏水一路流亡。出了郢都城门便痛切地思念啊，甲日的早晨我启程上路。

发郢都而去闾兮^①，荒忽其焉极^②？楫齐扬以容与兮^③，哀见君而不再得。望长楸而太息兮^④，涕淫淫其若霰^⑤。过夏首而西浮兮^⑥，顾龙门而不见^⑦。心婵媛而伤怀兮^⑧，眇不知其所蹠^⑨。顺风波以从流兮，焉洋洋而为客^⑩。凌阳侯之氾滥兮^⑪，忽翱翔之焉薄^⑫。心絓结而不解兮^⑬，思蹇产而不释^⑭。将运舟而下浮兮^⑮，上洞庭而下江^⑯。去终古之所居兮^⑰，今逍遥而来东⑱。羌灵魂之欲归兮⑲，何须臾而忘反⑳。背夏浦而西思兮㉑，哀故都之日远。登大坟以远望兮㉒，聊以舒吾忧心。哀州土之平乐兮㉓，悲江介之遗风㉔。当陵阳之焉至兮㉕，淼南渡之焉如㉖？曾不知夏之为丘兮㉗，孰两东门之可芜㉘？

【注释】

①闾(lú)：本义是里巷的大门，也可用来指称居民区。这里当是指楚国贵族"昭"、"屈"、"景"三氏聚居之所在，即"三闾"。

②荒忽：神思恍惚的样子。

③楫(jí)：船桨。容与：形容船徘徊不进的样子。

④长楸(qiū)：即高大的梓树。太息：长声叹息。

⑤淫淫：这里形容眼泪流而不止的样子。霰(xiàn)：小雪珠。

⑥夏首：夏水从长江分流而出的地方。西浮：从西面顺水漂流。一说"西浮"为"疾浮"。

⑦龙门：郢都的东城门。

⑧婵媛：眷恋，牵挂。

⑨眇(miǎo)：远。蹠(zhí)：踩，踏，落脚。

⑩焉：于是。洋洋：这里形容漂泊不定的样子。

⑪凌：乘，凌驾。阳侯：传说中司波浪的神，这里指其所掀起的波浪。氾滥：这里形容大水漫流的样子。

⑫忽：快速地。薄：停留，止息。

⑬絓(guà)：这里形容内心情感郁结牵缠而愁苦烦闷的样子。

⑭蹇(jiǎn)产：形容情思屈曲而无法舒展的样子。

⑮下浮：顺着江流而向下游漂浮。

⑯上洞庭而下江：这里指船行至洞庭湖汇入长江之处时的情形，若船南向驶入洞庭湖则逆流而上，以入沅湘水系，若东

向沿长江行驶则顺流而下。

⑰终古之所居：楚国历代先祖自古以来居住的地方，即郢都。

⑱逍遥：飘荡，流落。

⑲羌：楚地方言，句首发语词。

⑳须臾(yú)：顷刻，片刻。

㉑夏浦：即夏口，今汉口。西思：这里是思念西方郢都的意思。

㉒坟：江中岛屿沙洲。

㉓州土：荆楚大地。平乐：土地平坦富饶，人民安居乐业。

㉔介：间。一说是边上、侧畔的意思。遗风：楚先人世代遗传下来的美好风习。

㉕当：到，抵达。陵阳：地名，《汉书·地理志》载丹扬郡陵阳县，在今安徽青阳南。

㉖淼(miǎo)：水面阔大无边的样子。南渡：指往南渡过大江而登岸抵达陵阳。

㉗夏：高大的房屋。丘：丘墟，废墟。

㉘两东门："两"疑有误，或为"网"字，考量计较的意思。东门即郢都东城门，亦即上面提到的"龙门"。

【译文】

从郢都出发离开故土啊，神思恍惚不知该去向何方？桨一齐划动，船却徘徊不前啊，哀痛的是不能再见到君王。看那故国乔木我长声叹息啊，眼泪如同雪珠一样流淌。船过夏浦向东漂荡啊，回头看那郢都龙门已踪影难觅。心里牵挂不舍充满哀伤啊，前路邈远不知在何方落脚？顺风而行，随着流水啊，于是漂泊无依，流寓他乡。乘着水神掀起的巨浪啊，如鸟儿一般飞起却不知落在何方？心乱如麻难以解开啊，情思郁结无法舒怀。将要驾船顺流而下啊，上溯是洞庭下流是长江。离开先人世代居住的土地啊，而今漂泊流落来到东方。灵魂它想要回归故土啊，何尝有片刻忘记还乡？离开夏口思念郢都啊，哀伤距故都日渐遥远。登上沙洲纵目远眺啊，姑且舒散我忧愁的心情。哀怜荆楚大地曾富饶安乐啊，悲伤的是江上故俗遗风。抵达陵阳后该往哪里去啊，南渡浩淼大江后又将去何处？不知高大的宫殿楼台是否已成为丘墟啊，谁能料到郢都东门是否化为荒芜？

心不怡之长久兮，忧与愁其相接。惟郢路之辽远兮，江与夏之不可涉。忽若不信兮①，至今九年而不复。惨郁郁而不通兮②，蹇侘傺而含慼③。外承欢之汋约兮④，谌荏弱而难持⑤。忠湛湛而愿进兮⑥，妒被离而鄣之⑦。尧舜之抗行兮⑧，瞭杳杳而薄天⑨。众谗人之嫉妒兮，被以不慈之伪名⑩。憎愠忨之修美兮⑪，好夫人之忼慨⑫。众踥蹀而日进兮⑬，美超远而逾迈⑭。

【注释】

①忽：迷惘，恍惚。不信：当作"去不信"。去，离开。信，两天，这里形容时间很短。
②惨：忧愁。郁郁：形容忧愁的样子。不通：这里指心情忧愁烦闷、郁结不畅。
③蹇(jiǎn)：句首发语词。侘傺(chà chì)：惆怅失意的样子。
④汋(chuò)约：本指柔美的样子，这里形容小人谄媚的样子。
⑤谌(chén)：确实，实在。荏(rěn)：弱，软弱。
⑥湛湛(zhàn)：厚重。
⑦被离：分离，离散。鄣：壅蔽，阻塞。
⑧抗：高，高尚。
⑨瞭：明。杳杳(yǎo)：高远的样子。薄：迫近，靠近。
⑩被(pī)：加。不慈：不爱自己的儿子，指尧舜禅让天下于他

人而不传给自己的儿子。伪名：与事实不符的名声。
⑪愠忳(Yùn lǔn)：大约是形容怨思蕴积于心的样子，当是就忠贞君子而言。
⑫夫(fú)人：这里指谗佞小人。忼(kāng)慨：即"慷慨"，形容情绪激昂奋发的样子。
⑬众：这里指表面上故作慷慨之态的谗佞小人。踥蹀(qiè dié)：形容行走的样子。
⑭美：忠贤君子。超：远。逾：跃进，行进。迈：远走高飞。

【译文】

心中长久不快啊，忧和愁绵绵不绝。想到回郢都的路那么遥远啊，江水夏水已难以渡过。恍惚中仿佛刚刚离开故土啊，到如今已有九年未曾回去。心情忧郁愁闷不畅啊，惆怅失落一腔凄楚。小人们表面上奉承君王，一副媚态啊，实际上软弱不堪，难以辅国。忠厚之士愿有所作为啊，谗妒小人却从中阻挠。圣王尧舜德行高尚啊，他明智高远直逼苍穹。谗佞小人心怀嫉妒啊，给他加上不慈爱的恶名。君王嫌恶正直忠贤的君子啊，却喜爱那故作慷慨姿态的伪善小人。众多谗佞小人竞相奔走，日益得势啊，忠臣贤士被日益疏远，却远走高飞。

乱曰：曼余目以流观兮①，冀壹反之何时？鸟飞反故乡兮②，狐死必首丘。信非吾罪而弃逐兮，何日夜而忘之？

【注释】

①曼：本义是引而使长，这里指张大双眼。流观：四处观看。
②"鸟飞"以下两句：这是当时流行的成语。鸟飞虽远，终将返回故乡；狐狸死时，头必朝向其所出生的山丘。比喻对故土深厚而炽热的爱恋情怀。

【译文】

乱辞称：睁大我的眼睛环顾周围啊，盼望什么时候能回去一次？鸟儿远飞终究要返回故林啊，狐狸死时头必朝着故土山丘。实在不是我有罪过啊而被流放，何尝有一日一夜忘怀故都？

抽 思

【题解】

"抽思"取自少歌部分首句"与美人之抽思兮"中的二字。蒋骥《山带阁注楚辞》以为："抽，拔也。抽思，犹言剖露其心思，即指上陈之耿著言。"即剖陈心迹、将心中郁结的情思抒发出来的意思。

关于本篇的创作时地，由于王逸《楚辞章句》笼统地认为《九章》诸篇都是作于顷襄王在位期间，屈原被放逐于江南之野的时候，所以长期以来人们都沿袭《抽思》作于顷襄王时、江南之野的说法，如汪瑗《楚辞集解》、王夫之《楚辞通释》即持这种说法。清人林云铭则提出本篇是屈原在怀王时作于汉北，他在《楚辞灯》中说："屈子置身汉北，无所考据。刘向《新序》止云怀王放之于外，并未有汉北字样。即《史记》亦但云疏绌不复在位，其作《离骚》虽有放流等语，亦未有汉北字样。今读是篇，明明道出汉北不能南归一大段，则当年怀王之迁原于远，疑在此地，比前尤加疏耳，但未尝羁其身如顷襄之放于江南也。"蒋骥《山带阁注楚辞》也同意这一观点，其认为："此篇盖原怀王时斥居汉北所作也。"他在《楚辞余论》中又提出："《骚经》当作于《惜诵》之后，《抽思》、《思美人》之先。"其说大致可信，今人也大体遵循林、蒋二人的说法。

《抽思》表达屈原被怀王疏远而蛰居汉北时，仍忧心国事、思念郢都、意欲回归的拳拳之情，以及心系怀王、而心境无由上达的愁苦。

本篇的特色首先在于独特的篇章结构：除"乱曰"外，又有"少歌曰"、"倡曰"。跟"乱曰"一样，它们本来也是音乐组织形式的术语，这里则用来表示文章的篇章结构。由此构成本篇的二元结构，即"倡曰"之前部分与"倡曰"之后部分。之前部分以"少歌"作小结，倡辞则自成一段，最后以"乱辞"总结。

本篇的另一特色是出色的心理刻划，尤其是"倡辞"中"望孟夏之短夜兮"到"魂识路之营营"一段的离魂、魂游描写。作者以梦境中灵魂出窍、回返郢都的瑰奇想象，抒发了自己对于宗国、故乡的强烈怀念与刻骨依恋。这种魂游描写影响后人颇深。沈约《别范安成诗》"梦中不识路，何以慰相思"，杜甫《梦李白》二首之一"恐非平生魂，路远不可测。魂来枫林青，魂返关塞黑"，都可以看到其影子。

心郁郁之忧思兮[1]，独永叹乎增伤。思蹇产之不释兮[2]，曼遭夜之方长。悲秋风之动容兮[3]，何回极之浮浮[4]。数惟荪之多怒兮[5]，伤余心之忧忧。愿摇起而横奔兮[6]，览民尤以自镇。结微情以陈词兮，矫以遗夫美人[7]。

【注释】

[1]郁郁：忧愁的样子。

②蹇(jiǎn)产：情思屈曲而不得舒展的样子，即忧思郁结之义。
③动容：意即动摇。容，即"搈"，动。
④回极：回旋的天极。浮浮：变动不定的样子。
⑤数(shuò)：多次，频频。惟：思。荪：一种香草，这里用来比喻君王。
⑥摇起：迅速地起身、跃起。横奔：大步流星地疾急奔跑。
⑦矫：举起。美人：这里代指怀王。

【译文】

心中忧愁思绪烦乱啊，独自长叹又增感伤。情思郁结不能化解啊，漫漫长夜睡意全无。悲叹秋风猛烈撼动外物啊，何以竟使回旋的天极也变动不定？多次想起君王屡屡发怒啊，使我心伤忧苦无边。我愿疾起大步狂奔啊，看到百姓动辄得罪又静下心来。总结幽隐情思来陈词啊，面向君王表白心意。

昔君与我诚言兮①，曰黄昏以为期②。羌中道而回畔兮③，反既有此他志。憍吾以其美好兮④，览余以其修姱⑤。与余言而不信兮⑥，盖为余而造怒⑦。愿承间而自察兮⑧，心震悼而不敢⑨。悲夷犹而冀进兮⑩，心怛伤之憺憺⑪。

【注释】

①诚言："诚"当作"成"。成言即已约定的言语。成，定。
②黄昏：日落的时候，古代于此时举行昏礼(即今婚礼)。屈原作品多以男女关系比喻君臣关系。
③羌：楚地方言，句首发语词。回畔：改道，改路。
④憍(jiāo)：同"骄"，骄傲，矜夸。

⑤览:向他人展示。修姱(kuā):美好。
⑥不信:不守信用,不可靠,即言而无信。
⑦盍(hé):通"盍"。何,为什么。造怒:发怒,生气。
⑧间(jiàn):间隙,机会。自察:自我表白。
⑨震悼:内心惊恐、震恐的样子。
⑩夷犹:犹豫。进:进言。
⑪怛(dá):痛苦,忧伤。憺憺(dàn):因忧惧惊恐而心情动荡不安的样子。

【译文】

从前君王和我曾约定啊,说好相会在黄昏时分。半路上他却改了主意啊,转身而去有了别的想法。向我矜夸他的美好啊,对我展示他的才能。跟我说好的话不算数啊,为什么还对我怒气冲冲?我希望寻找机会表白自己啊,心里又惊惧不敢随意行动。悲伤犹豫盼望能进言啊,心中痛苦忧愁难安。

兹历情以陈辞兮①,荪详聋而不闻②。固切人之不媚兮③,众果以我为患④。初吾所陈之耿著兮⑤,岂至今其庸亡⑥?何毒药之謇謇兮⑦,愿荪美之可完⑧。望三五以为像兮⑨,指彭咸以为仪⑩。夫何极而不至兮,故远闻而难亏⑪。善不由外来兮,名不可以虚作。孰无施而有报兮,孰不实而有获?

【注释】

①兹历:当作"历兹"。历,陈列,列举。兹,此。
②详(yáng):通"佯",假装。
③切(qiè):正直,恳切。媚:谄媚,讨好。
④众:这里指跟屈原对立,专以谄媚君王为能事的谗佞小人。

⑤耿著：光明，明白。
⑥庸：乃。亡：忘。
⑦何毒药之謇謇兮：当作"何独乐斯之謇謇兮"。謇謇，形容忠贞切直的样子。
⑧完：当作"光"，发扬光大。
⑨三五：三指三王，即禹、汤、周文王；五指春秋五霸。一说指三皇五帝。像：法式，榜样。
⑩彭咸：传说是殷商时的贤人。仪：法式。
⑪闻：名声，声誉。亏：缺失，消歇。

【译文】

列数心事来陈辞啊，君王却假装耳聋听不见。本来正直的人就不会阿谀谄媚啊，一众小人果然把我当作祸患。当初我所陈说的话明明白白啊，难道如今竟全都忘却？为什么总是这样忠贞耿直啊，是希望君王美德能发扬光大。仰慕三王五霸以他们为榜样啊，指着古贤彭咸以他为楷模。假若如此，还有什么终极不能达到啊，从此声名远播将会永远流芳。善心不会自外产生啊，名声不会凭空出现。谁能不给予便有回报啊，谁能不播种就有收获？

少歌曰①：与美人抽怨兮②，并日夜而无正③。憍吾以其美好兮④，敖朕辞而不听⑤。

【注释】

①少歌：即《荀子·赋篇·佹诗》的"小歌"，是古代乐章结构的组成部分，对前一部分内容起小结、收束的作用。
②怨：朱熹《楚辞集注》本作"思"。
③并日夜：即夜以继日，日夜不分。并，合。无正：无从论

证、评断是非。

④恔(jiāo)：同"骄"，骄傲，骄矜。

⑤敖(ào)：同"傲"。

【译文】

少歌说：跟君王剖白心迹啊，夜以继日却得不到评判。向我夸耀他的美好啊，傲慢地将我的言语抛在一边。

倡曰①：有鸟自南兮②，来集汉北③。好姱佳丽兮，牉独处此异域④。既茕独而不群兮⑤，又无良媒在其侧⑥。道卓远而日忘兮⑦，愿自申而不得。望北山而流涕兮⑧，临流水而太息。望孟夏之短夜兮⑨，何晦明之若岁⑩！惟郢路之辽远兮，魂一夕而九逝⑪。曾不知路之曲直兮，南指月与列星⑫。愿径逝而未得兮⑬，魂识路之营营⑭。何灵魂之信直兮，人之心不与吾心同！理弱而媒不通兮⑮，尚不知余之从容⑯。

【注释】

①倡：同"唱"，古代乐章的结构组织形式之一，作用是发端启唱。

②鸟：屈原自喻为鸟。南：这里指郢都。

③汉北：汉水以北的地方，屈原当时被迁于此。

④牉(pàn)：分离，离别。异域：他乡，这里指汉北迁所。

⑤茕(qióng)：孤独。

⑥良媒：好的媒人，这里指能够为作者和怀王之间沟通关系的人。

⑦卓：同"逴(chuō)"，远。日忘：这里指被怀王一天天地淡忘。

⑧北山：当是郢都附近的山，或谓即郢都纪南城北的纪山。
⑨孟夏：阴历四月，初夏时节。
⑩晦明之若岁：形容度日如年，难以入眠。晦明，由夜至曙。晦，昏暗，黑夜。明，白昼。
⑪一夕而九逝：是说灵魂在一夜之内多次前往郢都，表达了对郢都的刻骨思念。夕，晚上。逝，去，往。
⑫南指月与列星：这里是说在由汉北往南去往郢都的路上，靠着月亮与群星来辨认方向。
⑬径逝：一直前往，返回郢都。
⑭识(zhì)：辨认。营营：形容来回走动的样子。
⑮理：媒人，媒介。
⑯从容：举动，行为。

【译文】

倡说：有只鸟儿从南边来啊，飞来栖息在汉北。容貌美好清丽动人啊，却独在异乡离群而居。既已孤身一个不能合群啊，又没好的媒人在旁扶持。道路遥远日渐被人遗忘啊，想要自己陈说却没有机会。望着北山落泪啊，对着流水叹息。初夏夜晚本来短暂啊，为何度日如年却难以入眠？想起回郢都的路途那么遥远啊，灵魂一夜之间多次前往。不知那道路是曲是直啊，只好靠着星月指认南去的方向。多想一直前往到达郢都却不被君王接纳啊，只有灵魂辨认那来往的路途。为何灵魂那么忠信正直啊，别人的心思和我却不一样！信使孱弱，没媒人通路子啊，还有谁知道我的言行思想。

乱曰：长濑湍流①，泝江潭兮②。狂顾南行③，聊以娱心兮。轸石崴嵬④，蹇吾愿兮⑤。超回志度⑥，行隐进兮⑦。低佪夷犹，宿北姑兮⑧。烦冤瞀容⑨，实沛徂兮⑩。愁叹苦神⑪，灵遥思兮。路远处幽,又无行媒兮。道思作颂⑫,聊以自救兮。忧心不遂,斯言谁告兮。

【注释】

①濑(lài):沙石滩上的水流。湍(tuān):急流。
②泝(sù):逆流而上。潭:水深的地方。
③狂顾:心神迷乱而左右顾盼。南行:向着南方郢都的方向而行。
④畛(zhěn):通"畛",田间道路。崴嵬(wēi wéi):形容石头高低不平的样子。
⑤蹇(jiǎn):通"謇",使……艰难。
⑥超回:徘徊。志度:通"跮踱",意即踯躅,徘徊不前。
⑦隐进:指一点点慢慢前进。
⑧北姑:大约是汉北一带的地名。
⑨烦冤:形容心中忧愁烦闷的样子。瞀(mào)容:当为"瞀俗",心情烦乱不安。瞀,乱。容,通"俗",不安。
⑩沛徂(cú):即颠沛困苦地行进。徂,去往。
⑪苦神:伤神,损伤精神。
⑫道:通"导",表达,表述。颂:即指本文。

【译文】

乱辞说:长长的沙石滩上流水湍急,沿着深潭逆流而上啊。心神迷乱顾盼南行,聊且抚慰我的心伤啊。路上石头高低不平,让我回家的路途艰难啊。徘徊踯躅,慢慢前行啊。迟疑犹豫,停歇在北姑啊。愁闷烦乱,走得实在艰辛啊。忧愁叹息,黯然神伤,灵魂仍在思念故乡啊。路途遥远,居处幽僻,又没人为我通报啊。表达忧思写下歌词,姑且自我解脱啊。忧郁心绪不得舒畅,这些话该向谁倾诉啊!

九章

怀 沙

【题解】

关于"怀沙"的含义，大致有两种说法。一种说法认为"沙"是"沙石"的意思，所谓"怀沙"意即怀抱沙石而自沉。这种说法在汉至宋间颇为流行。东方朔《七谏·沉江》已有"怀沙砾以自沉兮，不忍见君之蔽壅"的诗句。司马迁《史记·屈原贾生列传》说："于是怀石，遂自沉汨罗以死。"蔡邕《吊屈原文》曰："顾抱石其何补？"郭璞《江赋》曰："悲灵均之任石。"《后汉书·逸民列传》："与夫委体渊沙，鸣弦揆日者，不其远乎。"李贤注："谓屈原怀沙砾而自沉也。"洪兴祖《楚辞补注》、朱熹《楚辞集注》等也持这一观点。另一种说法认为"沙"指"长沙"，所谓"怀沙"即沙念长沙。明代汪瑗在《楚辞集解》中认为："世传屈原自投汨罗而死，汨罗在今长沙府。……怀者，感也。沙指长沙。题《怀沙》云者，犹《哀郢》之类也。"李陈玉《楚辞笺注》、钱澄之《庄屈合诂》也认为"沙"指"长沙"而言，是地名。蒋骥《山带阁注楚辞》则进一步指出："《怀沙》之名，与《哀郢》、《涉江》同义。沙本地名，《遁甲经》：'沙土之祇，云阳氏之墟。'《路史》纪云阳氏、神农氏，皆宇于沙，即今长沙之地，汨罗所在也。曰怀沙者，盖寓怀其地，欲往而就死焉耳。……长沙为楚东南之会，去郢未远，固与荒徼绝异，且熊绎始封，实在于此，原既放逐，不敢北越大江，而归死先王故居，则亦首邱之意，所以惓惓有怀也。"今人游国恩、姜亮夫、马茂元等也同意"怀沙"为怀念长沙。此说或优于"怀抱沙石"之旧说，但亦未必完全正确。

关于本篇创作时间，学者们基本都认为是屈原自沉前不久，主要问题在于其是否为屈原绝命辞。由于《七谏》与《史记》均提出屈原"怀沙砾以自沉"的说法，后世如洪兴祖、黄文焕、林云铭、屈复等都认为《怀沙》即屈原绝命辞。朱熹《楚辞辩证》对此提出质疑，他说："《骚经》《渔父》《怀沙》，虽有彭咸、江鱼、死不可让之说，然犹未有决然之计也，是以其词虽切而犹未失其常度。……至《惜往日》《悲回风》，则其身已临沅湘之渊而命在晷刻矣。"蒋骥《山带阁注楚辞》也认为："虽为近死之音，然纡而未郁，直而未激，犹当在《悲回风》《惜往日》之前，岂可遽以为绝笔欤？"今则颇有学者以为屈原绝笔为《惜往日》，两说并录以参。

诗篇虽未必是屈原的绝命辞，但距其投水而死理应不远。本篇一方面重申自己虽然屡受打击挫折，却始终不改高洁的志节；另一方面将批判的矛头指向楚国昏乱颠倒的政治与社会，述说谗佞当道，国君昏愦，"人心不可谓"的深深绝望和将死前的愤激和悲哀。全诗言辞激切，情调哀惨。

滔滔孟夏兮①，草木莽莽②。伤怀永哀兮，汩徂南土③。眴兮杳杳④，孔静幽默⑤。郁结纡轸兮⑥，离愍而长鞠⑦。抚情效志兮，冤屈而自抑。

【注释】

①滔滔：这里形容夏季暑热之气旺盛的样子。孟夏：阴历四月，初夏时节。
②莽莽：这里形容草木茂盛的样子。
③汩(yù)：快速地行走。徂：去，往。

④眴(xuàn):看。杳杳:昏暗,幽深。
⑤孔:很,甚。幽:幽深,深沉。默:寂静无声。
⑥郁结:形容心中忧郁的情思缠结积聚的样子。纡轸(yū zhěn):形容内心情感扭曲而伤痛的样子。
⑦愍(mǐn):哀痛,悲哀。鞠(jū):困苦。

【译文】

暖洋洋的四月初夏啊,草木茂盛葱郁。心情伤感,哀思绵长啊,匆匆又往南迁。眼前景象昏暗幽深啊,静谧幽深万籁悄然。愁绪纠结,内心痛苦啊,遭受悲哀,困苦无边。抚慰忧伤,考量心志啊,暗自压抑内心沉冤。

刓方以为圜兮①,常度未替。易初本迪兮②,君子所鄙。章画志墨兮③,前图未改。内厚质正兮,大人所盛④。

【注释】

①刓(wán):削,剜刻。圜(yuán):同"圆",圆形。
②本迪:常道,本来的路径。
③画:规划,计划。墨:即绳墨,木工画直线用的工具。
④大人:有三种说法:一指君子。二指居高位之人。三指有圣德之人。

【译文】

把方的削成圆的啊,正常的法度不能废弃!改变本心更替常道啊,这向来为君子所鄙薄。彰显原则标举准绳啊,前人的法度不曾更改。内心敦厚品格方正啊,大人君子盛赞不已。

楚辞

巧倕不斲兮^①，孰察其拨正^②。玄文处幽兮，矇瞍谓之不章^③。离娄微睇兮^④，瞽以为无明^⑤。变白以为黑兮，倒上以为下。凤皇在笯兮^⑥，鸡鹜翔舞^⑦。同糅玉石兮^⑧，一概而相量^⑨。夫惟党人鄙固兮，羌不知余之所臧^⑩。任重载盛兮，陷滞而不济。怀瑾握瑜兮^⑪，穷不知所示。邑犬之群吠兮^⑫，吠所怪也。非俊疑杰兮^⑬，固庸态也。文质疏内兮^⑭，众不知余之异采。材朴委积兮^⑮，莫知余之所有。

【注释】

①倕(chuí)：传说是虞舜时能工巧匠的名字。斲(zhuó)：砍，削。
②察：知道，了解。拨：弯曲。
③矇瞍(méng sǒu)：瞎子。
④离娄：古代传说中视力超强的人。睇(dì)：眼睛微眯着看。
⑤瞽(gǔ)：瞎子。
⑥笯(nú)：笼子。
⑦鹜(wù)：鸭。
⑧糅(róu)：错杂，混杂。玉石：指君子和小人。玉，比喻德行端正的君子。石，比喻谗佞小人。
⑨一概而相量：用一个度量衡标尺来衡量的意思，比喻善恶不分。概，古代称量米粟等时用来刮平斗斛的木板，这里引申为标准、尺度。量(liáng)：衡量。
⑩臧(cáng)：指自己所具备的美好品质。
⑪瑾(jǐn)：美玉。
⑫邑：城镇，城市，人口聚居的地方。
⑬非俊疑杰：非，毁谤，诋毁。俊、杰，都是指才能出众、智

识过人的人。
⑭文质：外在和本质。文指外表。质指本质。疏：疏阔，阔略，没有太多繁文缛节。内(nè)：木讷，不善言辞。
⑮材朴：可以使用的木材、木料，这里比喻人的才干。委积：堆积。

【译文】

巧匠倕如果不砍不削啊，谁会知道是曲是直？黑色花纹隐在暗处啊，瞎子也说它不明显。离娄眯着眼睛看啊，盲人认为他没眼力。把白变成黑啊，把上下颠倒过来。凤凰被关进笼子啊，鸡鸭却肆意飞舞。美玉顽石掺杂在一起啊，用一个标尺衡量它们。结党营私之徒卑鄙顽固啊，不知我内蕴的美好。负担太重装载过多啊，陷没停滞难达目标。怀抱美玉，手握宝石啊，身处困境，不知向谁展示。城里的狗一起狂叫啊，对着它们眼中怪异的人事叫嚣。毁谤俊才，猜忌贤才啊，本来就是庸人的常貌。外表质朴秉性木讷啊，众人不知我出众的文采。栋梁之材堆积一旁啊，我的才能无人知晓。

重仁袭义兮①，谨厚以为丰。重华不可遌兮②，孰知余之从容③！古固有不并兮④，岂知其何故？汤禹久远兮，邈而不可慕⑤。

【注释】

①重(chóng)：积累，重叠。袭：重累，重叠。
②遌(è)：遇。
③从容：行为，举动。
④不并：指圣君与贤臣不生在一个时代。

⑤邈(miǎo)：远。慕：仰慕，思念。

【译文】

积累宽仁培养忠义啊，谨慎敦厚充实自身。圣王重华不能与他相遇啊，有谁能了解我的言行举动？明君贤臣自古就不常生在一个时代啊，怎知其中的原因？汤禹距今如此久远啊，时代太早让人无从表达思慕之情。

惩连改忿兮①，抑心而自强。离愍而不迁兮②，愿志之有像③。进路北次兮，日昧昧其将暮④。舒忧娱哀兮⑤，限之以大故⑥。

【注释】

①惩：止住。连：当从《史记·屈原贾生列传》作"违"，恨的意思。
②愍(mǐn)：同"愍"，祸难。
③像：法则，榜样。
④昧昧：形容昏暗的样子。
⑤舒忧娱哀：舒散、发泄忧愁，使悲哀的情绪快乐起来。
⑥限：限度，期限。大故：死亡。

【译文】

克制心中怨恨改掉自己的愤怒啊，平抑心情自我勉励。饱受哀愁却不变心啊，希望志节有所依归。向北进发暂且停歇啊，天色昏暗已到黄昏。舒散忧愁排遣悲哀啊，期限已到死亡将临。

乱曰：浩浩沅湘，分流汩兮①。修路幽蔽，道远忽兮②。怀质抱情，独无匹兮。伯乐既没③，骥焉程兮④。万民之生，各有所错兮⑤。定心广志,余何畏惧兮?曾伤爰哀⑥,永叹喟兮⑦。世溷浊莫吾知,人心不可谓兮。知死不可让,愿勿爱兮。明告君子,吾将以为类兮⑧。

【注释】

①汩(gǔ):水流湍急的样子。
②忽:荒忽,茫茫,辽远阔大的样子。
③伯乐:古代传说中善于识别、挑选马匹的人。没(mò):通"殁",死亡。
④骥:好马,良马。程:衡量,测量。
⑤错:安置。
⑥曾:重累。爰:哀伤不止。
⑦喟(kuì):叹息。
⑧类:法则,标准,榜样。

【译文】

乱辞说:沅湘之水阔大,湍急向前奔流啊。长路幽深昏暗,辽远苍茫无际啊。内心修美品格坚贞,无可匹敌啊。伯乐已死,好马又该怎样衡量啊。万民降生,各有自己的命运啊。安心骋志,我还有什么好畏惧啊。满腹哀伤无休无止,叹息长久不绝啊。世间混浊无人理解,我对人心已无话可说啊。知道死亡不可避免,宁愿不再爱惜自己啊。明白地告诉大人君子,我将以此作为法则啊。

思美人

【题解】

"思美人"由篇首语"思美人兮,擥涕而伫眙"而来,所谓"美人",有"怀王"或"襄王"之说,后人多认同王逸《楚辞章句》的"怀王"说。"思美人",如王逸所说"言己忧思,念怀王也"的意思。《思美人》抒发了思念君王、却得不到表白心志的机会,无法接受变节以从俗邀宠的郁怨,也坚定了始终执守高洁人格与美政理想、宁死不变节的信念。

本篇的创作时地,多沿袭王逸的流放江南时的说法。至清代林云铭《楚辞灯》则提出:"与江南之野所作无涉。"屈复《楚辞新集注》也指出:"此亦迁汉北时作也。"近代沈德鸿、姜亮夫、陈子展等人也认为此篇是屈原于怀王时作于汉北,兹从后说。

本篇在创作上的特色在于"依诗取兴,引类譬喻"手法的运用。其以"思美人"名篇,"美人"便是用来指称"怀王"。屈原作品往往喜欢用男女爱情关系来比喻君臣关系,本篇即是一例。除"美人"喻外,本篇还大量运用了"香草"喻。全文下半部分诗人沿着江水、夏水散心消忧时所采摘的"芳芷"、"宿莽"等,都可视为他心目中美好德行、理想人格的象征,这同时可以在《离骚》等作品中得到印证。

思美人兮,擥涕而伫眙①。媒绝路阻兮②,言不可结而诒③。蹇蹇之烦冤兮④,陷滞而不发⑤。申旦以舒中情兮⑥,志沉菀而莫达⑦。愿寄言于浮云兮,遇丰隆而不将⑧。因归鸟而致辞兮，羌宿高而难当⑨。

【注释】

①擥(lǎn)涕：擦干、收起眼泪。擥，同"揽"。伫眙(zhù chì)：久久站立，注视前方。
②媒绝：指自己孤单一人，无人为自己和君王沟通。绝，断绝。路阻：这里比喻自己和君王之间存在隔阂，无法互相了解、沟通。
③诒(yí)：赠送。
④蹇蹇(jiǎn)：形容情绪滞塞、郁结而不通畅的样子。烦冤：形容心情烦乱而郁积不得发泄的样子。
⑤陷滞而不发：指愁闷烦乱的情绪郁积于内，无法发泄舒散。
⑥申旦：由夜至曙，通宵达旦。中情：屈原作品习语，即内心情感。
⑦沉菀(yùn)：形容心思郁积而不通的样子。
⑧丰隆：古代神话传说中云神的名号。不将：不听从命令。
⑨羌：楚地方言，句首发语词。宿：当作"迅"，即速度快。当：遇到。

【译文】

思念我那美人啊，擦干眼泪久久伫立，望眼欲穿。媒人断绝了消息，路途多有险阻啊，有话对君王说却言不成句。烦闷愁苦郁积我胸中啊，陷滞停留却难以舒泄。由夜至曙我想要抒怀啊，心思缠结却又无法传达。愿把话儿托付给浮云啊，碰上云神不听我言。想靠归鸟为我传辞啊，它迅疾高飞，转瞬不见。

高辛之灵盛兮①，遭玄鸟而致诒②。欲变节以从俗兮，愧易初而屈志。独历年而离愍兮③，羌冯心犹未化④。宁隐闵而寿考兮⑤，何变易之可为！知前辙之不遂兮⑥，未改此度。车既覆而马颠兮，蹇独怀此异路⑦。勒骐骥而更驾兮⑧，造父为我操之⑨。迁逡次而勿驱兮⑩，聊假日以须时。指嶓冢之西隈兮⑪，与纁黄以为期⑫。

【注释】

①高辛：五帝之一"帝喾"的名号。灵盛：神灵旺盛充沛。

②玄鸟：燕。致诒：传送礼物。诒，礼物。

③离愍(mǐn)：遭遇忧愁。

④冯(píng)：愤怒，愤懑。

⑤隐闵：隐忍，沉默不言。寿考：终身。

⑥前辙：前面、未来的道路。遂：通达，顺利。

⑦蹇(jiǎn)：通"謇"，句首发语词。异路：与世俗之人不同的道路。

⑧勒：本义是套在马首上的笼头，这里释为驾驭、控御。骐骥：一种骏马的名称。

⑨造父：周穆王时人，以善于驾车著称。操：执辔驾车。

⑩迁：迁延不进的样子。逡(qūn)次：徘徊不前的样子。

⑪嶓冢(bō zhǒng)：山名。大约是蜿蜒于陕甘交界处的山脉名称，汉水的发源处。隈(wēi)：山崖。

⑫纁(xūn)黄：日落、黄昏的时候。

【译文】

古帝高辛神灵多么荣盛啊，遇上玄鸟为他传送礼物。想要改变志节追随流俗啊，我又以改变节操委屈心志为愧。常年独自经受忧痛熬煎啊，一腔怨懑依旧不能化解。宁愿隐忍不言了此穷苦一生啊，又怎能改辙变节呢？明知前方道路艰难不通啊，却不更改这种处世原则。车已颠覆，马已颓倒啊，这路与众不同却仍是我的选择。勒住骏马，重套车驾啊，造父为我执辔驾驭。要他慢慢前行且莫纵马疾驰啊，姑且偷闲一番等待时机。指着嶓冢山的西面山崖啊，约好黄昏时分在那里相见。

开春发岁兮，白日出之悠悠。吾将荡志而愉乐兮①，遵江夏以娱忧②。擥大薄之芳茝兮③，搴长洲之宿莽④。惜吾不及古人兮⑤，吾谁与玩此芳草？解萹薄与杂菜兮⑥，备以为交佩⑦。佩缤纷以缭转兮，遂萎绝而离异。吾且儃佪以娱忧兮⑧，观南人之变态⑨。窃快在中心兮，扬厥凭而不竢⑩。芳与臭其杂糅兮，羌芳华自中出⑪。纷郁郁其远承兮⑫，满内而外扬。情与质信可保兮⑬，羌居蔽而闻章。

【注释】

①荡志：放纵情思，开怀。荡，放荡，放纵。
②娱忧：排解忧愁。
③擥：持取，摘取。薄：草木丛生的地方。茝(zhǐ)：香草名，或即白芷。
④搴：拔取。长洲：即形状长而大的沙洲。洲，沙洲，岛屿。宿莽：一种越冬生长的草本植物，或即卷葹草。
⑤不及古人：未能和古代的圣贤君子同处一个时代。
⑥萹(biān)薄：丛生的萹蓄。萹，萹蓄，一名萹竹。蓼科，一年生平卧草本植物。薄，丛生的杂草。
⑦交佩：两两相交的佩饰物。
⑧儃(chán)佪：徘徊不前的样子。
⑨南人：郢都以南之人。变态：不正常的情态。

⑩凭：愤懑，愤怒。竢(sì)：等待。
⑪羌：句首发语词，楚地方言。芳华：即芬芳的花朵。华，同"花"。自中出：从里面凸显出来。
⑫纷：疑当作"芬"，芳香之气。郁郁：这里形容香气浓郁的样子。远承：指香气向远处飘散。"承"即"烝"，气味向外飘扬发散。
⑬情：指人的外在感情。质：指人的内在本体的特质、特征，即本质。

【译文】

春天到来新年开始啊，白天的时间越来越长。我将敞开心扉寻找快乐啊，沿着江水、夏水消解忧愁。摘下丛林里芬芳的苴草啊，拔取大沙洲上生长的宿莽。可惜我没能生在古代先贤的时代啊，如今与谁一起玩赏这些芳香的花草？采折丛生的蒿蓄杂菜啊，备作左右相交的佩饰。它们缤纷繁盛缭绕周身啊，最终却枯萎凋落，被扔在一旁。我且徘徊闲行消愁解闷啊，瞧瞧这些南人不正常的情态。一丝快意暗自浮上心头啊，舒散愤懑不必再有所期待。虽然芳香、浊臭混杂在一处啊，花朵的芬芳依旧难以掩盖。浓郁香气远远飘散啊，充盈于内自然会发散于外。我的心志若能真的保持啊，居处虽然蔽塞，也能名声显扬。

令薜荔以为理兮^①，惮举趾而缘木。因芙蓉而为媒兮，惮褰裳而濡足^②。登高吾不说兮^③，入下吾不能。固朕形之不服兮，然容与而狐疑^④。广遂前画兮^⑤，未改此度也。命则处幽^⑥，吾将罢兮^⑦，愿及白日之未暮^⑧。独茕茕而南行兮^⑨，思彭咸之故也。

【注释】

①薜荔:香草名,一种缠绕着树木生长的藤本植物。理:媒人,媒介。
②搴(qiān):通"攓",提起。濡(rú):沾湿,浸湿。
③说:通"悦",喜爱,喜欢。
④容与:形容徘徊不前的样子。
⑤遂:道路。画:分布。
⑥处幽:居处于幽暗僻远的地方,这里指被疏遭逐而出居汉北荒凉之地。
⑦罷:同"罢",即休止,作罢。一通"疲",指疲乏,疲劳。
⑧白日之未暮:比喻尚有时日,要抓紧时间,及时有所作为。
⑨茕茕(qióng):形容孤独的样子。

【译文】

命令薜荔去做信使啊,却恐怕如同抬脚攀援树木。依靠芙蓉去做媒人啊,却担心提起裤子将双脚弄湿。向高处攀爬我不喜欢啊,往低处行走我也不愿。本来是我的形貌不适应当世啊,我却仍然犹豫不决徘徊踯躅。广阔道路向前方延伸啊,我却仍然不改一贯法度。命中注定居于幽僻之地,我将就此停止下来啊,但仍愿趁年轻有所作为。独自一人往南行走啊,这是思念彭咸的缘故。

惜往日

【题解】

本篇亦以篇首三字为题。

关于本篇真伪，历来颇多争议。南宋时人魏了翁《鹤山渠阳经外杂钞》因篇中提到伍子胥，怀疑本篇及《悲回风》为伪作。明人许学夷《诗源辨体》和清人曾国藩《求阙斋读书录》亦因作品语气而致疑。清人吴汝纶《古文辞类纂评点》以《怀沙》为屈原绝笔，又因文词浅显而疑本篇非屈原所作。今人陆侃如、冯沅君《中国诗史》，刘永济《屈赋通笺》、谭介甫《屈赋新编》、胡念贻《屈原作品的真伪及其年代》均对本篇是否屈作提出疑问，但所举理由说服力不够，故无法令人信从。

本篇是屈原临终前的作品，学者们大多没有异议，但是否为绝笔，则有不同看法。林云铭《楚辞灯》以《怀沙》为绝笔，王夫之《通释》以《悲回风》为绝笔，但也颇有人认为本篇为屈原绝笔，如蒋骥《山带阁注楚辞》、夏大霖《屈骚心印》、陆侃如《屈原评传》、郭沫若《屈原研究》、游国恩《楚辞论文集》、姜亮夫《楚辞今绎讲录》等。细绎文义，篇中说："宁溘死而流亡兮，恐祸殃之有再，不毕辞而赴渊兮，惜壅君而不识。"则亦可以本篇为绝命词。

关于本篇内容，姜亮夫《屈原赋校注》说："言己初见信任，楚几于治。而怀王不知君子小人之情，以忠为邪，以谮为信，贞臣无辜，遂以见逐。然楚君昏暗，任私无法，而秦方朝夕以谋东略，则国亡无日，义恐再辱，遂欲赴渊，又惧无益君国，徒死无用，遂剀切以陈，思以牖启昏暗；然法度已隳，罔可救药，故毕辞赴渊以成其忠爱之忱矣！"其说颇为允当。而钱澄之在《庄屈合诂》中进一步引申说"《惜往日》者，思往日之王之见任而使造为宪令也。始曰'明法度之嫌疑'，终曰'背法度而心治'，原一生学术在此矣。楚能卒用之，必且大治；而为上官所谗，中废其事，为可惜也。原之惜，非惜己身不见用，惜己功之不成也。"此见解甚为精辟。

惜往日之曾信兮①，受命诏以昭诗②。奉先功以照下兮③，明法度之嫌疑④。国富强而法立兮，属贞臣而日娭⑤。秘密事之载心兮⑥，虽过失犹弗治。心纯厖而不泄兮⑦，遭谗人而嫉之。君含怒而待臣兮⑧，不清澈其然否。蔽晦君之聪明兮⑨，虚惑误又以欺⑩。弗参验以考实兮⑪，远迁臣而弗思。信谗谀之溷浊兮，盛气志而过之。何贞臣之无罪兮，被离谤而见尤⑫。惭光景之诚信兮⑬，身幽隐而备之⑭。

【注释】

①往日：这里指屈原青壮年时被怀王信任并重用的那一段时期。
②命诏：君王发布的命令或文告。昭：明。诗：当从朱熹本作"时"，时世。
③先功：指楚国前代君王的功业、业绩。功，指对国而言的事功、功绩。照下：昭示下民。
④法度：指国家的章程、法令、制度。嫌疑：指法度中不明确或有疑难的地方。
⑤属(zhǔ)：托付。娭(xī)：游乐，嬉戏。
⑥秘密：即"黾勉"，勤勉，勤恳。
⑦厖(máng)：敦厚，厚道。不泄：出言谨慎，不随便乱说话。泄，泄漏。
⑧君含怒而待臣：《史记·屈原贾生列传》："怀王使屈原造为宪令，屈平属草稿未定。上官大夫见而欲夺之，屈平不与。因谗之曰：'王使屈平为令，众莫不知，每一令出，平伐其功，曰以为非我莫能为也。'王怒而疏屈平。"大约即指此事。
⑨蔽晦：遮蔽、蒙蔽从而使之昏暗不明。聪明：聪就听觉而言，明就视觉而言，所谓"耳聪目明"，即视听感官敏锐的

意思。引申则指判断、辨别是非善恶的能力。

⑩虚：空虚不实，假而伪。惑：使……疑惑。误：使……行为举动颠倒错讹。

⑪参：参互比较。考实：考察、考核事实真相。

⑫被：蒙受。离：当从洪兴祖及朱熹本作"讟"，诽谤。尤：罪过，罪责。

⑬景(yǐng)：同"影"。

⑭幽隐：这里形容其居所的偏僻荒凉。备：具备。

【译文】

痛惜年轻时曾受信任啊，传达君王的诏令昭明时世。承袭先王的功业昭示下民啊，辨明法度决断疑难。国家富强法度建立啊，国政托付忠臣而君王轻松游乐。勤于国事时刻在心啊，即使有过失也没有治罪。心性敦厚而不随便说话啊，竟遭谗佞小人妒嫉。君王满含怒火对待臣下啊，不去澄清其中对错是非。小人蒙蔽了君王耳目啊，用假话误导君王又欺骗了他。君王不去比较核查事情的真相啊，远远把我放逐不加考虑。君王听信谗言奉承的话啊，对我怒气冲冲大加责备。为何忠臣本无罪过啊，却遭到诽谤承受罪过？惭愧的是日月光影真实无伪啊，身处僻远之地也得蒙其光辉。

临沅湘之玄渊兮①，遂自忍而沉流？卒没身而绝名兮，惜壅君之不昭②。君无度而弗察兮③，使芳草为薮幽④。焉舒情而抽信兮，恬死亡而不聊⑤。独鄣壅而蔽隐兮⑥，使贞臣为无由。

【注释】

①玄渊：水呈黑色的深渊。

②壅(yōng)君：被壅蔽、蒙蔽的君王。
③度：法度，客观的衡量标准。
④薮(sǒu)幽：水泽幽暗的地方。
⑤恬：安适，安静。聊：苟且偷生。
⑥鄣壅：阻塞，阻隔。鄣，同"障"。壅，义近"障"，又写作"雍"。

【译文】

走近沅湘这深渊啊，就此忍心自沉江流？最终身死名声磨灭啊，痛惜君王被蒙蔽而不觉悟。君王没有原则不能明察啊，把香草丢弃在深暗水沼。该如何打开心扉、展示诚信啊，安静地死亡，我决不苟且偷生。只因有着重重阻碍啊，令忠贞的臣子无从接近君王。

闻百里之为虏兮①，伊尹烹于庖厨②。吕望屠于朝歌兮③，宁戚歌而饭牛④。不逢汤武与桓缪兮，世孰云而知之？吴信谗而弗味兮⑤，子胥死而后忧⑥。介子忠而立枯兮⑦，文君寤而追求⑧。封介山而为之禁兮⑨，报大德之优游⑩。思久故之亲身兮，因缟素而哭之⑪。

【注释】

①百里：即百里奚，春秋时人。初为虞国大夫，晋献公灭虞时被俘，后作为陪嫁媵臣入秦国。后又亡秦入楚，为楚人所执。时秦穆公闻其贤能，遣人至楚，以五张羊皮赎得其身，用为大夫，故又称之为"五羖(gǔ)大夫。"
②伊尹：商初成汤的大臣，名挚，尹是官名，因其母居伊水，故称伊尹。庖(páo)厨：厨房。庖厨烹饪之事古代视为下贱者所为。

③吕望：即俗称所谓姜太公、姜子牙。其佐周文、武王，乃灭商功臣，后封于齐，为齐国始祖，其族世代为姬周姻亲。朝(zhāo)歌：古地名，殷纣时国都，在今河南淇县。
④宁戚：春秋时卫人，曾至齐国国都经商，喂牛而歌，为齐桓公所闻，桓公认为他是贤人，遂任用其为大夫。
⑤吴：这里指吴王夫差。
⑥子胥：即伍子胥。后忧：指日后的亡国之忧。
⑦介子：介子推。春秋时晋国人，曾跟随晋文公重耳在外流亡十九年，文公归国继位后，介子推携母隐于绵上山中。立枯：抱着树而被烧死。
⑧文君：晋文公，晋献公子，大戎女所生，姬姓，名重耳，"春秋五霸"之一。寤(wù)：觉醒，醒悟。
⑨介山：古代山名。因介子推而得名，在今山西介休。禁：禁止民众上介山砍柴打猎，因为晋文公将介山作为介子推的封地。
⑩优游：形容德行至高至大。
⑪缟(gǎo)素：本义是白色的织物，这里指白色的丧服。

【译文】

听说百里奚做过俘虏啊，伊尹在厨房里烹制过食物。吕望在朝歌做过屠夫啊，宁戚边唱歌边喂过牛。若非遇到商汤、周武王、齐桓公、秦穆公啊，世上谁会说知道他们的好处？夫差听信谗言不加思量啊，伍子胥死后国家败亡。介子推忠于晋文公却被烧死啊，晋文公醒悟后立刻去访求。将介山作为他的封地禁止樵猎啊，来报答他的仁厚大德。怀念他是多年亲密的故人啊，穿上白色丧服痛哭泪流。

或忠信而死节兮，或訑谩而不疑①。弗省察而按实兮②，听谗人之虚词。芳与泽其杂糅兮③,孰申旦而别之④?何芳草之夭兮⑤,微霜降而下戒。谅聪不明而蔽壅兮⑥,使谗谀而日得。

【注释】

①诧谩(tuó mán):欺骗,诈伪。
②省(xǐng):检察,审察。按:考察。
③泽:当为"臭"字之误。
④申旦:意即日复一日。申,重复。旦,天亮。
⑤夭(yāo):夭折,死亡。
⑥谅:确实,的确。聪不明:即听觉不敏锐,引申就是偏听偏信,不辨是非忠奸。

【译文】

有人忠贞诚信却为节操而死啊,有人欺诈虚伪却没有人怀疑。不审察验证核对事实啊,却听信小人的不实之言。芳香腐臭混杂一处啊,谁能日复一日来加以辨析?为什么芳草过早夭亡啊,寒霜从天而降,给以警示。实在是君王偏听偏信受到蒙蔽啊,才使谗谀之徒日益得势。

自前世之嫉贤兮,谓蕙若其不可佩①。妒佳冶之芬芳兮,嫫母姣而自好②。虽有西施之美容兮③,谗妒入以自代。愿陈情以白行兮④,得罪过之不意。情冤见之日明兮⑤,如列宿之错置⑥。

【注释】

①蕙若:两种香草的名称。

②嫫(mó)母：传说是黄帝的妃子，貌丑。后世作为丑女的代名词。这里比喻奸邪小人。姣：容貌美丽。

③西施：春秋时越国人，以貌美著称，越人将其献于吴王夫差，令夫差荒淫不理政事，后卒亡吴国。

④白行：表白、说明自己的所作所为。

⑤情冤：指是非曲直。情，真情，真实。冤，冤枉，委屈。见(xiàn)：同"现"，表现，显现。日明：一天天地变得明白起来。

⑥列宿：排列在天幕上的众多星宿。错：通"措"，放置，安放。

【译文】

自古以来小人嫉贤妒能啊，都说芬芳的蕙草、杜若不可佩带。妒忌佳人芳美袭人啊，丑妇嫫母却自认为美丽而装出媚态。即使有西施那样的美艳容貌啊，谗妒小人也要钻进来取代。希望陈述衷情，表白所为啊，却无意之间招致罪过。事实与冤屈终究会得到澄清啊，就像天上星宿般排列有序。

乘骐骥而驰骋兮，无辔衔而自载①；乘氾泭以下流兮②，无舟楫而自备。背法度而心治兮③，辟与此其无异④。宁溘死而流亡兮⑤，恐祸殃之有再。不毕辞而赴渊兮，惜壅君之不识。

【注释】

①辔(pèi)：马缰绳。衔：马嚼子。

②氾泭(fàn fú)：筏子。

③心治：依着一己的私心去治理。

④辟：通"譬"，譬如，好像。

⑤溘(kè)：忽然，快速。流亡：随流水而去。

【译文】

骑上骏马我自由驰骋啊，没有缰绳和衔铁自行驾驭。乘着筏子顺流而下啊，却无船桨而要自己准备。背离法度自行治理啊，这跟以上情形没有两样。宁愿突然死去随流水飘逝啊，只怕再一次遭受祸殃。不把话说完便投赴深渊啊，痛惜君王被蒙蔽却一无所知。

橘　颂

【题解】

橘是一种常绿小乔木或灌木，枝有刺，花呈黄白色，果扁球形，熟时呈橙黄色或淡黄红色，果皮疏松，瓤肉易于分离，产于我国南方。颂一则为动词，是称赞、歌颂、赞美的意思；一则为文体的名称，即《诗经》所谓"风""雅""颂"之颂。所谓"橘颂"，洪兴祖《楚辞补注》说："美橘之有是德，故曰颂。"意即对橘的美好品德的称颂赞美。

关于本篇创作时地，王逸以为《橘颂》当是屈原晚年流放江南时的作品，这从王逸释"南国"为"江南"即可见出。明人汪瑷《楚辞集解》则怀疑"此篇乃平日所作，未必放逐之后之所作者也"。清人陈本礼《屈辞精义》则进一步指出："其曰'受命不迁'，是言禀受天赋之命，非被放之命也；其曰'嗟尔幼志'，'年岁虽少'，明明自道，盖早年童冠时作也。"认为《橘颂》是屈原青年时代的作品。今人林庚、胡念贻、陈子展等赞同此说。其中，陈子展在《楚辞直解》中推测《橘颂》可能是屈原担任三闾大夫一职时的作品。本书倾向于"早期说"。

本篇以细腻生动的笔触从橘树外形开始描绘，全景观照、细节刻画、内外结合、总分交汇，在有限的篇幅内腾挪变化，成功地塑造了橘树的美丽外表。随后由外转向里，将橘树绰约风姿比拟为坚守操守、保持公正无私品格的君子，挖掘其超乎寻常的品性：独立不迁、深固难移、遗世独立、闭心自慎、柔德无私。创设出咏橘述志，描物喻人的圆融诗境。

《橘颂》是我国文学史上第一首文人咏物诗，开后世咏物诗的先河。曹丕在《典论·论文》中说："如（王）粲之《初征》《登楼》《槐赋》《征思》，（徐）幹之《玄猿》《漏卮》《圆扇》《橘赋》，虽张、蔡不过也。"这说明从东汉中后期以来咏物赋创作大兴之后，"橘"已成为文人关注的题材之一。虽然徐幹《橘赋》已佚，无法目睹全貌，但我们有理由推断其中必有《橘颂》的流风余韵。晋人郭璞在《山海经·中山经图赞》中更是对《橘柚》为诗题大加赞誉说："厥苞橘柚，奇者维甘。朱实金鲜，叶蒨翠蓝。灵均是咏，以为美谈。"

后皇嘉树①，橘徕服兮②。受命不迁③，生南国兮④。深固难徙，更壹志兮。绿叶素荣⑤，纷其可喜兮⑥。曾枝剡棘⑦，圆果抟兮⑧。青黄杂糅⑨，文章烂兮⑩。精色内白⑪，类可任兮⑫。纷缊宜修⑬，姱而不丑兮⑭。

【注释】

①后：后土。后土是古人对土地的尊称，大地在古人心目中地位极为崇高，是具有神性、神格的事物。

②徕(lái)：来。服：习惯，适应。
③迁：迁移，迁徙。橘是南方特有的植物，所以说"不迁"。
④南国：泛释之为南方之义。在屈原的时代南方即楚国之地。
⑤素：白。荣：花。
⑥纷：这里形容橘树花叶茂盛的样子。
⑦曾：层层叠叠。剡(yǎn)：尖，锐利。棘：刺。
⑧抟(tuán)：圆。
⑨青黄：橘的果实未成熟时外皮呈青色，成熟时则呈黄色。杂糅：各种不同的东西混杂在一起，这里指青、黄两色交织、混杂。
⑩文章：文采，错综华美的色彩或花纹。文，同"纹"。章，文采。烂：色彩鲜明灿烂。
⑪精色：指橘实外表皮色明亮。内白：指橘实内部瓤肉色泽洁白。
⑫类可任兮：如同肩负重任的君子。当依洪兴祖、朱熹等校语作"类任道兮"。类，似、好像。任，承担，担任，肩负。
⑬纷缊(yūn)：纷繁茂盛，是针对橘树枝、叶、花、果各个方面而言的。宜修：修饰得宜，恰到好处。
⑭姱(kuā)：美好。

【译文】

后土皇天的美好橘树，它生来适应这片土地啊。禀承天地之命决不外迁，扎根生长在南方大地啊。根深牢固难以迁移，更加具有专一的心志啊。绿色的叶子白色的花朵，缤纷茂盛惹人喜爱啊。层叠的树枝尖锐的利刺，圆圆的果实簇聚成团啊。青黄两色混杂在一起，色泽文采多么美丽啊。外表鲜丽，内在纯洁，如同肩负重任的君子啊。风姿美盛，修饰得宜，美丽没有一点瑕疵啊。

嗟尔幼志^①,有以异兮。独立不迁,岂不可喜兮?深固难徙,廓其无求兮^②。苏世独立,横而不流兮^③。闭心自慎^④,不终失过兮^⑤。秉德无私,参天地兮^⑥。愿岁并谢^⑦,与长友兮。淑离不淫^⑧,梗其有理兮。年岁虽少,可师长兮。行比伯夷^⑨,置以为像兮^⑩。

【注释】

①嗟(jiē):表示感叹语气的虚词。
②廓:广大,空阔。这里指橘树的心境、品格的阔大,申言之即超脱旷达的意思。
③横:充满。不流:不随波逐流、媚俗从众、与世沉浮。
④闭心:将心灵关闭,如此则能排除外界的诱惑与干扰,保持自身内心世界的纯净。
⑤不终失过:当作"终不失过",即始终不犯错误。
⑥参:三。这里指与天地相配,合而成三。
⑦谢:离去,这里指岁月流逝。
⑧淑离:鲜明美好的样子。
⑨伯夷:商代末年孤竹国国君的长子,因与弟叔齐互相谦让王位而双双去国弃位,来到周国。后谏阻周武王伐纣,武王不纳其言,遂双双逃隐于首阳山,耻食周粟而饿死在山里。
⑩置:建立,树立。像:法式,榜样。

【译文】

惊叹你从小志向便与众不同啊。巍然独立而不变更,怎能不令人欢喜啊。根深蒂固难以移动,胸襟开阔无所欲求啊。清醒卓立在人间浊世,志节充盈,决不随波逐流啊。闭敛心扉,摒除物扰,保持审慎,始终不犯过错啊。秉持道德,公正无私,和天地同在啊。愿与岁月一起流逝，和你长久相伴永远为友啊。心灵美好而不淫乱，坚强正直而有条理啊。年纪虽小，可为人师啊。高洁德行与伯夷比肩，把你作为榜样来学习啊。

悲回风

【题解】

本篇以篇首三字为题。

《悲回风》也存在真伪之争。南宋人魏了翁《鹤山渠阳经外杂钞》以本篇风格不似屈原而类似宋玉、景差之作，因此怀疑为伪作；明人许学夷《诗源辨体》以语气不似屈原而质疑；清人吴汝纶《古文辞类纂点勘记》以本篇文字太奇而疑为伪作；今人陈钟凡《楚辞各篇作者考》等也从各个角度出发，认为本篇非屈原作。但这些理由都不足以推翻对本篇为屈原作品的认定。

关于本篇的写作时间，主要有四种意见：第一，陆侃如《屈原评传》认为是怀王十六年放逐汉北时作。第二，林云铭《楚辞灯》、夏大霖《屈骚心印》、郭沫若《屈原研究》等认为是襄王六、七年间作品。第三，蒋骥《山带阁注楚辞》认为是屈原自沉汨罗前一年秋天的作品。第四，王夫之《楚辞通释》、王闿运《楚辞释》认为是自沉时所作的绝笔。以上诸说以蒋说最为近似。因为从篇中所流露的感情来看，可判定是在自沉汨罗前不久。

关于本篇的内容题旨，汪瑗《楚辞集解》说："此篇因秋夜愁不能寐，感回风之起，凋伤万物，而兰独芳，有似乎古之君子遭乱世而不变其志者，遂托为远游访古之辞，以发泄其愤懑之情。然而遍游天地之间,愈求而愈远,其同志者,终不可得一遇焉,故心思之沉抑而竟不能已也。"概括较为允当。

《悲回风》没有叙事成分,全篇为诗人内心的独白。由诗人见"回风之摇蕙"的观物之感,联想到美好事物因遭受暴力摧残而毁灭,内心感情沉郁,意境迷离,充满了悲伤的气氛和绝望的情绪。关于这一点,姜亮夫《屈原赋校注》说:"全章皆以思理惑,不知所释为主;而最为萦惑者,则是非善恶,本不相容,而又实不能显别;因而心伤,作为伤心之诗。诗中描绘心思,出入内外远近不同之情,上下左右前后之态,而仍不知所止,悲感与思理相挟持,而遂思入眇茫,从彭咸之所居。既至天上,忽又感烟雨之终不可永久浮游上天,遂思追踪介子、伯夷。既申徒之死而无益,又自迴惑不解。大体情辞苦,惶惑不安。"评述精确。

悲回风之摇蕙兮①,心冤结而内伤②。物有微而陨性兮③,声有隐而先倡④。夫何彭咸之造思兮⑤,暨志介而不忘⑥!万变其情岂可盖兮,孰虚伪之可长!鸟兽鸣以号群兮,草苴比而不芳⑦。鱼葺鳞以自别兮⑧,蛟龙隐其文章。故荼荠不同亩兮⑨,兰茝幽而独芳。惟佳人之永都兮⑩,更统世而自贶⑪。眇远志之所及兮⑫,怜浮云之相羊⑬。介眇志之所惑兮,窃赋诗之所明。

【注释】

①回风:疾风,旋风。蕙:一种香草。
②冤结:形容心情忧伤、愁闷的样子。伤:悲伤,哀痛。
③物:这里指蕙而言。陨(yǔn):陨落,凋丧。性:生命,性命。

④声：这里指风声。隐：这里指风声藏匿无形。倡：起始，先导。
⑤造思：树立的思想。造，制造，造就。
⑥暨(jì)：与，和。介：坚固，坚定，坚贞。
⑦苴(chá)：枯草。比：合在一起。
⑧茸(qì)：整理，修饰。
⑨荼(tú)：苦菜。荠(jì)：一种味甘的野菜。
⑩惟：思念。佳人：这里或是屈原自谓。佳，美好。都：美好。
⑪更：经历，经过。统世：经过几世几代，历时久远。貺(kuàng)：给与，赐与。
⑫眇(miǎo)：远。及：至，到达。
⑬相羊：形容飘浮、游荡、没有凭依的样子。

【译文】

悲悯疾风摇落蕙草啊，内心忧伤愁思郁结。蕙草微小而丧失了性命啊，风声隐匿无形却能发出声响。为什么彭咸树立的思想啊，和他那坚定志节让我无法忘怀？情态万变，怎能掩盖内心的真实啊，虚伪的事物哪会绵延久长？鸟兽鸣叫招呼同类啊，荣草、枯草不能一起散发芳香。鱼儿修饰鳞片显示其与众不同啊，蛟龙则将身上文采隐藏。所以苦菜和甘荠不能在同一块田里生长啊，兰花芷草在幽僻之地独自散发芬芳。想起君子永远那么美好啊，经历几世几代却自求多福。志向远大与天比高啊，怜惜浮云游荡无依。我志向远大坚定让世人迷惑啊，暗自写作诗篇表明心志。

惟佳人之独怀兮①，折若椒以自处②。曾歔欷之嗟嗟兮③，独隐伏而思虑。涕泣交而凄凄兮④，思不眠以至曙。终长夜之曼曼兮,掩此哀而不去。寤从容以周流兮,聊逍遥以自恃⑤。伤太息之愍怜兮⑥,气於邑而不可止⑦。纠思心以为纕兮⑧,编愁苦以为膺⑨。折若木以蔽光兮⑩,随飘风之所仍⑪。存髣髴而不见兮⑫,心踊跃其若汤⑬。抚珮衽以案志兮⑭,超惘惘而遂行⑮。岁忽忽其若颓兮⑯,时亦冉冉而将至⑰。薠蘅槁而节离兮⑱,芳以歇而不比⑲。怜思心之不可惩兮,证此言之不可聊。宁逝死而流亡兮⑳,不忍为此之常愁。孤子吟而抆泪兮㉑,放子出而不还。孰能思而不隐兮,照彭咸之所闻。

【注释】

①惟:思念,想念。独怀:独特的胸襟、怀抱。怀,胸怀,襟怀。

②若:杜若,一种香草的名称。椒:一种芳香的植物,或即花椒。

③曾(céng):重累。歔欷(xū xī):哭泣,哽咽。嗟嗟(juē):不断叹息。

④凄凄:形容悲伤的样子。

⑤逍遥:遨游嬉戏以自适其心怀。恃:怙恃,依赖,依靠。

⑥愍(mǐn)怜:怜悯。

⑦於邑(wū yì):呜咽,哽咽。

⑧纠(jiū):编结,缠扎。纕(xiāng):佩带。

⑨膺:大约是紧贴前胸的衣物。

⑩若木:古代神话传说中的神木。

⑪飘风:疾风,旋风。仍:跟从,跟随。

⑫髣髴(fǎng fú):仿佛,好像。

⑬踊跃:跳动,跳跃。汤:热水。

⑭珮：玉佩，一种玉制的装饰品。衽(rèn)：衣襟。案：抑制。

⑮超惘惘(wǎng)：惘怅，怅惘。

⑯召召(hū)：即"忽忽"，这里形容时间流逝的样子，有迫促、迅疾的含义。颓：下坠，流逝，过去。

⑰时：这里指老年，老境。冉冉：形容渐渐前进的样子。

⑱蘋(fán)：一种水草的名称。蘅(héng)：一种香草的名称，即杜蘅。槁(gǎo)：枯。节离：枝节脱落、断开。

⑲不比：即不再茂盛，不再显得生机勃勃。比，茂盛。

⑳宁逝死而流亡兮：当作"宁溘死而流亡兮"。这是屈赋成句，又见于《离骚》、《惜往日》等。

㉑吟：叹息。抆(wěn)：擦拭。

【译文】

想那美人有独特的胸襟啊，采折杜若芸椒独自居住。哭泣不止，频频叹息啊，独自隐居，思索考虑。涕泪交流如此悲伤啊，沉思无眠直到天亮。熬过这漫漫长夜啊，压抑心头哀愁却萦绕不去。醒来后优游四处观览啊，姑且畅怀自我娱乐。伤感长叹实在可怜啊，气息哽咽无法抑止。缠扎忧心作为佩带啊，编结愁苦作为心衣。折下若木遮蔽阳光啊，随着疾风任意飘摇。仿佛存在的一切已经模糊不见啊，心如沸水猛烈悸动。抚摸玉佩、衣襟来抑制情绪啊，在惘怅迷惘中起身前行。岁月流逝匆匆过去啊，时光冉冉人生也将渐入老境。白蘋、杜蘅已然枯落啊，芳香消散生机全无。可怜思念君国的心绪无法悔改啊，证明克制忧愁的话靠不住。宁愿快点死去而随流水飘逝啊，不能忍受这没完没了的愁苦。独自叹息，擦拭泪水啊，被放逐的人一去不返。谁能想到这些不忧伤啊，我明白了彭咸的传说的真假。

登石峦以远望兮①，路眇眇之默默②。入景响之无应兮③，闻省想而不可得④。愁郁郁之无快兮，居戚戚而不可解⑤。心鞿羁而不形兮⑥，气缭转而自缔⑦。穆眇眇之无垠兮⑧，莽芒芒之无仪⑨。声有隐而相感兮，物有纯而不可为⑩。藐蔓蔓之不可量兮⑪，缥绵绵之不可纡⑫。愁悄悄之常悲兮⑬，翩冥冥之不可娱⑭。凌大波而流风兮⑮，托彭咸之所居。

【注释】

①峦：小而锐峭的山。一说指形状狭长的山。

②眇眇(miǎo)：遥远的样子。默默：寂静的样子。

③景：同"影"，阴影。

④闻省想：耳听目视心想。闻，听。省，看，审视。想，心想，思考。

⑤居：疑为"思"之误。戚戚：忧愁、愁苦的样子。

⑥鞿(jī)羁：鞿，马嚼子，马缰绳。羁，马络头，马笼头。鞿和羁都是控御马匹的用具，这里引申作束缚解。形：当作"开"，排解，开释。

⑦缭转：纠缠、缠绕，无法排解的样子。缔：缠结在一起而无法解开。

⑧穆：深远，幽微。垠：边际，涯岸。

⑨莽：苍莽，广大。芒芒：空间广阔的样子。仪：景象，容仪，仪貌。

⑩纯：精纯，粹美。不可为：有无能为力，无可奈何的含义。

⑪藐：通"邈"，远。蔓蔓：与"漫漫"声义相同，漫长、久远的样子。量(liáng)：计算，度量。

⑫缥(piāo)绵绵：细微绵长的样子。纡：弯曲，萦绕。

⑬悄悄(qiǎo)：忧愁的样子。

⑭翩：快速地飞。冥冥：形容飞得又高又远的样子。
⑮淩：乘。流：跟随，跟从。

【译文】

登上小山眺望远方啊，路途遥远寂静无声。进入空旷阴影万籁俱静啊，耳听目视心想都已徒然。忧愁苦闷心不快乐啊，思绪忧苦愁郁不解。内心纠缠不得排解啊，气息郁结不能发散。四周幽远无垠无际啊，莽莽苍苍茫茫无边。仿佛有幽微的声音在相互感应啊，纯洁美好的事物却无奈陨殁。思绪悠远不能测量啊，细微绵长而无法绕回。忧愁满怀常自悲苦啊，远走高飞也无欢娱。乘着滚滚波浪随风飘逝啊，投身于彭咸所在的深渊。

上高岩之峭岸兮①，处雌蜺之标颠②。据青冥而攄虹兮③，遂儵忽而扪天④。吸湛露之浮源兮⑤，漱凝霜之雰雰⑥。依风穴以自息兮⑦，忽倾寤以婵媛⑧。冯昆仑以瞰雾兮⑨，隐岷山以清江⑩。惮涌湍之磕磕兮⑪，听波声之汹汹⑫。纷容容之无经兮⑬，罔芒芒之无纪⑭。轧洋洋之无从兮⑮，驰委移之焉止⑯。漂翻翻其上下兮⑰，翼遥遥其左右⑱。氾潏潏其前后兮⑲，伴张弛之信期⑳。观炎气之相仍兮㉑，窥烟液之所积㉒。悲霜雪之俱下兮，听潮水之相击。借光景以往来兮㉓，施黄棘之枉策㉔。求介子之所存兮㉕，见伯夷之放迹㉖。心调度而弗去兮，刻著志之无适㉗。

【注释】

①岸：这里指山崖的侧畔，即崖壁。
②雌蜺(ní)：古人称彩虹色彩较暗淡的外环部分为蜺，因其暗淡，则属阴、属雌，所以叫作雌蜺。与之相对，彩虹色彩较

明亮的内环部分则叫做虹,其属阳、属雄,所以又叫雄虹。标颠:顶端,最高处。

③青冥:青天,天空。摅(shū):舒展。

④儵(shū)忽:迅疾,快速。扪(mén):抚摸。

⑤湛:浓重,浓厚。浮源:疑本作"浮浮",形容露水浓重的样子。

⑥雰雰(fēn):形容霜雪缤纷的样子。这里当是就霜而言。

⑦风穴:古代神话传说中的一个洞穴,是产生风的地方。

⑧倾寤:全都明白了。倾,全,都。寤,领悟,明白。婵媛:伤感,悲伤。

⑨冯(píng):凭依,依靠。瞰(kàn):俯视。

⑩隐:凭依,依靠。岷山:即岷山。清江:看清江流的面貌。一说作"清澈的江水"解。

⑪磕磕(kē):本指石头发出的声音。这里当指水石相激而发出的声音。

⑫洶洶(xiōng):波浪澎湃相击发出的声音。

⑬容容:形容变动不居、纷乱的样子。无经:没有法度,缺乏条理。

⑭罔(wǎng):怅惘,惆怅。芒芒:这里形容迷乱的样子。纪:头绪。

⑮洋洋:彷徨而不知何去何从的样子。

⑯委移(wēi yí):同"逶迤",曲折前行的样子。

⑰漂:漂浮,飞动。翻翻:形容上下翻飞、不安定的样子。

⑱翼:飞动。遥遥:摇摆。

⑲氾(fàn):氾滥。潏潏(yù):形容水流奔涌而出的样子。

⑳张弛:这里指潮水的涨落。弛,同"弛"。信期:潮水涨落是有一定的时间、期限的,仿佛信守约定一般,所以叫作"信期"。

㉑炎：通"焰"，火焰。仍：跟从，跟随。
㉒烟：指云。液：指雨。
㉓光景：这里是时日、岁月的意思。景，同"影"。
㉔黄棘：是一种带刺植物的名称。枉：弯曲。策：鞭子，马鞭。
㉕介子：即介子推。所存：即所在，指介子推生前居住过的地方。
㉖放：为放逐。一说作远、故旧解。
㉗刻著志：下定决心，打定主意。刻，刻镂，铭刻。著，附着而不分离。

【译文】

登上高高山陡峭崖壁啊，处在彩虹的最高点。倚靠苍穹，舒展一道虹彩啊，于是刹那间抚摸到青天。吸吮浓厚的露水啊，含漱着飞落的凝霜。凭依风穴独自停歇啊，忽然领悟一切的奥秘，不禁忧思伤感。倚靠昆仑俯瞰云雾啊，凭依岷山看清江流湍急。激流冲击岩石发出骇人响声啊，听到波浪汹涌涛声震天。心里纷乱没个条理啊，情思芜杂缺乏头绪。要止住彷徨却不知如何下手啊，悲愁纠缠，何处才是终点？心绪漂荡上下翻飞啊，高高飞起徬徨不定。如同氾滥水流前后涌动啊，伴随着潮水涨落的固定约期。看那火焰与烟气相随而生啊，窥见云雨聚积显现。悲伤那霜雪一齐降下啊，听取那湍水击荡的巨响。借时间的光影驰骋往来啊，用那黄棘制成的弯曲神鞭来驾驭。访求介子推生前的居所啊，去看伯夷远遁的高山。心中思量，不能释怀啊，下定决心，决不离开。

曰①：吾怨往昔之所冀兮，悼来者之愁愁②。浮江淮而入海兮，从子胥而自适③。望大河之洲渚兮④，悲申徒之抗迹⑤。

骤谏君而不听兮⑥，重任石之何益⑦。心纠结而不解兮⑧，思蹇产而不释⑨。

【注释】

①曰：这里的"曰"的作用类似"乱曰"，用来总结全篇。
②愁愁(tì)：形容忧虑、恐惧、不安的样子。
③自适：意即自求适意，自适己志。适，安适，逸乐。
④洲：水中的陆地。渚：水中的小块陆地。
⑤申徒：指申徒狄。传说其谏君不听，不容于世，于是投水自尽。其年代则说法不一。抗：高，高尚。
⑥骤：屡次。
⑦任：背负。一说为抱。
⑧纠(guà)结：心中郁结。
⑨蹇(jiǎn)产：思绪郁结，不顺畅。

【译文】

乱辞说：我哀怨以前所抱的期望啊，悲悼未来感到忧惧不安。顺着江淮漂流入海啊，追随伍子胥以求心安。望着大河中的洲渚啊，为申徒狄的高尚行为而伤感。屡次向君王进谏却不被接受啊，抱石投水又有何益处？心绪纠结难以解脱啊，思理不畅无法释怀。

远 游

【题解】

本篇作者问题存在争议，大致可分为两种观点，即屈原创作说与汉人拟作说。第一种屈原创作说以王逸为代表，后世如朱熹、陈第、陆时雍、王夫之、林云铭、胡文英等人均受其影响，应该说这也是由汉至清绵亘千年的主流看法。第二种汉人拟作说，属晚起的一派，以清人胡濬源、吴汝纶等人为代表。如胡濬源《楚辞新注求确》认为："《远游》一篇，犹是《离骚》后半篇，而文气不及《离骚》深厚真实，疑汉人所拟。"近人廖平又进一步指出《远游》与"相如《大人赋》如出一手，大同小异"（《楚辞讲义》），这引发后来疑古论者将《远游》归为司马相如所作的倾向。第二种看法注意到了《远游》与屈原其他作品的显著不同，但放大这些差异并将其作为汉人拟作或伪作的论据则显得不妥。对后一种说法反拨较有力的应属陈子展《楚辞直解》、姜亮夫《屈原赋校注》、姜昆武与徐汉澍《远游真伪辨》（《文学遗产》一九八一年第三期）等。姜昆武及徐汉澍从屈原全部作品出发，从《远游》的文风、文法与其他作品的统一性角度进行论述，最终将《远游》确定为屈原作品，洵为定论。

关于本篇的创作主旨，一般认为是屈原流放之后抒发忧愤之情而作，如朱熹《楚辞集注》称："屈原既放，悲叹之余，眇观宇宙，陋世俗之卑狭，悼年寿之不长，于是作为此篇。"但也有称此篇为屈原殉身寓言的,如屈复《楚辞新集注》称:"《远游》,寓言也。自沉汨罗,即是远游。远游之乐,即是自沉之乐。"此论深刻,发人深省。

关于《远游》的创作时间,王逸认为是受谗后,朱熹也认为是放逐期间,汪瑗认为在遭谗前,王夫之认为是怀王时,林云铭说是在江南时,今人陈子展以为是"屈子初放汉北"时,姜亮夫先生认为作于晚年,"可能是在《怀沙》之前,屈原写好《远游》后怀沙而死"。本书认同姜亮夫先生之论。

《远游》在内容上分为两部分:一是描写诗人神游天上,感受超离世风恶浊后的由衷快乐;二是从"重曰"开始到篇末,写诗人养生炼形,充满了道家的出世思想。特别是篇中所描绘的想象活动,是诗人精神与灵魂在天上漫游或虚幻的朦胧梦想,表达了对卑污世俗的谴责和对纯真世界的追求,开后世"游仙诗"之先河。

《远游》在文学史上对后世影响较大,最显著的例子莫过于对司马相如《大人赋》的影响。洪兴祖引《大人赋》相关语例补注《远游》的地方有十一处之多,难怪其评价说:"司马相如作《大人赋》,宏放高妙,读者有凌云之意。然其语多出于此。至其妙处,相如莫能识也。"另外,《远游》开创了后世游仙诗创作的先河,洪兴祖称"古乐府有《远游》篇,出于此",是很有道理的。像以《游仙诗》十四首闻名的郭璞,他在诗中写道:"逸翮思拂霄,迅足羡远游"(其五)、"六龙安可顿,运流有代谢"(其四)、"蓐收清西陆,朱羲将由白"(其八)、"登仙抚龙驷,迅驾乘奔雷。鳞裳逐电曜,云盖随风回。手顿羲和辔,足蹈阊阖开,东海犹蹄涔,昆仑若蚁堆。遐邈冥茫中,俯视令人哀。"(其九)我们可以明显看到里面闪烁着《远游》的影子。总之,《远游》在屈原作品中虽争议较大,但其固有的魅力和价值却不容忽视。

悲时俗之迫阨兮①,愿轻举而远游②。质菲薄而无因兮③,焉托乘而上浮④。遭沉浊而污秽兮⑤,独郁结其谁语!夜耿耿而不寐兮⑥,魂茕茕而至曙⑦。

【注释】

①迫阨(è):困阻灾难。迫,胁迫,逼迫。阨,阻塞,困厄。
②轻举:升,登仙。
③质:素质,禀性。菲薄:鄙陋,指德才等,常用为自谦之词。
④托乘:指攀附仙人之车乘,比喻得人援引。
⑤沉浊:污浊,多喻指风俗败坏的时世。
⑥耿耿:烦躁不安,心事重重。
⑦茕茕(qióng):孤独的样子。

【译文】

悲伤时俗使人困厄啊,真想飞升登仙去远处周游。禀性鄙陋又没机缘啊,怎能攀附仙车上天周游?生逢浑浊尘世充满污秽啊,心中郁闷向谁倾诉?夜里心事重重反侧难以入睡啊,孤单独守直到天明。

惟天地之无穷兮,哀人生之长勤①。往者余弗及兮②,来者吾不闻。步徙倚而遥思兮③,怊惝怳而乖怀④。意荒忽而流荡兮⑤,心愁悽而增悲。神儵忽而不反兮⑥,形枯槁而独留。内惟省以端操兮⑦,求正气之所由⑧。漠虚静以恬愉兮⑨,澹无为而自得⑩。

【注释】

①勤:艰辛,愁苦。

②往者：过去的人事。
③彽倚：徘徊不定，逡巡。
④怊(chāo)：惆怅，失意。惝恍(chǎng huǎng)：惆怅，失意，伤感。乖：背离，违背。
⑤荒忽：恍惚，神思不定。流荡：心神不定，无所依托。
⑥儵(shū)忽：形容迅速的样子。反：通"返"，回归，回返。
⑦惟省(xǐng)：思索，审察。
⑧所由：所由来的途径和方法。
⑨漠：清静淡泊。虚静：清虚恬静。
⑩澹(dàn)：恬淡，淡泊。无为：道家主张清静虚无，顺应自然，称为"无为"。

【译文】

想到天地无穷无尽啊，哀叹人生愁苦艰辛。过去的我没能赶上啊，未来的我也无法闻知。我徘徊不定而思绪邈远啊，惆怅失意而违背初衷。意绪恍惚而心神不定啊，心中愁苦而悲伤日深。我的灵魂忽然远去而不复返啊，只留下枯槁的肉身。内心审察以端正我的操守啊，寻求天地正气从何而生。我清虚恬静以安然自乐啊，淡泊无为而怡然自得。

闻赤松之清尘兮①，愿承风乎遗则②。贵真人之休德兮③，美往世之登仙。与化去而不见兮④，名声著而日延。奇傅说之托辰星兮⑤，羡韩众之得一⑥。形穆穆以浸远兮⑦，离人群而遁逸⑧。因气变而遂曾举兮⑨，忽神奔而鬼怪⑩。时髣髴以遥见兮⑪，精晈晈以往来⑫。绝氛埃而淑尤兮⑬，终不返其故都。免众患而不惧兮，世莫知其所如。

【注释】

①赤松：即赤松子，相传为上古时神仙。清尘：比喻清静无为的境界。
②遗则：前代留下来的法则。
③真人：道家称存养本性或修真得道的人，亦泛称"成仙"之人。休德：美德。
④化：变化，转化。这里有改变形体固有状态，羽化升仙，与天地造化共往来的意思。
⑤傅说(yuè)：殷高宗武丁的贤相，传说他死后，精魂乘星上天。辰星：星宿名，此指二十八宿中的房星，位于东方天幕。
⑥韩众：古代传说中的仙人。得一：道家术语，即得道，"一"即"道"。
⑦穆穆：宁静，静默。浸：渐渐。
⑧遁逸：隐逸，避世隐居。
⑨曾(zēng)举：高举，向上高高飞升。
⑩神奔而鬼怪：形容神出鬼没的样子。
⑪髣髴(fǎng fú)：同"仿佛"，好像，类似。
⑫精：精灵，灵魂。皎皎(jiǎo)：明亮的样子。
⑬氛埃：污浊之气，秽浊之物。淑尤：到达奇异的境界。

【译文】

听说赤松子无为自得高风超俗啊，我愿禀承他的遗则风范。崇尚得道之人的美德啊，羡慕古人能得道升天。形体虽然物化消失不见啊，名声却显著而流传。惊奇傅说死后能乘星上天啊，羡慕韩众得道成仙。形体寂静而渐渐远去啊，离开人群而避世隐逸。凭借精气的变化而高飞天上啊，飘飘忽忽就像神鬼出没。仿佛远远看见啊，精灵闪闪正来来往往。超越浊世到达奇异的境界啊，不再返回故国。摆脱群小再无所畏惧啊，世人都不知道我的去处。

恐天时之代序兮①，耀灵晔而西征②。微霜降而下沦兮，悼芳草之先零。聊仿佯而逍遥兮③，永历年而无成。谁可与玩斯遗芳兮，晨向风而舒情。高阳邈以远兮，余将焉所程。

【注释】

①天时：天道运行的规律，亦指时序。代序：时序相代。
②耀灵：太阳的别称，亦喻指帝王。晔(yè)：闪闪发光。
③仿佯(páng yáng)：同"彷徉"，彷徨，徜徉，徘徊。

【译文】

担心岁月流逝啊，太阳闪闪发光向西下行。薄薄的秋霜降下而沉沦啊，伤悼香草最先凋零。我姑且徘徊聊以散心啊，年复一年却事业无成。谁能和我同赏这残留的芳草啊？清晨迎着清风舒怀心情。古帝高阳离我已太邈远啊，我将如何承继他的风轨？

重曰①：春秋忽其不淹兮，奚久留此故居②？轩辕不可攀援兮③，吾将从王乔而娱戏④！餐六气而饮沆瀣兮⑤，漱正阳而含朝霞⑥。保神明之清澄兮，精气入而麤秽除⑦。顺凯风以从游兮⑧，至南巢而壹息⑨。见王子而宿之兮，审壹气之和德⑩。

【注释】

①重：表示动作行为的重复，相当于"再""又""重新"。这里应该是乐章歌节的名称，如同"乱曰""少歌曰""倡曰"之类。
②奚(xī)：为何，为什么。
③轩辕：古代帝王黄帝的名字，传说姓公孙，居于轩辕之丘，故名曰轩辕。曾战胜炎帝于阪泉，战胜蚩尤于涿鹿，诸侯尊为天子。后人以之为中华民族的始祖。

④王乔：传说中的仙人，传说是周灵王太子晋，即王子乔。
⑤六气：大约是指朝旦之气（朝霞）、日中之气（正阳）、日没之气（飞泉）、夜半之气（沆瀣）、天之气、地之气。沆瀣（hàng xiè）：夜间的水气、露水，或谓是仙人所饮。
⑥漱：吮吸，饮。正阳：日中之气。
⑦麤（cū）秽：粗浊污秽之气。
⑧凯风：和暖的风，指南风。
⑨南巢：南方古国名。壹息：稍稍歇息一下。
⑩壹气：元气，纯一不杂之气。和德：大约指一种高妙的修养境界。汪瑗《楚辞集解》："和德，言正气之中和也。"

【译文】

又说：春去秋来光阴不停留啊，又何必长久滞留此故地？圣君轩辕不可攀附相援啊，我将跟随王子乔嬉戏游赏。吞食天地六气而啜饮清露啊，吸着正阳之气含着朝霞的芬芳。保持精神心灵清明澄澈啊，把精气吸入把浊气排弃。我乘着南风到处游历啊，到了南巢国稍作休息。看见王子乔我且停下脚步啊，向他询问成仙之道。

曰：道可受兮①，不可传②；其小无内兮，其大无垠；无滑而魂兮③，彼将自然④；壹气孔神兮⑤，于中夜存；虚以待之兮，无为之先；庶类以成兮⑥，此德之门。

【注释】

①受：心领神会。
②传：说，描述，用语言表达。
③滑（gǔ）：乱。而：你。
④彼：即上面的"魂"。自然：天然，非人为。

⑤孔：甚，很。
⑥庶类：万物，万类。

【译文】

王子乔说："道"只可以心领神会啊，却无法口说言传；它小到不能再分啊，大到没有边缘；不要搅乱你的神魂啊，它自然而然地就会出现；这一元之气非常神秘啊，往往在半夜寂静之时留存；请虚心安静等待着它啊，不要先有接物的心愿；万物都是这样生成啊，这就是得道的法门。

闻至贵而遂徂兮①，忽乎吾将行。仍羽人于丹丘兮②，留不死之旧乡。朝濯发于汤谷兮③，夕晞余身兮九阳④。吸飞泉之微液兮⑤，怀琬琰之华英⑥。玉色频以脕颜兮⑦，精醇粹而始壮⑧。质销铄以汋约兮⑨，神要眇以淫放⑩。嘉南州之炎德兮⑪，丽桂树之冬荣⑫。山萧条而无兽兮，野寂漠其无人⑬。载营魄而登霞兮⑭，掩浮云而上征⑮。命天阍其开关兮⑯，排阊阖而望予⑰。召丰隆使先导兮⑱，问大微之所居⑲。集重阳入帝宫兮⑳，造旬始而观清都㉑。

【注释】

①至贵：非常珍贵，即要言妙道。徂：往，去。
②仍：因，就此。羽人：神话传说中的仙人。丹丘：传说中神仙所居之地，或谓其地昼夜常明。
③濯（zhuó）：洗。汤（yáng）谷：即旸谷，古代神话传说中日出之处。
④晞（xī）：晒干，曝晒。九阳：古时传说旸谷有扶桑树，上枝有一个太阳，下枝有九个太阳，十个太阳轮流值班一天。
⑤飞泉：谷名，即飞谷，在昆仑西南。微液：微，细微，精

细。液,汁液。
⑥琬琰(wǎn yǎn):泛指美玉。华英:这里指玉的精华。
⑦颒(pīng):面色光润。腕(wàn):有光泽,美好。
⑧醇粹:精纯不杂,纯粹完美。
⑨质:这里指凡庸、世俗的形体、形质。销铄(shuò):消亡,熔化。汋(chuò)约:绰约,姿态柔媚。
⑩要眇(miào):精深微妙。淫放:这里形容精神充沛旺盛。
⑪南州:泛指南方地区。炎德:火德。阴阳家将东、西、南、北、中分属五行,南方属火,故称。
⑫丽:与"嘉"互文见义,都是"赞美"的意思。
⑬寂漠:同"寂寞"。
⑭营魄:魂魄。
⑮掩:遮没,遮蔽。这里指被云气缭绕覆盖。上征:向上飞升。
⑯天阍(hūn):天帝的守门人。关:本指门闩。《说文·门部》:"关,以木横持门户也。"这里指门。
⑰阊阖(chāng hé):神话传说中的天门。
⑱丰隆:古代神话中的雷神,后多作雷的代称。一说云神。
⑲大微:亦作"太微",古代星名,神话传说中天庭之所在。
⑳重阳:指天。
㉑旬始:星名。清都:神话传说中天帝居住的宫阙。

【译文】

听了至理妙言就想前往啊,匆匆忙忙我就起程。跟随仙人到达丹丘仙境啊,停留在神仙的不死之乡。早晨在汤谷洗洗头发啊,傍晚在九阳之中晒干我的全身。吸饮昆仑飞泉的美液啊,怀抱美玉的精华。我的面色如玉光泽鲜润啊,精神纯美气息渐强。凡胎脱尽而显得柔美啊,神气幽远而精神充沛。赞美南国气候温暖啊,赞美桂树冬天也吐芬芳。山林萧条没有野兽啊,原野寂静不见人踪。载着魂魄登上彩霞啊,拥披着浮云而飞升。我叫帝宫门神打开天门啊,他推开大门朝我打量。我招来丰隆作我的先导啊,访问天庭太微星所在的地方。升上九天进帝宫游览啊,造访旬始星参观天庭清都。

朝发轫于太仪兮①,夕始临乎于微闾②。屯余车之万乘兮,纷溶与而并驰③。驾八龙之婉婉兮,载云旗之逶蛇④。建雄虹之采旄兮⑤,五色杂而炫耀⑥。服偃蹇以低昂兮⑦,骖连蜷以骄骜⑧。骑胶葛以杂乱兮⑨,斑漫衍而方行⑩。撰余辔而正策兮,吾将过乎句芒⑪。历太皓以右转兮⑫,前飞廉以启路⑬。阳杲杲其未光兮⑭,凌天地以径度。风伯为余先驱兮,氛埃辟而清凉。凤皇翼其承旂兮⑮,遇蓐收乎西皇⑯。擥慧星以为旍兮⑰,举斗柄以为麾⑱。叛陆离其上下兮⑲,游惊雾之流波。时暧曃其曭莽兮⑳,召玄武而奔属㉑。后文昌使掌行兮㉒,选署众神以并毂㉓。路曼曼其修远兮,徐弭节而高厉㉔。左雨师使径侍兮,右雷公以为卫。欲度世以忘归兮㉕,意恣睢以担挢㉖。内欣欣而自美兮,聊媮娱以自乐㉗。涉青云以汎滥游兮㉘,忽临睨夫旧乡㉙。仆夫怀余心悲兮,边马顾而不行。思旧故以想像兮㉚,长太息而掩涕。氾容与而遐举兮㉛,聊抑志而自弭。指炎神而直驰兮㉜,吾将往乎南疑㉝。

【注释】

①发轫(rèn):拿掉支住车轮的木头,使车前进。借指出发、起程。太仪:天帝的宫廷。
②于微闾:神话传说中的山名,在东北方,盛产美玉,即所谓"医巫闾",也叫"微母闾"。
③溶与:即"容与",迟缓不进。

④逶蛇(wēi yí):同"逶迤",形容车旗迎风飘扬的样子。
⑤雄虹:古人认为彩虹由两部分组成,外侧较鲜艳的部分称为虹,属雄性;内侧较暗较少光彩的部分称为霓,属雌性。采旄(máo):用旄牛尾装饰的彩旗。
⑥炫燿:闪耀,光彩夺目。燿,同"耀"
⑦服:古代一车驾四马,居中的两匹称服。偃蹇(jiǎn):形容马匹高大矫健。低昂:起伏,这里就马奔跑时的状况与姿态而言。
⑧骖(cān):驾车时位于两边的马。连蜷:这里形容骖马矫健、健美。骄骜:纵恣奔驰。
⑨骑:指车马。胶葛:交错纷乱的样子。
⑩斑:这里形容车骑排列得缤纷盛多而显得错杂的样子。漫衍:绵延伸展的样子。方行:并行,一齐前行。方,合并,并在一起。
⑪句(gōu)芒:古代神话传说中的主木之官。又为木神名。
⑫太皓:即"太皞",传说中古帝名。
⑬飞廉:风神。启路:开路。
⑭杲杲(gǎo):明亮。
⑮旂(qí):古代画有两龙并在竿头悬铃的旗。
⑯蓐(rù)收:古代神话传说中的西方神名,司秋。西皇:古代神话传说中西方的尊神。
⑰旌(jīng):亦作"旍",古代用牦牛尾以及五彩羽饰竿头的旗子。
⑱斗柄:北斗柄。指北斗的第五至第七星,即玉衡、开泰、摇光。北斗,第一至第四星像斗,第五至第七像柄。麾(huī):古代用以指挥军队的旗帜,后又成为宫廷演奏音乐时的指挥工具。
⑲叛:纷繁。

⑳曖曃(ài dài)：昏暗不明的样子。瞠(tǎng)莽：晦暗朦胧的样子。
㉑玄武：古代神话传说中的北方之神，其形为龟，或龟蛇合体。奔属(zhǔ)：追随，跟随。
㉒文昌：星座名，共六星，在斗魁之前，形成半月形状。亦指星神。掌行：带领从行的队伍，犹领队。
㉓选署：选择，部署安排。并毂(gǔ)：车辆并行。毂，车轮中心的圆木，周围与车辐的一端相接，中有圆孔，可以插轴。
㉔弭节：驻节，停车。高厉：上升，高高腾起。
㉕度世：犹"出世"，即超脱尘世为仙。
㉖恣睢(zì suī)：放任自得的样子。担挢(jiē jiāo)：高举。
㉗媮(yú)：同"愉"，乐。
㉘涉：徒步过河。汎滥游：四处漫游。
㉙临睨(nì)：俯视，察看。
㉚想像：想见其形象，即思念、缅怀、回忆的意思。
㉛遐举：远行，飞行。
㉜炎神：南方火神祝融。
㉝南疑：即九疑山，山在南方，故称。王逸《楚辞章句》："过衡山而观九疑也。"

【译文】

早晨从天宫出发啊，傍晚到达医巫闾山。万辆马车聚集一处啊，从容安详并驾向前。驾着八匹神骏迤逦而行啊，载着云旗飘扬飞动。竖起插着旄头绘有颜色鲜艳的雄虹的彩旗啊，五色缤纷光彩夺目。居中的马高大矫健俯仰自然啊，两边的马健壮而纵恣奔驰。车马参差交错杂乱啊，队列绵绵不绝并行向前。我抓紧缰绳握好马鞭啊，将经过那东方木神句芒。经过东帝太皓再向右转啊，让风伯飞廉在前开路。明亮的太阳尚未放射光芒啊，超越天地径直向前。风伯为我做车队的先驱啊，扫荡尘埃迎来清凉。凤凤的彩翼连接着云旗啊,在西帝那里遇见金神蓐收。摘下彗星充当旌旗啊,举起斗柄用以指挥。五色斑斓上下闪耀啊,在云海波涛中漫游流连。天色渐暗四周朦胧啊,我叫来玄武跟随相伴。让文昌在车后为我掌管行程啊,安排众神列驾前行。前方道路多么漫长遥远啊,我掌控车节缓缓驰向云天。左边让雨师相伴随侍啊,右边让雷公保驾扈从。想超脱尘世而忘却归去啊,放纵心志而高飞远举。我心中喜乐自认为美好啊,所以姑且娱戏以自乐。飞越层云漫游四面八方啊,忽然俯瞰到故乡田原。车夫感怀我心悲伤啊,车驾两侧的马也频频回望不肯向前。思念故友想见到他们啊,我长长叹息涕泪滂沱。从容泛游而逍遥远去啊,聊且抑制情感而自我宽慰。追寻南方火神径直奔驰啊,我将前往九疑山。

　　览方外之荒忽兮①,沛罔象而自浮②。祝融戒而还衡兮③,腾告鸾鸟迎宓妃④。张《咸池》奏《承云》兮⑤,二女御《九韶》歌⑥。使湘灵鼓瑟兮⑦,令海若舞冯夷⑧。玄螭虫象并出进兮⑨,形蟉虬而逶蛇⑩。雌蜺便娟以增挠兮⑪,鸾鸟轩翥而翔飞⑫。音乐博衍无终极兮⑬,焉乃逝以徘徊。舒并节以驰骛兮⑭,逴绝垠乎寒门⑮。轶迅风于清源兮⑯,从颛顼乎增冰⑰。历玄冥以邪径兮⑱,乘间维以反顾⑲。召黔嬴而见之兮⑳,为余先乎平路。经营四荒兮㉑,周流六漠㉒。上至列缺兮㉓,降望大壑㉔。下峥嵘而无地兮㉕,上寥廓而无天。视倏忽而无见兮㉖,听惝恍而无闻㉗。超无为以至清兮,与泰初而为邻㉘。

【注释】

①荒忽:形容朦胧恍惚的样子。
②沛(pèi):形容水流动的样子。罔(wǎng)象:本指水怪或水

神名。此处引申指水势盛大。

③祝融：神名，帝喾时的火官，后尊为火神，命曰祝融，亦以为火或火灾的代称。还衡：回车。衡，车辕前木，此指代车。

④腾告：传告。宓(fú)妃：神话传说中的洛水女神。

⑤《咸池》：古乐曲名。相传为尧乐。一说为黄帝之乐，尧增修沿用。一说为舜乐。《承云》：传说为黄帝乐曲。或曰是颛顼时乐曲。

⑥二女：这里指尧之二女，即娥皇、女英。御：侍奉弹奏，吹奏。《九韶》：亦作"九磬"、"九招"，舜时乐曲名。

⑦湘灵：古代神话传说中的湘水之神。

⑧海若：古代神话传说中的海神。冯(píng)夷：古代神话传说中的河神，即河伯。

⑨玄螭(chī)：玄，黑色。螭是龙一类的神物。虫象：一种水中生物，大约颇有灵异之处。

⑩蟉虬(liú qiú)：屈曲盘绕的样子。逶蛇：又写作"委蛇"、"逶迤"等，形容蜿蜒曲折的样子。与上面"蟉虬"意义相近。

⑪便(pián)娟：轻盈美好。挠：缠绕。

⑫轩翥(zhù)：高飞。

⑬音乐：古代音、乐有别。《礼记·乐记》："音之起，由人心生也。人心之动，物使之然也，感于物而动，故形于声。声相应，故生变，变成方谓之音。比音而乐之，及干戚、羽旄，谓之乐。"博衍：这里形容乐声博大广远、舒展绵延的样子。

⑭并节：两两相并的马鞭。驰骛(wù)：疾驰，快跑。

⑮逴(chuō)：远。绝垠：极远的地方。寒门：古代神话传说中北方极寒冷的地方。

⑯轶(yì)：本义是后车超前车。引申为超越。迅风：疾风。清源：指北极寒风的源头，传说中的八风之府。

⑰颛顼(zhuān xū)：上古帝王名，"五帝"之一，号高阳氏。

增冰：层层积累的冰雪，乃北方严寒景象。
⑱玄冥：北方水神。邪径：斜路，弯路。
⑲间维：指天地之间。古称天有六间，地有四维，故称。
⑳黔嬴(qián yíng)：造化之神。
㉑经营：周遍往来。四荒：四方荒远之地。
㉒周流：遍游，四处游观。六漠：犹"六幕"、"六合"，指天地四方。
㉓列缺：亦作"列缺"，指高空中闪电所显现的空隙。
㉔大壑(hè)：大海。
㉕峥嵘：深远，深邃。
㉖儵(shū)忽：这里形容看不清楚。儵，同"倏"。
㉗惝怳(chǎng huǎng)：这里形容听起来模糊不清。
㉘泰初：道家指天地未分之前的混沌元气，后亦指天地形成前的时期。

【译文】

遥览世外浩渺无垠啊，我仿佛在汪洋大海里上下浮游。火神祝融劝告我掉转车头啊，我传告鸾鸟去迎接宓妃。张设《咸池》之乐，演奏《承云》之曲啊，娥皇、女英奏起《九韶》之歌。让湘水之神敲奏瑟乐啊，让海神与河神共同跳舞。黑龙与水怪一起戏乐啊，形体屈曲婉转自如。彩虹轻盈层层环绕啊，青鸾神鸟高翔飞舞。音乐宏博没有终止啊，我于是远去周游徘徊。放松缰绳任马狂奔啊，远到天边北极的冰寒之地。超越急风来到清气之源啊，跟随颛顼到达冰天雪地之所。通过水神的崎岖小路啊，在天地之间顾盼不已。召唤造化之神前来相见啊，叫他为我先行铺平道路。我往来四方荒凉之地啊，周游六合广漠之境。向上直触闪电之至高空隙啊，向下俯瞰大海之至深。下面高远深邃不见大地啊，上面辽阔空远不见苍天。模模糊糊什么也看不见啊，恍恍惚惚什么也听不清。超越无为清静的境界啊，和太初原始结伴为邻。

楚辞

卜 居

【题解】

"卜",问卜;"居",居处。卜居即"谓所以自处之方"(蒋骥《山带阁注楚辞》)的意思。古人以占卜决疑,"卜居"就是说通过占卜,来解决自己"何去何从"的疑惑,即该采取怎样的态度来对待社会现实。

关于本篇的作者至今多有争议,王逸说:"《卜居》者,屈原之所作也。屈原履忠贞之性,而见嫉妒。念谗佞之臣,承君顺非,而蒙富贵。己执忠直,而身放弃,心迷意惑,不知所为。乃往至太卜之家,稽问神明,决之蓍龟,卜己居世何所宜行,冀闻异策,以定嫌疑。故曰《卜居》也。"这段话很好地解释了作者及题义,历代无异辞。至清人崔述乃认为是"假托成文",此说在学术界一直颇有争议。近现代一些楚辞研究者,如郭沫若、游国恩、陆侃如等人均认同"伪作说",以致许多文学史都将《卜居》、《渔父》排除在屈赋之外。但陈子展《楚辞直解》将"伪作说"的各种理由一一驳斥推翻,辩之甚详。姜亮夫、汤炳正、蒋天枢等人亦持赞同看法。本书认为在没有新材料出现来"证伪"之前,仍当以传统说法为是。

本篇采用散文笔法叙述,通篇一连提出十几个问题来卜问处世方式,表达了屈原对黑暗现实的激愤和抗争、对美善的坚持和对丑恶的弃绝,以及对人生态度的选择及选择之后的痛苦心情。

事实上,屈原并无待决之疑,他的选择取舍,早已通过问话一目了然。最后郑詹尹的回答也极富哲理警策,"夫尺有所短,寸有所长,物有所不足,智有所不明",这是对屈原的开导、安慰,让其顺应自然,于顺应中找方法,于自然中觅出路。这种问答体常为后人称颂,被视为后世辞赋杂文宾主问答体的滥觞。

屈原既放,三年不得复见。竭知尽忠①,而蔽鄣于谗②。心烦虑乱,不知所从。往见太卜郑詹尹曰③:"余有所疑,愿因先生决之④。"詹尹乃端策拂龟⑤,曰:"君将何以教之⑥?"屈原曰:"吾宁悃悃款款朴以忠乎⑦?将送往劳来斯无穷乎⑧?宁诛锄草茅以力耕乎?将游大人以成名乎?宁正言不讳以危身乎?将从俗富贵以媮生乎⑨?宁超然高举以保真乎⑩?将哫訾栗斯⑪,喔咿儒儿以事妇人乎⑫?宁廉洁正直以自清乎?将突梯滑稽⑬,如脂如韦⑭,以洁楹乎⑮?宁昂昂若千里之驹乎?将氾氾若水中之凫乎⑯,与波上下,偷以全吾躯乎?宁与骐骥亢轭乎⑰?将随驽马之迹乎?宁与黄鹄比翼乎⑱?将与鸡鹜争食乎⑲?此孰吉孰凶?何去何从?世溷浊而不清,蝉翼为重,千钧为轻⑳;黄钟毁弃㉑,瓦釜雷鸣㉒;谗人高张㉓,贤士无名。吁嗟默默兮㉔,谁知吾之廉贞!"詹尹乃释策而谢,曰:"夫尺有所短,寸有所长,物有所不足,智有所不明,数有所不逮㉕,神有所不通。用君之心,行君之意,龟策诚不能知事㉖。"

【注释】

①知:同"智",智慧,才干。

②蔽鄣：遮蔽，阻挠。蔽，雍塞，蒙蔽。鄣，通"障"，阻塞。
③太卜：古代官名，周时属春官，为卜官之长。郑詹尹：太卜的姓名。一说郑，表示郑国，或即是姓；詹，即"占"，占卜、占筮的意思；尹，官名。
④因：通过，凭借，依靠。决：分辨，判断。
⑤端：摆放整齐。策：古代卜筮用的蓍草。龟：龟甲，古代用作占卜之具。
⑥教：告诉。
⑦宁：宁可，宁愿，愿意，想做。悃悃(kǔn)款款：忠诚勤勉的样子。朴：本性，本质。
⑧送往：送别去者。劳来：慰问、劝勉归服的人。来，归服，此指归服的人。
⑨媮(tōu)生：苟且求活，无所作为地生活。
⑩超然：形容远走高飞、遗世独立的样子。高举：远离尘嚣，这里指退隐山林。
⑪哫訾(zú zī)：阿谀奉承。栗斯：献媚之态。
⑫喔咿(wō yī)：献媚强笑的样子。儒儿：强颜欢笑的样子。
⑬突梯滑(gǔ)稽：委婉从顺，圆滑随俗。
⑭韦：本指熟牛皮，此处意为"柔软"。
⑮楹(yíng)：厅堂的前柱。
⑯氾氾：飘浮、浮行的样子。亦作"汎汎"。凫(fú)：野鸭。乎：一本无"乎"字，当从之。
⑰亢轭(kàng è)：齐驱并驾。
⑱黄鹄(hú)：鸟名，这里喻指高才贤士。
⑲鸡鹜(wù)：鸡和鸭，这里喻指小人或平庸的人。
⑳千钧：代表最重的东西。古制三十斤为一钧。
㉑黄钟：古乐中十二律之一，是最响最宏大的声调。这里指声调合于黄钟律的大钟。

㉒瓦釜：陶制的锅，这里代表鄙俗音乐。
㉓高张：居高位而嚣张跋扈。
㉔吁嗟(xū jiē)：感慨，叹息。默默：形容无话可说的样子。
㉕不逮：比不上，不及。
㉖知事：一作"知此事"，当从之。

【译文】

屈原已经遭到放逐，三年没有再见到楚王。他竭尽智慧与忠诚，却因小人的逸言而受到冤蔽。心中烦闷，思虑烦乱，不知应该怎么办。就去拜访太卜郑詹尹，屈原说："我心里有所疑虑，特请教先生帮我决断。"詹尹就摆好占卜用的蓍草，拂拭灵龟，说："不知您想说什么事？"屈原说："我应该诚实勤恳、朴实忠厚呢，还是无休无止地应酬、周旋？我是应该锄草铲田过此一生，还是游说权贵求取功名？应该忠言直谏奋不顾身，还是追求富贵苟且偷生？应该超然世外保持真性，还是像取媚妇人一样奴颜婢膝？应该廉洁正直洁身自处，还是圆滑世故，如油脂滑腻，似熟牛皮柔能缠柱？应该气宇轩昂像矫健的千里马，还是浮游不定像水中的野鸭为保全性命而随波逐流？应该与骏马并驾齐驱，还是跟劣马亦步亦趋？应该与黄鹄比翼齐飞，还是和鸡鸭一道争食？这些事哪个吉利，哪个凶险？哪样不能做，哪样可以干？这世道浑浊，是非不清，薄薄的蝉翼被认为很重，千钧之物却被认为太轻；音响宏亮的黄钟被毁坏抛弃，鄙俗的瓦釜却作乐器雷鸣震天；谗佞小人嚣张跋扈，贤能之士则默默无名。不说了吧，谁了解我的廉洁忠贞！"詹尹于是放下筹策辞谢，说："一尺有嫌它太短之处，一寸有觉其太长之时，万物都有不足之处，智者也有不懂的地方，卦数有时会推算不到，神灵的法力也有所不至。就随您的心意而为，龟卜蓍占实在不能料知此事。"

楚辞

渔 父

【题解】

关于本篇作者，王逸曰："《渔父》者，屈原之所作也。屈原放逐，在江湘之间，忧愁叹吟，仪容变易。而渔父避世隐身，钓鱼江滨，欣然自乐。时遇屈原川泽之域，怪而问之，遂相应答。楚人思念屈原，因叙其辞以相传焉。"后人基本采用屈原所作之说，如朱熹《楚辞集注》称："《渔父》者，屈原之所作也。渔父盖亦当时遁隐之士。或曰亦原之设词耳。"蒋骥《山带阁注楚辞》称："或云此亦原之寓言。然太史公采入本传，则未必非实录也。"因此传统说法并不怀疑屈原创作的真实性。清代崔述较早提出本篇为伪作，姜亮夫《屈原赋校注》予以驳斥说："至近世崔述以庾信《枯树赋》之称桓大司马，谢惠连《雪赋》之称相如，因以定《渔父》《卜居》之称屈原为假托成文。假托成文，固亦《庄子》寓言之例，而尤以为辞赋家之常事；……史公非可以伪托欺者也，何以尚录之本传？又沧浪之歌明载乎《孟子》，其为江汉民间流行之曲，能假为《渔父》之文者，未必不读《孟子》，而渔父之歌之可供采择者亦至多，托伪者乃不之采，而取孺子所歌，大义与上文了不相属，又未必为渔者至高之境界，此不为当时直录所历，不计巧拙，亦将无以解于此疑。"所辨甚明，故本书亦从旧说，以之为屈原所作。

渔父

《渔父》是篇思想性和可读性很强的优美辞篇。因屈原遭楚王放逐,心情沮丧、形容枯槁,在漫步江畔、且歌且行之际,遇到渔父。渔父见屈原憔悴不堪,便向屈原发出两个疑问:一问其身份,二问其如此落魄的原因,由此引出屈原的答话。通过屈原与渔父的问答,揭示了屈原的处世态度,表现了他洁身自好、不与世俗同流合污的节操以及不惜舍生取义的精神。而渔父是位主张"与世推移"、高蹈遁世、游戏人生的隐者,明王夫之云:"江汉之间,古多高蹈之士,隐于耕钓,若接舆、庄周之流,皆以全身远害为道,渔父盖其类也。"(《楚辞通释》)他随俗俯仰、与时浮沉的处世思想与屈原形成强烈的对比:一方面是屈原面对黑暗现实执著坚守自己清白高洁的人格精神和宁可抛弃珍贵的生命也决不与污秽尘俗同流合污的决心;一方面是渔父看透尘世纷扰而恬淡自安、随性自适、寄情于自然、乐天知命的隐者劝诫。全诗在对比中进行问答,简短而凝练地塑造出两种对立的人生态度和处世哲学。

有意思的是,后人对《渔父》的推崇一般都撇开了"三闾大夫"的洁身自好的人格理想,却偏偏钟情于过着萧散自由生活的"渔父"。如洪兴祖《楚辞补注》说:"《卜居》《渔父》,皆假设问答以寄意耳,而大史公《屈原传》、刘向《新序》、嵇康《高士传》或采《楚词》《庄子》渔父之言以为实录,非也。"姑不论洪氏以来以为《渔父》非实录的观点如何,他的这一段评价倒反映出《卜居》《渔父》对汉魏以来文人的影响。像晋人王胡之在《与庾安西笺》中要求宽政说:"百姓投一纶、下一筌者,皆夺其渔器。不输十疋,则不得放。不知漆园吏何得持竿不顾,渔父鼓枻而歌沧浪也。"(《全晋文》卷二〇)从中可以看出他们对"渔父"生活方式的向往。至如唐宋以来,歌咏"渔父"的诗文则更多。如北宋范仲淹有《出守桐庐道中》诗云："笑解尘缨处，沧浪无限清。"南宋严羽自名诗话为《沧浪诗话》，且在开篇《诗辨》中称学会作诗前"先须熟读楚辞，朝夕讽咏以为之本"，足以看出屈骚对其的影响。另外，《渔父》对七言诗的发轫及发展也有一定影响。明徐祯卿《谈艺录》即称："七言始起，咸曰柏梁。然宁戚扣牛，已肇《南山》之篇矣。其为则也，声长字纵，易以成文。故蕴气雕词，与五言略异。要而论之：《沧浪》擅其奇，《柏梁》宏其质，《四愁》坠其隽，《燕歌》开其靡。"其虽仅指《沧浪》数句，但它却是《渔父》整篇必不可少的一部分，故亦可以说《渔父》是七言诗嬗变过程中必不可缺的一环。

屈原既放，游于江潭，行吟泽畔，颜色憔悴①，形容枯槁②。渔父见而问之曰③："子非三闾大夫与④？何故至于斯？"屈原曰："举世皆浊我独清⑤，众人皆醉我独醒⑥，是以见放。"渔父曰："圣人不凝滞于物⑦，而能与世推移。世人皆浊，何不淈其泥而扬其波⑧？众人皆醉，何不餔其糟而歠其醨⑨？何故深思高举⑩，自令放为？"屈原曰："吾闻之：新沐者必弹冠⑪，新浴者必振衣⑫。安能以身之察察⑬，受物之汶汶者乎⑭？宁赴湘流，葬于江鱼之腹中。安能以皓皓之白，而蒙世俗之尘埃乎？"渔父莞尔而笑⑮，鼓枻而去⑯。

【注释】

①颜色：面容，脸色，气色。
②形容：形态，容貌。枯槁：这里是形容清瘦的样子。
③渔父(fǔ)：打鱼的老人。父，对老年男子的尊称。这里的渔父是隐士的化身。

④三闾大夫：楚国官职名，掌管教育楚国王族屈、景、昭三姓宗族子弟。
⑤举世皆浊我独清：浊、清，指品德行为而言。汪瑗《楚辞集解》："清，比己之洁，而浊比世之秽也。"王夫之《楚辞通释》："没于宠利曰浊。"
⑥众人皆醉我独醒：醉、醒，指对楚国形势的认识而言。蒋骥《山带阁注楚辞》："昧于危亡曰醉。"蒋天枢《楚辞校释》："醒，己虽处沉昏之世，仍有所灼见。"
⑦凝滞：拘泥，固执。
⑧淈(gǔ)：搅混，扰乱。
⑨餔(bū)其糟：本义指吃酒糟，比喻为屈志从俗，随波逐流。《说文·米部》："糟，酒滓也。"歠(chuò)其醨(lí)：本义指饮薄酒，比喻为随波逐流，从俗浮沉。歠，饮，喝。醨，通"漓"，薄酒。
⑩深思：思虑很深，即"独醒"。高举：高出流俗，即"独清"。
⑪沐：洗头。《说文·水部》："沐，濯发也。"弹(tán)冠：弹去冠上的灰尘，整冠。
⑫浴：洗澡。振衣：抖衣去灰尘。
⑬察察：清洁，洁白的样子。
⑭汶汶(mén)：玷辱、污浊的样子。
⑮莞(wǎn)尔：形容微笑的样子。
⑯鼓枻(yì)：亦作"鼓栧"，划桨泛舟。

【译文】

屈原被流放以后，在江边游荡独行，他一边行走一边吟哦，面容憔悴，模样枯瘦。有位打鱼的老人看见他，便问道："您不是三闾大夫吗？为什么会沦落到这步田地？"屈原答道："世上的人都混浊，只有我清白；大家都醉了，只有我清醒着，因此被放逐。"渔父问："有圣德的人不被事物所束缚，而能随着世道一起变化推进。既然世上的人都混浊，你何不搅混泥水，扬起浊波？既然大家都醉了，你何不吃酒糟，喝薄酒？为什么要思虑深远，行为高尚，使自己被放逐？"屈原说："我曾听到古人说：刚洗过头的人一定要弹弹帽子上的灰尘，刚洗好澡的人一定要整理一下衣服。怎能让清白无比的身体，沾染上污秽不堪的外物？我宁愿跳入湘江，葬身鱼腹。怎能让洁白纯净之身，蒙上世俗的尘泥？"渔父听了，微微一笑，摇起船桨动身离去。

歌曰："沧浪之水清兮①，可以濯吾缨；沧浪之水浊兮，可以濯吾足。"遂去，不复与言。

【注释】

① "沧浪之水清兮"以下四句：以上渔父所唱的《沧浪歌》，亦名《孺子歌》，又见于《孟子·离娄上》，可能是流传于江湘一带的古歌谣。沧浪，古水名。有汉水、汉水之别流、汉水之下流、夏水诸说。濯(zhuó)：洗涤。缨：系冠的带子，以二组系于冠，结在颔下。

【译文】

唱道："沧浪之水清又清啊，可以洗我的帽缨；沧浪之水浊又浊啊，可以洗我的双脚。"渔父于是远去，不再和屈原说话。

宋玉

九 辩

【题解】

本篇为宋玉的代表作。宋玉，楚人，生卒年代不详，关于他的生平行状，《史记·屈原贾生列传》说："屈原既死之后，楚有宋玉、唐勒、景差之徒者，皆好辞而以赋见称。然皆祖屈原之从容辞令，终莫敢直谏。"其他如《韩诗外传》卷七"第十七章"、《新序·杂事》等零星记载了他与楚襄王的一些事迹，看来他有类似文学侍臣一样的身份，余不可考。据《离骚》、《天问》、《山海经·大荒西经》的说法，《九辩》与《九歌》一样，也是夏启从天上带来的乐曲，实为古乐曲名，宋玉是借用其名而自铸新词。"九辩"是"九阕"或"九遍"的意思，是指由若干乐章组合而成的一种曲调。自王逸以下，一般认为《九辩》是宋玉哀怜其师屈原而代为作词，这未免有些牵强。

《九辩》是继《离骚》之后又一首自述性长篇抒情诗。作品以衰败的楚国社会现实为背景，通过叙经历、叹遭际、抒情志，以悲秋、思君为主题，表现了诗人忧国、忠君的高尚节操，从中反映出的社会状况及个人忧思具有很强的时代感和民族性。

《九辩》开篇即把萧瑟的秋景与贫士的遭际联系起来加以细致描摹，接着反复抒写悲秋的原因，将个人不能为世所用的孤独感与绵长不尽的悲哀倾注其间。诗人清醒地认识到楚国君臣的腐败无能，他不愿顺从世俗，丢弃自己的人格与尊严，为不受世俗污染，诗人欲远走高飞，然而，现实社会中，秋天仍然草木凋落，贫士依旧难为世用。通过现实与想象的强烈对比，把悲秋主题渲染得淋漓尽致，给读者带来悲怆的情感冲击。

《九辩》是宋玉的代表作，全诗各章既各有宗旨，又彼此关联，整体结构精美。其中秋景的描绘历来脍炙人口，成为后世学习典范。如汉武帝《秋风辞》、曹植《秋思赋》、曹丕《燕歌行》等无不从"萧瑟兮草木摇落而变衰，憭慄兮若在远行，登山临水兮送将归，沆寥兮天高而气清"中汲取语源和灵感。当然，《九辩》中还有很多屈骚的影子，这反映出宋玉对屈原作品的借鉴和模仿。如"圜凿而方枘兮，吾固知其鉏铻而难入"句，即从《离骚》"不量凿而正枘兮"及"何方圜之能周兮"两句发展而来；又"尧舜之抗行兮，瞭冥冥而薄天。何险之嫉妒兮，被以不慈之伪名"亦明显化自《哀郢》"尧舜之抗行兮，瞭杳杳而薄天。众谗人之嫉妒兮，被以不慈之伪名"；又"憎愠怆之修美兮，好夫人之慷慨。众踥蹀而日进兮，美超远而逾迈"与《哀郢》相比，除"慷"作"忼"外，竟四句全同。这些均说明《九辩》与屈骚是一脉相承，乃至水乳交融的。

悲哉秋之为气也！萧瑟兮草木摇落而变衰①，憭慄兮若在远行②，登山临水兮送将归，沆寥兮天高而气清③，宋廖兮收潦而水清④，憯悽增欷兮薄寒之中人⑤，怆怳懭悢兮⑥，去故而就新，坎廪兮贫士失职而志不平⑦，廓落兮羁旅而无友生⑧。惆怅兮而私自怜。燕翩翩其辞归兮⑨，蝉寂漠而无声⑩。雁廱廱而南游兮⑪，鹍鸡啁哳而悲鸣⑫。独申旦而不寐兮，哀蟋蟀之宵征⑬。时亹亹而过中兮⑭，蹇淹留而无成⑮。

【注释】

①萧瑟：草木被秋风吹拂所发出的声音。

②憭慄(liáo lí)：亦作"憭栗"，形容凄凉的样子。

③泬寥(xuè liáo)：亦作"沉寥"、"泬寥"，形容晴朗空旷，天高气清的样子。

④宋崟(jì liáo)：清澄平静的样子。宋，即"寂"。潦(lǎo)：雨水，积水。

⑤憯(cǎn)悽：悲痛，感伤。欷(xī)：叹息。薄寒：秋天轻微的寒气。中(zhòng)：侵袭，伤害。

⑥怆怳(chuàng huǎng)：失意悲伤。怳悢(kuǎng lǎng)：失意怅惘。

⑦坎廩(lǐn)：坎坷不平，这里指困顿，不得志。

⑧廓(kuò)落：空虚孤寂。羁旅：作客异乡。羁，寄居在外。旅，旅行者。友生：友人，朋友。生，语缀，无实义。

⑨翩翩：飞行轻快的样子。

⑩宋(jì)漠：同"寂寞"。静默无声的意思。

⑪雝雝(yōng)：这里指雁鸣声。

⑫鹍(kūn)：鹍鸡，古代像鹤的一种鸟。啁哳(zhāo zhā)：形容声音烦杂而细碎。

⑬宵征：夜行。

⑭亹亹(wěi)：行进不停的样子。过中：过了中年，趋于老境。

⑮蹇(jiǎn)：发语词。淹留：滞留，久留。

【译文】

悲凉啊秋天！大地萧瑟啊草木在凋零陨落而衰黄，心中凄凉啊好像人在远行，又像登山临水送人踏上归程，空旷清朗啊天宇高远空气清爽，平静清澈啊积水消退水流澄清，凄凉叹息啊微寒袭人，恍惚惆怅啊离乡背井前往新地，世途坎坷啊贫士丢官心中不平，空虚孤独啊流落在外没有亲朋。失意悲伤啊自我怜悯。燕子翩翩辞北归南啊，寒蝉静寂没有声音。大雁鸣叫着向南飞翔啊，鹍鸡不住地啾啾悲鸣。独自通宵达旦难以入眠啊，蟋蟀的彻夜哀鸣勾起了我的悲伤。时光流逝已过了半生啊，仍然滞留在外而一事无成。

悲忧穷戚兮独处廓①，有美一人兮心不绎②。去乡离家兮徕远客③，超逍遥兮今焉薄④？专思君兮不可化，君不知兮可奈何！蓄怨兮积思，心烦憺兮忘食事⑤。愿一见兮道余意，君之心兮与余异。车既驾兮朅而归⑥，不得见兮心伤悲。倚结軨兮长太息⑦，涕潺湲兮下霑轼⑧。忼慨绝兮不得⑨，中瞀乱兮迷惑⑩。私自怜兮何极，心怦怦兮谅直⑪。

【注释】

①穷戚：困顿。戚，通"促"，迫促，局促。廓：空旷辽廓，这里指空虚寂寞的地方。
②绎(yì)：通"怿"，喜悦。
③徕(lái)：字同"来"，一本即作"来"。
④超：远。逍遥：这里指漂泊无依。
⑤烦憺(dàn)：烦闷忧愁。
⑥朅(qiè)：离去。
⑦结軨(líng)：车栏，古代车箱的前、左、右三面，用木条一横一竖交叉结成许多方格，形似窗棂。
⑧涕：眼泪。潺湲(chán yuán)：本指水流不断的样子，这里形容泪流不断。轼：古代设在车箱前供立乘者凭扶的横木。
⑨忼慨(kǎng kǎi)：激昂，愤激。
⑩瞀(mào)乱：昏乱，烦乱。

⑪怦怦(pēng)：心急的样子。

【译文】

悲愁困顿啊独处空寂大地，有一位美人啊心中郁结。远离家乡啊身为异客，漂泊无依啊去哪里？一心思念君王啊不可改变，君王不知道啊该怎么办？蓄满哀怨啊积满思虑，心中烦闷啊饭都不想吃。但愿见一面啊诉说我的心意，君王的心思啊却和我迥异。驾好马车啊驶去又返回，不得见君王啊伤悲郁悒。倚靠着车栏啊长长叹息，泪水涟涟啊沾湿车前的横木。愤激不平想决绝啊又做不到，心中烦乱啊心惑神迷。独自哀怜啊何时终了，忧心如焚啊诚实正直。

皇天平分四时兮①，窃独悲此廪秋②。白露既下百草兮，奄离披此梧楸③。去白日之昭昭兮，袭长夜之悠悠。离芳蔼之方壮兮④，余萎约而悲愁⑤。秋既先戒以白露兮，冬又申之以严霜。收恢台之孟夏兮⑥，然欿傺而沉藏⑦。叶菸邑而无色兮⑧，枝烦挐而交横⑨；颜淫溢而将罢兮⑩，柯仿佛而萎黄⑪；萷櫹椮之可哀兮⑫，形销铄而瘀伤⑬。惟其纷糅而将落兮⑭，恨其失时而无当⑮。擥骐辔而下节兮⑯，聊逍遥以相佯⑰。岁忽忽而遒尽兮⑱，恐余寿之弗将。悼余生之不时兮，逢此世之俇攘⑲。澹容与而独倚兮⑳，蟋蟀鸣此西堂。心怵惕而震荡兮㉑，何所忧之多方！卬明月而太息兮㉒，步列星而极明㉓。

【注释】

①皇天：对天及天神的尊称。
②窃(qiè)：私下，私自。多用作谦词。廪秋：犹言寒秋。廪，通"凛"，寒冷。

③奄(yǎn):快速。离披:形容树叶凋零,树枝扶疏的样子。梧楸(qiū):梧桐与楸树。二木皆逢秋而早凋。

④芳蔼:芳香而繁盛。

⑤萎约:萎靡而穷困。

⑥恢台:亦作"恢炱","恢胎",形容旺盛、广大的样子。

⑦然:与"焉"同,用为句首发端词。欿傺(kǎn chì):停止,敛藏。

⑧菸(yū)邑:因枯萎而呈黯淡之色。

⑨烦挐(rú):牵缠,纷乱。

⑩颜:形貌。淫溢:形容体貌枯槁瘦弱的样子。罢(pí):疲劳,衰弱。

⑪柯:草木的枝茎。彷彿:亦作"仿佛",犹模糊,指颜色不鲜明。

⑫萷(shāo):树梢。椮(xiāo sēn):形容树木光秃秃的样子。

⑬销铄:销毁,摧残。瘀(yū)伤:气血郁积成病。瘀,血液凝积。

⑭惟:思,想。纷糅:众多而杂乱。这里指枯枝败草相杂。

⑮恨:遗憾,痛惜。当(dāng):值,遇到。

⑯掔:抓住。骓(fēi)辔:指马缰。骓,驾在车辕两旁的马。辔,缰绳。下节:停鞭,使马徐行。

⑰相佯:亦作"相羊"、"相徉",徘徊,盘桓。

⑱忽忽:形容时光流逝之快。遒(qiú)尽:迫近于尽头,终了。遒,迫近。

⑲徰(kuāng)攘:纷乱不安的样子。

⑳澹(dàn):恬淡,淡泊。容与:闲散的样子。倚:凭靠。

㉑怵(chù)惕:亦作"怵愁",戒惧,惊惧。震荡:心神不定。

㉒卬(yǎng):同"仰",仰望,抬头向上。

㉓步:行走。列星:罗布天空,定时出现的恒星。

【译文】

皇上平分一年为四季啊,我独为这寒秋黯然悲伤。秋天的露水已经降落在百草上啊,衰黄的树叶瞬间飘离梧楸枝头。离别光明的白日啊,继之以漫漫的长夜。告别了壮年的繁茂芬芳啊,衰老困窘令我悲入愁肠。秋天先用白露来警示啊,冬天又加上层层寒霜。收尽了盛夏草木繁茂的景象啊,万物的生机都深深隐藏。叶子枯萎没有光彩啊,枝条纷乱杂错无章;色泽黯淡将要凋零啊,枝干枯朽已然干黄;树梢光秃秃令人悲怆啊,外形颓败似乎内有瘀伤。想到草木错杂将凋零啊,怅恨错失了美好时光。抓住缰绳停鞭徐行啊,姑且逍遥徘徊游荡。岁月匆匆流逝待尽啊,恐怕我的寿命也难以久长。伤感我生不逢时啊,遭逢这世道纷乱不宁。淡漠闲散独自靠立啊,听见蟋蟀在西堂哀鸣。内心忧惧而心神不定啊,为何百感交集如此忧伤!仰望明月长长叹息啊,徘徊在星光下直到天明。

窃悲夫蕙华之曾敷兮①,纷旖旎乎都房②。何曾华之无实兮,从风雨而飞飏③。以为君独服此蕙兮,羌无以异于众芳。闵奇思之不通兮④,将去君而高翔。心闵怜之惨悽兮,愿一见而有明。重无怨而生离兮⑤,中结轸而增伤⑥。岂不郁陶而思君兮⑦?君之门以九重⑧。猛犬狺狺而迎吠兮⑨,关梁闭而不通⑩。皇天淫溢而秋霖兮⑪,后土何时而得漧⑫!块独守此无泽兮⑬,仰浮云而永叹。

【注释】

①蕙华:蕙草的花。华,同"花"。曾(céng):通"层",重叠。敷:展布,开放。

②旖旎(yǐ nǐ)：盛多美好的样子。都：广大，美盛。
③飞飏(yáng)：飘扬，飘荡。
④闵：哀伤，怜念。后多作"悯"。
⑤重：深深思考。无怨：言行无可埋怨，即无罪。生离：被生生隔离，指被弃逐。
⑥结轸(zhěn)：形容内心忧思缠结、悲愁不已的样子。
⑦郁陶：形容忧思积聚的样子。
⑧九重：旧说天子之门有九重，此极言其深邃难进。洪兴祖《楚辞补注》："天子九门，谓关门、远郊门、近郊门、城门、皋门、库门、雉门、应门、路门也。"
⑨狺狺(yín)：犬吠声。
⑩关：本义为门闩，这里引申作"关塞"解。
⑪淫溢：过度，这里指久雨连绵。秋霖：秋日的淫雨。
⑫后土：本指土神，这里泛指土地，泥土。漧(gān)：同"乾"，干燥。
⑬块：孤独。无泽：荒芜的水泽。无，或为"芜"的借字。

【译文】

暗自悲叹那层叠开放的蕙花啊，繁盛娇美布满华美的宫殿。为何花朵累累却没有结果啊，随着风雨四处飘扬。原以为君王独爱佩带这蕙花啊，谁知在他眼里与众花没什么不同。伤心出众的谋略不能通达于君王啊，我将要离开君王远走他方。内心多么忧愁凄凉啊，希望见君王一面倾诉衷肠。念自己无罪却要被弃逐啊，内心郁结沉痛更加悲伤。哪能不忧思郁结思念君王啊？怎奈君门幽深重重关防。守门的猛犬迎面狂叫啊，关塞和桥梁都闭塞不通。上天降下连绵秋雨啊，大地何时才能干燥！独守在这荒芜的沼泽啊，仰望浮云长声哀叹。

九辩

何时俗之工巧兮，背绳墨而改错①！却骐骥而不乘兮②，策驽骀而取路③。当世岂无骐骥兮，诚莫之能善御。见执辔者非其人兮，故駉跳而远去④。凫雁皆唼夫梁藻兮⑤，凤愈飘翔而高举⑥。圜凿而方枘兮⑦，吾固知其鉏铻而难入⑧。众鸟皆有所登栖兮，凤独遑遑而无所集⑨。愿衔枚而无言兮⑩，尝被君之渥洽⑪。太公九十乃显荣兮⑫，诚未遇其匹合。谓骐骥兮安归？谓凤皇兮安栖？变古易俗兮世衰，今之相者兮举肥⑬。骐骥伏匿而不见兮，凤皇高飞而不下。鸟兽犹知怀德兮，何云贤士之不处⑭？骥不骤进而求服兮⑮，凤亦不贪馁而妄食⑯。君弃远而不察兮，虽愿忠其焉得？欲寂漠而绝端兮，窃不敢忘初之厚德。独悲愁其伤人兮，冯郁郁其何极⑰！霜露惨凄而交下兮，心尚吞其弗济⑱。霰雪雰糅其增加兮⑲，乃知遭命之将至。愿徼幸而有待兮⑳，泊莽莽与埜草同死㉑。愿自往而径游兮，路壅绝而不通㉒。欲循道而平驱兮，又未知其所从。然中路而迷惑兮，自压桉而学诵㉓。性愚陋以褊浅兮㉔，信未达乎从容㉕。

【注释】

①绳墨：本指木工画直线时用的墨斗、墨线，这里比喻规矩、法度。

②骐骥：骏马，这里比喻贤士。

③策：本义指马鞭，这里是驾驭、驱使的意思。驽骀（nú tāi）：劣马，喻庸人。

④駉（jú）跳：跳跃。

⑤凫雁：野鸭与大雁，有时单指大雁或野鸭。唼（shà）：水鸟或鱼吃食。粱：粟米。藻：植物名，指藻类植物，含叶绿素和其他辅助色素的低等植物。

⑥高举：高飞远去。这里有小人居位，贤者遁世的含义。

⑦圜：同"圆"。凿：榫眼，插孔。枘(ruì)：榫头。

⑧龃龉(jǔ yǔ)：亦作"龃吾"，互相抵触，格格不入。

⑨遑遑：匆忙，往来不定。这里形容凤凰无处可栖而不安的样子。集：鸟栖止于树。

⑩衔枚：原指横枚衔于口中，以防喧哗或叫喊。这里谓闭口不言。枚，形如筷子，两端有带，可系于颈上。

⑪被：蒙受，受到。渥(wò)洽：深厚的恩泽。

⑫太公：即太公望吕尚。

⑬相(xiàng)：看，观察。举肥：相马只选肥壮，这里讽刺当政者只根据表面现象来挑选人才。

⑭处(chǔ)：留，留下。

⑮骤进：疾速前进。服：驾车。

⑯餧(wèi)：喂养。妄：胡乱，随便。

⑰冯：通"凭"，愤懑。

⑱幸：同"幸"，希望。济：成功。

⑲霰(xiàn)：雪珠。雰(fēn)：雨雪纷飞的样子。糅：混杂。

⑳徼(jiǎo)幸：希望获得意外成功或由于偶然的原因而得到成功或免去灾害。徼，通"侥"。

㉑泊(bó)：留止，止息。莽莽：草类茂盛的样子。壄：同"野"。

㉒壅(yōng)绝：阻塞，断绝。

㉓压：克制，按捺。桉(àn)：通"按"，克制。学诵：学习写宜于读诵的韵文。

㉔褊(biǎn)浅：心地、见识等狭隘短浅。褊，原指衣服狭小，后泛称小。

㉕达：通晓，明白。从容：举动，行为。

【译文】

为什么时下风气是善于投机取巧啊，违背法度且改变正常的举措！拒绝骏马不去骑乘啊，却鞭赶劣马去上路。当世难道真的没有骏马啊，实在是没有人能好好驾御。看见拿缰绳的人不合适啊，骏马就会扬蹄飞奔而去。野鸭、大雁吞食着粟米水藻啊，凤凰则更加飘然高举。圆榫孔配上方榫头啊，我本来就知道两者相抵触而难以插入。群鸟都有了栖身之所啊，只有凤凰难寻安身之处。我本想闭口不语啊，但又难忘曾受君王深厚恩泽。姜太公九十岁才得显贵荣耀啊，实在是之前没遇上明主。良马啊归宿在哪里？凤凰啊栖息在何处？改变古风旧俗啊世道衰微，如今的相马人啊只看马的膘肥。骏马都藏匿起来不出现啊，凤凰都高高飞翔不落凡尘。鸟兽尚知道怀恩报德啊，怎能说贤士不肯留于仕途？骏马不会为了求进用而甘愿驾车啊，凤凰也不会贪图喂饲而乱吃。君王远弃贤士不能明察啊，贤士虽愿效忠又怎么能够？想自甘寂寞断绝对君王的眷恋之情啊，私下里又不敢忘记当初的恩德。独自悲愁多么伤人啊，满腔愤懑哪有终极！霜露齐降悲惨又凄清啊，心中还希望它们的破坏不会成功。雪珠雪花纷杂越下越大啊，才知道厄运即将要降临。想心存着侥幸再等待啊，却将与无边野草一同枯败。想径自前行畅游一番啊，道路阻塞断绝不能通行。想遵循大道平稳地驱驰啊，却又不知道何去何从。走到半路内心迷惑啊，只好克制情感作歌吟诵。本性愚笨孤陋而又狭隘肤浅啊，实在不知道如何行事。

　　窃美申包胥之气盛兮^①，恐时世之不固。何时俗之工巧兮？灭规矩而改凿^②。独耿介而不随兮，愿慕先圣之遗教。处浊世而显荣兮^③，非余心之所乐。与其无义而有名兮，宁穷处而守高^④。食不媮而为饱兮^⑤，衣不苟而为温^⑥。窃慕诗人之遗风兮^⑦，愿托志乎素餐^⑧。蹇充倔而无端兮^⑨，泊莽莽而无垠⑩。无衣裘以御冬兮，恐溘死不得见乎阳春⑪。

【注释】

①窃美：私下、暗自赞美。美，称赞，赞美。申包胥：春秋时楚国大夫。公元前506年冬天，吴国伐楚，占领郢都，楚昭王逃到随国。申包胥到秦国请派救兵，在宫廷上痛哭七昼夜，终于感动秦哀公出兵救楚，使昭王复国。
②规矩：画圆形和方形的工具，比喻法度。凿：当作"错"。错，通"措"，措施，法度。
③显荣：显赫荣耀，多指仕宦而言。
④穷处(chǔ)：穷，处境艰难、困窘。处，居。高：清高，高尚。
⑤媮(tōu)：苟且，怠惰。
⑥苟：随便，马虎，不审慎。
⑦诗人：指前代的先贤圣哲们。遗风：前代或前人遗留下来的风教。
⑧素餐：本指无功受禄，不劳而食，这里指俭朴的饮食。
⑨蹇：通"謇"，句首发语词。充倔：断绝阻塞。
⑩泊莽莽：无边无际。
⑪溘(kè)：突然。

【译文】

暗自赞美申包胥志气高扬啊，恐怕时世和那时不同。为什么时下风气是善于投机取巧呢？要毁弃规矩改变法度。我光明正直不随波逐流啊，愿取法前代圣贤的遗范。身在浑浊的世界而得到显贵荣耀啊，绝不是我心中所乐意的事。与其没有道义而徒有虚名啊，宁愿身居困穷境地而保持操守。不能为饱腹而苟且求食啊，不能为穿暖而苟且索衣。暗自追慕诗人的遗风啊，在粗茶淡饭中磨砺志节。媒理断绝无路可走啊，就像荒野没有边际。没有皮袄来抵御寒冬啊，怕会突然死去看不见春日。

靓杪秋之遥夜兮①，心缭悷而有哀②。春秋逴逴而日高兮③，然惆怅而自悲④。四时递来而卒岁兮⑤，阴阳不可与俪偕⑥。白日晼晚其将入兮⑦，明月销铄而减毁⑧。岁忽忽而遒尽兮⑨，老冉冉而愈弛⑩。心摇悦而日㚔兮⑪，然怊怅而无冀⑫。中憯恻之悽怆兮⑬，长太息而增欷⑭。年洋洋以日往兮⑮，老嶚廓而无处⑯。事亹亹而觊进兮⑰，蹇淹留而踌躇。

【注释】

①靓(jìng)：通"静"，平和。杪(miǎo)秋：晚秋。杪，本义是树枝尽头，多指年月或季节的末尾。
②缭悷(lì)：亦作"缭戾"，形容忧思萦绕缠结的样子。
③春秋：代指时间，这里指年纪、年龄。逴逴(chuō)：愈走愈远的样子。高：这里指时光流逝，一天天地老去。
④然：与"焉"同，用为句首发语词。
⑤递(dì)：同"递"，交替，轮流。
⑥俪(lì)偕：偕同，在一起。
⑦晼(wǎn)：太阳偏西，日将暮。
⑧销铄(shuò)：亏缺，消损。
⑨遒(qiú)尽：迫近于尽头，终了。
⑩弛：同"弛"，本义指放松弓弦，这里指放松，松弛。
⑪摇悦：喜悦，犹心旌摇荡。㚔：同"幸"。
⑫怊(chāo)怅：犹"惆怅"。
⑬憯(cǎn)恻：悲痛。悽怆：凄惨悲伤。

⑭欷(xī)：悲伤地叹息。
⑮洋洋：形容岁月匆匆流逝的样子。
⑯嵺(liáo)廓：同"寥廓"，空虚，空阔。
⑰亹亹(wěi)：勤勉不倦的样子。觊(jì)：希望，企图。

【译文】

寂静的暮秋长夜啊，心里缠结着无限悲愁。岁月如流年事渐高啊，令人惆怅自感悲凉。四季交替一年将尽啊，冬夏不同不能同时出现。太阳昏暗将要西下啊，月亮亏缺而消损。一年匆匆将要过完啊，老境渐至而身心释然放纵自己。心旌摇荡天天抱着侥幸的想法啊，但最终布满忧虑失去希望。心中惨痛凄然欲绝啊，声声长叹增加悲伤。时光匆匆一天天流逝啊，老来倍感空虚无处托身。不断勤勉企图进取啊，滞留不前徒自彷徨。

何氾滥之浮云兮①，猋壅蔽此明月②！忠昭昭而愿见兮③，然霠曀而莫达④。愿皓日之显行兮⑤，云蒙蒙而蔽之⑥。窃不自聊而愿忠兮⑦，或黕点而污之⑧。尧舜之抗行兮⑨，瞭冥冥而薄天⑩。何险巇之嫉妒兮⑪，被以不慈之伪名⑫？彼日月之照明兮，尚黯黮而有瑕⑬。何况一国之事兮，亦多端而胶加⑭。

【注释】

①氾：亦作"汜滥""泛滥"，这里形容浮云层层涌现。
②猋(biāo)：本为犬奔貌、群犬奔貌，引申为疾进貌。
③见：同"现"，显现，显露，剖白心迹。
④霠(yīn)：同"阴"，乌云蔽日。曀(yì)：天阴而有风，天色阴暗。

⑤皓日：明亮的太阳，比喻君主。显行：光耀地运行。显，光明。
⑥蒙蒙：形容幽暗、模糊不清的样子。
⑦聊：同"料"，考虑，估量。
⑧黕(dǎn)点：污垢。
⑨抗行：高尚的行为。
⑩瞭(liǎo)：明亮。冥冥：深远。薄：逼近，靠近。
⑪险巇(xī)：亦作"险戏"，崎岖险恶，这里指奸险小人。
⑫被(pī)：加在身上。
⑬黯黕(àn dǎn)：昏暗不明。瑕：斑点，瑕疵。
⑭胶(jiāo)加：乖戾，缠绕无绪。

【译文】

为什么浮云漫天涌现啊，迅速飘动遮蔽了明月！忠心耿耿愿剖白心迹啊，但乌云蔽日难以如愿。希望太阳光明显耀地运行啊，迷蒙的云气却把它遮罩。奋不顾身只想着效忠啊，有人却无端诽谤把我污蔑。唐尧和虞舜的高尚德行啊，光辉明亮直上云天。为什么险恶小人如此嫉妒啊，使他们蒙受不慈的冤名？太阳和月亮光辉朗照啊，尚且有昏暗出现斑点之时。何况一个国家的政事啊，更是头绪纷繁、杂乱无绪。

被荷裯之晏晏兮①，然潢洋而不可带②。既骄美而伐武兮③，负左右之耿介④。憎愠怆之修美兮⑤，好夫人之慷慨⑥。众踥蹀而日进兮⑦，美超远而逾迈⑧。农夫辍耕而容与兮，恐田野之芜秽⑨。事绵绵而多私兮⑩，窃悼后之危败。世雷同而炫曜兮⑪，何毁誉之昧昧⑫！今修饰而窥镜兮⑬，后尚可以窜藏⑭。愿寄言夫流星兮，羌儵忽而难当⑮。卒壅蔽此浮云兮,下暗漠而无光。尧舜皆有所举任兮,故高枕而自适。谅无怨于天下兮,心焉取此怵惕⑯?弃骐骥之浏浏兮⑰,驭安用夫强策⑱?谅城郭之不足恃兮⑲,虽重介之何益⑳。遭翼翼而无终兮㉑,忳惽惽而愁约㉒。生天地之若过兮㉓,功不成而无效。愿沉滞而不见兮㉔,尚欲布名乎天下㉕。然潢洋而不遇兮㉖,直怐愁而自苦㉗。莽洋洋而无极兮㉘,忽翱翔之焉薄?国有骥而不知乘兮,焉皇皇而更索㉙?宁戚讴于车下兮㉚,桓公闻而知之。无伯乐之善相兮㉛,今谁使乎誉之。罔流涕以聊虑兮㉜,惟著意而得之㉝。纷纯纯之愿忠兮㉞,妒被离而鄣之㉟。

【注释】

①荷:植物名,即莲,多年生水生宿根草本,夏天开花,色淡红或白,有清香,供观赏。裯(dāo):祗裯,贴身短衣。晏晏(yàn):漂亮轻柔的样子。

②潢洋:这里形容衣服宽大、宽松的样子。

③骄美:自负有美德。伐:自我夸耀。

④负:依恃,凭借。左右:近臣,侍从。耿介:这里指近臣的貌似雄武。

⑤愠怆(yùn lún):心有所蕴积而不善表达。

⑥夫人:那些小人。夫,发语词。慷慨:巧言令色,能说会道。

⑦踥蹀(qiè dié):奔走,小步趋进。

⑧美:有美德的人。超远:引身远去。逾(yú)迈:亦作"踰迈",过去,消逝。

⑨芜秽:荒芜,指土地因缺少整治而杂草丛生。

⑩绵绵:形容长而细小,且连续不绝的样子。

⑪雷同:这里比喻世人随声附和、众口一词。炫曜(yào):夸

耀，吹捧。

⑫昧昧：昏暗，模糊不清，这里指是非不明。

⑬修饰：梳妆打扮，这里指整顿国家事务。

⑭窜(cuàn)藏：隐匿，潜藏，这里指逃过危险，谨慎自保。窜，伏匿，隐藏。

⑮羌：句首发语词。当：值，遇到。

⑯怵惕：亦作"怵愁"，戒惧，惊惧。

⑰椉：同"乘"，坐驾。浏浏：本义指水流清澈。这里形容马匹如水流动一般奔跑，即行云流水，顺畅无阻的意思。

⑱驭(yù)：驾驭车马。策：驱赶骡马役畜的鞭棒。

⑲城郭：亦作"城廓"，城墙。城，指内城的墙。郭，指外城的墙。

⑳重介：厚重的铠甲。

㉑邅(zhān)：难行不进。翼翼：恭敬谨慎的样子。

㉒忳(tún)：忧郁，愁闷。惽惽(hūn)：精神昏愦，神志不清。愁约：悲愁困苦。

㉓若过：若白驹过隙，形容时间过得快。

㉔沉滞：沉抑埋没，不得伸展。

㉕布名：扬名。天下：古时多指中国范围内的全部土地。

㉖潢洋：形容无所遇合的样子。

㉗怐愗(kòu mào)：亦作"怐瞀"，愚昧，愚钝。

㉘莽洋洋：形容荒野辽阔的样子。

㉙皇皇：即"惶惶"，形容惶惑、迷惑的样子。

㉚宁戚：春秋卫人，齐大夫。讴：清唱，唱歌。

㉛伯乐：春秋时人，善于相马。

㉜罔：同"惘"，忧愁，怅惘。聊虑：深思。

㉝著(zhuó)意：集中注意力，用心。

㉞纯纯：形容忠诚、诚挚的样子。

㉟被离:通"披离",纷乱的样子。鄣(zhàng):同"障",阻隔,遮掩。

【译文】

披上荷叶短衣漂亮而轻柔啊,但是太过宽松不能束腰带。自我夸耀美德和武功啊,依恃貌似雄武的近臣。嫌弃不善表达的忠诚之士啊,喜欢小人的巧言令色。群小竞相钻营愈来愈腾达啊,贤士孤傲脱俗愈来愈疏远。农夫停止耕作放任闲散啊,恐怕田地将要荒芜。事情琐细又充满私欲啊,暗自担心国家以后会败亡。世人随声附和相互夸耀啊,好坏不分是非不明!如今修饰容貌照照镜子啊,今后还能够逃过危险。想托流星传语君王啊,但它飞掠迅速难以追遇上。终于被浮云遮蔽啊,世间暗淡没有光亮。唐尧虞舜都能选拔任用贤士啊,所以高枕无忧从容安逸。确实不受天下人埋怨啊,心中哪来忧惧不安?乘着骏马畅快地奔驰啊,驾驭之道岂在马鞭的劲悍?内城外郭实在不足依恃啊,即使盔甲再厚重又有什么用?谨慎前行看不到结果啊,忧郁烦闷穷愁潦倒。生于天地之间若白驹过隙啊,功业无成没有结果。想要埋没于人群无所表现啊,又想在世间声名远播。然而世事茫茫很难知遇贤君啊,只是愚钝不堪自讨苦吃。荒野辽阔没有边际啊,飘忽飞翔在哪停宿?国家的骏马却不知道驾乘啊,为什么糊里糊涂另外索求?宁戚在牛车下唱歌啊,齐桓公听了便知道他才能出众。没有伯乐相马的好本领啊,如今谁能使骏马被称扬?怅惘流泪姑且思量啊,用心访求才能得贤士。满怀热忱愿效忠君王啊,却被形形色色的嫉妒所阻碍。

愿赐不肖之躯而别离兮①,放游志乎云中。桀精气之抟抟兮②,骛诸神之湛湛③。骖白霓之习习兮④,历群灵之丰丰⑤。

左朱雀之茇茇兮⑥,右苍龙之躩躩⑦。属雷师之阗阗兮⑧,通飞廉之衙衙⑨。前轾辌之锵锵兮⑩,后辎乘之从从⑪。载云旗之委蛇兮,扈屯骑之容容⑫。计专专之不可化兮,愿遂推而为臧⑬。赖皇天之厚德兮,还及君之无恙⑭。

【注释】

①不肖:自谦之称。
②精气:阴阳精灵之气,古谓天地间万物皆秉之以生。抟抟(tuán):形容凝聚如团的样子。抟,聚集。
③骛(wù):追求,追逐。湛湛:聚集在一起的样子。
④霓:处于彩虹外侧色泽较暗淡的部分。习习:形容频频飞动的样子。
⑤群灵:群神,指众多星宿之神。丰丰:众多。
⑥朱雀:星宿名,二十八宿中南方七宿的总称。茇茇(pèi):形容飞翔的样子。
⑦苍龙:星宿名,二十八宿中东方七宿的总称。躩躩(qú):蜿蜒而行的样子。
⑧属(zhǔ):联接,跟着。阗阗(tián):形容声音洪大,这里指雷声而言。
⑨通:当作"道",开路、引导。衙衙(yú):行走的样子。
⑩轾(zhì):车顶前倾的样子。辌(liáng):古代的卧车。锵锵:形容金石撞击发出的洪亮清越的声音,这里指车铃声。
⑪辎(zī)乘:辎重车辆。辎,古代有帷盖的载重车。乘,同"乘",后亦泛指车辆。从从:车铃声。
⑫扈(hù):随从,护卫,多指随侍帝王。屯骑(jì):聚集车骑。屯,聚集。容容:形容车驾侍卫众多,场面盛大的样子。
⑬臧(zāng):善,好。

⑭无恙：没有忧患烦恼，幸福安康。恙，传说中的一种啮虫，人们以之为祸患，所以"恙"有忧患、祸患义。

【译文】

请赐我远去啊，我将纵情于江湖云水之中。乘着天地的一团团精气啊，去追随一群群的神灵。驾着飞动的白虹啊，穿过闪烁的繁星。左边的朱雀翩翩飞舞啊，右边的苍龙蜿蜒前行。雷师跟着咚咚敲鼓啊，风伯在前习习开路。前有卧车锵锵作响啊，后有辎车隆隆轰鸣。载着云旗首尾绵延啊，随从车骑聚集蜂拥。我心专一不可改变啊，但愿能推广成为善行。仰仗上天的深厚恩德啊，保佑楚国君王无灾无病。

屈原

招 魂

【题解】

《招魂》的作者及招魂的对象是历来颇有争议的问题，归纳起来主要有两种观点。第一种认为《招魂》为宋玉招屈原而作。王逸《楚辞章句》说："《招魂》者，宋玉之所作也。招者，召也。以手曰招，以言曰召。魂者，身之精也。宋玉怜哀屈原忠而斥弃，愁懑山泽，魂魄放佚，厥命将落，故作《招魂》，欲以复其精神，延其年寿，外陈四方之恶，内崇楚国之美，以讽谏怀王，冀其觉悟而还之也。"梁代萧统编《文选》所收《招魂》题宋玉作，知其亦沿用王逸之说。唐人李善、李周翰，宋人朱熹，明人陈第、陆时雍、周拱辰，以及清人王夫之，均赞同王逸的说法。第二种认为是屈原自招而作，或屈原招楚怀王之魂而作。两种说法的共同之处，在于都认为《招魂》为屈原作，其最早史证为司马迁《史记·屈原列传》中"余读《离骚》《天问》《招魂》《哀郢》，悲其志"的记载。

第一种说法因王逸《楚辞章句》、萧统《文选》、朱熹《楚辞集注》、王夫之《楚辞通释》等的支持，对后世影响甚大。但就本篇内容而言，亦有扞格难通之处，如写宫室之美、侍女之众、舞宴之丰、狩猎之盛，如以怀王当之，似更妥帖；而且，乱词中有对狩猎中误惊灵兽青兕，隐喻国运亡征的描写，则似作于怀王系囚于秦,甚至客死于秦之后。因此,本书更倾向于屈原招怀王说。它应是屈原任三闾大夫期间所写最后一篇职务作品。

"招魂"原本只是一种巫术仪式,在屈原手中则将它吸收、改造成了一种独特的叙述手法。它对天地四方罪恶艰危的诅咒及对故园闾里舒适惬意的赞美形成了强大的艺术张力;结束曲中又将对被招魂者的深切同情升华为对国家民族前景的忧虑。刘勰《文心雕龙·祝盟》说:"若夫楚辞《招魂》,可谓祝辞之组丽也。"梁启超称《招魂》"实全部《楚辞》中最酣恣、最深刻之作"(《楚辞要籍解题及其读法》),实不为过。

《招魂》"凄入肝脾,哀感顽艳"(繁钦《与魏文帝笺》),被后人誉为楚辞中仅次于《离骚》的优秀作品。它对后世文学的影响也是显而易见的。其铺陈的手法、铺张扬厉的风格对汉代及以后的辞赋乃至诗文创作有着深远影响。此外,其具体的艺术手法与文学主题也对后世创作有着较大影响。如对宫室、女乐、歌舞、游猎等的描写表现便在汉赋中广而大之,得到长足发展。更重要的是《招魂》中所体现出的深重的忧患意识得到了后世文人的共鸣。梁元帝萧绎在《玄览赋》中写道:"鼓洪涛于万里,曾未动于汨罗。……见旧楚之凄凉,试极目乎千里。何春心之可伤,其旧渚宫也。"又在《登江州百花亭怀荆楚》一诗中写道:"极目才千里,何由望楚津。"从中即可看出《招魂》乱辞的影响。

朕幼清以廉洁兮①,身服义而未沫②。主此盛德兮③,牵于俗而芜秽④。上无所考此盛德兮,长离殃而愁苦。帝告巫阳曰⑤:"有人在下⑥,我欲辅之⑦。魂魄离散⑧,汝筮予之⑨!"巫阳对曰:"掌梦⑩。上帝其难从。""若必筮予之⑪,恐后之谢,不能复用巫阳焉。"

招魂

【注释】

①朕：我。廉洁：行为正派、高洁无私。廉，本义指堂室边缘，后引申为正直端方。

②服：践行，履行。沬(mèi)：昏暗不明。

③主：固守，秉持。盛德：充实、充盛的德行。

④牵：牵制，拖累。芜秽：借喻污浊混乱的现实环境。芜，指田地中野草丛生。秽，杂草。

⑤帝：天帝。巫阳：叫作阳的神巫，古神话中的神医。

⑥有人：此指杰出人才。在下：在下界，人间。

⑦辅：原意指附于车辐中心的圆木，起加固作用，后引申为辅佐，祐助。

⑧魂魄：魂即独立于人身体之外存在的精神。魄，古人认为是依附肉体存在的精神。

⑨筮(shì)：用筮草占卜。予：给予，这里是使魂魄返还其身的意思。

⑩掌梦：专管解梦之官。掌，本指手心，引申为主管。

⑪若：你，指巫阳。这里是天帝对巫阳称"若"。

【译文】

我自小就高洁无私啊，亲身践行道义而未昏暗不明。固守这种充盛的德行啊，却受制于流俗，埋没于污浊的现实。上天不能明察这种大德呀，令我长久遭受祸患而愁思终日。天帝诏告巫阳说："有位贤人在下界，我打算帮助他。他的魂魄就要飘散，你可以用占卜的方式为他还魂！"巫阳回答道："这是解梦官的事，天帝你的命令我难以遵从。""你必须卜筮还魂给他，晚了它们就要消散，那时再用你巫阳也无济于事了。"

乃下招曰：魂兮归来！去君之恒干①，何为四方些②？舍君之乐处,而离彼不祥些!魂兮归来!东方不可以托些。长人千仞③,惟魂是索些。十日代出,流金铄石些④。彼皆习之,魂往必释些。归来兮!不可以托些。魂兮归来!南方不可以止些。雕题黑齿⑤,得人肉以祀,以其骨为醢些⑥。蝮蛇蓁蓁⑦,封狐千里些⑧。雄虺九首⑨,往来倏忽,吞人以益其心些。归来兮!不可以久淫些⑩。魂兮归来!西方之害,流沙千里些。旋入雷渊⑪,麋散而不可止些⑫。幸而得脱,其外旷宇些⑬。赤蚁若象⑭,玄蜂若壶些⑮。五谷不生⑯,藂菅是食些⑰。其土烂人,求水无所得些。彷徉无所倚,广大无所极些。归来兮!恐自遗贼些。魂兮归来!北方不可以止些。增冰峨峨⑱,飞雪千里些。归来兮!不可以久些。魂兮归来!君无上天些。虎豹九关,啄害下人些⑲。一夫九首,拔木九千些。豺狼从目⑳,往来侁侁些㉑;悬人以娭㉒,投之深渊些。致命于帝㉓,然后得瞑些㉔。归来!往恐危身些。魂兮归来!君无下此幽都些㉕。土伯九约㉖,其角觺觺些。敦脄血拇㉘,逐人驱驱些㉙。参目虎首㉚,其身若牛些。此皆甘人㉛,归来!恐自遗灾些。魂兮归来!入修门些㉜。工祝招君㉝,背行先些㉞。秦篝齐缕㉟,郑绵络些。招具该备,永啸呼些。魂兮归来!反故居些㊱。

【注释】

①去:离开。恒干:这里指魂魄平常所寄托的躯体、躯壳。恒,常。 干,躯干,躯体。

②四方:去四方,为古代祭礼仪式。些(suò):楚语中常用的语末助词,类同"兮"、"焉"、"矣"等。

③长人:神话传说中东方的巨人族。仞(rèn):为古制长度单

位,周制八尺,汉制七尺,东汉末为五尺六寸。
④金:古代金属通称。铄(shuò):高温销熔。
⑤雕题:此指南方蛮夷国度。雕,描画。题,额头。在额头上描画花纹图案是南方民族的习俗。黑齿:东南、华南一带民族有将牙齿染黑的风习。
⑥醢(hǎi):得人肉以祀,以其骨为醢,大约是一种杀人以祭祀的风俗。醢,肉酱。
⑦蓁蓁(zhēn):形容聚集、众多的样子。
⑧封狐:大狐。
⑨虺(huǐ):蛇。
⑩淫:淹留。
⑪旋(xuàn):旋转,卷入。雷渊:古水名。
⑫靡(mí)散:像粉末那样被碾碎。
⑬旷宇:空无一人的荒野。旷,空阔,广大。宇,荒野。
⑭蚁:红色蚂蚁。
⑮玄蜂:即土蜂,体黑,较木蜂略大,土中作巢,呈圆壶形。
⑯五谷:古指五种谷物,后泛指一切谷物。
⑰藂(cóng):同"丛",草木丛生的样子。菅(jiān):又称菅草、苞子草,茎可编绳、织幔覆盖房顶。
⑱增冰:层积高累的冰块或冰山。增,通"层",厚积貌。峨峨:形容高耸的样子。
⑲啄害:咬害,吞噬。啄,本指鸟用喙取食,此泛指一般动物的咬食动作。
⑳从目:眼睛竖长。从,通"纵"。
㉑侁侁(shēn):众多的样子。
㉒嬉(xī):同"嬉",玩弄,戏弄。
㉓致命:复命。致,传达,回复。帝:天帝。
㉔瞑(míng):假寐,小睡。

㉕幽都：古指北方极地，日落于此，物象昏暗，故称。幽，昏暗，都，城邑。

㉖土伯：土地神。伯，古指地方长官，此指神名。九约：形容土伯身上插满矛戟，杀气腾腾。约，即"矟"，矛。

㉗觺觺(yī)：形容尖利的样子。

㉘敦脄(méi)：厚实的脊背。拇：大拇指。

㉙駓駓(pī)：形容疾行的样子。

㉚参(sān)目：三只眼。参，通"三"。

㉛甘人：以人为美味，食人之义。甘，美味。

㉜修门：高大城门，此指楚郢都城门。

㉝工祝：即"巫祝"，巫祝都是主持祭祀仪式的人。巫以乐舞降神娱神，祝则主要负责诵读祷词。工，巫。

㉞背行先：巫者背向前方，面向魂灵，倒退而行，来为魂作导引。

㉟"秦篝(gōu)"以下两句：篝、缕、绵络(luò)，都是招魂时所用器具。篝，竹笼。缕，丝线。绵络，丝絮之类织物，编缀于竿头，作为招魂的灵幡。

㊱反：同"返"，回归，回返。

【译文】

巫阳于是下界招魂说：灵魂啊回来！为什么离开躯体四处游荡？离弃你的乐土，却遭受那些灾殃！灵魂啊回来！不能到东方安身啊。巨人族高达千仞，专门索要魂灵啊。十个太阳交替出现，金属石块全能销熔啊。它们都习惯了高温，灵魂一到必然离散啊。回来吧！那里不能落脚啊。灵魂啊回来！不能在南方停留。土著们在额头刺青，涂黑牙齿，以人牲祭，用人骨作肉酱啊。毒蛇丛聚，巨狐驰骋千里啊。九头雄蛇转瞬来去，吃人满足它们的贪欲啊。回来吧！不要长时间逗留啊。灵魂啊回来！西方险恶，有方圆千里的流沙啊。裹挟流入雷渊便会被碾成碎末，千万不能逗留啊。即使侥幸

招魂

逃脱,外面是人迹罕至的荒野啊。红蚁如象一般庞大,土蜂鼓腹与葫芦相仿啊。各种谷物不能生长,它们只能以丛生的营草为食啊。这里的地温能将人蒸烂,水源到处找寻不到啊。徘徊游荡无所凭依,广阔辽远走不到尽头啊。回来吧!恐怕你招来祸害啊!灵魂啊回来!不能在北方停留啊!冰山高耸,雪花飘飞弥漫千里啊。回来吧!不要再耽搁了啊。灵魂啊回来!不要登上天去啊!虎豹把守九座关口,吞噬伤害下界的人啊。有怪物长着九个脑袋,一口气拔掉树木九千啊。豺狼眼睛倒竖,群来群往片刻不停啊;将人悬挂起来戏弄,然后投到深渊里去啊。它们向天帝复命,之后才能小睡一会儿啊。回来吧!去了恐怕危及生命啊!灵魂啊回来!不要北上到日没的幽暗之处啊。土神剑戟森森,头角锐利啊。厚厚的脊背,血淋淋的手爪,急速地追着人们乱跑啊。他有虎头三眼,身体像牛一样啊。这些都以人为美味,回来吧!恐怕要自受其害啊!灵魂啊回来!从郢都国门进入啊。巫祝为你招魂,他背对前方,倒走为你作先导啊。秦地竹笼,齐地丝线,用郑国丝絮做成的灵幡啊。招魂的器具一应全备,再就是长声叫喊啊。灵魂啊回来!回到你的故园啊!

天地四方,多贼奸些①。像设君室②,静闲安些。高堂邃宇③,槛层轩些④,层台累榭⑤,临高山些。网户朱缀,刻方连些⑥。冬有突厦⑦,夏室寒些。川谷径复⑧,流潺湲些⑨。光风转蕙⑩,氾崇兰些⑪。经堂入奥⑫,朱尘筵些⑬。砥室翠翘⑭,挂曲琼些⑮。翡翠珠被⑯,烂齐光些。蒻阿拂壁⑰,罗帱张些⑱。纂组绮缟⑲,结琦璜些⑳。室中之观,多珍怪些。兰膏明烛㉑,华容备些㉒。二八侍宿㉓,射递代些㉔。九侯淑女㉕,多迅众些㉖。盛鬋不同制㉗,实满宫些。容态好比㉘,顺弥代些。弱

楚辞

颜固植㉙,謇其有意些㉚。娇容修态㉛,絙洞房些㉜。蛾眉曼睩㉝,目腾光些。靡颜腻理㉞,遗视矊些㉟。离榭修幕㊱,侍君之闲些。翡帷翠帐,饰高堂些。红壁沙版㊲,玄玉梁些㊳。仰观刻桷㊴,画龙蛇些。坐堂伏槛,临曲池些㊵。芙蓉始发,杂芰荷些㊶。紫茎屏风㊷,文缘波些㊸。文异豹饰㊹,侍陂陁些㊺。轩辌既低㊻,步骑罗些。兰薄户树㊼,琼木篱些。魂兮归来!何远为些?

【注释】

①贼奸:危害,险恶,即上文所陈说的害人、怖人之物。
②像:楚地旧俗,人死后设其遗像于室中供拜祀。
③邃(suì):深邃的房屋。邃,深。宇,房屋。
④槛(jiàn):栏杆。层:多重。轩:楼板,建筑物的上层结构部分。
⑤层台:多层的高台。台,四方而高的建筑物。累榭:累,重叠。榭,台上起建的高屋。
⑥方连:即方正形状叠和相连,是一种装饰图案。
⑦突(yào):同"窔",深邃。厦,高大的堂屋。
⑧径复:径或为"往"之误,往复即水流曲折、回环往复的意思。
⑨潺湲(chán yuán):水流动的样子。
⑩光风:晴朗的日子里,风吹动蕙草,令其翻动,其叶子在日光映照下显得闪闪发光,所以叫光风。转:摇动。
⑪氾:摇动。崇:通"丛"。
⑫奥:室内西南角,指屋子深处。
⑬尘:遮隔尘土的幕布。筵(yán):竹席。
⑭砥(dǐ)室:平整的屋室,有如砥石、磨刀石一般。翠翘:翠鸟羽毛,作装饰用。翠,鸟名,即青羽雀。翘,鸟尾的长羽

毛。

⑮曲琼：弯曲之玉，即玉钩。用来挂衣物。

⑯翡翠：鸟名，嘴长而直，生活在水边，以鱼虾为食，羽毛有蓝、绿、赤、棕等色，可做装饰品。

⑰蒻(ruò)：一种蒲草，可以制席。这里即指蒲席。阿(ē)：细缯，一种织物。拂(fú)：这里指把蒻阿铺在壁上。

⑱罗：绮罗，丝织物。帱(chóu)：帐子。

⑲纂(zuǎn)组：都是丝带。纂，赤色带子。绮缟(qǐ gǎo)：都是丝织物。绮，素地织纹起花的丝织物，织采为文称绵，织素为文称绮。缟，白绢。

⑳琦璜(qí huáng)：都是玉器。琦，美玉。璜，半圆形玉璧。

㉑兰膏明烛：用兰草来熬制油脂，以此来做成蜡烛。膏，一种油脂。

㉒华容：这里或是形容灯具上饰纹的华美。

㉓二八：一说即二列，古代乐舞表演以八人为一列，二八即女乐十六人。一说即十六岁。

㉔射(xī)：通"夕"，夜晚。

㉕九侯：殷代诸侯，纣以姬昌(周文王)、九侯、鄂侯为三公，九侯有美女送给纣，纣不喜欢，把她杀掉，并把九侯剁成肉酱。

㉖多迅众：盛多貌。

㉗盛鬋(jiǎn)：鬓发盛美。鬋，鬓。制：发型样式。

㉘好比：美丽温柔。比，温柔和顺，易于亲近。

㉙弱颜固植：外表柔弱，内心坚贞。

㉚謇(jiǎn)：楚地方言，发语词。

㉛姱(kuā)容修态：姱容，美好的容貌。姱，美好。修态，美好的仪态。修，本义修饰，引申则为美好义。

㉜絙(gèng)：通"亘"，连续周遍，此处指美丽的侍女罗列、

周遍于房室之内。洞房：深邃的内室。

㉝蛾眉：女子细长而好看的眉毛。蛾，形容眉毛细长如蚕蛾的样子。睩(lù)：目明貌。

㉞靡(mǐ)：细密。理：肌理。

㉟遗视：目光停留。遗，停留。矊(mián)：远视貌。

㊱离榭：离宫别馆。修幕：长大的帷幕。

㊲红壁：用红色垩土粉刷墙壁。沙版：以丹砂涂饰隔板。沙，通"砂"，即丹砂。版，堂室间的隔版。

㊳玄玉梁：玄玉梁即用黑玉装饰的屋梁。玄，黑色。梁，屋梁。

㊴榙(jué)：椽子。

㊵曲池：堂前因地建池，形制曲回，故称。

㊶芰(jì)：菱，俗称菱角。

㊷屏风：水葵，又称凫葵，一种水生植物。

㊸文缘波：紫茎屏风的纹理随着水波上下摇曳浮动。

㊹文异豹饰：侍从们以豹皮为服饰，其纹彩颇为奇异。

㊺陂陁(bēi tuó)：山坡水岸高低不平处。陂，泽畔障水之岸。陁，倾斜貌。

㊻轩辌(liáng)：轩，一种曲辕有幡的车，为卿大夫及诸侯夫人所乘。辌，卧车。低：停止，停下。

㊼薄：形容草木丛生的样子。

【译文】

天地上下，四面八方，多是狡诈害人的东西啊。你的遗像摆在中堂，显得如此宁谧安详啊。堂室高大，屋宇深广，回廊曲合，围栏绵延啊。台榭层叠，依山而建，自然居高临下啊。房门漆红网状文饰，其间刻镂连方图案啊。冬天房屋深幽宽敞，夏天内室清凉怡人啊。溪流注入低谷动荡往复，水声淙淙动听啊。晴风吹动蕙草闪闪发光，又使兰丛摇摆不定啊。由正屋进入内室，里面有红色隔尘的竹席啊。室壁平整饰以翠羽，又有玉钩悬挂衣物啊。衾被

招魂

内充鸟羽镶有珠玉，光辉灿烂夺目啊。蒲席、细缯蒙着墙面，绮帐设置其间啊。红白绶带、素洁的绮缟，缀结起美玉、圆璧啊。内室中的陈设，多是世所罕见啊。兰花混制的蜡烛通彻明亮，富丽堂皇的景象无以复加啊。妙龄女子服侍起宿，看厌就让其轮值更换啊。她们如同九侯献送的美女，多得不可胜数啊。鬓发浓密发型各异，充满栋宇宫室啊。容貌仪态娇媚柔婉，和顺可人举世无双啊。柔心弱骨而坚贞不渝，她们都意态缠绵啊。美丽面容姿态闲雅，连绵不绝充满房屋啊。美丽眉宇曼妙相视，秋波神光腾越荡漾啊。红颜光洁肌理细腻，凝视远方久久不移啊。别馆长幕，庭院深深，在你悠闲时倾心服侍啊。饰有翠羽的帷帐，挂满高大的厅堂啊。朱砂漆遍墙壁、隔版，屋梁嵌有黑色的美玉啊。抬头观望刻花的椽子，上面有龙蛇雕绘满眼啊。坐在中堂凭栏远望，目下正是庭院曲池啊。莲花初开，芰荷接天，碧色无穷啊。水葵紫色茎株，其纹理随波映漾啊。侍从们的服装绘有奇纹、带有云豹的绘饰，在岸边等待侍候啊。轻便的轩车、卧车停下，徒步、乘马的随从纷陈罗聚啊。丛生的兰花在门外种植，以玉树作为篱障啊。灵魂啊回来！为什么要去危险的远方啊？

室家遂宗①，食多方些。稻粢穱麦②，挐黄粱些③。大苦醎酸④，辛甘行些⑤。肥牛之腱，臑若芳些⑥。和酸若苦，陈吴羹些。胹鳖炮羔⑦，有柘浆些⑧。鹄酸臇凫⑨，煎鸿鸧些⑩。露鸡臛蠵⑪，厉而不爽些⑫。粔籹蜜饵⑬，有餦餭些⑭。瑶浆蜜勺⑮，实羽觞些⑯。挫糟冻饮⑰，酎清凉些⑱。华酌既陈⑲，有琼浆些⑳。归来反故室，敬而无妨些。肴羞未通㉑，女乐罗些。陈钟按鼓㉒，造新歌些。《涉江》《采菱》，发《扬荷》些㉓。美人既醉，朱颜酡些㉔。娭光眇视㉕，目曾波些㉖。被文服纤㉗，丽而不奇些㉘。长发曼鬋，艳陆离些㉙。二八齐容㉚，起郑舞些㉛。袵若交竿㉜，

393

抚案下些㉝。竽瑟狂会㉞，搷鸣鼓些㉟。宫庭震惊㊱，发《激楚》些㊲。吴歈蔡讴㊳，奏大吕些㊴。士女杂坐，乱而不分些。放陈组缨㊵，班其相纷些。郑卫妖玩㊶，来杂陈些。《激楚》之结㊷，独秀先些。菎蔽象棋㊸，有六簿些㊹。分曹并进㊺，遒相迫些㊻。成枭而牟㊼，呼五白些㊽。晋制犀比㊾，费白日些。铿钟摇簴㊿，揳梓瑟些㉛。娱酒不废，沉日夜些。兰膏明烛，华镫错些㉜。结撰至思㉝，兰芳假些㉞。人有所极，同心赋些㉟。酎饮尽欢，乐先故些。魂兮归来！反故居些。

【注释】

①室家：家人及宗族。遂宗：闾里宗族。

②粢(zī)：稷，粟米。穛(zhuō)：早熟的麦子。

③挐(rú)：杂糅。

④大苦：特别苦的味道。

⑤行：味道调和组成。

⑥臑(ěr)：通"胹"，形容熟烂的样子。若：而。

⑦胹(ěr)：煮。炮(páo)：烧烤。羔：小羊。

⑧柘(zhè)浆：蔗浆，糖浆。柘，通"蔗"。

⑨鹄：天鹅，似雁而大，颈长，羽毛纯白，能高飞。酸：用酸的调料熟制鹄肉。腌(juǎn)凫：用少量汁水烹制凫肉。腌，少汁。凫，野鸭。

⑩鸿：大雁。鸧(cāng)：一种鸟类，大如鹤，青苍色或灰色。

⑪露鸡：露天生长的鸡。臛蠵(huò xī)：把大龟做成羹汤。臛，肉羹。蠵，大龟。

⑫厉：味道浓烈。爽：败坏、变质或口感差。

⑬粔籹(jù nǚ)：搓面成细条，组之成束，扭作环形，油炸，今称馓子。蜜饵(ěr)：掺和蜂蜜制成的糕饼。饵，糕饼。

⑭饧餭(zhāng huáng)：饴糖之类的食品。

⑮瑶浆：指美酒。瑶，美玉。蜜勺：甜酒。勺，通"酌"，引申为酒。

⑯羽觞(shāng)：刻有鸟雀羽纹的酒杯。觞，酒杯。

⑰挫糟：挤压清除酒糟。挫，挤压。糟，酒糟，带有渣滓的酒。冻饮：冷饮。

⑱酎(zhòu)：经过多次反复酿成的美酒。

⑲华酌：华美的酒斗。酌，盛酒的容器，酒斗。

⑳琼浆：像红色美玉颜色的仙汁。琼，红色的玉。

㉑肴：酒肉之类的荤菜。羞：同"馐"，美味。通：这里是菜上齐的意思。

㉒按：击打。

㉓发：歌唱，演奏。《扬荷》：与《涉江》、《采菱》皆为楚乐。

㉔酡(tuó)：饮酒微醉，面颊红润。

㉕娭(xī)光：目光、眼神俏皮的意思。娭，嬉戏。眇视：微视，偷看。

㉖曾波：眼波频送、眉目多情的意思。曾，通"层"。

㉗被文服纤：被、服都是穿的意思。文，有花纹的丝织衣物，纤，轻薄细软的丝织衣物。

㉘奇(jī)：单一、单调。

㉙陆离：形容美艳的样子。

㉚二八：十六人，将十六位舞者分列两厢，奏乐起舞。

㉛郑舞：郑地舞蹈。郑，古国名，本为西周王畿内之地，周宣王封季弟友于此。其后郑武公迁居东都畿内，都新郑，即春秋时郑国，战国时为韩所灭。

㉜交竿：颇难解，兹录数解，以备参考：第一，"竿"通"干"，即盾牌。何剑熏《楚辞拾沈》认为交竿即交干，也

即起舞时，彼此飞袿交接如盾牌并举。第二，"竿"当作"笄"，即簪子。王泗原《楚辞校释》："或当作笄，则'袿若'谓舞人袿袖皆随旋转而顺向；'交竿'谓舞人首饰交接皆整齐。"第三，"袿若交竿"犹言舞者襟袖上的皱纹有如竹竿相交。第四，"竿"作羽毛解。姜亮夫《楚辞通故·文物部》："袿若疑为烓若之误，言舞容委蛇柔弱也；竿当指舞者所持之羽，即《陈风·宛邱》所谓'无冬无夏，值其鹭羽'之羽。"

㉝抚：循依。案下：按节奏徐缓前行。案，即"按"，按照节拍。

㉞竽瑟：竽，管乐器名。瑟，弦乐器名。狂：猛烈。

㉟摶(tián)：击打，敲击。

㊱宫：堂屋，房室。庭：堂前之地。

㊲激楚：古代楚国乐曲名，或是取声音高亢凄清之意。

㊳吴歈(yú)：吴地歌曲。吴，古国名，可参《史记·吴太伯世家》。歈，歌曲。蔡讴：蔡地歌曲。蔡，周时国名，周武王弟叔度封蔡，可参《史记·管蔡世家》。讴，歌唱，歌曲。

㊴大吕：古代乐律律调名。据《汉书·律历志》：古乐按音的高低分十二律，阴阳各六，六阳律称律，六阴律称吕，第四阴律为大吕。

㊵放陈：放，解开。陈，陈列。组：丝带。缨：系在颔下固定帽子的绳子。

㊶卫：古国名，周武王弟康叔封地，可参《史记·卫康叔世家》。妖玩：妖，艳丽。玩，供玩赏的什物或人。

㊷结：发髻，特指《激楚》之舞者特异的发式。

㊸菎蔽(kūn bì)：一种竹制的赌具。菎，通"筼"，竹名。蔽，通"箅"。象棋：以象牙制作的棋子。棋，古时博弈用的器物。

㊹六簿(bó)：古代簿戏的一种。因为簿箸有六根，棋子双方各六枚，故俗称六簿。簿，同"博"。

㊺分曹：两两对局。曹，偶。

㊻逎(qiú)：急迫。

㊼枭：本指猫头鹰，此指簿戏采名。枭，通"骁"。博弈中棋子先期到达者称"骁棋"，亦"成枭"之义。牟：同"侔"，相等，即势均力敌。

㊽五白：五枚竹片内侧向上，此法用于两方均"成枭"后决定谁最后胜出。

㊾晋：古国名，周成王封弟叔虞于唐，叔虞子燮父改国号为晋。参《史记·晋世家》。犀比：将犀牛角集中作赌具的加工原料。犀，犀牛角。比，集中。

㊿铿钟：击钟。铿，撞击。簴(jù)：支持簴的两根立柱。古代悬钟、磬、鼓的木架，其横木谓之簴，簴旁所立二柱谓之簴。字又作"虡"。

㈤揳(jiá)：弹奏。梓(zǐ)瑟：梓木制成的瑟。梓，树名，木质轻，易割，古常用作琴瑟及棺椁的木料。

㈥错：这里指灯上错镂雕饰的花纹。

㈦结撰(zhuàn)：构思写作。至思：穷思竭虑。

㈧假：至，到来。

㈨赋：诵读，带有一定的韵律节奏。

【译文】

闾里宗族聚集一处，饮食丰盛花色众多啊。稻谷稷麦，杂糅着黄灿灿的粟米啊。苦、咸、酸味道纯正，加以甜、辣两味调和相成啊。肥牛的肌腱，煮熟后香味扑鼻啊。调剂酸、苦，将吴地风味的肉羹摆出啊。笼蒸龟鳖烧烤羊羔，一并浇上糖浆啊。风干天鹅和野鸭，烹煮大雁和鸧鹄啊。晾制风鸡煎煮龟羹，味道浓烈而不变质败坏啊。油炸馓子蜜蘸糕饼,还有糖饴食品啊。琼浆玉酿蜜制甜酒,倒满雕刻羽纹的酒杯啊。抉别糟粕将酒冷却,美酒甘醇清冽啊。摆好华美的酒器,里面盛满晶莹透亮的酒浆啊。回到以前居住的地方,众人毕恭毕敬毫无违碍啊。佳肴、珍馐尚未上齐,歌妓舞乐列队侍候啊。敲起钟来打起鼓,演奏新制的歌曲啊。《涉江》《采菱》奏响,《扬荷》一曲清扬啊。美人醉酒后,双颊更加红润啊。俏皮的目光偷偷微视,秋波频送眉目传情啊。身着文饰斑斓轻缓的绢素,雍容华贵而纷繁富丽啊。鬓发修长,风采华艳,令人目眩神迷啊。十六名艺妓容仪一致,跳起郑舞翩翩高举啊。舞动的衣襟飞起交叠,依循节奏徐缓行进啊。吹竽鼓瑟强烈交织,击打鼓面铿铿作响啊。满堂瞠目惊骇,只因《激楚》高奏啊。吴歌蔡曲合声共唱,弹奏大吕这一宏大的调式啊。男男女女混坐一起,打破礼防不分彼此啊。系冠丝带散开放下,低垂纷乱难解难分啊。郑卫两地奇美珍玩,随意弄来摆放一地啊。《激楚》舞姬发髻特异,奇特秀美独一无二啊。菎蔽和象牙棋子,还有博弈的六簿啊。两两对局齐头并进,厉声催促分毫不让啊。双方骁棋功力悉敌,喧哗一片高呼五白啊。晋地的犀角赌具聚集一处,旷日持久欲罢不能啊。钟声铿铿磬鸣悠扬,弹起梓木制做的琴瑟啊。饮酒欢娱不肯中止,夜以继日沉迷不返啊。兰花膏油浇制成通透的蜡烛,华丽的灯具错彩镂金啊。精心构思弹思竭虑,以芳洁兰花借喻斯人啊。众人竭尽才智,一心一意颂扬赞美啊。欢饮醉酒不留遗憾,娱乐祖先,宴会故旧啊。灵魂啊回来!回到你的故居啊。

乱曰:献岁发春兮[①],汨吾南征[②],菉萍齐叶兮白芷生[③]。路贯庐江兮左长薄[④],倚沼畦瀛兮遥望博[⑤]。青骊结驷兮齐千乘⑥，悬火延起兮玄颜烝⑦。步及骤处兮诱骋先⑧，抑骛若通兮引车右还⑨。与王趋梦兮课后先⑩。君王亲发兮惮青兕⑪，朱明承夜兮时不可以淹⑫。皋兰被径兮斯路渐⑬。湛湛江水兮上有枫⑭，目极千里兮伤春心。魂兮归来哀江南⑮！

【注释】

①献岁：岁星又增一躔度，新的一年开始了。献，进。岁，岁星，即木星，其十二年运行一周天，称为一纪。发春：春天来临。

②汩(yù)：急速貌。

③菉(lù)萍：菉，草名，又称王刍，可制黄色染料。萍，植物名，又称田字草，生浅水，叶有长柄，夏秋开小白花。齐叶：指叶子长齐。

④庐江：在今湖北宜城县一带。长薄：高大浓密的树林。薄，丛生植被。

⑤倚：站立。沼：水池，水泽。畦：成块的田。瀛(yíng)：池沼，水泽。博：广大平整。

⑥骊(lí)：黑色的马。结驷：一车四马谓之驷，结驷即车乘相连。齐千乘：众多马车一齐进发。齐，一齐，一同。乘，四马驾一车为乘。

⑦悬火：夜间打猎而点起火把。延起：光焰四射，连成一片。玄颜：黑暗的天色。玄，黑色，此指玄天，即天空。颜，色。烝(zhēng)：光热上腾。

⑧步：徐行。骤：奔跑。处：歇止。诱：引导，导路。

⑨抑骛：或进或止。抑，停止。骛，快跑。若：顺畅。

⑩梦：云梦，这里泛指楚王狩猎区。课：考核，比较。

⑪发：射箭。惮：通"殚"，杀死。兕(sì)：兽名。

⑫朱明：太阳。承：接续。淹：停留
⑬皋兰：水边兰草。渐：掩盖，淹没。
⑭湛湛(zhàn)：形容江水平稳深广的样子。枫：树名，枫叶似白杨，叶圆而分角，秋时呈红色，可分泌树脂，有香味。
⑮江南：长江以南楚国土地。

【译文】

乱辞称：一年复始春意发萌啊，我将匆匆南下，王刍、青萍叶刚长齐啊，白芷刚好欣欣向荣。征途要通过庐江啊，我的左边是高大浓密的树林，站在池塘田界之间啊，远远眺望楚地广袤无边。黑色骏马以驷驾连结啊，齐整阵容多达千乘，高挂夜灯火光蔓延啊，蒸腾的火气照亮黑色的天空。或徐行，或追逐，或奔驰，或歇止啊，向导们一马当先，指挥进退通畅自如啊，向右掉转车头胜利而还。我与先王在云梦狩猎啊，考课猎物多少与追猎中的表现。国君御驾亲狩啊，射杀了贞祥的青兕，太阳破晓而出啊，不能够再作盘桓。水边的兰草布满小路啊，这条路芜没不见。清澈的江水啊，高处还有红枫，纵目千里一望无垠啊，充满春愁的心低落伤感。魂魄啊归来！为如今的江南楚地而哀叹！

大 招

【题解】

《大招》的作者以及招谁之魂，尚没有定论。关于其作者大致有四种说法：

一是认为屈原或景差所作。王逸《楚辞章句》云："《大招》者，屈原之所作也。或曰景差，疑不能明也。屈原放流九年，忧思烦乱，精神越散，与形离别，恐命将终，所行不遂，故愤然大招其魂。盛称楚国之乐，崇怀襄之德，以比三王，能任用贤，公卿明察，能荐举人，宜辅佐之，以兴至治，因此风谏，达己之志也。"

二是认为景差所作。朱熹《楚辞集注》云："《大招》不知何人所作，或曰屈原，或曰景差，自王逸时已不能明矣。其谓原作者，则曰词义高古，非原莫及。其不谓然者，则曰《汉志》定著原赋之二十五篇，今自《骚经》以至《渔父》，已充其目矣。其谓景差则绝无左验，是以读书者往往疑之。然今以宋玉大小言赋考之，则凡差语，皆平淡醇古，意亦深靖间退，不为词人墨客浮夸艳逸之态，然后乃知此篇决为差作无疑也。"周拱辰、王夫之同意这种说法。

三是确认为屈原所作。林云铭《楚辞灯》："《大招》一篇，王逸既谓屈原所作，又以或言景差为疑，尚未决其为差作也。……玉与差皆原之徒，若招其师之魂，何以见差之招当为大，玉之招当为小乎？后人守其说而不敢变，相沿至今，反添出许多强解，附会穿凿，把灵均绝世奇文，埋没殆尽，殊可叹也。"

四是认为乃秦汉之际摹拟之作。今人梁启超、游国恩、刘永济等持此观点。朱季海《楚辞解故》认为是淮南王刘安或其门客所作。

至于招谁之魂，则主要有两种观点，一为招屈原之魂；二为招怀王之魂。

关于本篇的作者，自东汉王逸以来已不能定，这是因为文献不足征的缘故。但从本篇铺陈描写的名物、制度及场景来看，其所招之魂的身份当非帝王诸侯莫属，这一点跟《招魂》颇为类似，故而或即招"怀王"之魂。

尽管《大招》的文章主旨一直聚讼纷纭，但它与《招魂》并称"二招"而独具特色。从内容上看，《大招》没有叙文与乱辞，全文皆为招魂辞。与《招魂》所招对象应为同一人。据史料记载，怀王被骗入秦国后，在顷襄王三年（前296）卒于秦，后归葬于楚国，这中间有相当长一段时间。因此，怀王死讯传到楚国时，楚应在国内举行招魂仪式，以招其魂归国不离散。到归葬时，则又举行更隆重的国葬仪式，因而须有二篇招魂辞，这或许正是《招魂》与《大招》的来历。《大招》在内容上可分两部分：一是极力渲染四方的种种凶险怪异，二是着意烘托楚国故居之美，最后又大力称颂楚国任人唯贤、政治清明、国势强盛等，以诱使灵魂返回楚国。

青春受谢①，白日昭只②。春气奋发，万物遽只③。冥凌浃行④，魂无逃只。魂魄归来！无远遥只。

【注释】

①青：在上古人的观念中，是把东方、春季、青色、草木联系在一起的。这里的青春即春天、春季的意思。谢，去，离去。
②昭：光明，灿烂。只：语气词。如同《招魂》之"些"字。
③遽(jù)：竞相，争相。
④冥：幽冥，幽暗。这里或指北方之神玄冥。凌：驰骋。浃(jiā)：遍，周遍。

【译文】

冬去春来，阳光多么明媚灿烂啊。春的气息喷薄而出，世间万物竞相生长啊。幽冥之神遍行于天地之间，魂你不要逃啊。魂魄归来，不要远远离开啊！

魂乎归来！无东无西，无南无北只。东有大海，溺水㳋㳋只①。螭龙并流②，上下悠悠只③。雾雨淫淫④，白皓胶只⑤。魂乎无东！汤谷寂只⑥。魂乎无南！南有炎火千里，蝮蛇蜒只⑦。山林险隘，虎豹蜿只⑧。鰅鳙短狐⑨，王虺骞只⑩。魂乎无南！蜮伤躬只⑪。魂乎无西！西方流沙，漭洋洋只⑫。豕首纵目⑬，被发鬤只⑭。长爪踞牙⑮，诶笑狂只⑯。魂乎无西！多害伤只。魂乎无北！北有寒山，逴龙赦只⑰。代水不可涉⑱，深不可测只。天白颢颢⑲，寒凝凝只。魂乎无往！盈北极只⑳。

【注释】

①溺水：这里指水很深，容易使人沉没于其中。㳋㳋(yóu)：形容水流迅疾的样子。
②螭(chī)：传说中一种没有角的龙。
③悠悠：形容游动、行走的样子。

楚辞

④淫淫：形容连绵不断的样子。
⑤皓胶：形容烟雨蒙蒙，天地间白茫茫一片的样子。
⑥汤(yáng)谷：古代神话传说中的日出之地。
⑦蝮(fù)蛇：大蛇。蜒(yán)：形容长的样子。
⑧蜿(wǎn)：形容行走的样子。
⑨鲵鳙(yú yōng)：神话传说中一种鱼的名称。短狐：神话传说中一种能含沙射人的动物。王逸《楚辞章句》："短狐，鬼蜮也。"
⑩王虺(huǐ)：大蛇。骞(qiān)：抬头，昂首。
⑪蜮(yù)：即短狐。躬：身体。
⑫漭(mǎng)洋洋：这里形容流沙广大、无边无际的样子。
⑬豕(shǐ)首：猪头。纵：竖。
⑭被：同"披"。鬤(ráng)：形容毛发蓬乱的样子。
⑮踞(jù)牙：锋利的牙齿。踞，通"锯"。
⑯诶(xī)笑：嬉笑，这里似指让人感到厌恶的狰狞的笑。
⑰逴(chuō)龙：当为古代神话传说中的"烛龙"，是居于北方的神祇。赩(xì)：赤色。据《山海经》，则烛龙神体呈"赤色"。
⑱代水：水名，大约是古代传说中的北方大河。
⑲颢颢(hào)：白茫茫。
⑳北极：北方至极至远之地，严寒之所在。

【译文】

魂啊归来！不要往东，不要往西，不要往南，不要往北啊。东面有浩瀚海洋，水深流急啊。螭龙随着水流，上下游动啊。烟雾雨水绵绵不绝，天地间白茫茫一片啊。魂啊不要往东！日出之地的汤谷死一般寂静啊。魂啊不要往南！南面有火焰千里，巨大的蝮蛇长得吓人啊。山林险峻狭隘，虎豹横行啊。又有怪鱼鲵鳙和含沙射人的短狐，大蛇昂着头啊。魂啊不要往南！鬼蜮短狐会

404

伤害你的身体啊。魂啊不要往西！西方有流沙，无边无际啊。那里的怪物长着猪的脑袋，眼睛竖长，披头散发，乱蓬蓬啊。长长的爪子，利齿如锯，发出狞笑，十分颠狂啊。魂啊不要往西！那里有太多害人之物。魂啊不要往北！北方有寒冷的山岭，烛龙神遍体通红啊。又有代水无法渡过，它的水深得无从测知啊。天空一片白茫茫，寒气冻结了大地啊。魂啊不要前往！整个北极都是冰天雪地啊。

魂魄归来，闲以静只。自恣荆楚①，安以定只。逞志究欲②，心意安只。穷身永乐，年寿延只。魂乎归来！乐不可言只。

【注释】

①恣(zì)：无拘束，任凭。
②逞：快意，称心。究：穷尽。

【译文】

魂魄归来，这里闲适又安静啊。在荆楚大地上自在遨游，是多么安定啊。合你心意，穷尽你的喜好，一切如愿，心情可以安适畅快啊。终身长乐，延年益寿啊。魂啊归来！这儿的快乐妙不可言啊。

五谷六仞①，设菰粱只②。鼎臑盈望③，和致芳只④。内鸧鸽鹄⑤，味豺羹只⑥。魂乎归来！恣所尝只。鲜蠵甘鸡⑦，和楚酪只⑧。醢豚苦狗⑨，脍苴蒪只⑩。吴酸蒿蒌⑪，不沾薄只⑫。魂兮归来！恣所择只。炙鸹烝凫⑬，煔鹑陈只⑭。煎鰿䑋雀⑮，遽爽存只⑯。魂乎归来！丽以先只⑰。四酎并孰⑱，不歰嗌只⑲。清馨冻歙[20]，不歠役只[21]。吴醴白蘖[22]，和楚沥只[23]。魂乎归来！不遽惕只[24]。

【注释】

①仞：长度单位，古代以七尺或八尺为一仞
②菰(gū)粱：菰米，可煮食。菰，茭笋，又名"蒋"，多年生水生宿根草本植物。
③鼎：古代烹煮用的器物，多用青铜制成，圆形三足两耳，也有方形四足的。臑(rú)：熟烂。
④和致芳：调和五味，以使其芳香。
⑤内：通"肭(nà)"，肥美。鸧(cāng)：一种形似雁与鹤，青黑色的鸟，鹄：天鹅。
⑥味：调和味道。豺：兽名，俗称豺狗，犬科动物，形似狼，较瘦小，吠声如犬。
⑦蠵(xī)：大龟。
⑧酪(lào)：乳浆。
⑨醢(hǎi)：肉酱。豚(tún)：小猪。苦：用胆调和肉酱以使苦。
⑩脍(kuài)：细切。苴蒪(jū pò)：蘘荷，姜科，多年生草本植物，根状茎淡黄色，有辛辣味。
⑪吴酸：吴地人调和酸咸，腌制菜肴。吴，吴地，吴地人。蒿蒌(hāo lóu)：两种草本植物的名称。王逸《楚辞章句》："蒿，蘩草也。蒌，香草也。"
⑫不沾薄：即味道不浓不淡。沾，多汁。薄，无味。
⑬炙(zhì)：烤肉。鸹(guā)：鸟名。《说文·鸟部》："鸹，麋鸹也。"烝：同"蒸"，用火烘烤使熟。凫：野鸭。
⑭煔(qián)：把肉浸在锅里，即煮肉。鹑：鸟名，即鹌鹑。

⑮鲫(jì)：鲫鱼。臛(huò)：不加菜，全用汤煮，做成肉羹。
⑯遽爽：极其爽口。
⑰丽：美，美味。
⑱四酎(zhòu)：四重酿之醇酒。
⑲歰(sè)：即"涩"，滞涩，不顺滑。这里是使喉咙感到苦涩、不顺滑的意思。嗌(ài)：咽喉。
⑳清馨：这里是形容酒的气味清冽芳香的样子。冻歆(yǐn)：冰镇后饮之。歆，即"饮"，一本即作"饮"。
㉑歠(chuò)：饮，喝。役：卑贱之人。
㉒醴(lǐ)：一宿熟的甜酒。蘖(niè)：做酒的曲。
㉓沥(lì)：清酒。
㉔遽(jù)：恐惧。惕：警惕，戒惧。

【译文】

这里的五谷高高堆积，还摆设着菰米饭啊。大鼎里煮熟的食物满眼都是，调和滋味使它散发芳香啊。肥美的鸧、鸽子、天鹅，调和着豺肉做的羹汤啊。魂啊归来！任随心意来品尝啊。新鲜的大龟，可口的肥鸡，调和了楚地的乳酪啊。乳猪做成的肉酱，胆汁浸渍的狗肉，再切点蘘荷放在里面啊。吴人腌制的蒿菜蒌芽，不浓不淡，味道正好啊。魂啊归来！随你心意来挑取啊。烤鸧鸟，蒸野鸭，煮了鹌鹑来摆开啊。煎鲫鱼，煮雀肉，味道极佳，让你口齿留香啊。魂啊归来！众多美味已经摆放上来啊。四重酿造的美酒都熟了，喝起来不滞涩喉咙啊。气味清冽芳香，适合冰镇后再饮，不是奴仆有福享用的啊。吴地的甜米酒，白酒曲酿造，掺上楚产的清酒啊。魂啊归来！不要害怕，不要有戒惧之心啊。

代秦郑卫①，鸣竽张只②。伏戏《驾辩》③，楚《劳商》只。讴和《扬阿》④，赵箫倡只⑤。魂乎归来！定空桑只⑥。二八接舞⑦，投诗赋只。叩钟调磬⑧，娱人乱只⑨。四上竞气⑩，极声变只⑪。魂乎归来！听歌譔只⑫。朱唇皓齿，嫭以姱只⑬。比德好闲⑭，习以都只⑮。丰肉微骨，调以娱只⑯。魂乎归来！安以舒只。嫮目宜笑⑰，娥眉曼只⑱。容则秀雅⑲，稚朱颜只⑳。魂乎归来！静以安只。姱修滂浩㉑，丽以佳只。曾颊倚耳㉒，曲眉规只。滂心绰态㉓，姣丽施只㉔。小腰秀颈，若鲜卑只㉕。魂乎归来！思怨移只㉖。易中利心㉗，以动作只。粉白黛黑㉘，施芳泽只㉙。长袂拂面，善留客只。魂乎归来！以娱昔只㉚。青色直眉㉛，美目媔只㉜。靥辅奇牙㉝，宜笑嘕只㉞。丰肉微骨，体便娟只㉟。魂乎归来！恣所便只。

【注释】

①代秦郑卫：古国名，这里是指四国的音乐。
②竽：一种管乐器的名称。张：音乐奏起。
③伏戏：即古代神话传说中的神王"伏羲"。《驾辩》：古曲名。
④讴：清唱。《扬阿》：古代楚地歌曲名，即《阳阿》。
⑤箫：一种管乐器。《说文·竹部》："箫，参差管乐，象凤之翼。"倡：领唱，这里指先行奏乐。
⑥定：调整琴弦，定下音位。空桑：瑟名。一说地名。
⑦二八：十六个舞女，即舞女以八人为一列，二列共十六人。
⑧叩钟调磬(qìng)：钟、磬，两种打击乐器的名称。
⑨乱：欢快。
⑩四上：指乐曲结构的四个组成部分。竞气：指乐曲中四个环

节的乐声依次强于前面环节。

⑪极声变：穷极乐音的曲折变化。

⑫谏(zhuàn)：陈述，表达。

⑬嫭(hù)以姱：嫭、姱，都是美丽、美好的意思。

⑭比：相同。好闲：仪态美好、娴静。

⑮习：熟悉礼节。都：仪容美好、高雅。

⑯调：性情和顺。

⑰嫭(hù)：同"嫭"，美好，这里用来形容眼睛。

⑱蛾眉：女子细长而好看的眉毛。蛾，形容眉毛细长如蚕蛾的样子。

⑲容：仪容，容态。则：举止，行为。

⑳稺(zhì)：字又作"稚"，幼小。

㉑姱修：美好，淑丽。滂浩：一本作"修广婉心"，当从之。"婉心"，性情柔顺的意思。

㉒曾：重累，层叠，这里指面颊丰满。颊：脸的两侧。倚耳：耳向后贴，不外张。

㉓滂心：心胸阔大。绰态：姿态柔美绰约。

㉔施：呈现。

㉕鲜卑：一种束在腰间的带子。

㉖思怨移：消除、忘怀忧怨的情思。移，去除。

㉗易中利心：易中，内心机敏，反应快。"利心"与"易中"意义相近。中、心，指内心而言。易，轻易，不坚实。

㉘粉：化妆涂脸用的脂粉。黛：青黑色的颜料，古代女子用以画眉。

㉙芳泽：香膏，也是化妆用物品。

㉚昔：通"夕"，一本即作"夕"，夜晚。

㉛青色：青黑色，这里当指蛾眉的颜色。

㉜嫇(mián)：形容眼睛美的样子，这里有眼波流眄动人，显得

聪慧狡黠的意思。

㉝靥(yè)辅：又作"酽酺"，脸颊上的酒窝。奇牙：奇而好的牙。奇，殊异美好。

㉞嘕(xiān)：笑的样子。

㉟便(pián)娟：形容体态轻盈美丽的样子。

【译文】

这里有代、秦、郑、卫四地的音乐，吹起竽管，音乐奏起啊。有伏羲氏的《驾辩》，还有楚曲《劳商》啊。一齐清唱起《扬阿》之歌，由赵地箫乐来领唱啊。魂啊归来！为空桑之瑟调弦审音啊。十六个佳人一个接一个起舞，配合着诗赋雅乐的节拍啊。敲起钟，调好磬，演奏到歌曲末章，人们欢快无比啊。四个乐章依次演奏，叠相强进，音声变化无穷啊。魂啊归来！来聆听曲中之意啊。美人们唇红齿白，俏丽无比啊。才德不相上下，仪态美好娴静，习于礼节且又秀美高雅啊。肌肤丰腴，骨相纤秀，性情温顺，让人快乐啊。魂啊归来！你会感到安乐舒心啊。她们那漂亮的眼睛含着笑意，蚕蛾般的眉毛细又长啊。仪容举止秀美娴雅，红润的脸庞是如此娇嫩啊。魂啊归来！你会觉得宁静又安逸啊。她们容貌美丽，性情柔顺，真称得上是旷世之美啊。面颊丰满，两耳巧致，弯弯的眉毛如圆规画成啊。心胸阔大，姿态绰约，姣好美丽显现无遗啊。腰肢细小，脖子秀美，就像鲜卑带子束着一样啊。魂啊归来！你会忘怀那幽怨的情思啊。她们心思敏捷聪慧，从动作中表现出来啊。白的脂粉，黑的眉黛，再擦上香膏啊。长长的袖子轻轻擦过脸庞，善于殷勤待客，让人留连忘返啊。魂啊归来！晚上在这儿娱乐啊。黑而直的眉毛刚健婀娜，漂亮的眼睛流波动人啊。腮上有酒窝，牙齿奇又好，一笑嫣然，妩媚动人啊。身形丰满，骨节小巧，体态轻盈秀美啊。魂啊归来！随你喜好，任意行事啊。

夏屋广大①,沙堂秀只②。南房小坛③,观绝霤只④。曲屋步壛⑤,宜扰畜只⑥。腾驾步游,猎春囿只⑦。琼毂错衡⑧,英华假只⑨。茞兰桂树⑩,郁弥路只⑪。魂乎归来!恣志虑只。孔雀盈园,畜鸾皇只⑫。鹍鸿群晨⑬,杂鹜鸧只⑭。鸿鹄代游⑮,曼鹔鹴只⑯。魂乎归来!凤凰翔只。

【注释】

①夏屋:高大的屋子。

②沙堂:用丹砂涂饰成红色的殿堂。沙,丹砂,又称朱砂,是一种红色的矿物。

③房:堂屋两侧的房间。坛:这里当指庭院,是游观憩息的场所。

④观:宫门外高台上的望楼,可作观看眺望用。霤(liù):屋檐。

⑤曲屋:阁道,亦即长廊,因其上修建了类似屋顶的东西,且又回环曲折,所以叫曲屋。步壛(yán):长廊。

⑥扰:驯养。畜:家养之兽。

⑦囿(yòu):畜养禽兽的园林,有围墙,汉以后称"苑"。

⑧琼:美玉。毂(gǔ):车轮中心的圆木,周围与车辐的一端相接,中有圆孔,可以插轴。错:错综华美的文饰。衡:车辕上的横木。

⑨英华:华美。假:大,盛大。

⑩茞(zhǐ):香草名。

⑪郁:树木丛生,茂盛。

⑫鸾:古代传说中的一种神鸟。皇:通"凰",古代传说中的鸟王,雄的叫"凤",雌的叫"凰"。

⑬鹍(kūn):鹍鸡。群晨:清晨时分一起飞翔鸣叫。

⑭鹙(qiū)鸧：一种水鸟，头顶无毛，性凶猛贪恶。
⑮代：更替，轮流，这里有来来往往的意思。
⑯曼：绵长，延续。这里形容鹔鹴群飞，连绵不绝的样子。鹔鹴(sù shuāng)：一种神鸟的名称。

【译文】

这里的房屋又宽又大，丹砂涂饰的殿堂真是壮美啊。朝南的偏屋，小巧的庭院，楼观屋檐下有承水沟槽啊。回环曲折的阁道，长长的走廊，适宜驯养鸟兽啊。驰骋车驾外出漫游，春日时分在园林中打猎啊。美玉般的车轴，错金镂彩的辕上横木，真是盛大华美啊。苴草、兰草和桂树，路边到处都是啊。魂啊归来！顺随你的心意，任你游玩啊。孔雀满园子都是，还养着鸾鸟凤凰啊。鹍鸡鸿雁清晨时分一起飞翔鸣叫，还混杂着秃鹙的声音啊。鸿鹄来来往往，嬉戏游乐，鹔鹴群飞，连绵不绝啊。魂啊归来！神鸟凤凰在飞翔啊。

曼泽怡面①，血气盛只。永宜厥身，保寿命只。室家盈廷②，爵禄盛只③。魂乎归来！居室定只。接径千里④，出若云只⑤。三圭重侯⑥，听类神只⑦。察笃夭隐⑧，孤寡存只⑨。魂兮归来！正始昆只⑩。田邑千畛⑪，人阜昌只⑫。美冒众流⑬，德泽章只。先威后文，善美明只。魂乎归来！赏罚当只。名声若日，照四海只⑭。德誉配天，万民理只。北至幽陵⑮，南交阯只⑯。西薄羊肠⑰，东穷海只。魂乎归来！尚贤士只。发政献行⑱，禁苛暴只。举杰压陛⑲，诛讥罢只⑳。直赢在位㉑，近禹麾只㉒。豪杰执政，流泽施只。魂乎来归！国家为只。雄雄赫赫㉓，天德明只㉕。三公穆穆㉖，登降堂只㉗。诸侯毕极，立九卿只㉘。昭质既设㉙，大侯张只㉚。执弓挟矢，揖辞让只㉛。魂乎来归！尚三王只㉜。

【注释】

①曼泽：形容面色丰润、润泽的样子。怡：和颜悦色。
②室家：宗族。
③爵：官位，爵位。禄：俸禄，即官员的收入。
④接径：道路相交接，四通八达。千里：方圆千余里，泛指疆域广袤。
⑤出若云：这里指出行时护卫侍从众多。
⑥三圭：圭是古玉器名，长条形，上圆下方，古代贵族以之作为朝聘、祭祀、丧祭时的礼器。重侯：指子爵和男爵。
⑦听类神：听讼断狱精审，类似于神明。听，听审诉讼。即《九章·惜诵》"听直"之"听"。
⑧笃：通"督"，察。夭：年幼而死，短命。隐：处境困苦。
⑨孤：本指幼而无父，引申为孤独之义。寡：本指老而无夫，引申为孤独义。存：抚恤，慰问。
⑩始昆：先后。昆，后。
⑪畛(zhěn)：田间的道路。
⑫阜昌：形容人口众多。
⑬美：美善之行，美政。冒：覆盖，这里有溥及众生的意思。
⑭四海：偏远地区，蛮荒之地。
⑮幽陵：地名，即幽州，地在今河北北部、辽宁一带。
⑯交阯(zhǐ)：地名，在今两广及越南北部一带。
⑰羊肠：西方山名。
⑱献行：百官向上进其治状。
⑲压陛：能人贤士布满朝堂廷阶。陛，殿堂前的台阶。
⑳诛：谴责并黜退。讥：受人讥刺指责。罢：能力有限，不堪大任的庸人。

㉑直赢：正直之人。赢，直。
㉒近禹麾：亲附、听从圣明君主禹的指挥。
㉓豪：卓越的人物。
㉔雄雄赫赫：形容声势、声威盛大的样子。
㉕天德：德行堪与天相配，故曰"天德"。
㉖三公：古代辅佐君王的最高的三个官职。一种说法是太师、太傅、太保；另一种说法是司空、司马、司徒。穆穆：平和恭敬。
㉗登降堂：出入朝堂、殿堂。
㉘九卿：九个中央国家机关的长官。
㉙昭质：箭靶的中心。
㉚大侯：射箭时所立之布，类似于箭靶。
㉛揖(yī)：拱手行礼。
㉜三王：指夏禹、商汤、周文王。

【译文】

肤色润泽，面色和悦，气血旺盛啊。身心永远安适康健，长保寿命啊。宗族成员布满朝廷，官爵、俸禄丰盛啊。魂啊归来！住所已经安排定了啊。道路四通八达，绵延千里，出行时护卫侍从聚集如云啊。朝廷大员、君王股肱，听审狱讼，明察秋毫，有如神明啊。察知了解夭折的儿童与处境困窘者的情况，安抚慰问孤儿寡妇啊。魂啊归来！来确定施行仁政时次序的先后啊。楚国的乡野城邑间道路上千条，人口繁盛众多啊。美政教化溥及芸芸众生，明德恩泽彰明显著啊。先用严政，后施仁政，这样就能既善且美又光明正大啊。魂啊归来！楚国赏罚得当啊。名声好比太阳一般，光辉照耀四海啊。功德、荣誉与天相媲美，天下百姓都得到治理啊。北边到幽陵，南边到交趾啊。西边迫近羊肠山，东边直抵大海啊。魂啊归来！楚国尊崇贤士啊。君王向下发布政令，百官向上呈递治状，禁绝苛刻凶暴啊。任用能人智士，布满朝堂廷阶，斥责、黜退无能的庸人啊。正直之人进用居官，听从圣明君主的指挥啊。才华出众者掌管政权，恩泽遍及民间啊。魂啊归来！国家得到治理了啊。声威雄壮，德行清明，上比苍天啊。三公平和恭敬，进出朝堂啊。诸侯都来致敬，设立九卿职位啊。箭靶已经摆好，大布靶也已张设啊。拿着弓，持着箭，拱手行礼，互相推辞谦让啊。魂啊归来！崇尚先贤，取法三王啊。

楚辞

Theory on Literary Translation of the Chinese School

The theory on literary translation of the Chinese school owes its origin to traditional Chinese culture, including the Confucian and the Taoist school of thought respectively represented by *Thus Spoke the Master* and *Laws Divine and Human*.

It is said in the first chapter of *Laws Divine and Human* that truth can be known, but it may not be the truth you know, and that things may be named, but names are not the things. When applied to literary translation, this may mean that the theory on literary translation can be known, but it may not the unproven theory on the one hand, nor the scientific theory on the other, for neither literary translation nor its theory is science. As the names are not equal to the things, the translation cannot be equal to the original. As there is more difference than equivalence between the Chinese and the English language, the principle of equivalence can not be applied to the translation between them as between two occidental languages.

It is said in the last chapter of *Laws Divine and Human* that truthful words may not be beautiful and beautiful words may not be truthful. That is to say, there is contradiction between truth and beauty or between equivalence and excellence. A translation where equivalents are used may be called a faithful or truthful translation. When no equivalent can be found between two languages, the translator should make use of the best expressions or excellent expressions of the target language. That may be called theory of excellence.

In *Thus Spoke the Master*, Confucius said, "At seventy, I can do what I will without going beyond what is right." Professor Zhu Guangqian said that this has shown the mature state of an artist. I think it may also show the mature state of a literary translator. The literal translator has used the equivalents without going beyond the original in sound; the liberal translator has described the image without going beyond the original in sense; the literary translator has described the scene without going beyond reality. Not to go beyond the original is to be truthful or faithful, and the translator has reached the ordinary level of translation. To do what one will without going beyond the original is not only to be faithful but also to make his translation beautiful, in that case the translator has attained a higher level. To excel the original without going beyond the reality it describes is to attain the highest level.

What is literary translation? It is an art of solving the contradiction between faithfulness (or truth) and beauty. How to solve it? There are three methods, namely, equalization, generalization and particularization. When there is little or no contradition between truth and beauty, equalization or equivalents may be used. When there is contradction between them, generalization may be used to make the meaning clear, and particularization to make a deeper impression.

Confucius said in *Thus Spoke the Master* that it would be good to be understandable, better to be enjoyable and best to be delectable or delightful. When applied to literary translation, this principle means that an understandable translation is good, an enjoyable one is better and a delightful one is best. The ontology or theory of contradition between truth and beauty, the methodology or theory of equalization, generalization and particularization, and the teleology or theory of the understandable, the enjoyable and the delectable, all owe their origin to the Confucian and Taoist schools of thoughts.

But Confucius said less about what delight is and more about how to be delightful. In the beginning of *Thus Spoke the Master* he said it is delightful to acquire knowledge and put it into practice; In Chapter Six he told us how Yan Hui could find delight in reading though living in a humble lane with only a handful of rice to eat and a gourdful of water to drink; In Chapter Eleven, Zeng Xi told us his delight in an spring excursion. From these examples we can see Confucius' theory on delight or teleology, and his theory on practice or methodology. His theory is not scientific but artistic. Since literary translation is an art but not a branch of science, his theory can not only be applied to the practice but also to the theory of literary translation. As his theory has stood the test of time, it is as durable as scientific theories. A theorist on science who studies truth and the truthful should not go beyond what is truthful. A theorist on art or an artist who studies beauty and the beautiful may go beyond what is truthful and faithful.

The contradiction between truth and beauty in Chinese theory on literary translation has developed into a contradiction between equivalence and excellence. As Keats said, "Beauty is truth, truth beauty," we may even say beauty is a virtue, a kind of excellence. When we cannot find the equivalent, we may resort to generalization or particularization.

In short, literary translation is an art to create the beautiful.

This is the epistemology of the Chinese school. The contradition between truth and beauty or between equivalence and excellence is its ontology; the theory on equalization, generalization and particularization is its triple methodology; and the theory of the understandable, the enjoyable and the delectable or delightful is its triple teleology.

Xu Yuanchong
Oct. 2011

楚辞

代后记：中国学派的文学翻译理论

中国学派的文学翻译理论源自中国的传统文化，主要包括儒家思想和道家思想，儒家思想的代表著作是《论语》，道家思想的代表著作是《老子道德经》。

《老子道德经》第一章开始就说："道可道，非常道；名可名，非常名。"联系到翻译理论上来，就是说：翻译理论是可以知道的，是可以说得出来的，但不是只说得出来而经不起实践检验的空头理论，这就是中国学派翻译理论中的实践论。其次，文学翻译理论不能算科学理论（自然科学），与其说是社会科学理论，不如说是人文学科或艺术理论，这就是文学翻译的艺术论，也可以说是相对论。后六个字"名可名，非常名"应用到文学翻译理论上来，可以有两层意思：第一层是原文的文字是描写现实的，但并不等于现实，文字和现实之间还有距离，还有矛盾；第二层意思是译文和原文之间也有距离，也有矛盾，译文和原文所描写的现实之间，自然还有距离，还有矛盾。译文应该发挥译语优势，运用最好的译语表达方式，来和原文展开竞赛，使译文和现实的距离或矛盾小于原文和现实之间的矛盾，那就是超越原文了。这就是文学翻译理论中的优势论或优化论，超越论或竞赛论。文学翻译理论应该解决的不只是译文和原文在文字方面的矛盾，还要解决译文和原文所反映的现实之间的矛盾，这是文学翻译的本体论。

一般翻译只要解决"真"或"信"或"似"的问题，文学翻译却要解决"真"或"信"和"美"之间的矛盾。原文反映的现实不只是言内之意，还有言外之意。中国的文学语言往往有言外之意，甚至还有言外之情。文学翻译理论也要解决译文和原文的言外之意、言外之情的矛盾。

《论语》说："知之者不如好之者，好之者不如乐之者。"知之，好之，乐之，这"三之论"是对艺术论的进一步说明。艺术论第一条原则要求译文忠实于原文所反映的现实，求的是真，可以使人知之；第二条原则要求用"三化"法来优化译文，求的是美，可以使人好之；第三条原则要求用"三美"来优化译文，尤其是译诗词，求的是意美、音美和形美，可以使人乐之。如果"不逾矩"的等化译文能使人知之（理解），那就达到了文学翻译的低标准，如从心所欲而不逾矩的浅化或深化的译文既能使人知之，又能使人好之（喜欢），那就达到了中标准；如果从心所欲的译文不但能使人知之，好之，还能使人乐之（愉快），那才达到了文学翻译的高标准。这也是中国译者对世界译论作出的贡献。

翻译艺术的规律是从心所欲而不逾矩。"矩"就是规矩，规律。但艺术规律却可以依人的主观意志而转移，是因为得到承认才算正确的。所以贝多芬说：为了更美，没有什么清规戒律不可打破。他所说的戒律不是科学规律，而是艺术规律。不能用科学规律来评论文学翻译。

孔子不大谈"什么是"（What?）而多谈"怎么做"（How?）。这是中国传统的方法论，比西方流传更久，影响更广，作用更大，并且经过了两三千年实践的考验。《论语》第一章中说："学而时习之，不亦说（悦，乐）乎！""学"是取得知识，"习"是实践。孔子只说学习实践可以得到乐趣，却不说什么是

"乐"。这就是孔子的方法论,是中国文学翻译理论的依据。

总而言之,中国学派的文学翻译理论是研究老子提出的"信"(似)"美"(优)矛盾的艺术(本体论),但"信"不限原文,还指原文所反映的现实,这是认识论,"信"由严复提出的"信达雅"发展到鲁迅提出"信顺"的直译,再发展到陈源的"三似"(形似,意似,神似),直到傅雷的"重神似不重形似",这已经接近"美"了。"美"发展到鲁迅的"三美"(意美,音美,形美),再发展到林语堂提出的"忠实,通顺,美",转化为朱生豪"传达原作意趣"的意译,直到茅盾提出的"美的享受"。孔子提出的"从心所欲"发展到郭沫若提出的创译论(好的翻译等于创作),以及钱钟书说的译文可以胜过原作的"化境"说,再发展到优化论,超越论,"三化"(等化,浅化,深化)方法论。孔子提出的"不逾矩"和老子说的"信言不美,美言不信"有同有异。老子"信美"并重,孔子"从心所欲"重于"不逾矩",发展为朱光潜的"艺术论",包括郭沫若说的"在信达之外,愈雅愈好。所谓'雅'不是高深或讲修饰,而是文学价值或艺术价值比较高。"直到茅盾说的:"必须把文学翻译工作提高到艺术创造的水平。"孔子的"乐之"发展为胡适之的"愉快"说(翻译要使读者读得愉快),再发展到"三之"(知之,好之,乐之)目的论。这就是中国学派的文学翻译理论发展为"美化之艺术"("三美","三化","三之"的艺术)的概况。

许渊冲
2011年10月

图书在版编目（CIP）数据

楚辞：汉英对照 / 许渊冲译 . — 2版 . — 北京：五洲传播出版社，2020.1
（许译中国经典诗文集）
ISBN 978-7-5085-4359-8

Ⅰ . ①楚… Ⅱ . ①许… Ⅲ . ①古典诗歌 – 诗集 – 中国 – 战国时代 – 汉、英 Ⅳ . ①I222.3

中国版本图书馆CIP数据核字(2020)第013155号

楚辞

译　　　者：	许渊冲
策划编辑：	荆孝敏　郑　磊
责任编辑：	王　峰
中文译注：	林家骊
中文编辑：	宋凤娣
英文编辑：	马培武　程　阳
装帧设计：	北京正视文化艺术有限责任公司
出版发行：	五洲传播出版社
地　　　址：	北京市海淀区北三环中路31号生产力大楼B座6层
邮　　　编：	100088
电　　　话：	010-82005927，010-82007837
网　　　址：	http://www.cicc.org.cn　http://www.thatsbooks.com
印　　　刷：	中煤（北京）印务有限公司
版　　　次：	2012年1月第1版　2020年4月第2版第1次印刷
开　　　本：	140mm×210mm　1/32
印　　　张：	13.75
字　　　数：	400千字
书　　　号：	ISBN 978-7-5085-4359-8
定　　　价：	98.00元